FOR *richer,* FOR *poorer*

BOOK THREE IN
THE PASTOR MAGGIE SERIES

For Richer, For Poorer

BOOK THREE IN
THE PASTOR MAGGIE SERIES

BARBARA EDEMA

Pen-L Publishing
Fayetteville, Arkansas
Pen-L.com

Books by Barbara Edema:

THE PASTOR MAGGIE SERIES

To Love and To Cherish

To Have and To Hold

For Richer, For Poorer

Dedication

This book is dedicated to Pastor Elisha and Marta Asamoah,
Bernard Boateng (Nana Bee), Fifi Obodai, Isaac, Joe,
and all the other adults and children at United Hearts
Children Center. We are richer for knowing you.

In Memory

Mr. Gary Grossman. A kind, gentle, caring man. A man who was
truly "pure in heart." You shocked us all by leaving an
unbelievable gift to a little church in a little town. You taught us
all how to live more generously.

List of Characters

RESIDENTS OF CHERISH, MICHIGAN

Pastor Maggie Elliot – Pastor of Loving the Lord Community Church (LTLCC)

Dr. Jack Elliot – Family practice doctor, on the staff of Heal Thyself Community Hospital; husband of Maggie

Hank Arthur – Administrative Assistant at LTLCC; married to Pamela Arthur

Pamela Arthur – Hospital volunteer

Doris Walters – Custodian at LTLCC; married to Chester Walters

Irena Dalca – Organist at LTLCC; fan of miniskirts and vodka

Marla Wiggins – Sunday school superintendent; married to Tom, owner of The Cherish Hardware Store; mother of Jason and Addie

Howard and Verna Baker – Recent newlyweds

Officer Charlotte Tuggle – Cherish Chief of Police; married to gravel pit owner Fred; mother of twins, Brock and Mason, and daughter, Liz

Officer Bernie Bumble – Charlotte's inexperienced deputy

Martha Babcock – Nosy police dispatcher

Cate Carlson – Maggie worshiper and a student at The University of Michigan, soon to be studying for a semester in Ghana

Cole Porter – Owner and proprietor of The Porter Funeral Home; husband of the lovely Lynn and father of Penny, Molly, and Samuel

Harold Brinkmeyer – Successful young lawyer; in love with Ellen Bright

Ellen Bright – Nurse at Heal Thyself, good friend of Pastor Maggie, Jack Elliot's cousin, and Harold's girlfriend

Sylvia Baxter – Owner of The Garden Shop; married to Bill Baxter

Bill Baxter – Handyman and master of construction

Mrs. Polly Popkin – Owner and proprietress of The Sugarplum Bakery

William and Mary Ellington – Owners of The Grange Bed and Breakfast

Cassandra Moffet– Mother of Carrie and Carl Moffet

Jennifer and Beth Becker – Sisters and owners of The Page Turner Book Shop

Max Solomon – Always sits in the last pew

Julia Benson – Reporter for the *Cherish Life and Times*; mother of Hannah

Lacey Campbell – Owner of We Work Miracles Beauty Salon

Dr. Dana Drake – Veterinarian at Cherish Your Pets Animal Hospital

Winston Chatsworth – Friend of Howard Baker; can't seem to comb his hair

Dr. Ethan Kessler – Teacher of African Politics at the U of M; married to Charlene

Dr. Charlene Kessler – Family practice doctor and Jack's partner; mother of Kay and Shawn

Skylar Breese – Owner of Pretty, Pretty Petals Flower Shop

Judy – Hospice nurse

Arly Spink – Cherish artist and owner of Cherished Works of Art Gallery

Darcy Keller – Owner of The Mill

Priscilla Keller Sloane – Darcy's sister; a widow

Jim, Cecelia, Bobby, and Naomi Chance – A new family

Juan, Maria, Gabby, and Marcos Gutierrez – A new family

SHUT-INS IN CHERISH

Katharine Smits – Sylvia Baxter's mother

Marvin Green – Hates women ministers, supposedly

Various other old darlings

Resident of Ann Arbor, Michigan
Detective Keith Crunch

Residents of Blissfield, Michigan
Ken and Bonnie Elliot – Jack's parents

Residents of Zeeland, Michigan
Dirk and Mimi Elzinga – Maggie's parents

Residents of San Francisco, California and Bawjiase (Bo-gee-ossi), Ghana
Bryan Elzinga – Maggie's brother
Joy Nelson – Founder and CEO of Africa Hope; Bryan's boss

Residents of Bawjiase, Ghana
Adua, Hannah, Kofi, Kwashi – A family in the countryside
Dr. Obodai – Doctor at the local clinic
Pastor Elisha (or just "Pastor") and his wife Marta – Founders of United Hearts Children's Center
Fifi – Resident at United Hearts; cook for visitors, builder, baker, and entrepreneur; cares for everyone he knows and he loves living at United Hearts
Nana – Lives at United Hearts and runs the farm nearby
Isaac, Joe, and several other older boys who do work at United Hearts
Cynthia – Oldest girl at United Hearts; hardworking, loving, intelligent
Mary, Grace, and Amanda – Friends of Cynthia
The rest of the orphans who live at United Hearts

If you are interested in knowing more about the fictional organization Africa Hope, please visit the website of the real organization MAMAHOPE.ORG

The Mission

To connect the rich with the poor,
the healthy to the sick,
the educated and skilled to the uninstructed,
the influential to those of no consequence,
the powerful to the weak
to do the will of God on earth.
– Catherine McAuley, 1831

Prologue

January 4, 2016

A wave of hot air hit Maggie the moment she stood at the opened airplane door. Her nose was overwhelmed with the scents of steaming tarmac, burned and unburned refuse, and heavy wafts of jet fuel. The sun bore down on the top of her head as she made her way carefully down the rickety airline stairs. Maggie slung her carry-on bag over her shoulder and was knocked a little off balance by its weight. She gingerly walked down each metal step to the waiting bus ready to bring the passengers to the customs terminal.

The warm air of Accra, Ghana, had begun to melt the Detroit iciness out of Maggie. The brand-new year had begun with a trip to a brand-new continent and country.

When she reached the tarmac, Maggie reached up to the small gold cross around her neck and absently held it. She stopped for a moment, closed her eyes, and breathed in deeply. She didn't want to miss any sensation of being in that beautiful, mystical country. She had dreamt about it for months. She had heard God's many whispers about it. Maggie believed in God's whispers and listened for them constantly. Now the whisper was a roar of affirmation as the mighty winds blew through Accra from the powerful Atlantic Ocean. She felt the heat from the tarmac rise through her flip-flops. Once again, a poor choice of shoes. Maggie never seemed to wear the appropriate footwear. She tripped, fell, and stumbled her way through life with tiny pieces of floppy rubber on her feet.

With only two weeks to learn too many things about the land and its people, Maggie also had the added responsibility to lead a group of her own parishioners on the adventure. Fortunately, her brother, Bryan, would be in charge of the work on the trip. Maggie would be in charge of the human and spiritual cares.

Maggie let God's warm breath blow through her hair, her clothes, and her soul.

"Who will go for us?" God had asked in his holy court, way back when God was searching for a prophet, a messenger. Isaiah answered that time.

What Maggie didn't understand was that, if she acquiesced to God's bidding, the whispers could become startling shouts. Her simple assumptions of faith, life, right, wrong, good, bad, rich, and poor would certainly bring anguish, resistance, brokenness, loss, renewal, hope, and piercing joy.

But Maggie only heard the whisper. God's request.

"Who will go for us?"

"Here I am," Maggie whispered back Isaiah's words.

She was excited to meet God in Ghana.

"Send me."

1

Jennifer Becker buttoned up her coat and tied her scarf around her long, thin neck. Everything about Jennifer was tall, thin, and angular. At the age of fifty-four, she had the height and metabolism of her mother. Jennifer's younger sister, Beth, had inherited their father's shorter, rounder physique. Now, with both parents gone, they could see their mother and father in one another. It was comforting.

Jennifer's coat and scarf were worn habitually now, even though the month of October was acting like October. Warmth and cold playfully wrangled for a foothold each day, which kept the month unpredictable. Actually, almost one week into the month, it was a sunny seventy degrees. That didn't matter, of course, because as soon as September twenty-third had rolled around, indicating the first day of autumn, both Jennifer and Beth unpacked their sweaters and other winter clothing from their cedar chests. Their summer clothes were carefully packed away between sheets of tissue paper until spring (perhaps May or June in Michigan). Although that particular day was warm, the nights had slowly dropped in temperature. It was how autumn began its creation of crimson, gold, and orange leaves on the treelined streets of Cherish.

Jennifer shook with excitement because she had just received a shipment of novels at The Page Turner Book Shop less than an hour before. Jennifer and Beth had owned and operated The Page Turner for the past twenty-five years. Visitors and townspeople alike enjoyed browsing in the book shop, mainly because it smelled of books, a rarity in the new days of Kindles, Nooks, and other e-readers. The shop also smelled like cinnamon, apple, and nutmeg. Beth made her own potpourri each season. Autumn smelled delicious.

The new shipment of the morning had thrilled Jennifer because she had a very special delivery to make to a very special someone. Jennifer carefully wrapped *The Haunted Season* by G.M. Malliet in brown paper and tied it with a pink string. Then she set off on her journey by foot and left Beth to keep an eye on things at the shop.

Jennifer walked north on Main Street, past Skylar Breese's Pretty, Pretty Petals Flower Shop, then Lacey Campbell's We Work Miracles hair salon, O' Leary's Pub, and the newest Cherish business, Arly Spink's Cherished Works of Art Gallery. Jennifer made a right turn on Middle Street, then went straight up the old steps of Loving the Lord Community Church.

Opening one of the huge oak doors, Jennifer entered the sanctuary. She caught her breath as she saw the large plastic sheet covering what once was a beautiful stained-glass rose window. It was still a shock to everyone at Loving the Lord Community Church, that one of their own members had purposefully destroyed the original window in the sanctuary.

Redford Johnson, the perpetrator of the violence, was now awaiting trial—and most likely a long prison sentence—for the break-ins and physical damage he had wreaked upon the church in the past few weeks. Not only had he destroyed the historic rose window, he had also stolen money from the church, evaded child support for a child no one knew he had, and cheated many people out of their own retirement money through his financial planning business. Worst of all, he had violently assaulted the church janitor, Doris Walters. In short, Redford had broken not only the law but the hearts and trusts of the people in his church.

Redford had moved to Cherish five years earlier. He was young, single, and a financial wizard. He was also a predator. No one knew he had a previous life with a wife and child who had left him. No one knew that he looked at the people of Loving the Lord Church and saw a group of "suckers." His thievery and abuse began almost immediately. Fortunately for Loving the Lord, Redford's finances were frozen at the time of his arrest. Reassurance had been given to all of his victims that restitution would be made. The rose window was being repaired knowing the money would be provided following Redford's conviction.

Jennifer took a moment to remember the window and say a thankful prayer for its reparation. Then she quietly walked past Irena Dalca, who was perched on her organ bench, pounding out the somber notes of "If Thou but Trust in God to Guide Thee." Irena's hair was still the fluorescent blonde it had been for the recent wedding at Loving the Lord. She was so involved in her music, she didn't see the slim frame of Jennifer slip past toward the church assistant's office. Jennifer was relieved. Irena scared her. Jennifer was much too timid a person to know how to deal with the lightning bolt that was Irena.

Irena Dalca was a tiny powerhouse who was in charge of everything musical at Loving the Lord. Irena was four foot eight, eighty pounds, and frightened everyone who got in her way. With her Romanian heritage, she was direct, opinionated, and did not suffer fools. Her definition of "fool" was quite fluid.

Hank Arthur, Loving the Lord's happy administrative assistant, smiled broadly as Jennifer made her way into his office. She returned the smile then quietly asked, "Good morning, Hank. Is Pastor Maggie in?"

"Yessireebob, she sure is, Miss Becker. Go right on in!" Hank said, almost sparkling.

"It sure was a celebrative weekend, wasn't it, Hank?" Jennifer said in her soft voice.

"I don't think I've ever seen anything like it in my life. Nosireebob, never. Pastor Maggie got married good and proper, right here in her very own church with all the people who love her. And she never saw it coming!" Hank said with a double burst of pride and laughter.

Ever since Pastor Maggie Elzinga and Dr. Jack Elliot had tied the great big marriage knot just days before, Hank had been unable to stop smiling. The congregation had pulled off an undercover plot to give Dr. Jack and Pastor Maggie a dream wedding. The couple's original plan had been to marry quietly in the living room of Maggie's best friends from seminary, Nora and Dan Wellman. But Nora would have none of it. She understood Maggie and the church had been under siege with several break-ins and a young family in terrible crisis. But Nora insisted she would see her best friend married surrounded by her congregation. So Nora, Maggie's mother, Mimi, and Hank began the secret conspiracy.

Because a quiet elopement had been planned, Jack and Maggie never knew what hit them the morning of their wedding day. It was perfect. The congregation of Loving the Lord Church did what they did best. They gathered together, each using their own gifts and talents, and made a wedding day so special that Jack and Maggie were convinced they couldn't have planned anything better themselves. Flowers, music, decorations on pews and altar, and a delicious wedding meal. The best surprise was being married in their very own church.

Sitting at her desk, now a happily married lady, Maggie heard a soft knock on her office door. Jennifer entered, holding the brown package. Maggie had been sipping a cup of Lady Grey tea while working on something that had nothing at all to do with her church to-do list.

"Good morning, Jennifer."

Maggie smiled as she quietly slipped a large book under her desk, along with a stack of cards. Then she got up, thankful she could stand on her own two feet without crutches or cane. Thanks to Redford's first of several church break-ins, Maggie had slipped through a folding chair as she fell through a basement window a few weeks prior. A badly sprained ankle kept her on crutches then a cane for far too long, in her opinion. Now she moved around her desk and met Jennifer as they each took a seat in the two cream-colored visitor chairs.

"Good morning, Pastor Elliot," Jennifer said, blushing slightly. Jennifer had never been married, but imagined it was quite a satisfactory existence for most people.

Maggie laughed. She loved her new last name. It was so close to her maiden name, Elzinga, but was by far easier to pronounce. Parishioners normally just called her Pastor Maggie, but they had taken to dropping "Pastor Elliot" as well to honor her newly married status.

"I love the sound of that, Jennifer. Please say it again!"

"Pastor Elliot. Pastor Elliot. Pastor Elliot," Jennifer obliged.

"Thank you," Maggie said, giving a small nod of her head. "I may just turn into a high school girl and write *Pastor Maggie Elliot* over and over again on my blotter. It's kind of sickening, isn't it?"

"Of course not," Jennifer said, blushing. "But just in case you need a diversion from your new name, I have brought you a little gift that should take you out of Cherish and drop you right into G.M. Malliet's Nether Monkslip." Jennifer handed the brown package with pink string to Maggie.

"Oh! I completely forgot about her new book. Jennifer, thank you. I have missed Max Tudor."

Maggie unwrapped the brown paper and held the book in her hands. Maggie *loved* books she could hold in her hands. She thumbed through the pages and then sniffed. Since she was a child, Maggie loved opening new books and smelling the fresh pages. Actually, she enjoyed the smell of old books, as well. The mustier the better.

"Jennifer, thank you for remembering. I will begin this tonight. I may have to read it to Jack. He's a new Malliet convert." Maggie grinned.

Of course, that bit of intimacy immediately embarrassed Jennifer, who looked down at her hands, then stood to leave. Along with Jennifer, her sister, Beth, had never been married. Now in their fifties, it didn't appear marriage would be part of either of their lives. That was just fine with them. Maybe.

"I hope you, uh, both enjoy it," Jennifer said, still looking down.

Maggie stood and impulsively gave Jennifer a hug, the book sandwiched between them.

"I really mean it, Jennifer. Thank you for your thoughtfulness."

"Pastor Maggie," Jennifer said, after stepping back slightly and smoothing her coat, "your wedding was just beautiful. Beth and I both agreed we have never seen a more lovely ceremony. We are very happy for you and Dr. Elliot."

"We could feel the love and good wishes from everyone on Saturday," Maggie said quietly. "We'll never forget a moment of that day."

"Oh, I almost forgot." Jennifer surprised herself. "Beth and I have fifty brand-new books, picture books appropriate for infants all the way up to chapter books for adolescents. We want to donate them to the Ghana mission trip. We figure, if the children are learning English in school, these books will be just the thing to help them keep reading."

"Excellent!" Maggie said. "We want to fill up the library in the new school. Your variety of books will serve them all. Thank you for such a generous donation."

"We'll bring the box to the parsonage this week. We're happy to be part of the mission."

Jennifer was pleased to see Maggie's enthusiasm, lacking that altruistic piece of genetics herself.

Maggie was preparing to take a group from the congregation to Bawjiase, Ghana, where her brother, Bryan, was working to build a new school for United Hearts Children's Center, an orphanage near the village. Loving the Lord was all-in for the exciting new project. The people who weren't actually going to do the on-site physical work were contributing from home any way they could.

Maggie's office door flew open. Irena click-clacked in on her high heels. She carried a pile of music in her skinny little arms, clutching the stack with her black painted fingernails. They looked like talons.

Hank's voice followed her from his desk, "Irena! I told you she had someone in her office right now!"

Irena stopped and stared at Maggie and Jennifer, giving them a full view of her newest makeup creation. Since the latest kitchen sink disaster of her dyed blonde hair, Irena had also taken the pains to adjust her makeup to "complement" the hair color. The bright-blue sparkly eye shadow looked like something straight out of the 1960s. As usual, Irena's face was a horror show of vivid colors.

"Shut it, Hunk!" Irena shouted over her shoulder.

Hank did so. Irena was Pastor Maggie's problem now.

"Good morning, Irena," Maggie said quickly. "Jennifer and I are just finishing a chat."

"Gooot. Ve neet to talk ov Chrristmas."

Irena plunked her small rigid self right down in the chair where Jennifer had been sitting, similar to the way a tomcat might pee on his territory where an infidel cat has set an unwanted paw.

Jennifer took the opportunity to move to the door. It was time to get back to The Page Turner and unpack the rest of the Malliet books—in blessed peace and quiet.

"Good morning, Irena. Your music on Saturday was beautiful," Jennifer said kindly.

"Vat aboot Sunday?" Irena asked, her eyes narrowing.

Jennifer coughed nervously. "Of course. Every Sunday you play beautifully for us. The wedding was extra special, wasn't it?"

At that, Irena's easily ruffled feathers quickly unruffled. She gave Jennifer a queenly nod.

"Have a good day, Pastor Elliot." Jennifer winked at Maggie.

"And you, Jennifer. Thank you again for the book."

Maggie walked Jennifer the few steps to the door, then closed it behind her. She turned to face Irena, who was pawing through her music.

"Irena, you must stop barging in here when I am with someone," Maggie said, annoyed.

"Vy? Dees ees my verkplace. I am de prriorrty. Now, Chrristmas," Irena said, still digging.

Maggie remembered how last year Irena had wanted to do Handel's *Messiah* for a Christmas cantata. The problem was, Loving the Lord had a choir of only five people at the time, and no orchestra. That didn't seem to be a roadblock for Irena. Maggie had slyly talked Irena out of her grand plan through (somewhat) false praise and new promises of Irena playing extra pieces for Advent services. Thankfully, Irena had agreed. Maggie hoped to avoid a reprise of the same battle.

"I tink, I tink ve vill . . ." Irena was still ferociously clawing through the music when Maggie's door opened. There were no words from Hank's desk that time.

The faithful—albeit slightly cranky—church janitor, Doris, pushed her large rolling trash can into Maggie's office, her yellow apron wrapped around her sufficient waist, stuffed with cleansers and paper towels. A feather duster was in her hand.

Irena looked up and glared at Doris.

"Git out! Git out! Git out!" she screeched.

Maggie hid a smile. She knew Doris had arrived on purpose, probably with Hank's help, to give Irena a taste of her own selfish medicine.

"I work here too, Irena," Doris said calmly. "After the wedding, there is more than usual to clean up around here." Doris began to dust Maggie's windowsill. "Not that I mind cleaning up after the wedding," she said quickly, looking at Maggie.

"Thank you, Doris," Maggie said. "We certainly had no intention of dirtying up the church with a wedding. I'm afraid you will have to blame Pastor Nora, my mother, and Hank, of course."

Doris and Maggie both laughed. Irena glowered.

"Well, I guess I can come back and finish your office later, Pastor Maggie," Doris said, pushing her rolling trash can toward the door. "I'll go dust the organ now."

"Don't you touch dat orrgan!" Irena barked. "You vill mess up my stops!"

Maggie could hear Doris and Hank trying to stifle laughs in his office.

Irena went back to the music on her lap. But not before, oddly, she dropped her head to her right shoulder. Maggie wondered if Irena was all right. For the first time, Maggie noticed Irena's blouse was wrinkled and not tucked tightly into her miniskirt, as usual. Irena took a deep breath, popped her head back up, and dove into her purpose for being there.

"I tink ve vill do dees." Irena flourished several pages of something with musical notes sprinkled on them.

Maggie couldn't read music and was usually happy when Irena took care of all things musical. Usually.

"What is it?" Maggie asked, looking for some kind of title.

"Eet's called *Mangerr Baby*. I wrrote eet myself."

Irena sat back in her cream-colored chair, waiting for Maggie to bow down and worship in awe.

Maggie was stunned into silence. *Manger Baby? Oh, good grief!*

"Tell me about it," Maggie said once she was able to find her vocal chords.

Irena was still waiting to be fawned over but switched gears and dove right in to share her brilliance with Pastor Maggie.

"Vell, eet ees, ov courrse, about de tiny poor baby Jesus. I write eet frum de view of de cow in de stable. Poor animal watch de poor baby come into de worrld in de strraw. But den dis baby gets de prresents frrom de rich mens on dere rich camels. Dere ees a beeyootiful duet between cow and camel." Irena sat back in her chair again, quite self-satisfied.

Maggie kept a look of interest frozen on her face, but she had no idea what to say. Saying no to Handel was one thing. Saying no to Irena as the author of this Christmas nightmare could mean bodily harm.

"How long is it?" Maggie asked carefully.

"Eet's tree hours. I shorrtened eet. Ees perfect," Irena said, looking as though she was prepared to win the Best Musical Score award at the Oscars.

Three hours?

Suddenly, Maggie had a thought she assumed came straight from heaven.

"Irena, this sounds wonderful! But a church service isn't time enough to enjoy it in its entirety. What if we choose a Saturday afternoon, and it can be a complete concert? You will have the entire afternoon to shine and share your incredible music." Maggie didn't feel guilty anymore when she slipped little lies into conversations with Irena. It simply had to be done.

Irena's head lolled to the right again. Was she having a seizure?

"Irena, are you all right?" Maggie asked.

Irena's head popped back up and her eyes glowed.

"Ov courrse."

Irena could see it all. Her brilliant afternoon sharing her dazzling artistic talent with these musically challenged people.

Once Irena was satisfied that her composition would be celebrated appropriately, she left Maggie's office as quickly as she had arrived. The thought of Doris being anywhere near "her organ" had Irena irate. She brushed past Hank without a word, then click-clacked toward her corner of the sanctuary. She was relieved to find no sign of Doris's rolling trash can. One less righteous crusade to fight.

For now.

Irena climbed onto the organ bench. Normally, she would begin playing next Sunday's hymns without hesitation, but she closed her glittered eyelids for a moment. She let her nose drop to her right shoulder and took a whiff. The musky smell gave her a little shiver. Someone special had held her closely the night before as they watched television in Irena's small apartment. His cologne remained on her blouse. After he left, she went to bed in that blouse. She woke up in that blouse. She went to work in that blouse. She couldn't help it if her nose dropped over every few minutes to smell the scent. Irena had never experienced that kind of sensory excitement before. It was delicious and made her head spin just a little.

Then she heard her mother's ghostly voice in her head. "Irena! Vy you sit dere? Stop vasting de time! Prractice!"

Would her mother's voice ever leave her alone? But then Irena realized how much she hoped not. She missed her mother's commands and demands. She missed her mother.

She sniffed her shoulder one more time, then skipped Sunday's hymns and began playing the overture to *Manger Baby*.

2

January 4, 2016
Accra, Ghana

Going through customs at Kotoka Airport in Accra, Ghana, was hot and slow. But the little group from Loving the Lord was taking in every sight, smell, and sound. They had been anxiously waiting for months to be right there, beginning their journey. Maggie and Jack led the way, prepared with everything her brother, Bryan, and his boss, Joy, had told them to do ahead of time. They had their previously purchased entry visas, updated health record cards, and of course, had passports, all at the ready. Each member had to have a completed form that stated why they were coming to Ghana, who had invited them, and the address of where they would be staying. Thankfully, Bryan once again provided the information ahead of time.

Bryan's first trip to Ghana hadn't gone quite so smoothly. He had neglected to buy his visa in the United States, and he had misplaced the address of United Hearts Children's Center. The Ghanaian airport security had not been amused. Bryan had been held at the airport for three hours until Pastor Elisha rescued him, after paying a stiff fine. Bryan had learned his lesson.

Maggie and Jack, closely followed by the rest of the group, slowly made their way through the customs line. The air was hot, and everyone began removing the sweaters and sweatshirts that had kept them warm on the plane. They could hear the roars of planes taking off and landing due to the open doors to the tarmac. Maggie saw the bus rumble away to pick up another load of passengers.

Maggie looked at Jack. "I can hardly believe we're here," she said softly. "It's been a dream for so long. Now the adventure has begun."

Jack kissed the top of her head and smiled. "I think adventure is the right word."

Jack had no idea what to expect on the trip. That wasn't usually how he liked things to be. It always worked better if he had all the needed information ahead of time. He marveled at his wife, who dove into new situations with complete abandon. As much as Maggie liked to have a plan, she was always ready for Plan B. Sometimes that worked. But not always. Maggie's impetuousness got her into trouble from time to time.

Finally through customs, Maggie was thrilled to see "Republic of Ghana" stamped in her passport. The new arrivals were then direct-ed to their luggage. Each member of the mission team had brought two large suitcases and two very full carry-on bags. Most of what they brought were things for United Hearts and the school. They only brought things they knew they couldn't buy at Market in the village. All other needed supplies would be purchased in town to help the local economy.

When Maggie pulled her red suitcases from the luggage rotation, she noticed that the wheels on one of her bags had broken off dur-ing the flight. She grabbed it and dragged it anyway, looking around, trying to find everyone in the group. They were mixed in with all the other passengers from their flight. She saw Sylvia and Bill Baxter as they gathered their luggage. Jack helped Charlene Kessler lift a box from the rotation belt. The two doctors had carefully packed a CBC blood analyzer for the clinic in the village. The box had been wrapped with several strips of "fragile" tape. Charlene had paid the extra money for that particular piece due to the weight of the machine. Jack and Charlene were doing a quick check of the medical box to make sure the CBC machine was intact. Ellen Bright walked over to help. As a nurse, Ellen would help Jack and Charlene in the local clinic, although none of them knew exactly what that might mean.

Maggie saw Addie Wiggins's brown ponytail on the other side of the luggage area, but she didn't see the other members of the group yet. People and bags were crowded everywhere. Maggie stood by a pole near the exit, hoping the Loving the Lord folks would be able to find her. Wearing flip-flops didn't expand her five-foot-three-inch frame, but the group slowly found their way to her. They looked like a herd of lost and tired sheep.

A gentleman, appearing as if he had some authority over loitering foreigners, pointed and directed Maggie and the others to leave through the exit. He wasn't interested in the fact that the group hadn't all gathered together yet. Maggie led the rest of the group in the direction the man was pointing. Jack, Charlene, and the CBC machine brought up the rear. They walked to the waiting area where Maggie squealed as she dropped all of her luggage and bounced up and down.

"Bryan!" Maggie ran to her brother.

Standing next to him was Joy Nelson, the CEO of Africa Hope. She smiled as Bryan picked up his sister and swung her around.

"Sister Margaret, welcome to the happiest place on earth!" Bryan said.

"Didn't you just see each other at Thanksgiving?" Joy asked.

Her tanned skin, hazel eyes, and wavy honey-blonde hair were aglow. Joy actually looked like her name.

"Hi, Joy. It's so nice to meet you face-to-face. Skyping is all right but, wow, you're really tall," Maggie said, getting a little sidetracked. "Let me introduce you to our group," she said, realizing she was leaving everyone out of the grand welcome.

Just then, airport security moved people along once again to clear the passageway. Other passengers from another flight began moving past them with family members who had been waiting. Everyone looked so happy. Except maybe the security personnel, who just looked irritated and hot.

"Grab your luggage, everyone," Joy said. "I'll lead you to the tro-tro."

Maggie picked up her suitcases and began to roll one and drag the other. It was a pain. This time, she followed behind the rest of the group. As they made their way out of the waiting area and through the exit doors, they were hit with a wall of heat as they moved directly into the sun.

"Lady! Taxi?" a man called. Then another and another, and then a cacophony of voices. "Taxi! Taxi! Where you go?"

Maggie noticed a long line of taxis with eager drivers in shouting wars, wanting business. Some people got into taxis, others walked toward a large parking lot. Maggie was grateful Joy was so tall. She watched Joy's head bouncing ahead of them and followed along.

Joy shouted something Maggie didn't understand to several of the taxi drivers and made a shooing motion with her hands. There were other people with sealed baggies of water for sale. Maggie saw a woman with a huge platter of fried plantains balanced on her head and stopped for just a second to marvel at her.

"Dollar!" the woman demanded when she saw Maggie staring.

"No, no thank you," Maggie mumbled and began walking again.

Her senses were on overload. The taxis, honking nonstop, began to move with their new fares. Other street vendors holding Ghanaian flags, trays of bread, beaded jewelry, and many other items were along the road.

Joy once again looked back at the group. "Follow me!"

Her long legs moved at a quick pace. Maggie struggled to keep up rolling/dragging her suitcases through potholes and dirt. She kept getting whiffs of trash and burning hot tarmac.

"How're you doing?" Jack asked. He and Charlene had found her at the back of the pack.

"Good. Won't it be nice to get all this luggage to United Hearts and unpack?" Maggie was breathing hard.

"It looks like you lost some wheels," Jack said.

"They must have stayed on the plane," Maggie huffed.

"Yes. Hey, it looks like Joy is at the tro-tro."

"Thank goodness we're almost there," Charlene chimed in. "This machine is too heavy."

The tro-tro was a van capable of holding twelve people. Legally. But Jack and Maggie knew there were often four or five times as many people packed in for the ride. Sometimes children and adults rode five deep in one seat. Bryan had shown them pictures of special beach days for United Hearts. All the children, along with the adults, were packed into one tro-tro.

Waiting at the tro-tro was the driver, along with two smiling men. The two smiling men were so excited to see the small crowd of Americans, they began to laugh.

Bryan said, "I want you all to meet Pastor Elisha and Fifi. You have heard all about them, and they have heard all about you. They are very happy to see you here."

Pastor Elisha and his wife, Marta, had started United Hearts Children's Center several years earlier. Pastor Elisha and Fifi helped with bags while meeting Bryan's friends.

"We thank God you are here!" Pastor Elisha said.

Fifi gathered more suitcases and put them in the back of the tro-tro. Jack and Bill Baxter helped.

"Hi, Fifi. I am Jack, Bryan's brother-in-law." They shoved the suitcases as far back as they could. "And this is Bill Baxter. He likes to build things." Jack grinned at Bill, who reached out and shook Fifi's hand.

"Hi, Fifi. We have heard so much about you," Bill said with his shy smile.

"We are glad you came here. Bryan and Joy have told us so much about you," Fifi said.

"We have much to learn from you, Fifi," Jack said, knowing it was true, and that he had little idea what would be needed for the people of Bawjiase in the next two weeks.

The women of the group followed Joy's direction to get their luggage to the back of the tro-tro. Maggie watched as the five women dragged bags, then they stopped to shake Pastor Elisha's hand and impulsively hug Fifi.

Maggie stopped. She should be looking at six women, not five. Maggie searched the parking lot. Ethan Kessler joined Jack, Bill, and

Fifi. They picked up more bags and crammed them in the back of the tro-tro, but they dropped the bags they were holding when they heard Maggie yell. Everyone stared at her.

"Where's Addie?!" Maggie shouted over the roar of a jet engine and the departure of more taxis. "Where is Addie?"

Addie was the youngest member of the group, just a senior in high school. Her mother, Marla, was the Sunday school superintendent at Loving the Lord and one of Maggie's best friends. Now Addie was not with the group. Actually, Maggie hadn't seen Addie after the ponytail sighting in the luggage area.

Maggie dropped her bags and ran back toward the airport entrance. Joy and Pastor Elisha were close behind.

They had lost Addie.

3

Before Jennifer Becker's happy visit to Maggie's office, Maggie had carefully gathered her wedding cards and an empty scrapbook in the parsonage kitchen and placed them into a basket. Then she blissfully made her brief journey across the lawn to the church. Of course, everything she did was blissful since her wedding three days earlier.

She walked into Hank's office, basket in hand, and saw his face beam.

Hank looked as though he might just burst with delight. "Good morning, Pastor Maggie. What a beautiful day! Yessireebob, it's a beautiful day."

"It's been a beautiful almost four days, thus far," Maggie said joyfully, then lowered her voice. "Please don't tell anyone, but I am going to read through our wedding cards and begin a scrapbook. I'll try to have a sermon title for you tomorrow. Is that okay?"

"Absolutely! Great idea. You do that, Pastor Maggie. Would you like a cup of tea?"

"That would be lovely, Hank."

Maggie went into her office and closed the door. She set the cards on her desk and opened the scrapbook to look at the blank pages that would soon be filled.

After a quick knock on her door, Hank appeared with a steaming cup of Lady Grey tea.

"Thank you, Hank. I feel like royalty."

"As you should, M'Lady," Hank said, tipping an invisible hat as he departed.

Maggie laughed, then went back to her book. The card she would put on the first page was from Jo James. Jo was the widow of Maggie's beloved seminary professor, Ed James, who had died tragically of a heart attack in February. It was only October now, and Maggie had always dreamed Ed would officiate her wedding. But that wasn't to be. Jo had found the loveliest wedding card, and tucked inside was a small cross-stitched bookmark of Shakespeare's *Sonnet 116*.

SONNET 116
William Shakespeare

Let me not to the marriage of true minds
Admit impediments; love is not love
Which alters when it alteration finds,
Or bends with the remover to remove.
O no, it is an ever-fixed mark
That looks on tempests and is never shaken;
It is the star to every wand'ring bark,
Whose worth's unknown, although his highth be taken.
Love's not Time's fool, though rosy lips and cheeks
Within his bending sickle's compass come,
Love alters not with his brief hours and weeks,
But bears it out even to the edge of doom.
    If this be error and upon me proved,
    I never writ, nor no man ever loved.

Ed often used the sonnet when he officiated weddings. Jo had lovingly created the delicate piece of lacey poetry for Maggie and Jack. Maggie knew it came with Ed's now silent blessing. Maggie had loved the sonnet since Ed had first shared it with her. Love does not alter when it alteration finds. Love is an "ever-fixed mark."

Maggie had been surprised over the last few months when she'd begun to realize the truth of the sonnet. It wasn't difficult to see where people fixed their mark of love. Sometimes it was fixed on another person, sometimes it was a possession or money, and sometimes it was a love of wickedness and harmful behavior. She thought of Redford Johnson in the Wayne County Jail, awaiting trial. She shivered as she thought of Redford's endless desire to hurt others.

Maggie ran her finger down the delicate lace of Jo's stitched artwork, assured her love would be true, honest, and fixed. She loved God. And she loved Jack. She loved her family and her parishioners. Her love was fixed on all, in different ways. It seemed to Maggie that love had the capacity to grow and remain fixed—altering not when it alteration found. For Maggie, love moved beyond romance. She wondered what poor, tragic, romantic Shakespeare would think of that.

Not surprisingly, Maggie had spent the last three days doing what she was doing at that moment—rereading beautiful wedding cards and sentiments and reliving her nuptials. She had never been as surprised in her life as she was at her surprise wedding. And although she hadn't made one single decision about her ceremony and celebration, she wouldn't have changed a thing. Except, perhaps, that unfortunate accident between young Carl Moffet's head and the wedding cake table. But he would have his stitches removed in a week or so. And five-year-olds seemed to bounce back from those sorts of body/furniture collisions.

However, every time Maggie thought of Carl, her thoughts immediately turned to his mother, Cassandra. Cassandra had been diagnosed with terminal cancer just within the last few weeks. Maggie was now in the midst of helping a young mother make her way to the end of her life. One of the most difficult things Maggie had ever done was to be present with Cassandra when she told her two children, Carl and his seven-year-old sister Carrie, she was dying. It was a profound night, when the fears and woes of death were dealt with through grace, honesty, and a circle of women's arms so strong they were unbreakable. God had been in Cassandra's living room that evening. And God remained. Maggie watched Cassandra stare into the face of death with quiet acceptance. Cassandra had only one request, that her children be loved and cared for. Now the entire church had gathered around this family to do whatever they could to ease the Moffet's emotional fears and pain.

A new couple at church, William and Mary Ellington, owned The Grange Bed and Breakfast in Cherish. The couple had made a shocking discovery once they began to attend Loving the Lord Community Church. Actually, William had put the pieces together as he heard names mentioned and remembered the most horrific day of his own family's life. William and Mary's eighteen-year-old son, Michael, had been driving to their home in Ann Arbor from the University of Michigan. He had just completed an orientation for his first semester, which would begin in the fall. While he drove, his mother called his cell phone. As he shared his excitement about the orientation, his distraction on the phone caused him to crash into another car. Both drivers were killed. Eerily, the other driver had been Cassandra's husband, Calvin.

The indescribable pain of the accident had been sterilized by attorneys and insurance companies. William and Mary had never met Cassandra—who, after the accident, moved her small daughter and infant son to Cherish. Then, one Sunday, William and Mary showed up at Loving the Lord Church. They had left their home in Ann Arbor to purchase The Grange. While it had been an earlier dream, it now became a necessity in order to have a new beginning after Michael's death.

Church was where William heard Cassandra Moffet's name. There couldn't be that many Moffets in the Ann Arbor/Cherish area. William quietly asked more questions, discovered the connection was true, and gently told his wife. Since the accident, Mary's guilt over her phone call being the cause of so much tragedy had consumed her like a fire. She'd pulled herself into a dark shell and spent her time cleaning, baking, and being the hostess of The Grange. She was barely able to leave her home, except for the necessity of buying groceries. Mary had been living on autopilot.

The knowledge of Cassandra's cancer diagnosis had jolted Mary out of her isolation, guilt, and self-pity. It was as if someone released her from an emotional straightjacket. She stepped from her grief to walk alongside Cassandra. Mary's focus turned to the children. What would their fate be? She discovered there were no relatives able to take care of these little ones.

One afternoon, while William was feeding the animals in the barn at The Grange, Mary found him. She took the buckets of oats and corn from him and began filling troughs absentmindedly. The two cows, three horses, one donkey, and two sheep were pleased to receive more than the usual allotted amount as Mary poured out the grain along with her heart.

"William, I've been thinking. Carrie and Carl need a home, they need a family. We are intertwined with them in such a tragic way. I see this as some sort of sign. I know they are as old as our own grandchildren, but what do you think about bringing them into our family?"

William was rightfully dumbfounded. He took the buckets back from Mary, who had made one cow in particular very happy with an overflowing trough. He set the buckets down and took his wife in his arms. He silently thanked God for bringing her back to life. He thought he had lost her, but now her heart was beating again.

"Let's go inside and figure this out," William said, looking into her clear blue eyes.

Cassandra had asked Pastor Maggie and Dr. Elliot if they would consider adopting Carrie and Carl, once she knew the couple was engaged. When William and Mary turned up at the parsonage to tell Jack and Maggie what they had been praying about, the younger couple had been quietly relieved.

So, on a rainy September evening, William and Mary asked Cassandra if they might adopt Carrie and Carl and provide them a loving family.

Cassandra wept.

"My biggest fear was not knowing what would happen to Carrie and Carl," she said as she blew her nose and wiped her overflowing eyes. "You know I had asked Dr. Elliot and Pastor Maggie?"

"Yes," William said, "but Mary and I feel we have a certain connection with you and the children. It comes from, well, from a tragic place." William spoke calmly and softly. "Perhaps, caring for Carrie and Carl is a way to heal a great deal of pain. For all of us."

Mary cautiously took Cassandra's slim hand in hers. "If you think this is wise, we want to know your hopes, wishes, and ideas for Carrie and Carl. We'll do our best to make your wishes reality."

Cassandra nodded solemnly and wiped her nose again. She closed her eyes for a moment, then took a deep breath. Her children would be loved. That was the only thing that mattered.

The LTLCC family had been shocked by the unbelievable connection between William, Mary, and Cassandra. The news of the sad intertwining of losing a son in one family and a husband and father in another had many people dumbfounded. Except for Mrs. Verna Baker, who said practically, "It's not shocking. These kinds of accidents happen all the time in small towns. People can be anonymous in large cities. But in small towns, we just happen to know everything about everyone around us. It's not shocking, it's just plain heartbreaking."

Then she gave a curt nod of her head. Verna was brilliant at giving curt nods, tightening her lips in disagreement, and giving icy glares when necessary. She had softened only slightly following her wedding/elopement to Howard Baker the past spring. Actually, she had softened quite a bit, but she still enjoyed the power of being the church crank.

Maggie remembered that Cassandra, Carrie, and Carl would move to The Grange in two weeks' time. Many people from church would help with the move. Carrie and Carl would become accustomed to their new home while hospice care would be available daily for Cassandra. The biggest concern from Carrie and Carl was whether their two cats and two dogs could join them—which, of course, they could. An extra piece of good fortune was that they were moving to a farm. There was plenty of room for everyone.

Mary had invited the children to bring one special toy from home to The Grange each day prior to the move. She encouraged them to find special places in their new home for stuffed animals, dolls, Legos, and other toys. The transition had begun to work.

The entire story of the Moffets had the members of Loving the Lord in a steady state of grief for everyone involved, so they did what they did best. They brought food to Cassandra's home. They cleaned her house, they raked leaves, and they took the children on outings. They drove Cassandra to doctor's appointments. A gentle layer of compassion was wrapped around the little family. A mother saying goodbye to her children. Children hoping it would not be hard to visit their mommy in heaven. After all, someone must be able to drive them there.

Jennifer hadn't been gone long when Maggie was startled out of her ruminating by a slight knock on her door for the second time that morning. It was Hank.

"Sorry to interrupt, Pastor Maggie, but you seem to be very popular this morning. Lacey Campbell is here. May I send her in?"

"Of course," Maggie said as she shook off the heaviness of her thoughts.

"What about your wedding cards?" Hank whispered, trying to keep up with the secret scrapbook plot.

"Oh." Maggie smiled as she put the cards and scrapbook back under her desk. "Apparently, I shouldn't be trying to do anything but church work today. Drat."

Hank ushered Lacey into Maggie's office.

Lacey Campbell owned and operated the We Work Miracles Hair Salon on Main Street. Lacey was bright, funny, talented, in charge, and a natural gossip. She knew what was going on with everyone in Cherish. And if she didn't know, she found out within a day, depending on who was in her shampoo chair.

Lacey was dressed in black, which was her usual salon-wear. Her auburn hair was cut short on the sides and back, with longer bangs hanging down the right side of her face. By owning her own salon, Lacey had the fun of changing her own look and style whenever she wished. Her earlobes sparkled as each held several shiny stones. A delicate nose ring rested on her left nostril. A heart tattoo on her forearm was on full display, which perfectly matched Lacey's signature red lips.

Maggie found Lacey fascinating and exotic. She also enjoyed her as a new parishioner and friend. Maggie felt there was much to discover about Lacey. She looked forward to it.

"Good morning, Lacey. This is a nice surprise."

Maggie moved back to the visitor chairs, pointing to one for Lacey.

"Hi, PM. How's it going now that you have been married for not quite seventy-two hours?" Lacey sat down, her brown eyes laughing. "Are you going to keep him?"

Maggie laughed and snorted at the same time. She enjoyed people like Lacey who said what they thought whenever they thought it.

"Well, the jury's still out on that. I might have to give it . . . oh, I don't know, another fifty years, and then I'll have a better idea," Maggie said with a giggle.

"Okay. Keep me posted," Lacey said, crossing her legs as she settled into her chair. "Now, let's talk about something that really matters."

Maggie smiled. "Absolutely. Let's not waste our time on unimportant matters such as holy matrimony."

"Right. Here's the thing . . ." Lacey paused.

It seemed to Maggie that Lacey was—could it be *nervous*? Maggie waited.

"It's just that I think I would like to go on the mission trip to Ghana with you and everybody," Lacey said bluntly. "I don't know if I can do anything useful, but I think maybe I could try to do something."

Maggie opened her mouth to speak, but Lacey was on a roll.

"Don't worry about the money. I can pay my full way. I know I haven't been to any of the preparatory meetings, but perhaps you could catch me up. I figure we have about three months to get ready. I'm a fast learner. And don't worry about my shop." Lacey stopped to take a breath.

Maggie hadn't even thought about the salon.

"I am hiring a partner to help me out. The people of Cherish keep me awfully busy, and I'd like a Saturday off now and then." Lacey gave a slight toss of her auburn head. "I also have someone who can take care of my pets, so we're all good on that front as well."

Lacey seemed to have thought through everything. Maggie remembered that Lacey was the proud owner of two cats, Ned and Ted, a Chihuahua named Benedict, and a boa constrictor named Evelyn.

"You know I was raised in the church in Indiana," Lacey continued, "but I never understood what all the fuss was about. There was a lot of screaming and yelling about hell from the pulpit. And also at our kitchen table. My parents knew every person who was headed to hell, and they seemed to enjoy listing them off at dinnertime. My sister and I figured we didn't have a chance to make it to heaven. There were so many rules. I had friends who went to church. They mainly hated it too. But I like this church. It's kind of funky. You don't scream and yell, and Irena sure is a kick in the pants. I wish she would come into my salon and let me have a go at her crazy head." Lacey looked wistful as she dreamed about what she would do to Irena's hair if she could get her hands on it. "Anyway, I would like to go to Ghana and do something for those poor kids."

Maggie wondered if Lacey was finished. She waited.

Silence. Then she spoke.

"Lacey, I think it would be wonderful if you joined our group. We need all the hands we can get. There's nothing I can really do to prepare you because we don't know exactly what we'll be doing. We'll all learn on the job, so to speak. But we meet twice a month as a group for dinner. We also have a Skype call with my brother, Bryan, and his boss, Joy. They help us as they share information about the culture in the village, things we should bring, things we should not bring, what to expect as far as where we'll stay and what we'll eat . . . things like that. Oh, and we're all in the process of receiving necessary immunizations. Fortunately, with two doctors and a nurse on the trip, we are jabbed regularly with their vicious little needles." Looking at Lacey's tattoo and piercings, Maggie didn't think immunizations would faze the lovely Lacey at all. "Can you come to the parsonage on Friday night? It's potluck."

Lacey looked at Maggie, dumbfounded.

"You mean, that's it? I can go? Even though I didn't even go to all the new members classes? Am I even a real member?" Lacey asked quietly. "I thought maybe only real members could go on a mission trip."

"Lacey, what do you think church is, jail? Probation? High school? Rules and regulations?" Maggie laughed. "Maybe the church you grew up in had a different message, but we don't have laws. You don't have to jump through hoops to belong, you just belong. We love having you here. You're part of the family. Please come to Ghana with us."

Lacey smiled. "You know, PM, you're pretty cool."

Was there a slight catch in Lacey's voice?

"Ditto. Now, do you know how to cook? Because honestly, if you don't bring something delicious to the potluck on Friday, I might change my mind." Maggie tried to look serious, but it didn't work.

"Do I know how to cook? I'm an unbelievable cook. In fact, if I didn't work miracles in my hair salon, I would work miracles at the Cherish Café. I'll see you Friday with something that will knock your socks off." With that, Lacey stood up, and her nose ring gently dangled as she moved in and gave Maggie a hug. "I've got to get to my hair chair. Thanks, PM, for everything."

Lacey made her way past Irena, who ignored her, through the large oak doors of the church, and stood on the old stone steps. Irena was blaring something churchy on the organ. It was still a little foreign but sounded beautiful or hopeful. Or comforting. Lacey sat down on the steps and listened. Then she looked up to the blue sky, through leaves that were just thinking about changing color, and for the very first time in her life, Lacey really prayed.

"Thank you, Big G." Then she looked down at her purple painted fingernails. "Now, is there any chance you can actually forgive me and maybe love me?"

4

January 4, 2016
Bawjiase, Ghana

Maggie, Pastor Elisha, Joy, and Bryan made it to the airport waiting room all at the same time. Breathing hard, Pastor Elisha found a security guard and spoke loudly in the Twi dialect. The conversation was animated by both men. The security guard turned and led the group back to the luggage area.

Maggie looked frantically around the almost empty room. Back in the corner, she found Addie sitting on a pink suitcase, crying. Maggie ran across the room to the teenager.

"Addie, are you okay?" Maggie asked, even though it was obvious she wasn't.

"One of my bags didn't show up. I waited here, hoping it would come around on the belt. Once the belt stopped, I looked around, and the room was practically empty. I didn't know where our group was." Addie sniffled.

"That's Pastor Elisha," Maggie said, pointing. "He'll help us."

Pastor Elisha was talking to one of the luggage claim operators with the same speed and loudness he had with the security guard. Maggie liked the sound of the new language but remained focused on Addie.

"That man Pastor Elisha is talking to said, if I gave him one hundred dollars, he would see if he could find my bag," Addie said.

Joy and Bryan walked over to Maggie and Addie while Pastor Elisha continued speaking to the attendant. His voice got louder, and his arms began waving around.

"Addie was asked to pay one hundred dollars to possibly receive her bag by the man Pastor Elisha is speaking with," Maggie said quietly.

Bryan laughed and looked at Joy. She smiled.

"That happens to us sometimes," Bryan said. "We're getting good at fighting back. But everyone looks for a way to make some extra money. No one gets rich working here. But the worst airport we've experienced is in Lagos, Nigeria. We were trapped in that airport overnight once, weren't we, Joy."

Joy laughed.

"Is this really funny?" Maggie asked. "Addie was taken advantage of, probably due to her youth." Maggie turned to Addie. "What did you say when he asked for the dollars?"

"I told him that you had all the money. It was a lie, but I wasn't going to pay with my own money. I worked hard for that money at The Sugarplum." Addie moved from feeling frightened to feeling perturbed. "But then I realized I had no idea where any of you were."

"I'm sorry," Maggie said. "We will come up with some kind of buddy system from now on. We won't lose you again, or anyone else. What is it they do in preschool? Everyone has to have a buddy to hold hands with when they go on a field trip? Something like that."

Pastor Elisha came over, grinning. It seemed he was always grinning, when he wasn't yelling at airport attendants.

"Yes! It's done. Your bag will be here in the minute. No worries."

Maggie looked at Bryan. She was a mixture of indignation and frustration. She didn't have to speak as her eyes bored into his. Bryan pulled Maggie aside.

"Listen, this is the way it is," he said. "White people come here, and the people here think they are all very wealthy, which they are. Most white people come here and don't speak Twi. I won't go on a rampage about white privilege right now, but I could. It's not right, what happened to Addie, but it happens. It will happen every day for the next two weeks in some way or another. Whether it's a child in the village asking for dollars, or a taxi driver, or even one of our own kids at United Hearts, who have sadly learned that when white people show up they get loads of stuff. So relax yourself, Margaret. You are not in America. Respect the culture you are in and learn." Bryan was serious, more serious than Maggie had ever seen him before. "Maggie, your ideas of 'right and wrong' may be turned upside down on this trip. Get ready."

Maggie stared mutely at her brother. She didn't know what to think, therefore, had nothing to say.

The pink suitcase that matched the one Addie was sitting on rolled toward them with the luggage attendant pushing from behind.

"Your bag," he said and turned and walked away.

"Well, good. Let's go." Joy moved toward the exit. Obviously, there was no more time to chat about the situation.

Addie and Maggie stared at one another, then each pulled a pink rolling bag toward the exit. As they left the area, Maggie's eyes were drawn to the luggage belt. There were the wheels to her suitcase, smashed flat. *Drat!*

The small group made their way back to the tro-tro. No one had gotten in yet due to the heat, and everyone was relieved to see Addie and her pink bags. Ethan and Jack piled the last two suitcases on top of everyone else's in the back of the tro-tro. Soon they were settled inside. It was crowded, as everyone had to hold their own carry-on bags on their laps. But once they got going, the ride was thrilling.

As they drove through Accra, their eyes were overwhelmed with the sights. There were construction workers fixing parts of the road or working on new buildings. There were hundreds of people with stands selling food, clothing, beverages, jewelry, toys, and Ghanaian souvenirs. Along with the stands, people lined the roads, heads piled high with breads and cakes, fried plantains in plastic bags, more baggies of water, and Ghana flags. The driver moved in and out of traffic without fear. Maggie closed her eyes more than once when it looked like someone would get run over.

As the traffic started and stopped second by second, the music of car horns filled the air. At first, Maggie was discomforted by all the horns. In America, it was usually the sign of an angry driver. She looked at Bryan.

"It's how drivers talk to each other," Bryan said as he read her mind. "People honk for no reason sometimes. They know the traffic won't disappear if they honk, but they honk anyway."

Maggie sat back and took it all in. She smelled car exhaust, trash, cooking meat, and something spicy. She was hot just sitting in the tro-tro with her carry-on bags piled on her lap. She could feel sweat down the side of her face and a trickle moving down her back.

As she thought back to Bryan's "lecture" in the luggage area, Maggie felt irritated. She thought she understood the significance of different countries and cultures. Her time in Israel had taught her a great deal about how to respect these differences. But now she was in that new, beautiful, country and couldn't take her American eyes off the differences.

She needed Ghana eyes.

Lacey, after reapplying her red lipstick, pulled out a handful of hair ties from her carry-on bag and twisted her hair up into a messy bun on the top of her head. Sylvia was in the seat in front of Lacey. Lacey grabbed her hair and twisted it up too. Sylvia didn't know what was happening at first, then she laughed. Lacey turned to Dana, who sat next to her, and did the same thing.

"Ellen, your hair is too short. So is Joy's and Charlene's. But if you give me your head, Addie, I can help you out of this heat."

Lacey readied another tie. Addie leaned over Ellen and Jack and flung her long ponytail at Lacey. Lacey wrapped and wrapped Addie's long, thick hair around her head and used another tie to hold it in place.

"How much do I owe you?" Addie asked, giggling.

"You can't afford me. That's some pretty exquisite work I just did. Come here, PM," Lacey said, reaching for Maggie's head.

Maggie leaned in dutifully. Lacey pulled and twisted until Maggie yelped in pain and laughed at the same time.

"Ouch, Lacey, what are you doing?"

"You look a little cranky, so I thought I would pull your hair so you could have something different to be cranky about," Lacey said, giving Maggie's hair one last twist and anchoring it with a hair tie.

Cranky? I look cranky? Good grief! Maggie, pull yourself together.

"Lacey, you are good for my soul," Maggie said, rubbing the top of her head, "and my psyche. Maybe not my hair."

"I know," Lacey said with a toss of her head. "Now who wants to play 'I Spy'"?

Halfway through their journey, the tro-tro pulled into a small parking space in the midst of several stands.

"This is where we exchange money for the trip," Joy said. "We have found the office here has the best exchange rate. Maggie, you have the bulk of the church money, but does anyone else have money they would like to exchange while we're here?"

Everyone did. Joy pulled out a small pad of paper and a pen and jotted down each person's individual amount. Then she collected the money from each person. They had been told to bring one hundred dollar bills as the larger denomination would secure the best exchange rate. Joy and Pastor Elisha disappeared behind a small cinderblock building, each carrying a wad of one hundred dollar bills.

For one small second, Maggie wondered if they would ever see their money again. Then the second was gone. *Trust the people you are with. Ghana eyes.*

Maggie closed her eyes and thought back to the time she lived in Israel. It was right after college. For six months she had wandered the streets of Jerusalem, Bethlehem, Jericho, Tel Aviv, Gaza, and Galilee. She had climbed Masada and floated in the Dead Sea. There had been so many experiences. She had to learn how to exchange money and figure out what a shekel was worth. She had to navigate the Old City of Jerusalem, where different major religions lived and moved and had their being. She had heard bombs explode. She had smelled the spices as she passed local food stands in the Bazaar. She had picked fresh figs from trees and eaten them with goat cheese as she explored her surroundings. She had walked where her Bible told her Jesus had walked. Everything was foreign. Until Maggie had realized she was the foreigner. She had to stop comparing and just learn. She had to watch, listen, taste, and never say, "Well, in America we do it this way . . ." She had made mistakes, of course. But God had kept up the whispers. Maggie learned she had known a lot *about* God. But in Israel she had learned to *know* God, at least in a small way.

After about fifteen minutes, Pastor Elisha and Joy returned with Ghanaian cedis. One cedi was worth about one quarter in American money. Pastor and Joy had their hands full of fifty and twenty cedi notes. Joy dispersed the cedis to each participant, then gave Maggie the bulk of the money to keep for the projects they would complete during their visit.

Back on the road, they made their stop-and-go, horn-honking way toward Bawjiase. Fifi bought fried plantains and baggies of water for everyone. Maggie munched and sipped. She watched small children clinging to their mothers' legs. The mothers tried to sell whatever was being carried, seemingly without effort, on their heads. Dogs were running through the stands or lying in the sun, hoping for a morsel of food. People were talking and laughing as they plied their trades, ate a meal, or blasted loud Ghanaian music from loud speakers. The music was also coming from cars around them. It felt like a party that never ended.

Addie played "I Spy" with Lacey and Ellen. They watched all the action in the streets. Addie could hardly wait to get to United Hearts and meet the children. She had memorized the names of each child by the pictures Bryan had sent them.

Charlene and Dana were talking medicine. Since each woman expected to help on the medical side of things, they were trying to picture what that looked like. Dana would care for animals. Charlene would have human patients. Neither woman had ever done their work in a foreign country before.

"I think Jack, Ellen, and I will begin with simple checkups of the children. We'll go to the clinic in the village and do whatever we can," Charlene said. "I just don't know how people in the village will know about us."

"They already know," Joy said. "They've known for over a month. Word gets around. I think you will all have plenty to do for the next two weeks."

Sylvia looked at Joy. "I'm so excited to be able to help on the farm," she said.

"You will also have plenty to do," Joy said. "We have to water each plant individually by hauling water in buckets and watering cans every day. Sometimes twice a day. Nana is the young man who runs the farm for United Hearts. He will plant new vegetable plants while you're here."

"It's a treat to be able to work with plants in January," Sylvia said. "I usually have to wait until March to plant anything in my greenhouses. This sunshine is fabulous."

"I love it here," Joy said, more to herself than to Sylvia.

Bill Baxter and Ethan Kessler sat closest to the front.

"I'm interested in the school plans," Ethan said.

"Well," Bill's voice was so soft Ethan could hardly hear him, "I think we'll need help building the school."

Ethan laughed. "I've heard of something called a hammer, but I've never seen one with my own eyes."

"That's true," Charlene interjected. "He's my wonderful, completely *un*handyman."

"I will introduce you to a hammer," Bill said.

"Well, you're the expert. I only know how to lecture and grade papers," Ethan said self-deprecatingly. He was one of the most sought-after professors at the University of Michigan.

Bill could not put his finger on what he was feeling, but it was a good feeling. He was the building "expert" on this trip. He had never been an expert at anything before, or so he thought.

Jack looked at Maggie. "How are you doing?" he asked.

"Great. I just don't want to miss anything," Maggie said as she looked out the window. "I have a sneaking suspicion we will be back in a tro-tro going the opposite direction before we blink."

"I'm glad we get to do things like this together 'for as long as we both shall live.' I think that's how the vows went," Jack said.

"Yep. They did. You're stuck with me now, and I plan on living for a little while yet."

"Good. That's my plan too. We need to at least live through this trip." Jack laughed.

The tro-tro lurched hard to the right as the paved road quickly changed to a rocky and rutted red-dirt road. The remainder of the ride was one of bouncing, bouncing higher, sliding into one another, braking fast, and honking as herds of goats tripped merrily across the rough road. Finally, the tro-tro bumped its way past several cinderblock homes, through more herds of goats and sheep, and what appeared to be hundreds of chickens. The driver honked incessantly at all the beasts. The animals were responsible to get out of his way. Several children walked through the small neighborhood with buckets of water or grain on their heads. They waved at the tro-tro. Finally, the driver turned sharply in front of a house and stopped. The entire group lurched forward. The driver turned off the engine and everyone seemed to take a deep breath at the same time. Maggie wondered if they might all have whiplash.

Bryan, speaking Twi, thanked the driver and handed him several cedis for the trip.

"We're home," Joy said with a huge grin. "Welcome to the volunteer house."

5

October 6, 2015

Cherish, Michigan

Jack arrived at the parsonage on Tuesday evening a little later than planned. When he had finished his office work, he'd grabbed his coat, left the office building, gotten in his car, and driven straight to his condo. That's when he remembered he didn't really live there anymore. But since he was there, he grabbed a few things out of his closet, two houseplants, and three bags of books. Jack and Maggie had only begun to think about where they should live. They didn't even know how to be married yet, although they enjoyed figuring it out.

Jack drove to the parsonage and parked his black Jeep Cherokee behind Maggie's black Dodge Caliber. Even their cars looked married. Jack carried some of his belongings in through the kitchen door and smelled something delicious. He grinned. In the four years he had lived in his condo as a single family doctor, he had not once walked through the door and smelled something cooking. In fact, his kitchen looked as new and unused as the day he moved in. He breathed in the aroma of chicken, rosemary, onion, and something else spicy. Parsnips or rutabagas? This marriage thing was turning out to be a pretty good deal.

As he headed toward the stairs, three creatures came flying into the kitchen—one screeching, one sliding into the dishwasher, and one getting tangled up in Jack's legs. Dropping his briefcase and a bag of books, he fell against the wall, clumsily bracing himself with his shoulder as papers went flying.

There was another screech as another creature dashed into the room, but this time it came from Maggie.

"Are you all right?" she asked as she began collecting Jack's books, papers, calendar, pens, and sticks of spearmint gum.

"Those cats are going to kill me," he said, sounding perturbed as he righted himself. He wasn't used to being knocked off his feet by three furry terrorists.

Maggie turned to the delinquents. Marmalade, a large orange tom-cat, was sitting under the kitchen table, his eyes wide, looking as guilty as a cat is able to look. Cheerio, a fluffy calico, jumped on a chair to escape her tormenter, Fruit Loop, a tabby who spent his days chasing Cheerio around the parsonage. At that moment, the tabby sat by the dishwasher, shook his head, and tried to get his bearings after slamming into the appliance.

"Now listen, you three," Maggie said in her kitty voice. "You may not knock Dad down right when he gets home from work." Her voice got higher and more singsongy. "Dad loves you. Please stop trying to kill him." Then she gave each cat a pat on the head.

"First of all, I'm not their dad," Jack said, his hair uncharacteristically ruffled. "Secondly, I'm the one who should be getting nice physical attention since I'm the one they almost killed."

"Of course," Maggie said, still in her cat voice. "Poor Jackie! Let me fix your hair." She patted him on the head.

Jack watched as she winked at Marmalade. With that, he picked her up, swung her around, and dumped her on the once-white-now-gray couch in the living room. He was careful not to bump her ankle, just in case it was still tender.

"What's for dinner? And how did you have time to make anything? Didn't you see shut-ins today?" Jack asked, helping her up from the couch.

"It's called a Crock-Pot. After you left for work, I loaded it up with chicken, tomatoes, spices, and Sylvia's latest installment of root vegetables. Then I pressed the 'on' button. Voila! Dinner cooked all day long."

"You are brilliant and beautiful," he said.

He grabbed his books and made his way toward the stairs.

"That's your stomach talking. You can't fool me," Maggie said as she picked up his briefcase and followed him up the stairs.

They had made one decision about living arrangements and chosen one of the extra parsonage bedrooms to be a study for Jack. The next weekend Bill Baxter, his truck, and his muscles would help move furniture around the parsonage and bring Jack's desk and other personal items from the condo.

Maggie's office was on the main floor at the back of the parsonage. It had turned out to be her favorite room. Oak paneling, bookcases full of her school books, and a box stuffed with every note, letter, and gift from Ed James. That box made the study a sacred place for Maggie. She also loved the one large floor-to-ceiling window facing the backyard where three beautiful pine trees grew. There was a small red wagon full of colorful annual flowers that danced and bobbed beneath the trees. The flowers danced a little less as nights got cooler with autumn on the move. Eventually, she would remove the flowers and refill the wagon with pinecones and branches from the evergreens.

Maggie wrote her Sunday sermons in the quiet room. The trees gave her something to focus on when she experienced writer's block. The squirrels and birds that lived in the backyard easily drew her attention away from tasks at hand, and the cats went "kitty bananas" as they stared out the window that seemed to be made just for cats: floor level. The addition of birdfeeders gave everyone something to watch.

Maggie went back downstairs to finish prepping dinner, while Jack dropped off his books in the spare room and then changed out of his suit. Maggie felt as though she were living in a 1950's television show. All she needed was an apron. Fortunately, she found it delightful instead of restrictive—love without bounds. Neither Jack nor Maggie had expectations of the other, in traditional or non-traditional ways. Every act of love was a mini happy surprise party for the other.

"What's our to-do list for tonight?" Jack asked as he came back into the kitchen. "Wait, let me guess. We are going to do something with all these wedding cards. Please tell me we can eat first?" he pleaded.

"No wedding cards," she said, moving them off the table. "By the way, your mother is a saint for stocking our freezer with her applesauce."

She emptied one of Bonnie's containers into a bowl and took a whiff of the apples and cinnamon. "It's the only reason I married you."

"I know."

They sat down, and Maggie prayed. Then Jack grabbed his fork and shoveled a large bite of chicken and veggies into his mouth.

"I saw Arly Spink at the hospital today," Jack said after swallowing. "She is donating several works of her own art to the new cafeteria."

Heal Thyself Community Hospital had recently built a new cafeteria. Oddly enough, the hospital food had become so popular in Cherish, Heal Thyself saw an opportunity to open up the cafeteria to the community. Breakfast, lunch, and dinner were available to all. The hospital board also chose to have reduced and free meals for anyone in need. Jack had been behind the idea of the "cost of meal" options.

"That was nice of Arly. The hospital is lucky to have her art. She is so gifted. I sure would like to get her into church sometime. Not just because she's artistic and I could ask her to make some cool banners for the sanctuary, but she really seems like an interesting person to know."

Jack nodded. He had asked Arly to paint a picture of Loving the Lord as a birthday gift for Maggie earlier in the year. With very little time, the painting was finished, and Maggie was thrilled. Arly had even painted Maggie's name on the small painted sign in front of the church.

"Did you see Cassandra today?" Maggie asked, a little more subdued as she helped herself to a bite of noodles and parsnips.

"I did. The hospice nurse was with her, so I didn't stay long. She's relieved to be moving into The Grange next week. She mentioned how many people have stopped by to help, which she appreciates, but it has also taken away almost every shred of her privacy. People won't be able to just stop by at The Grange. Mary and the hospice staff will make sure of that." He took a bite of a piece of liberally buttered bread. "But even with people around, death can be a lonely journey."

Maggie set her fork down. It was true. People made that last journey alone. But, she thought, they make the journey with a promise of God with them—holding them and bringing them into healing and total love.

"You're right," she said, "being at The Grange will give Cassandra more privacy. Carrie and Carl will also have a chance to get used to their new home. There's so much to do."

"So tell me, what is our to-do list for tonight and the next week?" Jack asked again.

"You know, bits and bobs, odds and ends, this and that."

Jack stared at her. She smiled.

"Well, tonight we can do a little more rearranging. Then, for the coming week, we have our particular work schedules, of course. We need to be ready for the Ghana potluck on Friday. Lacey is going to join us for the potluck and the mission trip. That was a nice surprise today."

"What is she going to do on the trip?" Jack asked. "Cut everyone's hair?"

"She's going to do anything that needs to be done. I think she will keep us laughing. So, as far as our to-do list," she continued, "on Saturday we'll move some of your things from the condo. And, of course, celebrate our one week wedding anniversary." She grinned. "Sunday afternoon is the animal blessing service at church. You'll be in charge of our three inmates."

Maggie looked at Cheerio, who was curled up on Jack's lap.

"What do I have to do?" Jack asked tentatively as he gave Cheerio an absentminded pat.

"Put them in their cat carriers and walk across the lawn to church. Then I will bless them and we will all have treats."

Cheerio lifted her head when she heard the magical "T" word.

"I can't wait," Jack said resignedly, realizing he had new responsibilities as the pastor's spouse.

They finished dinner, and as Jack loaded the dishwasher, Maggie showed him the new G.M. Malliet book.

"Secretly, this was the best part of my day," Maggie said. "It was so nice of Jennifer to bring it over this morning. She had it wrapped and everything."

"Will you share it?" Jack asked.

"What do you think?"

"Great. So, Malliet . . . I think we should have a fire in the fireplace and begin reading it tonight," Jack said, but then he became distracted with a kiss.

Maggie dropped the book on the counter.

The Westminster chimes rang.

The amazingly distracting kiss was sadly interrupted.

Maggie instinctively looked at the clock on the wall. It was seven thirty. She opened the front door.

Cole Porter stood on the parsonage porch. Cole and his wife, Lynn, owned the funeral home in town. Maggie had learned so much from him about caring for the bereaved. She also learned how to be prepared for the suddenness of death.

Maggie looked at Cole. All she could say was, "Cassandra?"

Cole shook his head. "Katharine Smits. Sylvia just called, and I told her I would pick you up on the way. Katharine died about thirty minutes ago."

Maggie moved quickly. "I'll be right down, Cole," she said, climbing the stairs a little too fast until her ankle slowed her back down.

Once in her bedroom, she opened her closet door and immediately smelled Jack. His cologne wafted into the room. Maggie took a deep breath as she pulled black pants and a sweater from what was now her side of the closet. She was changed and back downstairs in two minutes.

"Love you," she said to Jack with a kiss. "I'll be back in a while."

Cole drove the hearse down the street to the Friendly Elder Care Center and parked near the rear entrance. Katharine would be going back with him. He treasured being able to care for the people of Cherish when loved ones died.

"Thanks for picking me up," Maggie said.

"No problem. It's what we do, right?" Cole smiled.

Cole and Maggie walked into Katharine's room, and Sylvia and Bill were there. Each held one of Katharine's still hands. Katharine's body was curled up and twisted, as it had been in life. Sylvia's silent tears made a slow stream down her cheeks. When she saw Maggie, she looked up and whispered, "Mother's gone now, Pastor Maggie.

The nurses helped her into bed for the night. When they came back to check on her, she was gone. Just like that."

Maggie walked to Sylvia's side, and Bill walked from the bed and stood behind his wife.

"I'm so glad for her," Maggie said, "and I'm sorry for you. You have been a faithful and loving daughter all your life."

Maggie remembered how Sylvia went to her mother's room every day to feed her lunch and often went back in the evenings to help with dinner.

Sylvia's tears flowed quietly. "She was the one who taught me how to love in the first place." Sylvia paused, then said, "Do you know what I'm most thankful for?"

Maggie shook her head.

"Her arthritis is all gone. She can walk again, and she can hold up her head and hug my father. Right after Jesus, of course."

Maggie thought about the many years Katharine had spent in a wheelchair, her body bent so badly it looked like all her bones were pointed in the wrong direction. After a lifetime of working hard in her garden and then buying and successfully running The Garden Shop, Katharine's body began to give out, bit by bit. After giving so much to others all her life, she finally had to be the recipient of every kind of help at the end. That lack of control caused occasional outbursts of frustration and anger, usually aimed at Sylvia, but her daughter took it with grace.

"How are you doing, Bill?" Maggie asked.

"I'm doing all right, Pastor Maggie. I'm glad she was my mother-in-law these last few months. I wish it could have been longer." Bill quickly brushed his hand across his eyes then looked at the ground in his normal shy way.

Cole waited until Maggie had prayed with Sylvia and Bill, then he carefully explained the next steps. He would be taking Katharine to the funeral home that night.

"Pastor Maggie will meet with you tomorrow," Cole said to Sylvia and Bill. He and Maggie had discussed this on the short ride to the

Friendly Elder Care. "I will join you, and we can plan Katharine's funeral."

"Would it be okay to meet in Pastor Maggie's office?" Sylvia asked, looking from Maggie to Cole.

"Of course," Cole said. "Let's meet at ten o'clock."

Sylvia and Bill said their quiet goodbyes to Katharine. Then Maggie walked out to the parking lot with them. She silently thanked God for Bill. Sylvia wouldn't have to be alone that night. Or any night.

"Pastor Maggie?" Sylvia took Maggie's hand. "I told my mother last week that I was going to back out of the Ghana trip. I felt that spending two weeks away from her would be too long. She needs . . . um . . . needed so much extra care." Sylvia looked at Maggie, then down at the ground.

"How do you feel about that tonight?" Maggie asked.

"It's weird." Sylvia sighed. "In a way, it feels as if she has given me a gift. Does that sound selfish?"

"Would your mother call you selfish?" Maggie asked.

Sylvia shook her head. "She told me I had to go because 'those babies needed to be hugged.'"

Maggie bit her lip and took a deep breath. "Your mother was right. I think you learned how to be selfless from your mother, never selfish. That's what makes you such a beautiful woman."

Maggie hugged Sylvia, then felt Bill's arms surround both of them.

"Would you like a ride, Pastor Maggie?" Bill asked after their tiny group hug.

"No, thank you. I think I'll walk. But I'll see you both in the morning."

They said goodnight to one another. Then Maggie pulled out her cell phone and called Jack.

"I'm walking home to you now," she said.

"I'll meet you halfway."

He actually met her farther than halfway, due to the fact that he had longer legs.

As they walked home, hand in hand, they saw Katharine pass by in Cole's hearse. She was already home.

6

January 4, 2016
Bawjiase, Ghana

Everyone poured out of the tro-tro once the doors were opened. Legs were stiff, but their owners were excited. Pastor Elisha needed to get back to United Hearts but said he would see them at dinner.

The volunteer house was a long, white cement structure with a front porch that went the length of the building. Several plastic chairs were lined up along the porch, and towels and T-shirts were hanging on the backs of some of the chairs. A stack of colorful buckets was piled at one end. Large palm trees surrounded the house, and the branches danced in the wind, the sound creating a natural wind chime. There were two clotheslines running along the side of the house, but nothing was hanging on them as they swayed in the wind.

Everyone helped unload the tro-tro, grabbing their luggage and following Bryan, Joy, and Fifi into the house. They turned to the right through large double doors and into what appeared to be a living/dining room. A long wooden table was in the center of the room with more plastic chairs set around it, and a jar of strawberry jam, a bowl of sugar, a small box with packets of tea, and several books were on the table. There was a spicy, peppery smell hanging in the air, and Maggie realized she was hungry.

Pieces of foam rubber were lying on the cement floor against the walls. On one wall there was a giant bookcase haphazardly filled with books, games, and art supplies. The walls were covered with photographs of the many volunteers who had been to United Hearts over the years. Each volunteer was holding one or more of the children in the photos. Lots of happy teeth were showing. In the corner of the large room, a refrigerator hummed.

"This is the dining room, but we also hang out here a lot in the evenings," Bryan said. "We play games or just talk and listen to music. It's a great way to debrief our day. The bookshelf holds many books that past volunteers have left here. I'm sure you will find something interesting if you need something to read." He grinned. "If you need a nap in the middle of the day, feel free to lie down out here on one of the foam rubber pads. It's usually cooler in here than the bedrooms." He took a breath and continued. "We have some children's books here for when the kids come over. We always let them read whatever is on the shelf and look at the pictures or color in the coloring books."

"We brought fifty new books for all ages of children," Maggie said.

"It will be wonderful for the library in the new school," Joy responded. "The books will be well used."

Just then, a dog ran out of what looked to be the kitchen and into the dining room and began jumping on each new person, licking hands and stopping to bark with excitement every few seconds. His tail was completely out of control.

"This is Obolo," Bryan said as he knelt down to pet the affectionate dog. "His name means 'fat,' and he lives here at the volunteer house. He'll be the healthiest dog you see here on your trip."

Dr. Dana stepped forward and knelt down next to Bryan. Obolo went right to Dana and immediately rolled on his back for a belly rub.

"He's been neutered. That's great!" Dana said.

"The local vet knows you are coming, Dr. Dana. I think you'll be interested in the pet clinic," Bryan said.

Dana smiled as she casually looked in Obolo's ears and at his teeth.

"He seems to live up to his name," she said. "He must get regular food."

"Bryan has made that happen," Joy chimed in. "He and Fifi plotted together. Bryan sends the money, and Fifi rides his motorbike to Kasoa to buy dog and cat food. We have a litter of kittens over at United Hearts." Joy smiled at Bryan and Fifi.

"Fifi, do you love animals?" Dana asked.

"Yes, I love animals. Many animals have a hard life here. We do what we can."

"The kitchen is through that door," Joy continued. "Fifi will cook your food these next two weeks. He is an excellent cook."

Fifi grinned under Joy's praise. He took great pride in being a good cook, and he often cooked for volunteers who stayed in the house. His best friend, Isaac, helped when there was a big crowd.

"But tonight, we'll be eating at United Hearts," Joy continued. "You will taste Fifi's handiwork at breakfast tomorrow."

"What do I smell?" Maggie asked. The spicy smell was delicious. It reminded her of the rice they had made for the special Ghana service at church to raise money for the trip.

"That is Ghana red pepper. You will smell a lot of it while you're here," Joy answered.

Maggie, who was starving, wanted to eat Ghana red pepper sprinkled on anything, right then and there.

The group took turns looking in the kitchen. There was one small sink and one countertop covered with a piece of thick wood. Several trays of eggs were at the end of the counter. There was a two-burner stove and a large rubber trash barrel filled with water for cooking and washing up.

"The water in the trash barrel is not to be used for drinking. Let me be very clear on that," Joy said, looking each participant in the eyes. "Once it's boiled, it is fine for cooking. But we have small bags of pure water for drinking." She pointed to a large pallet of plastic wrapped baggies. Maggie thought there might be a hundred baggies of water altogether. "We replenish these bags every day. Drink a lot of water every day. It is hot. You will walk miles per day, and it's important to stay hydrated."

Everyone nodded as they looked back into the kitchen.

Off to the side of the sink was a very small pantry that held bags of rice and beans and several pineapples and watermelons. There was a large bowl of what had to be the red pepper.

How can Fifi possibly cook for all of us with such a small and ill-equipped kitchen?

Maggie couldn't imagine trying to make food for such a crowd without her large stove and oven, her many countertops, her dishwasher, and every electric appliance under the sun. She thought back to Thanksgiving dinner at the parsonage six weeks earlier. She and Jack had used the parsonage kitchen along with the church's double ovens. She looked at Fifi's small kitchen once again. Then she remembered: *Maggie, stop. Ghana eyes.*

"There are three bedrooms," Joy continued. "Because we have only four males, you are all in this room."

She led the group to a small room off the dining room. There were three sets of bunk beds, all covered in mosquito netting. It was clear to Maggie that Bryan had already moved his things in. One bottom bunk was an absolute mess, with clothes and toiletries scattered on the bunk under his net.

"Jack, Ethan, and Bill, you can all pick a bunk in here."

The men did as commanded, and Jack quickly took the top bunk of one of the sets. Maggie knew Jack did it so others could have the bottom bunks, which were usually more comfortable and easier to get in and out of. It made her heart swell to witness such thoughtfulness.

"Women, if you would like to follow me, I'll show you to your rooms. Because there are eight of us, nine on weekends when Cate Carlson gets here, we have the luxury of two rooms."

The women's rooms were at the other end of the house. They had the same set-up, except there were four sets of bunk beds in one room and three in the other. Mosquito nets also enveloped each bed. Maggie quickly took Jack's lead and lifted the net on one of the top bunks in the room with three sets of bunks.

"Oh no, Pastor Maggie," Sylvia said, horrified. "You must take a bottom bunk."

"No, Sylvia, I mustn't. I love sleeping on the top bunk." *Lie* "I always chose the top bunk when I went to summer camp." *Lie* "We'll make Cate take another top bunk since she's just showing up for weekends."

Maggie laughed as she hauled a sheet out of her suitcase and began making her top bunk, which was quite difficult because of her short stature and the mosquito net that kept tangling itself around her arms and the sheet.

Lacey and Addie followed suit, pulled sheets out of their suitcases, and made their thin beds. They had been told to bring a travel pillow to sleep with, which they had done.

Joy, Charlene, Ellen, and Dana went into the next room and were each treated to a bottom bunk. Joy's bunk was already set up, looking nothing like Bryan's slop hole. The other three women made their beds, then placed their suitcases either above them on the top bunks or shoved them underneath their beds.

They were settled in and ready to work.

When Maggie finished making her bed, she shoved her two suitcases on the top bunk of the bed next to hers. The other women finished up, stepped out of their bedroom, and peeked to the right into a large cinderblock room. It had a cement floor with a drain in one corner. There was a window high up for light, and a rough wooden shelf was against one wall. The men joined them after throwing sheets on their beds and calling it good enough. Jack had a sneaking suspicion he was going to feel quite claustrophobic under the mosquito net.

Joy appeared with the women from the other bedroom.

"This is the shower room," she said.

Everyone looked around the walls. There was no shower. There wasn't even a hose.

"Where's the shower?" Lacey asked.

Joy pointed to a large rubber trash barrel. It was like the one in the kitchen, also full of water.

"When you wish to shower, you will have a 'bucket bath' using this water. Grab a bucket from the porch, bring your towel and toiletries into this room, along with a full bucket of water from the barrel. If you need more, bring in a second bucket. Rinse with the water, *but don't swallow it!* Suds up, then rinse again. It often feels good at the end of the day to have a cold bucket bath." Joy nodded her head, as if wishing for a bucket bath that very minute.

"Well, I'll be dipped!" Lacey said.

"No, you'll be sprinkled," Maggie retorted, thinking her little baptism joke quite hilarious.

No one laughed.

"Now, on to the toilet," Joy said.

They didn't have to move because the toilet stall was right next to the so-called shower room. One toilet sat in a tiny cement room. There was a toilet paper holder with a new roll of toilet paper attached. A small plastic trash can was next to the toilet.

Joy continued, "Yes, it is unusual to have a real toilet. Lucky you. We had this put in for volunteers. Toilets are somewhat rare in the village. Now, excuse my crassness, but here's how it goes. When you pee, just pee. There's no flushing for that. But before you do something with more substance, you will need a bucket of water in here with you. Do your business, then pour the bucket down the toilet. That's the only way to flush. *Never put toilet paper in the toilet!*" Once again, Joy looked everyone in the eyes. "We don't have the plumbing in the countryside to handle anything but human waste going through the pipes. Put your used toilet paper in the trash can. When it's full, we'll take turns burning it out back."

No one was quite able to restrain from making a face at that bit of news.

Gross! Maggie cringed.

"Needless to say," Joy soldiered on, "feminine hygiene products also go in the trash and will be burned. We'll all work together fetching water to keep both barrels full. The well is just a few minutes walk from here."

"Well, this is going to be fun," Lacey said, clapping her hands. "There will be thirteen of us, once Cate gets here. We'll keep this little toilet pretty busy."

"It may seem primitive," Joy said with a lighter tone, "but there are many in the country who don't have any plumbing at all. The new orphanage has six toilets. Three for the girls and three for the boys. It's quite luxurious." She smiled.

"When can we go to United Hearts?" Addie asked hesitantly. She had her mother's soft voice.

"If you would like, we can walk there right now." Joy raised an eyebrow questioningly.

"I'd love to go," Maggie said.

The others nodded in agreement. It appeared that everyone was eager to finally meet the children they had heard so much about.

"Then feel free to use the facility, if needed. Grab a baggie of water, and I think we all should put bug spray on before we leave. I know you are all taking your anti-malaria meds, but it never hurts to have a little added protection. Grab your flashlights, and off we go!" Joy sounded like Happy of the Seven Dwarfs.

Everyone took care of toilet needs, grabbed a bag of water, bug sprayed themselves, and lined up.

"Hey, Joy?" Bryan called. "Should we bring some groundnuts?"

"Great idea. Grab about forty baggies," Joy answered.

"Megs, can you help me?" Bryan asked with a wink.

Maggie followed Bryan to the kitchen. He pulled a large bucket from under the counter full of small baggies filled with something that looked like Spanish peanuts. The bags were tied shut. Bryan took a large canvas bag and filled it with the small bags, and Maggie joined in.

"Where did you get these?" Maggie asked as she counted.

"There is a woman in the village who grows groundnuts. We made a business deal with her. We promised to buy one hundred and fifty bags per week if she can produce them for us. She has them ready every week. We give groundnuts to the children for an extra boost of protein, and she is able to support her entire family because of what we buy."

Bryan kept counting.

Maggie marveled at that information.

"We also found a woman who sells oranges," he said. "We have set up a similar deal with her. Her son delivers them directly to United Hearts. The best part is, although Joy and I buy the groundnuts, United Hearts is now making enough money from their farm to buy the oranges. They are getting more and more self-sustainable." Bryan picked up the bag. "Joy and I are trying to work ourselves out of this job."

"What would that mean?" Maggie asked.

"United Hearts will definitely be able to sustain itself and no longer need our support. Then we move on to the next place. We ask them what they need. They tell us, and we do what we can to help them get to where they want to be. The people in the villages are much smarter about this than we are."

Bryan led Maggie out into the dining/living area as she considered what he had said. She was excited for him, and a little jealous. He would work himself out of job after job, only to go to new villages all over the countries in Africa. What amazing things he would see and hear. It made her life in Cherish seem dull.

Bryan poked Maggie in the ribs, and she jumped, snapped back to the present moment.

"Okay, friends, we each need a buddy," Maggie blurted, looking at Addie. "If you're married, your spouse is your buddy. If you're not, pick someone else."

Ellen grabbed Addie's hand. "We'll not be losing you again, missy!"

Addie smiled. Lacey and Dana buddied up, and Joy took the lead. Bryan and Fifi brought up the rear.

They began their journey down the long, winding, red-dirt road into the countryside and straight to the children who already had their hearts.

7

October 6-11, 2015
Cherish, Michigan

It was nine p.m. when Jennifer Becker finally locked up The Page Turner and walked north on Main toward her home on Dewey Street. She had packed up the box of children's books for the Ghana mission trip as her final task of the day. Beth had left earlier to begin dinner preparations. It was Jennifer's night to stay late.

Walking past the dark business buildings, she passed Middle Street, then crossed over the railroad tracks. Jennifer walked past The Mill, famous for "Easy Mix" corn muffin and other delicious mixes for baked goods. The Mill had been in Cherish since Jennifer and Beth were children. The two sisters had gone to school with the children of The Mill's founders, the Kellers, and had never known their school friends were multi-millionaires. It wouldn't have mattered if they had known. Children wanted friends, not money. The children at Cherish Elementary School wanted friends they could occasionally swap lunches with and chase around town on bikes. And they'd usually end up at the Keller home for treats afterward, long before the recipe for those treats became a national treasure.

Mrs. Keller was a wonderful baker, and her recipes filled the stomachs of the children who came home with her son, Darcy (Mrs. Keller was a huge fan of Jane Austen), and daughter, Priscilla (Mr. Keller was a huge fan of the Bible). When Darcy, Priscilla, and their hungry friends showed up after tearing around town on their bicycles, Mrs. Keller had plates of blueberry muffins and lemon tarts in summer time, apple biscuits in the fall, cherry muffins and cinnamon bread in the winter, and strawberry cake in the spring.

Mr. Keller had taken his wife's recipes to restaurants in Cherish and Ann Arbor in an attempt to sell them to different eateries. No one was interested. They didn't want new recipes with so many ingredients. Mr. Keller knew there would be a craving for his wife's delicious baked goods and knocked on doors until one day he met a baker in Ypsilanti who said, "Give me the ingredients already mixed. I'll try them out for a month."

What grew like warm yeast out of that exasperated request were fifteen dozen Mason jars with the ingredients for corn muffins, biscuit mix, brownies, and yellow cake. All the baker needed to add were eggs and milk.

"I need another fifteen dozen!" that baker bellowed to Mr. Keller over the phone after one week.

"The Mill" and "Easy Mix" were born.

Mrs. Keller's kitchen hobby turned into many a housewife's dream: making money from baking in their kitchens.

Mrs. Popkin, the owner of The Sugarplum Bakery in Cherish, mainly baked with her own family recipes, but she wasn't averse to using some varieties of the mixtures, throwing in her own secret ingredients to make her baked treats extra special.

All in all, The Mill and Easy Mix grew every year as the simple mixes were shipped far beyond the borders of Michigan, but Cherish kept its reputation as the only city in the world that made the mixes. It was a source of pride for the entire community.

Jennifer smiled as she passed The Mill. So many people from Cherish had made a good living there. Mr. Keller hired from his own town first and was a fair, generous, and honest employer. Jennifer's own father had worked his way up in the company from the mixing room to the executive offices.

As young teens, Jennifer and Darcy had gone from bike riding around town to walking in the park, eating ice cream at the drug store, and holding each other's hands and hearts. They had their own quiet relationship in junior high and high school. But after graduation, Darcy was sent to the University of Michigan to study business. Even though the U of M was close to home, Darcy found a new life. There wasn't an actual break-up between Darcy and Jennifer. He became more like a "missing person" in Jennifer's life. The young romance was slowly snuffed out.

Upon university graduation, Darcy married a young woman from New York City, who was also a U of M graduate. The marriage had been neatly arranged by the four parents, eager to merge two successful family businesses.

Jennifer had read about Darcy's wedding in the *Cherish Life and Times* and was faced with the photos of her high school sweetheart with his new bride. Jennifer never talked about Darcy, not even with Beth. Some things needed to stay hidden in the heart. At least that's what Jennifer thought.

As they got older, Jennifer and Beth were groomed by their father to begin their own business because he was confident in his daughters' keen intellects. Since they both had a passion for books, they decided to open the first book shop in Cherish: The Page Turner. They took classes at the local community college in accounting, economics, and business. After graduation, The Page Turner Book Shop was opened, thanks to their father's investment, and thrived under the sisters' ownership. The Cherish community appreciated not having to drive to Ann Arbor or Jackson to buy their books. For Jennifer and Beth, the long hours of work kept both women happily busy from dawn till dusk. Thoughts of romance and love had faded into the periphery of life. Beth had been aware of her sister's high school romance with Darcy, but once his marriage had taken place, life consisted only of education and The Page Turner.

Jennifer and Beth had remained friends with Priscilla, however. The friends didn't spend time talking about Priscilla's brother but kept their friendship revolving around life and events in Cherish. Priscilla spent some of her time at her home on Lake Michigan, but more and more she was in Cherish, living in the home she grew up in. Priscilla always had a smile on her face, and she loved popping into The Page Turner with large coffees and the latest gossip from around town. Both Jennifer and Beth felt a lift in their spirits when Priscilla was around. She was lively and knew how to tell a story.

Both Darcy and Priscilla were on the board of directors of The Mill. That meant Darcy flew home three times a year for meetings, but no one in Cherish ever saw him beyond those meetings. He flew in with his private jet, was driven to Cherish from Detroit in his limousine, and left the same way following the two-day meetings. Darcy had a large home on the east side of town, but he never stayed there. It had been locked up for years. He chose to stay with Priscilla in their childhood home on his short visits back. With both now parents gone, the two siblings were close.

One morning, the year before, right before Thanksgiving, Priscilla had bounced into the bookstore, her eyes flashing as she passed out coffees to Jennifer and Beth.

"There are some rumblings afoot," Priscilla announced conspiratorially. She blew on her coffee, then took a gulp. "It sounds like Darcy's wife has left him. And guess what? She's apparently dating his very best friend!" She took another large swallow, as if the hot coffee was fueling her words like gas to an engine. "Darcy is apparently devastated. I have begged him to come home to Michigan. He refused. Such an idiot! He claims his life is in New York. So there he is staying."

She took another swig of coffee and looked at the sisters, a little more intently at Jennifer.

Jennifer wasn't going to bite. Darcy was a memory so faded she couldn't even picture him anymore. He wasn't in her head. At all.

And she hadn't seen Darcy in the year since Priscilla's revelation. Jennifer thought back through the long years as she slowly walked past The Mill and toward home to Beth. Whoever first said "time heals all things" was right. The harsh colors of heartbreaks and devastations had smoothed into softer, gentler water colors as the years passed.

∞

Maggie could hardly keep up with her week as it turned from well-ordered into chaos. Katharine Smit's funeral was planned for Saturday, the tenth of October.

Besides the funeral, Maggie was trying to prepare file folders of information for all those attending the Ghana potluck on Friday evening. Joy and Bryan had sent a list of common Twi words for the group to learn and practice with one another.

Looking at Jack, Maggie said in exasperation, "I have to figure out a time to make the two pies for the potluck. I have to write my sermon for Sunday and plan the animal blessing service for Sunday afternoon. I've decided to give up sleep. It's the only way to manage."

Jack smiled at his wife. He rightly suspected every week was similar to that one, and somehow she managed just fine.

"Want me to write your sermon for you?" he teased. "Give up sleep if you will, but I won't."

Unfortunately, that's exactly what Jack did. He delivered three babies in four days: one on Wednesday night, one on Thursday night, and the third on Saturday, which was also the day he was supposed to move his things from his condo into the parsonage.

"Thank goodness for Bill Baxter and Fred Tuggle," Maggie said to Jack over the phone on Saturday morning. "They have already moved the furniture we wanted and the boxes you had ready. You just stay at the hospital and do that easy, cushy job of bringing a life into the world. We'll take care of the important things over here." She giggled, convinced she was incredibly funny.

"You do that, wife," Jack said and then clicked off.

He knew the church folk would help, and he was thankful. He yawned as he made his way back to the delivery suite.

The evening before, Maggie had been happy to see Lacey at the potluck but shocked to see Dr. Dana Drake. Dana owned the Cherish Your Pets Animal Hospital in town. She was also a new member of Loving the Lord. Dana was the only African-American member of the church. Or the entire town of Cherish. There was a noticeable lack of diversity for those with eyes to see.

"Dana, what are you doing here?" Maggie asked, confused.

"I'm sorry to crash your potluck, but I have been thinking about it and praying a lot. I would love to join the trip and maybe help with an animal clinic. Anything to help." Dana's brown eyes were serious.

Maggie's head whirled. "That's wonderful. I'm sure there are a million needs. You will be able to help in so many ways. There is a local vet in Bawjiase. You can meet him and find out about a developing country's veterinary medicine."

"Thank you," Dana said. "I am fascinated to learn. I can bring supplies if they're needed."

"We'll ask Joy and Bryan later when they Skype into the meeting," Maggie said. "It's time for dinner now."

"I don't cook, but I did bring some cat treats for your felines. I hope that's enough to get me into the meeting."

Dana handed the treats to Maggie, knowing the pastor was a complete pushover for anything involving her feline babies.

The rest of the group was thrilled when they discovered Lacey and Dana were joining their ranks.

"This trip is going to be *the bomb*!" Addie said. "When I'm not with the children, may I help with the animals?"

"Of course," Dana said. "I don't know what we'll do exactly, but we'll do all the good we can for whoever we find."

The potluck had gone well, and dinner was consumed with gusto. Then the mood changed when Maggie pulled out the list of Twi words they were supposed become familiar with. Twi was one of the dialects in Ghana. Even though the words were spelled phonetically, it was hard for the participants to get their tongues around the new sounds. Joy and Bryan came into the meeting via Skype and tried to encourage the group in the parsonage.

"I know it sounds odd at first," Joy said, "but these words will help when you speak with the adults at United Hearts. A few of them know some English, but most people in the village do not. The children learn English in school. They will be helpful translators for you."

Maggie knew the importance of learning at least some basics of the culture and language before traveling to any foreign country. It was a sign of respect.

"It's important to remember you are guests," Joy continued. "I can't tell you enough that to show respect for the country and village is the most important thing you can do. You do not know more than they do about where they live, how they live, and what they need. Learn everything you can from the experts: the people who are hosting you." Joy looked and sounded intense.

The group in the parsonage became quiet as the information sank in. They were not going with all the answers, or any answers. They would be foreigners.

Joy urged them to practice the dialect. They divided up into pairs and repeated words after Joy and Bryan said them. By the end of the night they were able to ask one another, "How are you?" Reply, "I am fine. How are you?" And ask other simple questions, such as:

"What's your name?"

"What do you like to eat?"

"Do you need help?"

They ended the evening by eating pie and chattering in Twi until they were laughing in hysterics.

Jack's things were moved from his condo without him, and Saturday afternoon Katharine's funeral commenced, attended by most of the town. It was beflowered beyond compare. Everyone knew exactly where the extraordinary flower arrangements had come from.

The owner of Pretty, Pretty Petals Flower Shop—Skylar Breese—had been good friends with Sylvia in school. Skylar left Cherish for ten years right after high school in an attempt to "find" herself. She returned after realizing home was the only place to bring her very broken heart, and she reconnected with Sylvia. The Garden Shop was so busy selling vegetables, flowers, and all possible gardening paraphernalia that Sylvia was delighted when Sky showed up with no job and no direction. Sky did, however, have money. And quite a lot of it. Sylvia was as curious as a cat as to where Sky made her fortune, but she did not have the temerity to ask.

The two old schoolmates schemed and planned together about how to open Pretty, Pretty Petals Flower Shop. It was a perfect match. Sky bought the store space, and she also bought Sylvia's flowers and sold the flowers and plants to the people of Cherish. And Ann Arbor. And Saline. And Ypsilanti. And Jackson. People came from all around for Skylar's creations, which were masterpieces, even though Sky usually appeared to be unable to add two plus two.

Sky could barely finish her sentences and dressed like a delicate fairy in scarves, flowing skirts, and blouses. Not to mention she was over six feet tall with the body of a supermodel and a waterfall of blonde hair cascading down her back. She was brilliant with flowers. She also had quite a head for numbers and could add much more than two plus two, despite how she came across to other people. Pretty, Pretty Petals began making a profit immediately, which was good for The Garden Shop as well.

Sky had recently joined Loving the Lord through the new members class. Maggie at first thought Sky to be a beautiful ditz, but she slowly discovered her keen brain. Sky was a puzzle of a human. One of the most positive things that came from Sky's presence at Loving the Lord was how she stealthily took over the weekly flower arrangements for worship. Prior to Sky's advent, Verna Baker, nee Abernathy, had filled the sanctuary every Sunday with her endless bouquets of zinnias. However, now a flower chart had been placed on the bulletin board, and everyone who signed up for a Sunday turned to Pretty, Pretty Petals and Sky's creations for weekly church flowers.

Skylar had designed the loveliest arrangements for Katharine's funeral, using brightly colored autumn leaves as "doilies" for the vases to sit on. Sky even used gourds, pumpkins, and other squash in displays around the church. It was an immediate reminder of what Katharine had spent her life doing with The Garden Shop. When Sylvia walked into the sanctuary the morning of her mother's funeral, she burst into tears at Sky's profound thoughtfulness.

Jack missed the funeral and the worship service on Sunday morning. He had to round at the hospital. By the time he cajoled, tricked, and crammed the cats into their carriers and got them all into the church on Sunday afternoon, he sat right down in the front pew and promptly fell asleep.

The cats were blessed anyway.

Maggie got the cats back to the parsonage, then went back to the sanctuary and gently shook Jack's shoulder.

"Jack," she whispered, "let's go home. It's time for a nap."

Jack slept for the rest of the afternoon, as did his wife.

As did the newly blessed cats.

When they awoke, they both had that foggy-brained, sick stomach feeling from sleeping too long after not sleeping long enough in prior days. Maggie dragged herself out of bed and made a beeline for her toothbrush. She was certain her teeth had grown fur that afternoon.

Jack rolled over and groaned.

"Whash the matter?" Maggie asked, quickly coming into the bedroom, toothbrush sticking out of her mouth and toothpaste dripping down her chin.

Jack focused his eyes, looked at her, and smiled.

"Whash sho funny?"

"You and your toothbrush. I'm just trying to figure out what day it is, and you're doing dental hygiene procedures." He laughed.

Maggie went into the bathroom, rinsed her mouth, wiped her chin, and went back to the bedroom. She sat down on the edge of the bed and gave Jack a very romantic kiss.

"Now, isn't that nice? All fresh and pepperminty?" she asked with a smile.

It was quite a while before they made their way downstairs for supper.

Eating bowls of vegetable soup, curried orange salad, and a baguette from Mrs. Popkin's Sugarplum Bakery, Jack and Maggie talked through the week's happenings and future events.

"So all three babies are healthy?" Maggie asked, then slurped her soup.

"Yes. Mothers, babies, and fathers are all doing fine. Two are home already, and I'll probably discharge the last family tomorrow afternoon."

Jack buttered his slice of baguette and took a big bite.

"I wonder if we will ever have a honeymoon," Maggie said, a little out of the blue, as she slid a piece of pie onto a dessert plate for Jack. "It doesn't seem possible. Going to Ghana will be challenge enough for both the church members and your patients. I don't think we will be able to leave again for quite a while."

"Yes. You and I are utterly indispensable," he said with mock seriousness. He put a bite of tart cherries and smooth chocolate into his mouth and closed his eyes in delight. "As are your pies. This is incredible."

"Thank you. I'm just trying to bribe you into not leaving me," Maggie said, covering the cherry-chocolate ganache pie and putting it back in the fridge.

"Wait! Don't put that away. I haven't been bribed enough yet," Jack said with his mouth full of red-and-brown goo.

Maggie set the pie back on the table. "Help yourself. But if you get fat, I may be the one to leave you." She giggled.

"I promise you, Maggie, we will have a honeymoon. It will not be in Ghana with half the church along. It will be just the two of us."

Jack quickly slid another piece of pie onto his plate before it disappeared into the fridge.

After the dishes were done, Maggie took *The Haunted Season* from the counter.

"It's time for some Malliet," she said. "Let's read a chapter each."

So with a fire glowing in the living room fireplace, Maggie and Jack spent the next two hours reading chapters to each other until Maggie felt the book slide out of her hands and her head jerk up. It was time to sleep. Jack put out the fire, and they crawled upstairs and into bed.

As she slept, Maggie found herself walking on a beach. It was warm, the sand was soft, and palm trees cheerfully waved in the wind. She was looking for Jack. It was their honeymoon. She looked behind her, then down the beach, then at the beautiful ocean water. She was surprised when a head appeared, rising from the ocean waves. Irena's platinum head swam toward her.

"Pastoor Maggie!" Irena screeched. "Vat about Chrristmas?"

Irena was fully dressed in a tight leopard print mini-dress, black fishnet stockings, and six-inch heels. She was also carrying a dripping-wet stack of music.

"Irena, what are you doing here on my honeymoon?" Maggie asked, perturbed.

"Dere is still verk to do! You can't just leave us!"

Irena began digging sand out of her shoe.

"I'm allowed to have a honeymoon with Jack," Maggie said emphatically. Then she turned and saw Lacey walking down the beach toward her, wearing black salon clothes.

"Hi there, PM. I'm just here to do your hair before dinner. Let's go back to the hotel," Lacey said brightly.

"Lacey, what are you doing here?" Maggie asked incredulously.

"Uh . . . you invited me to come along to do your hair on your honeymoon. Have you already forgotten?"

Lacey took Maggie's arm and tried to lead her back down the beach.

"Where's Jack?" Maggie asked.

"You know," Lacey said. "He had to go back to Cherish. Verna Baker is having a baby."

"Verna Baker is too old to have a baby," Maggie said, pulling her arm away.

"I'm just saying . . ." Lacey said nonchalantly.

"Vat about Chrristmas?!" Irena screeched.

Maggie saw a shadow behind a large palm tree. Jennifer Becker stepped shyly from behind it. She was carrying several packages wrapped in brown paper with pink strings. She wore her winter coat and scarf, along with heavy, sensible shoes that were sinking into the soft sand.

"Oh, hello, Pastor Maggie," Jennifer said barely over a whisper. "I just wanted to give you these books to enjoy. Did you know G.M. Malliet is writing one book per week now?"

Jennifer put the books in Maggie's arms then quietly went back behind the tree.

"Hello, sister Margaret!"

Maggie turned and saw Bryan coming toward her. She felt a little relief. Bryan would make sense of it.

"Bryan! I'm glad you are here. Have you seen Jack? We're on our honeymoon."

Maggie grabbed both his hands, and in the process, dropped all the wrapped books in the sand.

"I think you're confused, Megs. We've got to get back to United Hearts. The kids are waiting for dinner, and it's your night to cook. They want pie."

Bryan tried to lead Maggie one direction, while Lacey took her arm in another. Irena simply tried to get in the way of each of them. Jennifer quietly came back out from behind the tree and picked up all the books.

The alarm on Jack's phone went off. Maggie awoke with a start. Jack rolled toward her and held her close.

"Your heart is pounding," he mumbled. "Are you okay?"

Maggie took a deep breath and snuggled closer to him.

"I was just on our honeymoon. It was a nightmare."

8

January 4, 2016

Bawjiase, Ghana

The parade of obronis marched down the rutted road. The children by houses along the road shouted the word "obroni!" as loudly as they could at the "white people." Maggie watched as Joy greeted many of the children who ran into the road—and into her arms. The same thing happened at the back of the line with Bryan and Fifi. The children in the countryside knew Fifi, Joy, and Bryan. They knew they could always get a hug and often a treat. Fifi, Bryan, and Joy shared small bags of groundnuts with them. Maggie could tell the kids would have liked more than one baggie, but that was the limit. She marveled at the way the three leaders knew each child's name and also how to get a little extra nutrition into each child as they made their journey toward United Hearts.

The children were friendly as they came looking for hugs from the group of new obronis. Maggie and the entire group knelt down to hug the children. They also tried out several phrases and basic words Bryan and Joy had taught them in Twi.

"How are you?" Maggie tried to say to a little boy who had cuddled up to her. "E te sen?" she said carefully. She didn't trust her tongue to get the sounds right.

"Me ho ye," he said (I'm fine). "Na etsi sen?" (And how are you?)

"Me ho ye!" Maggie said, giving him a gentle squeeze.

"Groundnuts?" the boy asked. He had no problem with that English word.

"Bryan," Maggie said, pointing to her brother. Then she called, "Bryan! Groundnuts here, please!"

Bryan walked over and knelt down.

"This is Kweku. He's about four years old. The two girls by Charlene are his big sisters. This is one of the families that will benefit from the school. Their parents cannot pay the fees for the school in town, but they won't need to pay at our school. We want all these kids to be able to learn. You will hear lots of interesting names. Some are traditional Ghanaian names. Often their name is the day of the week they were born. But they usually have more than one name. You will hear many English names from when the British occupied Ghana. They began naming the children traditional British names during that time. It's a crazy mix." Bryan watched as Kweku chewed on his groundnuts.

Maggie felt another little hand slip into hers.

"This is Hannah," Bryan said. "She's a very good girl."

Hannah smiled. She must have been about six because her front teeth were missing.

Maggie smiled back. She thought of little Hannah Benson back in Cherish. The two Hannahs were close in age, but different in so many other ways.

"Hannah!" A woman's voice could be heard from one of the houses.

"Me bra!" (I'm coming!) Hannah called to her mother.

Bryan handed her three bags of groundnuts. Hannah grinned, then impulsively kissed Maggie's hand.

"Wo ho ye fe," (You are beautiful.) Hannah whispered to Maggie.

"Me da wo ase! Wo ho ye fe!" (Thank you! You are beautiful!) Maggie said back, giving Hannah a kiss on her dimpled cheek.

Hannah ran off toward home, laughing. Maggie watched and pondered on the two versions of "Hannah." Their name meant *grace*.

Joy finally got the obronis to move along, waving goodbye to the children.

"One more bend in the road, and we will be at United Hearts," Joy called out to her followers.

The road curved, and the obronis saw what they had planned for and travelled so far to see: a large green building, surrounded by palm trees. It looked bright and cheerful on the red dirt. Not far away were stacks of iron rods and bags of cement. A school-in-waiting.

"Hey! Where is everyone?" Joy yelled at the large doors fifty feet away.

No one could have prepared the small group of Loving the Lord volunteers for what happened next.

From the huge front doors of United Hearts came a rush of children. They were as fluid as a river. They were dancing, jumping, yelling, laughing, and barreling right toward Joy, et al.

Maggie watched as Addie impulsively ran forward, got down on her knees, and opened her arms wide. Things seemed to move in slow motion as the children, six of them, ran right into Addie's arms. The girl took the enthusiastic force with abandon and went flying backward with all six children landing on top of her. Lacey's handiwork was for naught. Addie's hair burst the tie, and her long, brown locks fanned out in the red dirt. She rolled back and forth, hugging the squealing children.

Maggie caught her breath at the vision of pure, unconstrained, chaotic joy.

Addie wasn't the only one bowled over. The children clung to any adult they could get their hands on. Soon the entire group was sitting in the dirt, laughing and introducing themselves.

Pastor Elisha, his wife, Marta, and several other adults were walking toward the elated group on the ground. Joy stood up, brushed herself off, and lifted a little boy named Dougie onto her hip.

"E te sen?" Joy said easily. The dialect rolled off her tongue.

"Me ho ye, pa pa pa pa," Pastor said, along with the others. "Pa pa pa pa" was used regularly to put emphasis on a sentiment. Pastor grinned. "Everyone! This is my wife, Marta. My beautiful wife!"

Marta was beautiful. She was wearing colorful fabric wrapped around her small frame, and her hair was wrapped around her head.

"Greetings! Welcome here!" She held out her hands to Joy, then leaned in to hug both Joy and little Dougie, who squealed at being made into a sandwich. Marta gazed at the disheveled crowd. Everyone from Loving the Lord was holding at least two children. "I wish to meet Bryan's sister." She looked carefully, then her eyes landed on Maggie. "This is you!" she said, taking Maggie's hands. "You and your brother have eyes that have seen life together. Your soul looks like his." Marta hugged Maggie and the little ones she held.

What a lovely way to say we look alike. Maggie looked at Bryan. She felt a sting in her eyes but sniffed the tears to the side. She had a feeling there would be many such moments that would surprise her ears, eyes, and her heart. She hoped she wouldn't sob continually for two weeks.

"It is a privilege to meet you, Marta," Maggie said. "We have heard so much about you from Joy and Bryan. You are a mother to many." Maggie looked around at the children.

"You are holding my own baby in your arms," Marta said. "This is Meshack, my baby."

Maggie looked at Meshack. He looked exactly like Pastor Elisha. Maggie was also holding the hand of a little boy named John.

"Groundnuts?" John asked.

Joy looked at Marta, who gave the consenting nod. The children erupted again—surrounding Joy, Fifi, and Bryan—and shouted for groundnuts.

"They're for me! They're for me!"

Their mouths quickly became gooey with smushed peanuts.

The rest of the group began to talk as everyone was introduced. They slowly walked to United Hearts. The other adult boys were punching Bryan in the arms, and they all spoke Twi to each other. Bryan was speaking so fast, Maggie was mesmerized. The Twi dialect was one that was fast and got louder as people were speaking to each other. But then, didn't every foreign language sound like that? Maggie remembered being told, when she lived in Israel, that Americans spoke too quickly and loudly. She hadn't thought so, but when she listened to her language for the first time with that idea, it was correct. American tourists in Israel were loud and often rude. She never wanted to be that way. Twi was much more playful, Maggie thought.

Pastor took them all on a tour of United Hearts. The entryway was huge and held a large table. There were toys scattered on the floor and what looked like school papers lying on the table.

"We eat here, and the children do homework," Pastor explained.

The entryway had two separate hallways, one going down the right side of the building and one down the left. In-between the hallways were three large rooms. One of these rooms was for study. The children could also do their homework in that quiet room. There was a bookshelf with some school books. There were also six computers, which Bryan had brought and installed on his last trip. The children could play games and do math and spelling activities on the computers, as long as the electricity from town was working.

Another room was a sick room, meant to keep anyone who was ill isolated from the rest of United Hearts. The third room was Pastor and Marta's room. To the left and the right of each hallway were the children's rooms. There were four rooms for the boys on the right and four for the girls on the left. The kitchen was also off to the left side. The bathrooms were at the very back: one large bathroom for the boys and one for the girls.

Part of the kitchen was inside United Hearts, and part was outside where there was a firepit for cooking. There were several benches for people to sit on as they prepared huge quantities of food for the large United Hearts family.

Maggie held Meshack as the children shouted out when their room would be seen next. Six children could comfortably fit into each large room. They had bunk beds covered in mosquito nets, and most of the children had a box or small suitcase in which to keep their clothes and personal possessions. Maggie could see the pride on each child's face when they pointed out their bed and box. Most of the younger children had a stuffed animal or a soft toy on their bed.

Meshack and his brother, Jonas, slept with their mom and dad in Pastor's and Marta's room. Their older sister, Amanda, slept with her best friends: Cynthia, Grace, and Mary. These teenage girls worked hard at United Hearts, sang and laughed together, bickered with one another, kept each other's secrets, and dreamt of going to university one day. Unlike the boys' rooms on the other side of United Hearts, the older girls kept their room as neat as a pin.

"This room is beautiful," Maggie said, looking at each of the girls.

The four girls burst out laughing and clapped their hands.

"Thank you," Cynthia said. "We are cleaner than the boys."

"Not just because we are girls," Amanda chimed in. "We are smart!"

More giggles erupted.

"Cynthia! Amanda! Grace! Mary!" Marta shouted. "Come now!"

The girls scurried out of the bedroom and headed to the kitchen. It was time to begin dinner preparations. They had special guests to-night.

Maggie stepped out of the kitchen door just in time to see one of the older boys ringing the neck of a chicken. Maggie cringed and looked away.

She had apparently just seen dinner.

9

Maggie ordered pizza for dinner. Ethan and Charlene Kessler had called the parsonage the Wednesday before Cassandra's moving day and asked if they could stop by. Maggie invited them for dinner and told them to bring along their two children, Kay and Shawn.

Over many slices of pizza from It's Not Your Mama's Pizza Parlor, Ethan and Charlene made an offer to Maggie she couldn't refuse. Kay and Shawn, who were ages thirteen and eleven, respectively, didn't fit into a Sunday school class because there was no one else at church in their age group.

"Our offer is this," Charlene said. "We would like to take over the high school class, but Kay and Shawn will join us. There is no need to come up with a new teacher for two. How does that sound?"

Maggie was thrilled. She had taught high school Sunday school since she'd arrived at Loving the Lord, and she was happy to share some of the work.

"What about a curriculum?" Ethan asked. As a university professor, he wanted to get right down to basics.

"I've found, the more you let the youth create what they want to do, the more invested they will be," Maggie said hesitantly.

"Yeah, Dad," Kay said with pizza sauce on her nose. "Church is already boring enough." She heard herself and gasped. She looked at Maggie. "I'm sorry, Pastor Maggie. I didn't mean it. Church is great."

Maggie laughed out loud. "I think you're right, Kay. There can be too much boring talk about very boring things, can't there?"

Kay slyly looked at her mother, hoping she wouldn't be in trouble later.

"Well, that makes it clear," Charlene said, wiping her hands on her napkin. "Absolutely no curriculum. Let's think of something else."

Kay smiled with relief.

Ethan was at a loss. Jack handed him the pizza box and smiled. Jack enjoyed being partners with Charlene in their doctors' office, and he knew she would come up with something for Sunday school even Kay would like.

Fortunately, Charlene not only had a scientific doctor's mind, she also had a colorful, creative side.

"What if we plan to make Thanksgiving baskets for people in Cherish who won't be able to afford a Thanksgiving dinner this year? I bet we could get some names from Grace in Action. The youth will come up with ways to raise money for food, and maybe even some hygiene and household products." Charlene knew from listening to some of her patients that there were basic needs not being met within the community. "Perhaps the kids could write 'commercials' and perform them during the incredibly boring church services we have to put up with." She laughed, and Kay blushed.

Charlene was now on a crusade. She took her phone out of her purse to check the calendar dates.

"If we begin this Sunday, October eighteenth, we will have six weeks until the Sunday before Thanksgiving, November twenty-second. We can assemble the items and deliver them that afternoon." She looked around the table, particularly at her children.

"That's brilliant," Maggie said, having no problem keeping up with Charlene's quicksilver mind. "I'll expect the first commercial this coming Sunday. Shawn and Kay, you will need to do it because no one knows about this yet. I can't wait to see what you come up with."

Shawn and Kay looked pleased, if not somewhat confused.

"Can we do whatever we want?" Shawn asked.

"As long as your mom and dad approve, it's fine with me. I will tell Hank to put a space for a Thanksgiving commercial in the bulletin."

Maggie picked up her phone and dialed.

"Hello?"

"Marla? It's Maggie."

"Oh, hi, Pastor Maggie. How are you?" Marla asked. Her voice sounded old.

"I'm great, and I think you might be too. I wanted to let you know that the Kesslers volunteered to teach high school Sunday school. Kay and Shawn will be in the class with them. You don't need to worry about finding a place for them or another teacher." Maggie was pleased to deliver that good news.

"Wow," Marla said slowly, "that's great." She didn't sound great. "A real relief." She didn't sound relieved.

Maggie picked up the cues in Marla's tone. She walked away from the table and said more gently, "I hope it eases a little stress for you, Marla. You have really worked so hard to accommodate everyone, not to mention all your work with Carrie and Carl the last several weeks."

Maggie heard Marla choke.

"Marla, are you okay?"

"I'm fine. Thank you for the news. I'll see you tomorrow, okay?" Marla actually hung up the phone without saying goodbye.

The Kessler's had given both Maggie and Marla a gift. They had no idea how badly it was needed. Perhaps, Maggie didn't know how badly it was needed either.

Early Saturday morning, on October 17, Cherish awoke to a crisp, cool, but sunshiny day. The members of Loving the Lord, all dressed in jeans and sweatshirts, descended on Cassandra's small home. Carrie and Carl were already at The Grange. Mary had helped them with their last boxes of small toys, books, and suitcases of clothes in the days prior. Mary and Cassandra agreed it would be better if the children were settled before the big move.

Most of Cassandra's furniture, clothes, kitchen items, and other belongings were going to Grace in Action. The local charity was a comforting lifeline to the poorer people of Cherish. There were, of course, those who refused to believe there were any "poor" living in Cherish. Those who actually believed that suffered from the malady of affluent blindness.

Mrs. Polly Popkin was the first to arrive at Cassandra's home, along with five stellar members of the youth group.

Mrs. Popkin ordered the youthful backs and arms of the younger folk to set up long tables on the lawn of Cassandra's home. Then the youthful backs and arms unloaded several large pink bakery boxes and thermoses of coffee and hot apple cider to set on the tables. Mrs. Popkin had been baking at The Sugarplum since the wee hours of the morning to make sure that, in the midst of the heaviness of that day, everyone would be fed and watered, so to speak.

"Hokey tooters! Brock, please lock that table leg into place. It's ready to fold under. Mason, you've already had three donuts. Please go get the rest of the thermoses from the van. Addie, thank you for thinking of tablecloths. Just like your mother, you are, that's for certain. Liz, grab the napkins and cups, will you, please? Oh, I see you already have. Bless you. Jason, once the van is empty, will you please move it onto the street, down a ways? We'll make some room for the other trucks that'll need the driveway. There, that's a dear boy." Mrs. Popkin said all these things with a toothy smile on her face, her white baker's hat waving in the breeze, and her large white apron making her visible to all in the vicinity.

She bustled right up to Cassandra's front door and knocked with purpose. She was surprised when Hank's wife, Pamela Arthur, opened the door.

"Well, hokey tooters! Pamela Arthur, what in the world are you doing here so early?"

Mrs. Popkin bustled her way through the front door, not waiting for an answer.

Pamela was one of the first people who had known about Cassandra's cancer. Pamela volunteered at the hospital and often found herself as a volunteer for patients once they left the hospital. Cassandra had been Pamela's "daily volunteer opportunity" since she was released from Heal Thyself Community Hospital.

The two women had laughed when Pamela painted Cassandra's toenails a vibrant orange. Pamela listened to stories of Cassandra's past and cried when she heard the story of husband Cal's death—that unbelievable day when Cassandra became a young widow. Pamela listened to Cassandra's struggles of being a single mom with a toddler and an infant. The loving care and true friendship lightened Cassandra's soul. The lessening of her emotional burdens helped ease her physical battle as well.

Pamela stepped aside as Mrs. Popkin pushed her way through the front door.

"Good morning, Mrs. Popkin," Pamela said. "I'm here to help Cassandra. We'll move her over to The Grange early so everyone else can get to work in here."

"That's a good idea. No need for dear Cassandra to sit here while the world marches in and out of her living room."

Pamela nodded.

"Now, I'd like to see Cassandra, if you think it would be okay with her," Mrs. Popkin requested.

"Of course. She's in her bedroom. I'm just doing a little work in the kitchen. Go on in." Pamela pointed to an open door.

Cassandra was putting her last few items of clothing and some sentimental keepsakes into a hard-sided green suitcase. She was ready for this day. There was no grief over leaving this home. Her husband, Cal, had never lived in it, so it had never been complete. Carrie and Carl were over the moon about living at The Grange. What a relief not to have to watch them mourn leaving home.

"Cassandra?" Mrs. Popkin's voice was only slightly lowered.

Cassandra jumped.

"I didn't mean to frighten you, my dear. I just wanted to give you a quick hug and let you know how loved you are today."

Mrs. Popkin hustled right on over and threw her small, round arms around the taller, much thinner woman. As she did so, Mrs. Popkin noticed the bed had been stripped and only a bare mattress remained. No pillows. There were rectangles visible on the walls where pictures had been removed. The closet held only a few wire hangers.

Mrs. Popkin caught her breath. The room looked dead.

Cassandra hugged Mrs. Popkin and unexpectedly laughed. She couldn't help it.

"Thank you, Mrs. Popkin. I feel loved, and I love you all back."

"Well, good. Because I can't stand around hugging you all day, trying to make you believe it. We've got work to do, and I hear you're going to get right out of our way. Thank goodness for that." She smiled broadly. "I've got to go and keep those kids from eating all the donuts."

She began to leave the room when Cassandra asked, "Donuts? You don't happen to have any pumpkin spice, do you?"

"Only about five dozen. Why?"

"I would love a pumpkin spice donut," Cassandra said, hoping she would be able to keep it down.

"I have a box ready for you to take to The Grange. Purple frosted donuts for Carl, chocolate for Carrie, and pumpkin spice for you. You don't think I would let you go through this moving day without proper sustenance, do you?"

Mrs. Popkin smiled again and left the room. As she stood in the living room, she looked around at the furniture that would soon be taken away, and she caught her breath. Cassandra was a warrior, she thought. Mrs. Popkin had been through her own wars but was safely on the other side of them. The dear younger woman was marching straight into battle. Mrs. Popkin closed her eyes. *She belongs to you, God, but we all love her. May every kind act and good word spoken today give her strength. Bless her, please. Amen.* Mrs. Popkin quickly wiped her eyes and then made her way into the kitchen to find Pamela.

"Pamela, which car should I put some baked goods in for the trip to The Grange?"

Pamela looked at one stray tear that was gently sliding down Mrs. Popkin's face. Her own eyes filled, but she kept her voice steady.

"We'll take my car. It's parked in front of the next-door neighbor's house. It's unlocked."

Pamela sighed. The two women stared at each other, full of understanding. Secondary sufferers. That's what they were. The ones who had to watch a beloved-one die.

"Well, that sounds just about right," Mrs. Popkin choked. "I'll get the boys to put the donuts in your backseat."

She turned and hurried out the front door. She had a job to do today. Crying would have to wait.

Pamela closed the lid and taped up the last box of dishes.

Maggie and Jack arrived at Cassandra's house and saw the youth group setting pink boxes and large thermoses on long cloth-covered tables. Maggie hadn't known what to expect on that day. In one way, it was a relief that Cassandra would be in a place where she had constant care. It was wonderful that Carrie and Carl already loved being at The Grange. But emptying the little home wasn't a celebratory day. It wasn't a fun church work day. Maggie watched as Mrs. Popkin bustled and ordered people about and thanked God. Polly Popkin would be the driving force of the day, gluing everything together with donuts and cider while shouting loving commands.

Several cars and three pickup trucks pulled up in front of the house. Bill and Sylvia Baxter, Harold Brinkmeyer—the town attorney, who had orchestrated legal details for Cassandra once her diagnosis was known—and his girlfriend, nurse Ellen Bright, were first. Ellen was also Jack's cousin and a member of the Ghana mission trip. They all arrived at the same time. Lacey pulled up right behind them wearing overalls and a purple scarf tied around her head, more for style than protection. Jack and Maggie joined the new arrivals, and they made their way to the magical pink boxes being governed by Mrs. Popkin.

"Good morning to the seven of you!" Mrs. Popkin greeted them. "Help yourself to some of these treats before the real work begins."

"Thank you, Mrs. Popkin," Ellen said as they all obeyed.

Lacey looked in the boxes and helped herself.

Jennifer and Beth Becker showed up with their friends Arly Spink and Priscilla Sloane. They were doing their best to entice Priscilla to come back to the church she grew up in and Arly to just give church a try. It was almost working.

Maggie looked around and smiled. Howard and Verna Baker were there with their constant appendage, Winston Chatsworth, Howard's best friend. Maggie hoped they wouldn't try to lift any furniture. Older men often thought they were stronger than they were.

"Good morning, Pastor Maggie," Verna said and went on briskly, "at least the sun is shining. This isn't the kind of job to do in the rain."

Maggie watched as Verna marched on toward the front door. She felt a light tap on her shoulder.

"Pastor Maggie, do you remember our friends Arly Spink and Priscilla Sloane?" Jennifer asked softly.

"Why yes, I believe I've met you before, Priscilla." Maggie somehow dug up the memory of someone telling her Priscilla Sloane was an heir to The Mill in Cherish. "And Arly, I've walked by your new gallery. Good morning to both of you. It's so nice of you to come today." Maggie was pleased with Jennifer and Beth's friendly tactics to bring new members to church, or at least to a "churchish" function.

"When I heard the story of this poor woman, my heart just broke," Priscilla said with sympathy. "I lost my husband. It's an unexplainable agony. Unless a wife doesn't like her husband in the first place, of course. Then it must be one huge relief to have him kick-off. But I loved my husband." Priscilla looked at Maggie with glistening bright-blue eyes, her short blonde hair ruffled by the wind. She was a petite woman, the same height as Maggie, and Maggie liked her right away.

Arly stepped forward and shook Maggie's hand. "Good morning, Pastor Maggie. I don't think we have actually met, but your husband commissioned a painting from me as a special gift for you. It's nice to meet you," Arly said with a smile.

"You painted the picture of the church. He surprised me with it for my birthday." Maggie's eyes lit up.

"Yes, he didn't give me a lot of time, but it was a joy to paint," Arly said.

"And now you've opened your own shop on Main Street."

"Yes, Cherished Works of Art Gallery. Stop in anytime," Arly said.

"How about this. I'll come to your shop, and then you come to mine? What do you say?" Maggie looked at Arly and then at Priscilla. "You too, Priscilla. I buy Easy Mix all the time. That's kind of like your shop."

Maggie's un-common sense made them laugh.

Sunday school superintendent Marla Wiggins and her husband, Tom, joined the group. Marla's eyes were red. It was obvious she had been crying. Maggie instinctively reached out and gave Marla a hug.

"Please don't, Pastor Maggie. I don't want anyone to see me crying. Just give me a job I can do by myself to help," Marla whispered. "I just can't believe this is happening." She made a gasping noise.

Marla had resented Cassandra's "bad mothering." Now the guilt of knowing the truth about Cassandra's illness was too much to bear.

Maggie thought quickly. "There are miscellaneous kids' toys and pet paraphernalia in the backyard. I told Cassandra yesterday that we would just get it moved and not to worry about it. It will probably take two or three trips to The Grange and back. Some large boxes are already back there. Hank dropped them off yesterday. How does that sound?"

"I'll get started."

Marla quickly moved to the side of the house, where a small gate let her through to the backyard.

Maggie made her way to the house just as Pamela and Cassandra were coming out of the front door. Cassandra leaned on Pamela's arm, and Pamela carried the hard-sided green suitcase. Maggie quick-ly moved forward, took Cassandra's other arm, and gave it a gentle squeeze. Cassandra smiled a thin smile.

"Hello, Pastor Maggie. We're heading to The Grange. I think my work here is done."

Maggie's heart wrenched.

"I wonder," Cassandra continued, "would you come with us to The Grange? It seems like enough people are here. Would you spend some time with the children and me?"

"Of course. Let me tell Jack. May I ride over with you?" Maggie looked at Pamela.

"Yes. I'm going to pull my car a little closer. Cassandra, just wait here."

Pamela took the suitcase toward her car. Maggie waved to Jack, who came over to the front steps.

"I'm going to The Grange with Cassandra and Pamela. I'll give you a call later, okay?"

"Absolutely. How are you feeling today, Cassandra?" Jack turned his kind brown eyes on the pale woman.

"I would like a donut," Cassandra said with a very slight chuckle. "I'm told I will have an entire dozen to myself once we get to The Grange."

"Enjoy them," Jack said as he smiled back at her. "I'll bring my black bag when I pick up Maggie later. How about a little check-up before you go to sleep in your new bed?"

"That will be fine," Cassandra said.

Then she looked past Jack. Cassandra stood very still for a moment and stared straight ahead.

As she, Jack, and Maggie stood on the front steps of the house, the church members in her yard formed two lines, making a walkway for Cassandra as she left her home for the last time.

Pamela pulled up in her car. Maggie and Jack walked Cassandra slowly across her front yard. One by one, the members of the congre-gation stepped forward to gently hug Cassandra, kiss her cheeks, or shake her hands. It was completely silent. No one spoke a single word. It was a walk of love.

Maggie paused at each new sign of affection, feeling the tears well up in her eyes. Cassandra's tears flowed freely, as did many others. They finally got to the curb, and Jack helped Cassandra get comfortably into the front seat as Maggie climbed in the back with the boxes of donuts. Maggie saw Jack wipe away his own tears. He looked at her.

"I'll see you in a while."

He closed the doors, and Pamela slowly pulled away from the curb.

Marla brought the children's outdoor toys and the pet paraphernalia in three trips as the day progressed. Children and pets were thrilled, and Marla was comforted to see where the children were now going to live. It was their busiest season of the year at The Grange, with lovely fall colors for visitor to come to town and enjoy, but the few guests Mary had booked were out and about and didn't notice the comings and goings that day.

Knowing that the Moffet family would make their transition to the Grange, Mary and William decided to accept very few guests until they knew how life was going to unfold. The weekend of Cassandra's arrival was the last weekend of out-of-town visitors. Marla and Mary had shared several discussions over the past few weeks as Mary gleaned needed information from Marla about the children's wants and needs. They were the priority now.

Mary had walked through The Grange with the little ones and asked Carrie and Carl if they would each like their own room or to share a room together.

"Well," Carrie said slowly and seriously, "Carl and I have always shared a room, but I am a big girl now, and I could have my own room."

Then Carrie looked at Carl and saw his stricken little face.

"But," Carrie continued, "I think I might be awful lonely, so we should probably just have that circle room together."

"The circle room?" Mary asked.

Carrie was talking about the turret room in The Grange. It was a lovely and peaceful room with windows all around and a huge oak tree brushing its branches against the side of the house. Mary had been using it as a sitting room, but she and William quickly removed the few chairs and end tables up to the third floor. "The circle room" was ready to become a bedroom.

Once furniture arrived on moving day, Mary took both children to the turret.

"Now, where should your beds go?" she asked.

"Can we each sleep by a window?" Carrie asked, making sure Carl was in agreement.

"Of course. That's a perfect idea."

Mason and Brock, who had ridden in the truck with the furniture, moved the beds to opposite windows. They stood silently and waited for the next order. It came from a small voice.

"My Mickey Mouse lamp always goes by my bed," Carl said, blinking.

"Mason, could you move this end table and the Mickey lamp by Carl's bed?" Mary asked kindly.

Mason moved the pieces and set them by the bed.

"Is this where you want it, Carl?" Mason asked.

Carl nodded mutely.

Brock got into the spirit of things. "And what about this pink nightstand? Does it belong in here anywhere?"

"Oh, that's mine," Carrie said, looking up at Brock. "My bedspread matches it. It's only for princesses."

Brock moved the nightstand next to the opposite bed.

"Is this right, Princess Carrie?"

Carrie giggled. "Yes."

The gentle question-asking throughout the afternoon gave the children a sense of control now that their lives were being slowly turned upside down.

The beds were made with clean sheets and covered with stuffed animals. Mason and Brock brought up a few boxes of children's books, a bookshelf, and a toy chest that had all been waiting in The Grange living room for a place to go. The circle room was filled with afternoon sunshine and the comfort of familiar items. Mary asked the children where each book and toy should go before placing anything. Carl and Carrie thoughtfully chose shelves and corners for their possessions. Mary finally got down on her knees to look at Carrie and Carl at eye level.

"Is there anything else you can think of to make your new room perfect?"

Both children shook their heads.

"Let's get some supper then," Mary said.

They all trooped downstairs, with a quick stop into Cassandra's room for kisses and a hugs from Mommy and Pastor Maggie.

Day One at The Grange seemed to be a success.

Joining them for supper was another little girl. Hannah Benson was the five-year-old daughter of Julia Benson. Julia had been at The Grange for a month, thanks to Mary and William's generosity. What no one knew when she arrived in Cherish with Hannah was that she was seeking the whereabouts of her ex-husband, who owed her a great deal of back child support for Hannah. The cruel, thieving Redford Johnson was Hannah's father.

Julia had gotten a part-time job at the *Cherish Life and Times* newspaper, procuring advertisements from local businesses. Hannah was signed up for kindergarten, and Mary helped watch her when Julia had to work. Julia had finally received some good news after years of struggle and resentment. She had been recently offered a salaried job as a local reporter for the newspaper. The weight that was lifted from Julia's burdened shoulders was monumental. For the first time in years, she could breathe and smile and love Hannah without the darkness and fear that had walled her in for so long. Julia told William and Mary that she would soon be looking for a place to live, and she and Hannah would be moving. Julia had even begun to look at apartments in Cherish.

Until that time, Hannah was a fun playmate for Carrie and Carl, her long, red curls flying in the wind as the children played in the hayloft of the barn—jumping and climbing and exploring every nook and cranny.

On that first night as permanent residents of The Grange, Carrie and Carl were happy to eat their grilled cheese sandwiches and homemade tomato soup with Hannah. Monday morning they would all three be dropped off at school together, and Mary's new version of motherhood would begin in earnest.

Julia came and sat with the children as they ate. She ruffled Hannah's curls and gave Carrie and Carl each a hug.

"How's moving day going for you two?" Julia asked gently, watching for signs of any distress.

"We have a new room, and it's a circle," Carrie said, taking a large spoonful of her soup. It was dripping down her chin.

"Owa toys all fit in and books too," Carl chimed in.

"Well, I would love to see your room after dinner," Julia smiled. "Will you show it to me?"

Both children nodded eagerly.

Julia and Hannah had gone to the park for the day to let the moving commence without two more people in the way. Feeling very much on the periphery of the family tragedy, Julia decided to watch and see where she could help as the days passed. Her heart, which had been caged for so long by fear and resentment, was set free. She wanted to keep the friendship between Hannah, Carrie, and Carl strong, especially after she and Hannah moved out.

"I want to see your room too," said Hannah, crunching into her sandwich.

"Maybe sometime we can all sleep together in our room," Carrie said, eyes wide. "We could have a . . . a . . . a lumber party!"

"I think you mean a *slumber* party." Julia laughed. "I'm sure we can work that out."

They finished their supper and headed to the turret room to show Julia and Hannah their new quarters. Julia watched the three children play, running in circles around the beautiful old room. She couldn't imagine what it would be like to be Cassandra, to know she would have to leave Hannah forever. Impetuously, she grabbed all three children as they ran by, dragged them to the floor, and began to tickle them and kiss them until they squealed.

There must be something else I can do, Julia thought to herself as someone's little elbow poked her in the stomach.

Earlier in the day, Marla had suggested that Mary and William might want to have a baby monitor set up in the children's room—hidden of course—just in case one or both of the children woke in the night afraid or confused. The Grange was so large, it might be difficult to hear them in the night. William had procured the monitor immediately and installed it at the back of a built-in shelf, high above the children's eye level. Mary set the other part of the monitor on the kitchen counter.

Now she heard Julia and the children as they laughed and squealed in the turret. She felt that odd sensation of a joyful heart. Breaking.

Throughout the day at Cassandra's old home, Polly Popkin had kept the group of church volunteers moving right along. She cheerfully ordered those about who didn't seem to know what to do next and encouraged those who knew how to move steadily from one task to another. The house had been emptied of furniture and boxes of generic items Cassandra didn't want to keep. Sentiment for possessions had been discarded once Cassandra knew where the children would live and that they would be loved. They would have a new life. She knew William and Mary had no need for boxes of items to be stored for years in their basement or attic. Nearly everything was taken to Grace in Action.

Once the house had been emptied, Hank, Marla, Verna, Doris, Chester, and Dr. Charlene Kessler went into cleaning operations. The little house was scrubbed from center to circumference, top to bottom. Walls washed, carpets cleaned, windows cleared of tiny handprints. The kitchen was scoured, as were the bathrooms. Jack and Tom Wiggins mowed the front and back lawns for the last time before cold weather set in.

At the end of the day, Jack, Hank, and Polly Popkin stood in the empty living room, surveying the work. Each of them individually sent up prayers for Cassandra, Carrie, and Carl. Then they locked the front door of the little home and left.

Jack drove out to The Grange. It had been a long day. When he got out of his car, he grabbed his black bag and walked up to the wrap-around porch. He was tired. His muscles ached, as well as his soul.

As he made his way into The Grange kitchen, he saw his wife sitting at the large pine table, sipping tea with Mary, William, and Julia. Jack only wanted to hold Maggie tightly to alleviate his own exhaustion and sadness, but he had to settle for a chaste hug as he kissed the top of her head before he sat down next to her.

"How did it go, Jack?" Mary asked while pouring him a cup of tea and sliding a plate of crackers and cheese toward him.

Jack relayed the work of the day, absentmindedly eating crackers and sipping his tea, which helped keep the tiredness out of his voice.

"How are Cassandra and the kids?" Jack asked, looking at all four of them.

"Judy, the nurse from hospice, and Pamela are with Cassandra right now," Mary said. "Carrie and Carl enjoyed a long bubble bath and are tucked into bed."

"I better go up and check on Cassandra," Jack said as he stood with his black bag.

He moved toward the stairs. Then stopped. A small voice floated into the room. Jack looked at Maggie quizzically.

"It's a monitor," Maggie whispered, pointing to the device on the kitchen counter.

They all listened.

"Carl?" It was Carrie's voice.

Small footsteps could be heard running across the floor above.

"Cawie, I can sleep with you, I think," Carl's small voice came through the monitor.

"Yes. Okay. Wait, watch out for Butterball and Dusty."

Rustling noises could be heard through the monitor, and one loud meow from Butterball or Dusty, the family's two cats.

"There," said Carrie. "Do you have enough blankets?"

"Yes," Carl answered. "Cawie?"

"Mmm?" Carrie sounded sleepy.

"Do you think, if we put owa toys in a box and owa clothes back in the suitcase, we can just go to heaven with mommy when she goes?" Carl's voice cracked slightly.

"I don't think so," Carrie said, yawning, "but we'll ask Miss Mary in the morning. She might figure out a way. She's smart and pretty."

Another yawn.

"Okay. Miss Mawy will help," Carl said. "Do you think heaven is fun?"

"I think so . . ." Carrie's voice trailed off.

"Why haven't we gone to heaven befoe?" Carl sounded wide awake.

"Um . . . I think Jesus has to invite us. It's like a birthday party." Carrie sounded like she just wanted to sleep.

"Pawty?" Carl said. "Then there will be cake!"

"Mmm hmmm. Go to sleep now, Carl," Carrie said, a little frustration creeping into her small voice.

The five adults in the kitchen looked at one another silently but couldn't see for the tears in their eyes.

10

January 5, 2016
Bawjiase, Ghana

That morning, Maggie woke up early to the sound of a rooster outside her window. It was still dark. At first, the mosquito net confused her. She felt it on her arm as she rolled over. When she opened her eyes, everything was dark and a little fuzzy. Then she remembered. She took some time to collect her experiences of the last two days of travel and being on the ground in Ghana. It felt like two weeks. The previous night they had followed Bryan and Joy in the dark, with flashlights and cell phones lighting the way. Then the weary and sweaty travelers had taken individual bucket baths. Maggie had waited to be last. The cold water on her skin chilled and refreshed her all at the same time.

And then everyone slept. Even the five hour time difference from Cherish didn't keep them from slumbering like the dead.

The rooster continued to crow, and soft light just barely began to come through the window. Maggie carefully lifted her mosquito net and, as quietly as possible, slid from her top bunk to the floor. She could see Sylvia, Lacey, and Addie still sleeping. Sylvia was making snuffling noises. Maggie quickly threw on a sundress, grabbed her sandals instead of the worthless flip-flops, and stepped out of the room. She heard some rustling noises in the kitchen. She tiptoed in and saw Fifi slicing a large loaf of bread. He had one of the cardboard trays of eggs next to a bowl.

"Good morning, Fifi," Maggie said softly.

Fifi looked over and smiled. His whole face lit up. "Good morning, Maggie. Did you sleep?"

"Yes, very well. I thought I might go for a little walk before breakfast. Is there time?"

The thick slices of bread looked delicious, and she smelled a whiff of spice. *Nutmeg.*

"Yes. Breakfast will be in one half-hour. Joy has already left for United Hearts. She'll be back soon." Fifi continued slicing.

"I'll be back before breakfast," Maggie said.

She sat on the front porch of the volunteer house and buckled her sandals. Then she began her walk. She decided to go toward United Hearts because that was the only direction she knew. No point in getting lost on Day Two in Bawjiase.

As she walked, she smelled the red earth. Every now and then she would smell urine or feces, but that was when she passed the outdoor cement structures used as bathrooms. The palm trees danced as the wind continued without pause, day and night. The ocean breezes blew across the land. The sun was bright, and Maggie felt her skin warm as she walked. There was something about that land. That country. That continent.

It was the oldest inhabited continent in the world. It was the birthplace of humankind. The oldest fossil evidence of the first humans was found on the eastern side of Africa. The blood of birth and death saturated the ground. The red earth. It was sacred land. It was holy ground. The history and stories of civilization rose up from that earth. The spiritual world, so different from Maggie's pristine and organized one, was full of unfettered spirits, wisdom, superstitions, magic, truths, tragedies, and miracles. Maggie stopped on the path and closed her eyes.

Her body jolted with a shudder. For a moment, Maggie felt the power of the earth. The power of the centuries, of those who lived and died on that land.

Maggie realized that God was so much bigger and came in so many clever disguises—more than she had ever imagined. The small God of

Maggie's Reformation religion exploded out of the tightly locked box of her over-explained and platitude-filled faith.

God wasn't explainable. God could only be experienced.

"E te sen? E te sen?" A small voice called over the wind and dancing palms.

Maggie was jolted again. She opened her eyes and felt her legs wobble just a little.

Maggie took a deep breath and looked toward the voice. It was Hannah, the little girl who had kissed her hand the night before. Hannah was running toward Maggie as fast as her little legs would carry her. She was waving her arms and smiling toothlessly.

Maggie turned toward the little girl, then watched as she hit something on the ground with her foot, tripped, and fell down hard, face first.

"Hannah!" Maggie yelled as she ran to the little girl.

The girl's mother was coming from their cinderblock home just as Hannah tumbled to the ground.

Maggie and the mother reached the little girl at the same time. Hannah was lying in the dirt, blood coming from her nose, or mouth, or chin. Then Maggie saw a gash on her forehead. The child wasn't making any noise, which scared Maggie more than anything else. She looked at Hannah's mother, who tried to roll the child over on her back.

"Me pa wo hyew," (I beg you) Maggie said. "Bra!" (Come!) Maggie pointed in the direction of the volunteer house.

Hannah's mother nodded mutely. Then she looked up as she heard other voices. Two little boys were calling to their mother. Maggie thought they must be Hannah's brothers. She looked at Hannah's mother and gestured to the boys to join them.

"Me mba," (My babies) Hannah's mother said.

The boys came and held on to their mother's dress. They looked at their sister, and the youngest one began to cry.

"G yae su," (Stop crying) his mother said, but then she took his hand.

Maggie gently picked up the little girl and looked at the gash down her forehead. Blood dripped down her nose and cheeks. Maggie walked as quickly as she could, carrying Hannah in her arms like a baby. Hannah's mother followed, holding onto her daughter's leg and her youngest son's hand. They moved in a little herd toward help.

When Maggie got to the door of the volunteer house, she heard the sounds of the others.

"Jack!" Maggie cried as she entered the dining room. "Charlene! Please help!"

The others were making cups of tea and coffee. Jack got up when he saw Maggie holding Hannah. The little girl's eyes began to flutter, but she wasn't aware enough to know where she was or what was happening. Hannah's mother saw Fifi and began a rapid exchange in Twi.

"This mother wants to take Hannah to the clinic," Fifi explained. "She says they will take care of this bleeding."

"We do have some medical supplies," Jack said slowly. "We could take care of this, if she would like us to."

Fifi shared the information with Hannah's mother. It was obvious she did not want this. Bryan looked at Fifi and said something in Twi. When Fifi responded, Bryan looked at the others.

"We need to get her to the clinic. It's about a ten-minute walk."

"She can certainly make that short trip, but we have everything we need right here to clean and stitch up her wound," Charlene persisted.

Bryan, ignoring her, picked up Hannah and walked out the door toward the clinic. Hannah's mother followed. Jack and Charlene followed last.

In the volunteer house, Fifi said something to the little boys in Twi. They sat down on one of the foam rubber mats. Fifi went back into the kitchen, and the boys looked as if they were going to cry.

Addie swooped down and gave them hugs, then took their hands. She walked them into her room and dug through one of the suitcases until she found two new coloring books and a box of crayons. The boys followed her to the large table in the dining room, and she helped them into chairs. The boys seemed shy at first, but then Addie opened the crayons and began coloring a picture in one of the books. She handed a crayon to the youngest boy. He took it and opened his book.

Ellen sat down next to the older boy. Soon, all four were coloring. Addie and Ellen would point at something in the pictures and ask the boys what it was. They received an impromptu Twi lesson. Then the boys did the same thing, wanting to know the English word. Even though they did not know the same language, the foursome enjoyed a creative conversation.

Maggie, Bill, Sylvia, Ethan, Lacey, and Dana also took seats at the coloring table.

"Do you think Hannah will be okay?" Maggie asked Ellen.

As soon as the boys heard Hannah's name, they looked up from their activity.

Ellen smiled at the boys. "Yes, she will probably need some stitches, and she'll have quite a headache, but she will be fine."

"It's wonderful to have a clinic here," Sylvia said thoughtfully. "What happens to the people who live in villages without any medical care?"

No one answered.

The front door opened, and Joy stepped through. She looked at everyone at the table and noticed Hannah's brothers.

"Good morning. What are Kofi and Kwashi doing here?"

She walked over and kissed each boy on the head. Then she asked them something in Twi. Kofi, the oldest boy, answered her quietly.

"Hannah fell," Maggie said when Kofi was done. "Bryan, Jack, and Charlene went with Hannah and her mother to the clinic. Can you tell us these boys' names again?"

"Kofi is this one," Joy said, rubbing his shoulder. "He's four. And this little one is Kwashi. He's two."

Joy gave Kwashi a little tickle around his ear.

Both boys had perked up when Joy came in. She was familiar. They began to chatter about what they were coloring, and Joy made all the appropriate oohs and ahhs.

"How about we fetch some water for the kitchen and the bathroom?" Joy said, looking at the adults. "Addie, you can stay here and watch the boys. We used up almost all the bathroom water last night after bucket baths, and Fifi always needs more water in the kitchen."

Everyone stared at her.

"Sure," Maggie finally said, standing up. "How and where?"

Soon all the adults, minus Addie, were following Joy down a dirt road going the opposite direction of United Hearts. They each carried a bucket. As they wended their way through the village, Maggie saw women outside their homes, cooking something over open fires. *Breakfast.* Maggie could smell the burning wood under the fires. Every odor smelled different than in America. Maggie wondered what those women were making for breakfast. There were goats running free around the single file group of volunteers. Chickens were everywhere. Small children looked shyly at the line of obronis walking past. Some of the older children shouted, "Obroni! Cedi!"

Joy shouted something back at them, but she was smiling. Everyone seemed to recognize Joy.

The small group finally got to the well. Joy had a smaller bucket on a rope and dropped it down into the well. She pulled up the small bucket and emptied it into her larger one.

"The thing to be careful of," she said, "and I'm telling you from too much personal experience, is to not let go of this rope on the smaller bucket. I have lost too many small buckets down the well." She kept pulling up water to fill the other buckets.

Soon some older children arrived with their empty buckets. Regular morning chores for the villagers. Joy greeted them, and the other Americans tried out their Twi. The children watched as Joy showed the adults how to hoist, and then balance, the heavy buckets of water on their heads.

That was a cause of great hilarity for the children.

Maggie spilled half her bucket down her back before she took one step.

Ethan stepped on a small tree branch, and his entire bucket went straight into the ground.

"Steady the bucket with your hands before you move," Joy instructed, sending her small bucket back down in the well. She was used to clumsy spills with newbies.

Lacey was determined to balance her bucket. She made it ten steps before water began slopping over the sides, drenching her dress and sandals.

Dana stood as tall and straight as she could and actually made great progress. Until she slowed down while going around a small curve of a house. Ellen hadn't noticed the slow down and crashed right into Dana's back.

Two buckets down. Two women soaked.

Joy began filling the buckets of the children who were waiting. Getting her group in order would take too much time.

Finally, Bill and Sylvia, with their buckets only three-quarters full, began the walk back to the volunteer house. With minimal spillage, they walked right up to the empty rubber trash bin and dumped their precious fluid cargo. The others followed and dumped whatever had remained in their buckets. Then they all stared.

"It's not even half full!" Lacey said. "And we haven't begun on the kitchen bin."

Addie, Kofi, and Kwashi stared at the dripping adults. The boys began to laugh.

"I think you're supposed to carry the water in the buckets, not on yourselves," Addie said with mock seriousness.

Lacey walked over and wrung out her hair on Addie's head. Addie squealed, and the boys laughed until they almost fell off their chairs.

"Maybe you should give it a try," Lacey said.

"I wish I could, but I'm babysitting." Addie grinned.

Three more trips to the well followed.

"My head hurts," Sylvia whispered to Bill, "and my shoulders are killing me."

"It's my arms," Dana said, coming up behind the couple.

"I have a feeling we will discover muscles we never knew we had," Bill said.

"That would be just about all my muscles," Ethan remarked.

"Can you imagine if this was how we had to get our water every day at home?" Maggie asked thoughtfully.

"It's a reason to have many children," said Ethan. "I would make Kay and Shawn do this, no problem."

As they made their way toward the clinic, Charlene looked at Hannah's mother, not knowing if the woman would have any idea what she was asking.

"What is your name?"

"Adua," the woman said. "Your name?"

Charlene was surprised at that but smiled and said, "Charlene, and this is Jack."

Hannah began to whimper in Bryan's arms. He walked faster. They arrived at the clinic within minutes. Bryan looked at Jack and Charlene.

"Come on in to see the clinic and meet Dr. Obodai."

Jack and Charlene followed Adua, who followed Bryan and Hannah. Backless benches were lined up in a large room meant to be a waiting area. Jack and Charlene saw many women, dressed beautifully, holding babies and small children. It was noisy with crying babies— children unhappy to have to sit still and wait, a universal sadness for all children.

Bryan walked up to one of the nurses at a table in the front of the waiting area. The nurse spotted Hannah's wound and the blood still dripping down her face. She looked at Bryan, then began speaking to Adua. The nurse had them follow her into a room to the side of the waiting area. There were several gurneys lined up. One young woman was lying down with an IV attached to her arm. On another gurney, a little boy was sleeping and sweating profusely.

Bryan said to Jack and Charlene, "Often malaria can cause dehydration and high fever. This clinic has been a Godsend to Bawjiase for extreme cases. Also, women can come here to deliver their babies. The blood analysis machine you brought is needed to help with all blood testing. I'll tell the doctor that we will bring the machine later today."

"This is impressive," Jack said. "Is this where the children from United Hearts come for things like immunizations and other medical care?"

"Yes. Ghana has a more advanced National Health Program than several other countries. We will spend time this week updating the insurance cards of everyone at United Hearts."

The nurse gestured toward a gurney. Bryan laid Hannah on the small bed. The nurse spoke to him in Twi again. Jack stepped aside as a tall man in a white coat entered the room.

"Hello. I'm Dr. Obodai. What do we have here?" He looked at Hannah, who was still whimpering. "It looks like some stitches are in order," Dr. Obodai said in a lilting accent.

Adua spoke to the doctor in rapid Twi. He put his hand on her shoulder as he listened. Then he responded softly. She sighed and nodded her head. It was clear she was relieved by whatever he said.

"Dr. Obodai is telling Adua to wait out in the larger room. I will go with her, but you two can stay," Bryan said to Jack and Charlene.

"It is a pleasure to have you here," Dr. Obodai said.

"Thank you. I'm Jack Elliot, and this is Charlene Kessler."

Jack shook Dr. Obodai's hand, followed by Charlene.

"Let's look at this little girl now."

Dr. Obodai turned to Hannah. The nurse had already brought in a small tray of medical supplies to clean and stitch up Hannah's gash. Dr. Obodai cleaned the wound carefully. Then he took a syringe of lidocaine and carefully injected Hannah's forehead.

Hannah yelped at the sting of the needle and burning sensation of the medicine, and the nurse took her hand. Dr. Obodai spoke to Hannah and must have said something funny because she smiled.

Jack and Charlene stood behind the doctor as he carefully stitched up the wound. Nine stitches later, with a large gauze bandage in place, Dr. Obodai helped Hannah sit up on the edge of the gurney. After bringing the mother back in, the nurse gave Adua a small bottle of acetaminophen for pain, along with instructions for the next week.

"It is good to know you now," Dr. Obodai said to the two American doctors. "I will look for you, when? Joy told us about the CBC machine. We are grateful for that and will make good use of it here."

"We are glad to be here," Jack said, "glad to bring the machine, and we are willing to do anything to help. We will bring the machine later today."

"Wonderful." Dr. Obodai nodded.

"Dr. Obodai, it has been a pleasure," Charlene said, shaking his hand again.

"I will see you later today, then," Dr. Obodai said as he moved to the gurney with the young woman.

The group left the clinic, and Bryan asked Hannah if he could give her a piggyback ride. She nodded. Bryan knelt down and carefully let Hannah climb on his back. She put her arms around his neck and gently laid her cheek on his shoulder. Then the small group headed back to the volunteer house.

Fifi had been working on Ghana French toast while the medical procedure was going on. Now he brought a steaming platter to the table and invited everyone to sit.

Before breakfast began, Addie went to the bedroom and returned with two brown teddy bears and a small stuffed pink elephant. She handed each of the boys a brown bear. Then she gave the elephant to Hannah. Hannah smiled wanly and took the soft toy.

Everyone gathered around the long table. Maggie prayed and thanked God for Hannah, the clinic, and for breakfast. She made it short for those who couldn't understand English.

"You know," Maggie said when everyone began helping themselves to the steaming French toast, "Hannah's name means *grace*. Isn't that beautiful?"

She used her fork to stab a slice of toast. She looked up and saw Lacey staring at her quizzically.

"What?" Lacey asked. "How do you know that? That Hannah means *grace*?"

"I like to know the meaning of names, especially biblical names. Hannah is one of my favorite women in the Bible. *Grace*. Isn't that beautiful?" Maggie looked at Lacey, who looked odd. "I think you need some breakfast, Lacey. You look as if you might fall over."

Lacey felt tired and was still pondering what Maggie had said about the name, but she accepted the heavy plate that was handed to her.

Jars of strawberry jam were opened and the jam spread on the thick slices of Fifi's French toast. The sweet nutmeg-spiced bread melted in their mouths. Even Hannah's appetite wasn't hindered once she had a bite. When Fifi saw how fast the breakfast was being devoured, he went back into the kitchen, and Maggie could hear him cracking eggs as fast as he could. He soon brought out several more slices of French toast. Hannah's little family ate and ate, and each of the children drank a water bag.

When the food had been exhausted, it was apparent to Fifi more food would be needed at lunchtime. Even without Adua's family. He would be making a trip to the little blue store near the volunteer house. At least they had the basics there. He wouldn't have time to go to Market.

Adua quietly told Joy that she and her family needed to go home now.

Maggie, Addie, and Ellen each carried a child on their back as they followed Adua to her home. Hannah looked sleepy, so they tucked her into bed to rest, grateful there was no fear of a concussion. Then the three women shook Adua's hand. And smiled. That was the extent of their communication. They waved goodbye as they left Hannah's house.

Maggie could see that not having Hannah to help around the house for a few days would put a burden on her mother.

"If Joy agrees, I think Addie and I may be back here," Maggie said. "You're too important, Ellen, being a medical professional and all. But Addie and I are nothing special. I bet we can help with something, even taking care of the little boys might be helpful."

Addie laughed. "As our friend Hank would say, yessireebob!"

11

October 18, 2015
Cherish, Michigan

The day after Cassandra was moved to The Grange, Maggie awoke early. She let Jack sleep as she quietly crawled out of bed. She couldn't run quite yet because of her ankle, but she could walk, so she put on her sweats and walked to the end of Middle Street. She arrived at the cemetery, which was bathed in gold and crimson as the rising sun glittered through the trees over the gray and white headstones. She took a few minutes to chat with God, and as she walked, she turned her sermon over and over in her head. She practiced saying it out loud, trying to cement her thoughts.

"It was about power and servanthood," Maggie said to the majestic gravestones. "Jesus had two disciples who were vying to sit, one on each side of him, once they reached heaven." Maggie's thoughts drifted to Carrie's statement about getting to heaven the night before. *I think Jesus has to invite us. It's like a birthday party.* She continued preaching to the great oak trees. "The disciples, James and John, wanted seats of honor at the party. Somehow, they thought they deserved to be front and center, to be in places of privilege and power." Maggie imagined that the trees were listening intently.

"Jesus dashed their dreams by saying, 'But whoever wishes to become great among you must be your servant, and whoever wishes to be first among you must be slave of all.'" Maggie continued passionately, focusing on a large pinecone dangling on an evergreen tree.

"And all I can say is: this very important lesson has not been learned wisely, or too well, over the course of history. Power has always been grasped and grabbed for by those with the most money and the biggest armies. From the Old Testament to present day, power rarely went to the poverty-stricken or the small-voiced." Maggie felt like she was in the zone. "There will certainly be a lot of surprised people in heaven. Can you just imagine those powerful folks, who will march straight to the head of the banquet table for a seat, only to be handed a tray of hors d'oeuvres and an apron and told to begin serving the other guests?" Maggie could think of certain recent politicians and world leaders she would love to see serving "the least of these."

"And then the meekest and mildest of all," she continued in a gentle voice, "the poorest in spirit, will be given lovely clothes that will lay softly on their skin, and they will sit on pillowed chairs surrounding Jesus as they eat the feast of peace and grace prepared for them."

Maggie again remembered the difficult work at Cassandra's house. She thought of the generosity of Mary and William, the deepest love shown to Cassandra by Pamela, and the countless ways the congregation was willing to give without question or complaint. That morning in church, Maggie could only tell them how very different they were from so many others. They had servanthood handled perfectly. She couldn't wait to tell her congregation how amazing they were.

Energized, she walked back to the parsonage and climbed the stairs to where Jack was still sleeping. Marmalade had laid a large white paw over Jack's forehead. Cheerio and Fruit Loop were both cuddled on his feet. Maggie crawled in next to him and kissed his nose. He opened his eyes and smiled.

"Wife of mine."

"Husband."

"Let's skip church today," Jack said groggily as he stretched.

"That's a great idea. We'll just stay here and have coffee and read the paper," Maggie said dryly.

"Wait," Jack said, yawning. "I think I have to usher. I guess I have to go, but you can stay home."

"Well, then, you'll be ushering and preaching a sermon. Have fun!" She tickled him under his arm.

"Hey! Stop it!"

He grabbed her more tightly so she couldn't tickle him again. The kitties were considerably perturbed with these shenanigans and all hopped off the bed.

"Let me go," Maggie squirmed. "We'll have to continue this war later. I have to get ready for church. I am the pastor. You would be wise not to forget that, my good sir."

Jack squeezed her more tightly, kissed her, then let her go.

"We'll pick up right where we left off after church. You can count on that, pastor."

Maggie cleaned up, pushed the Keurig button, and made two bowls of oatmeal with banana and maple syrup. Then she and Jack hurried through breakfast.

"What are you thinking about, Pastor Maggie?" Jack asked, staring at his wife. "You've gone away somewhere."

Maggie had slipped into her own thoughts. Again.

"Marla, Cassandra, the Kesslers, life, death, guilt, hope, love."

Maggie looked up into Jack's brown eyes, and Jack saw Maggie's eyes glistening.

"I'm glad you're our pastor. None of us ever wonder if you care. And I'm glad you're my wife. I'll never wonder if I'm loved."

After a short introduction by Pastor Maggie, Ethan and Charlene taught their very first Sunday school class, an hour before worship began. The high school students had received an email to meet at church instead of the parsonage for the morning. They were suspicious of the new development. They had gotten used to Pastor Maggie and liked her goofy sense of humor. They suspected an ambush. Charlene had been warned there would be a mighty uprising if the youth arrived and didn't find donuts on the premises. Thus, Charlene called in a standing order with Mrs. Popkin for two dozen donuts every Sunday. The students were not sure about meeting in the nursery instead of the cozy parsonage, but they settled down once they saw the familiar pink boxes. Maggie slipped out quietly as Charlene took charge.

Thanksgiving commercial ideas were discussed. Kay and Shawn displayed their own creative idea for that morning's worship to the rest of the class and asked for more participation. The Great Thanksgiving Basket Plan had begun.

Maggie looked over her sermon notes in her office, but she could hear the laughter coming from the nursery. It made her smile to think of the youth plotting and planning on how to make Thanksgiving special for people in Cherish—people who maybe had very little for which to be thankful. She couldn't wait to see what Kay and Shawn had come up with for their commercial.

Church began with Irena shushing the congregation. She could not abide the cheerful greetings congregants gave to one another as they entered the sanctuary. She expected silence, followed by awe, as she played the prelude. Maggie watched from her chair behind the pulpit as Irena hissed like a snake at the silence violators. Maggie also noticed Detective Keith Crunch sitting in the pew right next to the organ, grinning each time Irena hissed. At least he thought it was funny.

Irena played her own rendition of "There's a Wideness in God's Mercy," and worship was underway.

After the welcome and opening announcements, Maggie invited Kay and Shawn to come forward for a "Thanksgiving Commercial."

Kay and Shawn walked up the steps to the altar table carrying a large wicker basket. They plunked it down, and Kay stepped forward.

"I love Thanksgiving, don't you, Shawn?" She sounded slightly robotic.

"Yes, Kay, I do," Shawn said, feeling his stomach flutter as he saw the crowd in front of him.

"What's your favorite thing about Thanksgiving, Shawn?" Kay asked in a staccato voice.

"Dinner," Shawn squeaked out.

What Maggie could see, but the congregation could not, was Ethan in the front pew, holding cue cards by his feet for the youth to read.

There was a voice from the back of the sanctuary.

"I love turkey!" Liz Tuggle said.

She walked down the aisle carrying a frozen turkey, placed it in the basket, and then stepped next to Kay.

"I love corn pudding!" It was Jason Wiggins and a friend of his from school.

They got up from the middle of the sanctuary carrying corn muffin Easy Mixes, cans of creamed corn, and a tub of sour cream. They walked jauntily up to the basket and put the items inside. Then they stood next to Shawn.

"We love green bean casserole."

Brock and Mason climbed over their mother with cans of green beans and cream of mushroom soup. They deposited their gifts into the basket and stepped aside.

Maggie watched as the congregation looked around the sanctuary, trying to see who would pop up next. Carrie clapped her hands, unable to control her excitement at the unexpectedly fun church experience.

"I love rolls and butter!"

Cate Carlson, who was home from college for the weekend, quickly walked up the aisle with her donations, giving Maggie a wink as she placed them in the basket. Cate was Bryan's long-distance girlfriend and Maggie's good friend.

"I love cranberry sauce."

Addie Wiggins, along with two of her friends from school who now attended Loving the Lord, came from the "secret" door that led from the church offices to the sanctuary. They placed several cans of cranberry sauce in the basket, which was beginning to overflow.

Carrie couldn't control herself any longer. She jumped up on the pew in her yellow tutu and purple feather wand and shouted, "I love punkin' pie!"

"And ice cream," came Carl's small voice.

Charlene Kessler, sitting in the front pew with her husband, was holding pie ingredients. Charlene had been planning to bring them up herself, but motioned for Carrie to come forward. Carrie bounced her way to Charlene, who handed the little girl the items. Carrie twirled up to the basket and plunked down the cans. They immediately rolled out, one rolling down the stairs—*thump, thump, thump*—right back to Charlene. She picked up the can and walked up to her new Sunday school class, plus the one small infidel.

"What do you love for Thanksgiving?" Charlene asked the congregation.

Ethan stood up and said, "There are people here in Cherish who will not have a Thanksgiving dinner this year. To buy the food in this basket is beyond their means. But it's not beyond ours. For the next five Sundays, we will be working hard in our Sunday school class to raise food and money for the people of our town who have to go without."

Kay, who had gained immeasurable strength being surrounded by her new friends, said, "We don't want anyone to go without Thanksgiving dinner. We know you don't either."

"Please use the sign-up poster on the bulletin board if you can donate a turkey," Liz said, smiling.

"Bring canned goods anytime. We have a lot of baskets to fill," Jason said.

"How many?" Charlene asked Brock and Mason

"Twenty-two," the twins said in tandem.

At that, there was an audible gasp in the sanctuary. Discomfort and disbelief comingled in the pews.

"Yes, twenty-two," Cate chimed in.

"Our Sunday school class has promised Grace in Action that our church will provide these needed meals, along with other items for our neighbors," Addie said. "So, we all have work to do. If you wish to donate money, designate 'Thanksgiving Dinners' on your check or envelope."

"There is a list of other needed items next to the turkey sign-up sheet. Be generous." Ethan sounded like a professor.

"We will stay after church on the Sunday before Thanksgiving to put baskets together and then deliver them," Charlene said.

"And don't worry about reminders," Addie said. "We'll remind you every week!" Addie, Liz, and their two girlfriends began to giggle.

"Thank you for your attention. Now back to your regularly scheduled worship." Brock and Mason closed the commercial.

All the students sat back down in the sanctuary. The overflowing Thanksgiving basket stayed on the altar for the remainder of the service. Maggie's sermon about James and John's demand for high favor, and Jesus' command to serve one another, along with the idea of folks who wanted to be the greatest but had to be slaves of all, was made crystal clear with the Thanksgiving basket for everyone to see.

"I want you to know how proud I am to be one of you," Maggie said. "You are the most service-minded, other-focused group of people I have ever met. The work that was done yesterday for a dear family in our congregation," Maggie didn't mention Cassandra, Carrie, and Carl by name since Carrie and Carl were sitting right under her nose, "was true goodness. And the loveliest picture of serving others with joy."

They finished the service by singing "Called as Partners in Christ's Service." Irena ratcheted up the volume with each verse. By the end, the congregation was practically shouting the words.

As Maggie made her way from the gathering area to her office, her ears pricked up when she overheard scattered conversation.

"I know for a fact there aren't any really poor people in Cherish," a voice said.

"That's what I thought. This Thanksgiving dinner issue might be in Jackson or even parts of Ann Arbor, but our community doesn't have those kinds of people," a second voice chimed in.

"If there are poor people in Cherish, it's because they choose to be. In my experience, the poor are often just lazy. Lazy people don't deserve or need handouts. They need to work, like the rest of us." The third voice had an edge.

Maggie didn't bother to turn around. She thought she knew who the voices belonged to. She kept walking to her office, her body stiffening with frustration and anger. All the joy and hope of the worship service had been deflated by voices of ignorance and arrogance.

12

Maggie sat in the middle of the floor of the parsonage family room, sipping her second cup of Lady Grey tea. She was surrounded by dozens of large Ziploc bags, piles of colorful children's clothes, and two permanent markers.

The church had taken their job to clothe the orphans of Bawjiase seriously. The children often had clothes brought to them from other missionaries, but they were all hand-me-downs. Some fit, some didn't. Maggie had Skyped Bryan and Joy with an idea.

"I know we will bring money to spend at Market to support the Bawjiase economy, but would it be possible to bring each child new clothes that fit just right and can be their very own?"

Joy smiled. "That would be a great gift, Maggie. The children have little perception of what they wear. They put on clothes, ill-fitting or not. If Loving the Lord Church would like to send clothes, we'll enjoy sharing them with the children."

"That's just it," Maggie said. "For the people in the congregation not going to Ghana, this is a way to support the mission. Is there any way you could get the names, sizes, and favorite colors of each child?"

Joy laughed and looked at Bryan. "I see smart 'go-getting' is genetic in your family."

"Oh, I'm nothing like my sister," Bryan said, sadly shaking his head. "She is bossy, pushy, and annoying in every way."

Maggie rolled her eyes. "Yes, Joy, that is true. The only way Bryan got through school was because I wrote all his papers for him and helped him cheat on tests. He's a total dunce." She stuck her tongue out at Bryan. "And by the way, I'm not bossy. I'm *the boss.*"

"Okay, Beyoncé." Bryan grinned.

Joy moved on. "On to the matter at hand, I will call Pastor Elisha and get all the info you need to make the clothes personal for each child. Besides medical supplies and the CBC machine, most everything else will be bought at Market."

Maggie felt like she had heard that a million times.

Joy said goodbye, but Bryan and Maggie had a few minutes to talk.

"How's married life going?" Bryan asked.

"I think fine. It still feels like we're dating, in a way, except he sleeps over every night. It's amazing how life just keeps moving forward." Maggie realized she sounded a little bit sorry for herself.

"What do you mean?"

"We have been trying to figure out if we will ever have a honeymoon." Maggie thought of her dream on the beach and cringed. "But it seems it will have to wait until after Ghana. But then we will be getting close to Lent and Easter . . . and Jack has patients." Maggie sighed.

"I think you learned last year that the church is quite capable of being without you for a bit. You aren't that important. Maybe Jack is, but probably not." Bryan laughed.

"Thanks, you turd."

"I remember you told me, 'We all do what we want to do. There are no excuses for not getting things done.' I have come to believe that, sister Margaret. You will have a honeymoon when you want to have a honeymoon." Bryan nodded his head in agreement with himself.

"Well, look at you, throwing my words back at me. Although I believe it was Ed who said that. On another matter, I can't wait to see you for Thanksgiving. We are having the feast here in the parsonage, and it will be jammed with people. Including a tall, beautiful blonde with the initials CC."

Maggie was in love with idea of Bryan and Cate Carlson being in love.

"Yes. I'll fly into Detroit the Monday before. We've got a lot to do between now and turkey time, though. Joy and I will call on Friday and chat with the mission group again. It seems to be growing by leaps and bounds, which is great. There is work for everyone. Okay, I've got to get going. Love you, Megs."

"Love you, Bry."

They had clicked out of Skype.

A week after the call, a poster was put up in church with thirty names for the Loving the Lord congregation to choose from. The invitation was for donations of brand-new clothes for the children in Bawjiase.

Child's Name

Age

Clothing sizes

Favorite color

And the congregation responded overwhelmingly with brand-new, appropriately-sized clothes. Each girl would receive three sundresses, seven pairs of underwear, and flip-flops. Each boy would receive three pairs of shorts, three T-shirts, seven pairs of underwear, and flip-flops.

Now, sitting in the midst of the generosity of her congregation, Maggie put the initials of each child on the inside of their new clothes and then put each set of clothes in a large Ziploc bag with the child's name on it.

Maggie enjoyed this quiet, thoughtful task. Writing someone's name and their initials, over and over again, made her feel as if she was beginning to know them. She knew who the littlest ones were by their tiny sizes. She knew the tallest boy was named Promise. Cynthia was the tallest girl. As she wrote all the names and carefully placed the clothing in the bags, she began saying a prayer for each child.

God bless Leah today. She is a tiny baby. You made her. May the care she receives from Marta today be exactly what she needs. Amen.

Maggie knew some of the stories of the children. Parents who couldn't keep them. Parents who had died in floods and many in car accidents. Grandparents who just couldn't care for a baby. Pastor Elisha and his wife Marta found the children, or the children found them, and then there was one more place set at the table in the orphanage. It was always set with thanksgiving for another life being found and loved. Most recently that had been Leah. At two weeks old, she had been found stuffed in a paper bag and left in an abandoned building.

Jennifer and Beth Becker had put their names next to Leah's on the poster in church.

Maggie had made it very clear to the congregation, because Joy made it very clear to her: "The children may receive different styles and colors, but they must receive the same number of gifts. No one receives more than the others. It has to be fair for all."

Joy had seen other visitors to Bawjiase, thinking they were being helpful, unloading suitcase after suitcase of ill-fitting clothes, used toys, candy, and other things they thought "African" children would want. It was a nightmare. It was also condescending.

"The children become overwhelmed by these piles of toys and other items. Someone is always left out or doesn't get something they want because there is too much of one thing and not enough of another," Joy said on one Skype call, exasperated. "They don't need Western ideas of what they need, if that makes sense. They have the food they like here from Market. They enjoy having soccer balls to play with, but they don't need complicated games that have batteries or extra pieces."

Maggie kept praying as she placed the colorful clothes in the bags. *God bless Promise as he learns in school today. What a beautiful name. God bless Rahael and her sister Barbara. Thank you for keeping the sisters together and bringing them to Pastor Elisha.* Pretty sundresses went into bags.

There was a footstep and a creak of the floor. "Whatcha doing?"

Maggie looked up to see her favorite face.

"Oh, Jack, you're home. I lost track of time. Look at all these wonderful new clothes."

Maggie stood up, and several pairs of flowered underpants fell to the floor.

"I can't wait to hug you," Jack said and hugged her tightly with a kiss added in for good measure.

Jack looked at the floor and took in the scene. Thirty bags, some filled, some partially filled, and piles of clean new clothes neatly stacked.

"You've been working hard on this."

"Yes, and a nice quiet job it is. Are you hungry? We should probably eat and then get ready for ghouls and goblins to ring the Westminster chimes all night." Maggie had the Halloween candy all ready to pass out.

"It's too bad it's so chilly and rainy out," Jack said, walking to the kitchen.

"But it almost always is. Halloween weather in Michigan is a crap-shoot, emphasis on *crap*. Then the little ones get too cold and just need to be home in their beds . . . Are we going to take our kids trick-or-treating?"

"Well, I don't know. Do we have to decide that right now? Can I have some dinner first?" Jack asked as he opened the refrigerator.

"I guess, if you want to put our children at risk by not deciding this very pertinent and important question right this minute. Can you grab that salad and the butter, oh and some jam?" Maggie gave the soup a stir. "The soup committee at church made a bumper-crop batch, so to speak, of butternut squash bisque. Probably everyone in church has been given some. I also made Italian bread in our new wedding bread machine today. I think it worked. At least it doesn't feel like a brick."

The bread was a success.

"Another triumph, my dear!" Jack exclaimed, echoing the words of Bob Cratchit to Mrs. Cratchit on Christmas Day.

"Hey!' Maggie's brain logically leapt to Christmas. "We get to make our own brand-new Christmas traditions this year. I didn't even decorate last year. When can we get a tree? What do you think about lights on the three evergreens in the backyard? Are you afraid of heights? There's a church ladder around the back. What's your favorite Christmas cookie?"

She had at least a dozen more questions, but Jack stopped her the only way he knew how.

"Well," Maggie said with a sigh, "that was very pleasant. But I would almost think you were trying to keep me from making any more Christmas plans with a kiss like that."

Jack just grinned as he set the table. They ate quickly, blowing on the hot bisque and slathering jam on the homemade bread.

"Don't think you're getting out of Christmas questions that easy, Dr. Elliot," Maggie said with jam dripping onto her fingers. "I'm relentless."

"I'm discovering that. Fortunately, I know just how to shut you up," he said, handing her another napkin.

The dishes were just about loaded in the dishwasher when the first sound of the Westminster chimes rang out.

"I'll get it," said Jack.

He picked up the candy bowl and headed for the front door. Maggie heard squeals of laughter from three very familiar voices.

"Whao's Pasto Maggie?" Carl demanded from the doorway.

"Pasto Maggie! Pasto Maggie! Pasto Maggie!" Carl, Carrie, and Hannah shouted together and then dissolved into giggles.

Maggie came to the door and said, "BOO!"

More giggles.

"Carrie! Hannah! Carl! What are you doing out on a night like this?" Maggie said with mock surprise.

"Pastor Maggie," Carrie said seriously with her hands on her small hips, "it's Halloween."

Carrie was dressed in one of her many tutus, with a silver crown on her head and a golden, sparkly cape wrapped around her shoulders. Carl was dressed in striped overalls, a kerchief around his neck, and a small train engineer's cap on his head.

Hannah, dressed as a bright-red M&M, nodded awkwardly and said, "Halloween!!"

Maggie looked past the children and saw Mary and William standing on the porch steps. They both smiled, and William held a large umbrella over their heads.

"Oh, so it is. What do you say then?" Maggie asked.

"TRICK OR TREAT!" Carrie, Carl, and Hannah yelled.

Jack knelt down and let the children pick out several pieces of candy for their plastic pumpkins.

Maggie looked over at William and Mary and motioned them toward the end of the porch. Once out of the children's earshot she asked, "How's it going?" her eyebrows raised.

"It's going well," William said with his quiet smile, "but it seems we had a little more energy when our own children were young."

"That is because we are old now," Mary said and poked her husband with her elbow. She looked at Maggie and said softly, "The children are a delight. It's helpful to have Hannah around. The three of them are inseparable. We are adjusting to our 'new normal,' aren't we, William?"

"Yes. Carrie and Carl are comfortable at The Grange, they know their schedule for school now, and even though it's still new, we are setting a routine." William sounded optimistic, which eased Maggie's mind.

Everyone was watching and waiting to see how the new family arrangement would work for all involved. The hope was that Carrie and Carl would feel at home, comfortable in new surroundings, and loved when their mother died. Mary and William would be able to help the children grieve when Cassandra was gone without being filled with grief themselves. Their focus was the children.

"Miss Mary, Mr. William, we're ready to go!" Carrie's giggles bubbled out of her as she and her two cohorts began moving down the steps.

William took Carl's hand. The boy's stitches from crashing into Jack and Maggie's wedding cake table had been removed two weeks earlier, but his new caregivers were very protective of the accident-prone little boy.

"Bye, Pasto Maggie!" Carl waved his pumpkin in her direction.

"Thank you, Dr. Jack!" all three children shouted.

As they made their way to the house next door, Cole and Lynn Porter came up the parsonage walk with three little pigs.

"Hello, Porter family!" Maggie exclaimed.

Penny and Molly immediately began making little piggy noises.

"Good evening, Pastor Maggie," Lynn said. "We have some little piglets here who are eager for some candy."

The piggy noises became louder.

"Fortunately, we happen to have some candy right here in this bowl."

Maggie bent down and let the little pigs help themselves. Sammy squirmed in his daddy's arms, so Cole set him down on the porch, and he toddled over to the bowl. He watched his sisters, then began digging in the bowl and throwing candy on the porch. His small piggy snout slipped askew and covered his right eye. He looked like a piggy pirate.

As the evening progressed, so did the rain. Soggy witches, angels, Mickey Mouses, ghosts, and a variety of action heroes came up the steps of the parsonage to gather their treats.

"I wonder how many of these children you'll see in your office this week," Maggie said as the last group of middle schoolers left on their roller skates. "Colds, broken bones, tummy aches . . ."

"There often is a tiny surge after Halloween," Jack said. "Rain and roller skates are perhaps not the best combo."

They turned off the porch light and went into the kitchen. As they helped themselves to the last of the candy, Maggie picked up her phone and made a call.

"Hello? Maggie? Is everything okay?" Maggie's mother, Mimi, had just the tiniest tinge of anxiety in her voice.

"Oh, yes, Mom. Sorry to call this late, but I have a psychology question for you."

"Oh. We were just turning out the lights. We had quite a multitude of little goblins tonight. What's your question?" Mimi got straight to the point, as always.

"I'm wondering about Carrie and Carl and what to do for them when Cassandra dies. I mean, the practical things no one wants to talk about. Should they see her dead? Should they go to the funeral? They already know she's 'going to heaven,' but they don't understand what that means. They think we might be able to drive them there. They are only seven and five. What can they handle?"

Jack put another miniature Snickers bar in his mouth, then whispered through the chocolate, "Put her on speaker."

"Mom, I'm putting you on speaker. Jack is here too."

"Well, I certainly hope so," Mimi said. Then, after a moment to gather her thoughts, she continued. "Death and young children is somewhat tricky. It's important never to tell young children that a loved one is 'asleep' or has 'gone away.' They may be afraid to go to sleep themselves or think when someone goes away, to work or run errands, they won't return."

"What about 'closure'?" she asked her mother.

"Children as young as Carrie and Carl are unable to process many of the adult emotions of loss and grief. For instance, 'closure' is not something a five-year-old can process. So I would recommend they do not see their mother's body. Talking about heaven and Jesus is not always helpful, especially saying 'Mommy is happy with Jesus.' They may wonder why Mommy couldn't be happy with them.

"Keeping their schedule intact will be one of the most helpful things. Of course, their teachers will know what they are dealing with at the time and can help if the children feel bad or act out at school. Nothing they do will be out of the ordinary or wrong. They will process their mother's death in small chunks. Try to speak to them directly, without too much detail or flowery words. I think the best thing going for them is the fact they are settled in the home they will be raised in. When Cassandra dies, they won't have the trauma of a move and new changes they can't understand."

"What about the funeral?" Maggie asked.

"Will there be a casket?" Mimi asked.

"I . . . I don't know," Maggie admitted.

"Should there be?" Jack asked.

"Hello, Jack. You know, a casket can frighten small children because they don't want to know their mommy is in a box or going into the cold ground. These may be things to talk to Cassandra about. I would think she has opinions about her death and burial."

Maggie cringed. She always appreciated her mother's directness, but the thought of talking to Cassandra about it was intimidating.

"This may seem somewhat intimidating," Mimi continued, reading Maggie's thoughts, "but it gives Cassandra one more thing to be in control of at this time of being able to control little else."

"You're right," Maggie said. "Mom, how do you know all that stuff off the top of your head?" Maggie marveled, once again.

"I wrote a chapter on children and death in my Child Psychology textbook," Mimi said simply.

Jack shook his head in admiration. "You know, I only married Maggie so that I could have you for a mother-in-law."

"That makes sense," Mimi said, then chuckled.

Maggie rolled her eyes.

"Is Maggie rolling her eyes?" Mimi asked.

"Yes!" Maggie responded. She picked up Marmalade, who had just walked into the room. "I thought he only married me for my cats."

"Well, if you need any more info, give me a call or buy my book. You two have a nice evening. Your father and I love you," Mimi said.

"Love you too," Jack and Maggie chorused and hung up the phone.

"She's the most intelligent woman I know," Maggie said.

"I'm looking at the most intelligent woman I know." Jack smiled.

"Well, let's talk about that some more upstairs. Plus, I have a few more Christmas questions for you."

Maggie got up and turned off the lights.

Six round eyes glared in the dark. Marmalade, Cheerio, and Fruit Loop watched as the two figures retreated to the stairs. How many nights would it be before someone remembered to give them their nighttime treats?

13

Obolo the dog was licking up the last bits of breakfast, his tongue and tail simultaneously wagging. Although he had plenty of dog food, thanks to Bryan and Fifi, Obolo still enjoyed people food more and had made himself right at home with the new guests in his house. He had no qualms about sleeping on anyone's bed or sniffling through luggage. He was expectantly present at every meal, looking at each person sitting at the table—his large brown eyes pleading, smiling, and finally, victorious at getting various tidbits. He never failed to receive handouts.

Bryan seemed especially generous to Obolo that morning.

"What are you smiling about?" Maggie asked her brother too loudly.

Everyone looked at Bryan and agreed he did have kind of a goofy grin on his face.

"Are you excited to fetch water after breakfast?" Maggie asked.

"No," Jack said slowly, "he's excited because it's his turn to burn the toilet paper."

Everyone grimaced. Thus far Maggie, Jack, and Sylvia had been the designated TP burners at the back of the volunteer house. It was not a pleasant task.

"It's not because Cate is coming this afternoon, is it?" Joy asked, sprinkling salt on her boiled egg.

"You guys are jerks," Bryan said, but he was smiling. He hadn't seen his lovely Cate since Thanksgiving. Six whole weeks ago. Time had dragged way too slowly.

"I can't believe how time flies," Maggie said. "It's Friday already."

"Is everyone ready for the day?" Joy asked, looking around the table.

Obolo took the opportunity to sneak his nose up to Joy's plate and handily steal her entire boiled egg with one precise bite.

"Obolo!" Joy said. "You could have said please."

Fifi, who was just finishing his own egg, reached for the bowl, plucked out the last boiled egg, and put it on Joy's plate.

"Stop talking and eat your breakfast," Fifi said.

Fifi had become a fast friend to all of the Americans, and each of them watched and listened to him carefully. Fifi knew more than Joy or Bryan about United Hearts, each child, the farm, the needs for the new school, and the culture. It was his village. It was his country. Those were his people. He was patient with visitors, in spite of the fact that some visitors spoke to Fifi as if he knew nothing.

Fifi was also a man of great faith. He saw God's goodness everywhere and had complete trust in God's care for all creation. His faith was simple, but not simplistic. "All things work together for good, for those who love God." Fifi loved God with his entire being.

Often, Pastor Elisha led all-night church services. These occurred behind United Hearts in the church made of benches and covered by a large plastic sheet. There was a sound system with speakers and a microphone that ran on batteries, or when the power in town was working, it was connected to electricity. The music, prayers, lamentations, and joys were shared by all and lifted to God. The children twelve and older were in attendance and were expected to be in school the next day. United Hearts adults and people from the countryside were present as well.

Fifi never missed all-night church, and after being up all night singing and praying, he would bake breads and cakes to be sold in the village. He had recently purchased his own taxi, and after all-night church he would get his taxi driver up and out on the roads for the day. He had begun a pig farm a year earlier and donated all the money he earned to the orphanage. Fifi would help with anything needed at United Hearts. He loved his life and never wavered in his heart of thankfulness.

That week, and every week when volunteers visited, Fifi added the chore of cooking three meals a day to his already busy life. He also had to add extra trips to Market and the blue store to have enough food for the volunteers. He never complained, but Joy knew that Fifi sacrificed much when volunteers were in Bawjiase.

Joy smiled at Fifi to thank him for the egg and then looked around the table. "Are you ready for the day?" she repeated.

"Actually," Ethan said, "I thought we were going to be building at least part of the new school during this trip. But we haven't built anything at all. We've only got another week or so."

Bill and Ethan had gone to the site of the school each morning after breakfast. The young men from United Hearts were also there. Of course, it was only a few yards from the orphanage for them. The first day, they had waited for a truck from Accra to bring a cement mixer and tools, but the truck didn't arrive. Bill and Ethan learned about the back-breaking work of making bricks from the bags of cement and dirt mixed together with shovels. The young men from United Hearts also spent the first day making bricks and teaching Bill and Ethan how to make them exactly the same size.

"I don't mind making bricks," Bill said in his quiet voice. "I just thought we'd be laying a foundation or putting up a frame."

Some of the others had been confused (at best) and disappointed (at worst) by how the first few days had gone.

Jack and Charlene had brought the CBC machine to the clinic the day Hannah got her stitches. They carried it in the box it had flown in, and then, along with two of the nurses at the clinic, set up the machine in a small room used as a laboratory at the back of the clinic. The nurses were thrilled. Dr. Obodai came in the lab and also expressed his pleasure to have the CBC machine.

"We'll be able to test the blood of our patients now and make faster diagnoses. Until now, it has just been a guessing game."

Dr. Obodai had been trained in the United States. He then taught for a few years at the medical school in Accra, but his heart was in the countryside where he had grown up. The clinic had been his dream, and piece by piece, the dream was becoming reality.

"We want to stay connected with you and the clinic," Jack said. "You know best what you need here. If we can help you in any way, let us know."

"Thank you for your generosity. There is something you can do. The children at United Hearts need to have their National Health cards updated. Some will need booster vaccines. Would you be willing to organize those tasks?"

Paperwork like that wasn't exactly what Jack and Charlene had in mind when making the offer to help in the clinic. They were both highly trained doctors, after all.

"Certainly," said Charlene. "Ellen might be a good one for that. She's a nurse."

"Thank you," said Dr. Obodai. "That would be helpful. We don't have the extra staff here for that undertaking."

He thanked them again and then left to see patients in the room full of gurneys.

Jack and Charlene had left the clinic and walked back to the volunteer house, disappointed that there wasn't something more doctor-like for them to do.

Sylvia had gone to the farm each morning right after breakfast. The farm was fifteen minutes farther down the road past United Hearts. She walked as quickly as possible, eager to help Nana. Once there, she and Nana, the young man in charge of the farm project, would begin filling buckets from a mossy pond on the edge of the farm. Sylvia loved the smell of the algae-covered water, the rocky soil, and the warm air. All morning they would fetch water, then walk from plant to plant and water each one. One bucket watered about five plants. Nana took one side of the dirt road, Sylvia the other. At midday, Sylvia and Nana would walk back to the volunteer house. They were always late for lunch. They would eat quickly, then head straight back to the farm and water all afternoon. They never got every plant watered thoroughly by dusk.

"The plants need so much water in this heat, don't they?" Sylvia had asked Nana on one of their hot and exhausting journeys home.

"Yes, it is hard work, but this is what we eat, and now we are able to sell yams and cabbages at Market," Nana said with a grin.

"I grow vegetables in Michigan. I have a shop," Sylvia said. "But we don't have as much sunshine as you do here. I begin growing my seeds in what we call a greenhouse. The temperature is very cold outside. We have a lot of snow when I begin growing plants. I have to keep them warm. The greenhouse keeps them protected and allows them to get a head start."

"We have two seasons here," Nana said. "Dry season and rainy season. We are in the dry season now. That is why it is important to water our crops each day. The heat is too much for the plants."

Sylvia was thinking of how an irrigation system would save on the back-breaking work, but she had no idea how that could even happen.

"When there are no volunteers here, do you do this all by yourself?" she asked.

"Not all the time. The other men come with me. But now they will be busy building the school. I will do the watering until April. Then the rains should come and God does the watering." Nana smiled.

Each night, after a bowl of jollof rice and chicken, or whatever else Fifi had prepared, Sylvia would wait her turn to take a bucket bath and then fall straight into bed. She ached everywhere. Each morning, she awakened to roosters crowing, dressed hurriedly, ate her breakfast, and then made her way down the red road again.

After Hannah's accident, Maggie and Addie had asked Joy if it would be all right to go to Adua's house and help her while Hannah was healing from her fall.

Joy had thought about it, then said, "It should be fine. But follow her lead. She will not allow you to help with things like dishwashing or clothes washing, but she may appreciate you playing with the boys. I know I sound like a broken record, but respect the culture. It would be offensive if you entered her home and decided what she needed to have done."

That seemed to be a lesson everyone struggled with. The members of Loving the Lord all saw things that could be done to make life easier for the people at United Hearts and in the village. At least they thought they did.

Joy and Bryan had made it clear during their Skype calls to the group in Cherish that things didn't always go as planned, so it would be important to be flexible. The group had nodded and seemed to understand. The difficulty was, they each had begun to dream of what they could do to help. They wanted to make a difference. They wanted to use their skills to better the lives of the people of Bawjiase.

Now it was the first Friday of the trip, almost a week gone. Jack and Charlene hadn't been back to the clinic. There was no foundation poured for the school, just piles of bricks. Sylvia hadn't planted a single thing, just watered endlessly. Ellen had checked on Hannah once during the week, and the child was healing well so her nursing services were not required. Dana hadn't left the volunteer house because every day, when she thought someone was going to introduce her to the veterinarian in town, no one did.

Maggie and Addie had taken Kofi and Kwashi to United Hearts to play while Adua took care of her house and Hannah rested. Lacey walked every day to United Hearts and observed. She saw the older children leave for school in town. Then she saw Marta and two other women begin to wash breakfast bowls and the endless piles of laundry. All the washing, of dishes and laundry, was done in buckets using homemade soap. Then all items were placed on bushes in the sun to dry. Lacey offered once to help, but was immediately rebuffed by the women. They would never let a guest do their washing. So Lacey, Maggie, and Addie mostly played with the little ones at the orphanage as the week went on.

Everyone (except Sylvia, who went to the farm) helped fetch water every morning. Sometimes, one or two of them would go with Fifi to the blue store to buy bread, eggs, beans, and biscuits (cookies to the

Americans). They all took their turns washing up after meals. They had all done a little bit of laundry in the buckets on the porch of the volunteer house, but the group had spent quite a bit of time around the dining table talking or reading books from the bookshelf. It was not what they had envisioned for their mission trip.

That Friday morning, Joy sensed their feelings and frustrations.

"How is everyone doing?" Joy asked more pointedly, looking everyone in the eyes, as was her habit.

"To be honest," Jack said, "I have a feeling we all had some preconceived ideas of what we would be doing here. That we would be using our skills in some helpful way. But what I'm seeing is the people here know exactly what they are doing."

"We never know if a need will arise or not," Joy said. "We take everything an hour at a time around here, but I appreciate the fact that none of you have felt like you're wasting your time."

"I do." Dana Drake spoke from the end of the table. "I thought I could help with the animals here. I didn't know what to expect, but there are so many animals, many desperately needing care. I haven't met the veterinarian in town yet, but I have sat here waiting to do so. I was able to check on the cat and kittens at United Hearts and give them some deworming medicine. I put flea medicine on Obolo. I've tried to have a look at the wandering goats and the thousands of chickens everywhere, but I really don't know why I'm here." Dana ended with a deep sigh. "I'm sorry. I don't mean to complain. But I don't feel helpful at all."

"I'm sorry, Dana," Maggie said.

All of a sudden, Maggie felt guilty. She had gathered this group and, rightly or wrongly, they had all dreamed of doing something more tangible than what they were actually doing. Maggie turned to Joy.

"What can we do, Joy? What is the greatest need? We want to do anything but sit."

Maggie was polite but direct. She had never meant to bring that group of giving and gifted people to Bawjiase to do nothing. Regardless of what wasn't being said to Joy directly, Maggie knew by overhearing whispered conversations that there was a great deal of frustration not being shared.

"We're on Ghana time," Joy said.

"We wait and see what needs to be done," Bryan chimed in, backing his boss. To Maggie's ears, he sounded smug.

"Well, Bry, that's great. But we need a little direction now. We aren't just going to sit here waiting for your girlfriend to show up." Maggie immediately regretted the tone in her voice.

"Well, I know what I'm going to do," Lacey jumped in. "I've got some plans for the kids at United Hearts this afternoon. I could use a couple of volunteers."

Lacey was almost able to break the tension at the table with her breezy words and attitude, but not quite.

"That's great, Lacey. Count me in," Maggie said without enthusiasm. Then she looked back at her brother. He was the safe one to unload on with her lack-of-work frustrations. "We have brought money for food and building supplies. Is there a way to get food for United Hearts? Or order building supplies?" Maggie asked.

"Jack and I were asked to update the children's National Health cards and bring the kids in for needed vaccinations. We haven't done much with that yet," Charlene said, omitting the fact that she and Jack had figured Ellen, being a nurse, could do that mundane chore.

"What about all the bags of new clothes for the children?" Addie's sweet voice slightly lessened the tartness around the table. "We could bring the bags over, and after school, they could each receive their new things."

That seemed to catch on.

"Let's take pictures of them . . . if that's okay," Maggie looked at Joy but avoided Bryan, "and we can show the people back home. They can see the children wearing their new clothes."

"That's a great idea," Joy said.

Once again, she wanted to remind the group of what she and Bryan had told them over the months of preparation for the trip, but she could read the levels of frustration. It happened with every group.

There was usually a meltdown experience during a trip like this. But she also believed there weren't egos driving this group, the way she had seen in others. This group was bored, and that was due to the lack of her direction. Ghana time didn't mean do-absolutely-nothing time.

Joy had watched many groups come and go. Too many had come and decided to "fix" all the problems they perceived. They inserted themselves in ways that were not just ignorant, but rude and disrespectful. She would purposely slow down those groups, try to steer them in a different direction, remind them of cultural differences, and encourage them to learn, not teach. But this group wanted to do just that: learn from the people of Bawjiase.

"Listen," Joy said, "today is Market day. Market is open every Tuesday and Friday. If some of you would like to come, we can make a trip to fetch food we need for United Hearts. I'll call Pastor and find out what to buy." She pulled out her cell phone.

That had been one thing that surprised the group: every adult at United Hearts had a cell phone. They were constantly connected with one another.

"Who would like to be in on Lacey's secret scheme? Have fun doing whatever it is you are going to do," Joy said as Lacey looked around the table. Joy wisely chose not to vet Lacey's plan. She seemed down-to-earth and respectful of everyone there. It was time to let the group have some control. "If the medical staff would like to head to United Hearts with Bryan, you can get a group together and go to the clinic for their booster vaccines. If there is someone willing to go through the National Health cards, Pastor Elisha can tell you who needs updating."

"Also," Sylvia said shyly, "it would be great to have some help at the farm. Nana and I are watering almost every plant by hand. Twice each day. He's going to begin planting new plants, and I can't manage the watering by myself."

She stared down at her empty breakfast plate. The breakfast wasn't quite settling in her stomach.

"What about me?" Dana asked. She wasn't willing to be relegated from animal care.

"Dana, if I could make an animal care job for you, I would. But I can't," Joy said plainly. "I expect we'll hear from the local vet at some point, but we may need you to do something different today. Is that okay?"

From the look on her face, it was obvious it wasn't.

"I'll go to the farm with Sylvia," Dana said stoically.

She got up from the table, brought her dishes to the small plastic tub in the kitchen for washing, and went out on the porch.

Maggie shot a look at her brother, but it seemed like he didn't care. She set her breakfast dishes on top of his, then followed Dana out onto the porch.

Neither Maggie nor Dana spoke. They stood side by side and looked out at the sun-filled yard. Clothes that had been washed in buckets the day before waved cheerfully in the breeze. Chickens were pecking around the yard and clucking to one another in comradery. A mother goat passed through, scattering indignant chickens, her twin babies bleating after her.

Maggie got lost in the sights, sounds, and smells. She felt weary. Her mind drifted back to Cherish. She thought of her wedding. She thought of Irena, Irena's sadness. She thought of Thanksgiving baskets. She thought of Cassandra, which made her throat constrict. She thought of the quiet Christmas that year. And she thought of all the anticipation and excitement of going to Ghana on the church's first mission trip. All the planning and hopes of meeting new people, learning about a new culture, and working hard to maybe make a difference.

At that moment, all Maggie wanted to do was to go home.

14

The day after Halloween was All Saints' Day. Maggie had prepared the service with Irena over the past two weeks. Remembering loved ones who had died was a ritual the church could easily nourish. Doris, once again, would ring the church bell after each name was read. Irena had chosen impossibly depressing hymns, although she acquiesced to play "For All the Saints" at the close of the service.

As they prepared the service, Maggie had been surprised to find Irena continually disheveled and distracted. The organist had been spacey and unfocused throughout the planning sessions, and it drove Maggie slightly insane—even more so than usual.

Then, one afternoon, Irena handed Maggie a folded piece of paper and said, "Dees ees my muder. Herr name ees Catrina. I vould like to hev it red out loud dis yearr."

Maggie took the paper and wrote "Catrina Dalca" on her list of names. Maggie again noticed the wrinkled blouse, the runs in Irena's stockings, and the crooked miniskirt.

"When did your mother die?" Maggie asked carefully.

"Ven I was feefteen."

"Where were you?" Maggie slowly continued.

"Een Detroit. Ve hed a shop. She geeve museek lessons to de people. Ve sleep above de shop."

"What did you do when she died?" Maggie wondered when she would ask one question too many.

"I called funerral home. Police came to de shop. Dey see me alone and my muder ded. Ven dey say I vill be taken away, I hid so dey couldn't find me. My muder had de book of customers. I call dem and say, 'I vill be teaching de lessons in two veeks.' By den, no morre police. Dey too beezy. I teach and pay rent and save money. I tell many lies to keep my secret. My mama vant me to go to school, but I teach myself. Den I pass de tests and go to university. Den I play de orrgan and teach lessons morre. Den I come herre." Irena brushed her hands together, as if neatly wiping away the past.

Maggie had no idea that was part of Irena's story. *Only fifteen?* Irena had to hide from police and take up teaching her mother's students. She'd lost her mother, which was worst of all. Why didn't anyone ask questions? Why didn't the police follow up? Who would ignore a fifteen-year-old girl living alone?

"Did you go to your mother's funeral?" Maggie asked almost inaudibly.

A sigh from Irena. "No, I deed nut. No one told me, and I vas hiding. I dunt know vere she ees. I found her on de keetchen floor, vit no breathing. Dat's de last time I see herr." Irena was sounding a little less cavalier now, like she hadn't visited the memory in a while.

Maggie cautiously opened her mouth one more time.

"Irena, I'm so sorry you lost your mother." Did she dare continue? "Um . . . lately you have seemed a little . . . I don't know . . . preoccupied. Are you all right?" Maggie held her breath.

Irena's eyes narrowed into glittering green slits. "Vat you mean?"

"Well, you don't seem quite yourself. You seem . . . distracted or, I don't know, are you feeling sick?"

Maggie was sorry she had begun that line of questioning. They had actually had a calm conversation. Now, Irena was not looking pleased.

"I em nut seeck. I em fine," Irena said with a huff.

Getting called out had made thoughts of her mother quickly disappear. But then, what was it that Maggie saw?

Is Irena blushing?

Maggie grabbed Irena's black-nailed fingers with her own hands and held on to the small organist.

"Spill, Irena. What is going on? You are not acting normal!" *But then you never have.*

Irena looked into Maggie's clear, blue eyes.

"Okey, okey! You are annoying. I em heving a friend in my life. A nice boy. Eet makes me heppy."

Maggie blinked. "You have a boy who is a friend? Please tell me he is of age, Irena!" Maggie imagined Irena in dominatrix attire with some poor high school boy.

Irena looked confused.

"Who is your boyfriend?" Maggie said slowly and clearly.

"Vell . . ." In all honesty, Irena had been dying to tell someone about her first true love. Who wouldn't be? Irena blurted it out. "He ees my Captain Crrunch!" Irena said with a small toss of her badly colored head.

Well, if a cool breeze had blown into Maggie's office at that moment, it would have been enough to knock her straight over. Irena and Detective Keith Crunch were having a love affair.

"So vat? You hev noting to say?" Irena smirked.

Maggie stared mutely.

Irena laughed out loud. "You are nut de only one een luv, Pastoorr Maggie. Irena Dalca ees also een luv."

Maggie could not get her brain to accept that new information. Weren't all men scared to death of Irena? Didn't they just gape at her from afar, then run for the hills if she came too close? And Keith Crunch? What in the world?

Maggie rearranged her face as best she could. She tried to smile, but she was unnaturally using all of her teeth. It didn't look nice.

"Congratulations, Irena," Maggie said in a singsong voice. "I think he needs to be invited to Thanksgiving dinner, don't you? If you're going to be with us, he should be too. Would you like to ask him, or should I call him? What do you think?" Maggie told herself to shut up. It didn't work. "Do you know what his favorite pie is? I'll make one special. Well, this is just great news."

Irena chuckled. "Pastoorr Maggie, you look silly. I vill invite heem. Ees verry nice ov you. He likes blueberries. I know dis already." Irena smiled a knowing smile.

Good grief! "Great. Blueberry it is. I'll plan on you both. Now, how about we look over this service?"

The All Saints' Day service was beautiful. Maggie read names, so thankful she could say "Catrina Dalca" and look at Irena on the organ bench, who immediately looked down at her organ keys.

The youth did another commercial for Thanksgiving baskets, more subdued due to the day, but still a fun reminder to continue with donations.

At the end of the service, Maggie was ready to give the benediction when the breeze of the Holy Spirit moved her in a different direction. She looked at the congregation, all standing for the end of the service.

"A couple of weeks ago, our wonderful youth invited us to make Thanksgiving baskets for the people in our city who wouldn't be able to buy their own dinner." Maggie purposefully looked slightly over the heads of her congregation, careful not to make eye contact with anyone. "I would like to underscore today that poverty is an equal-opportunity devastation. It's not just in faraway developing countries. Poverty is not found only in large cities with high crime rates, lack of enough police, and too many citizens. Poverty affects people in every city, town, and village in the entire world. I hope you hear that." Maggie paused.

"*Poverty affects people in every city, town, and village in the entire world,*" she repeated with great emphasis. "There is not one place in the world where every person in the community has everything they need to live a decent life. Poverty exists in Cherish. It makes life hard for children, women, and men. Some people might think these people are lazy, and they're teaching their children to be lazy. Some people might think they are just gaming the system of our government. And maybe some of them are." *Breathe, Maggie, breathe.*

"But what about the ones who aren't? I'll tell you. The places where poverty lives and destroys is where Jesus lives. Those are the places where Jesus invites us to go, to follow him, and care and love and heal in his name."

Maggie now began to look each parishioner in the eye. She went from row to row, staring at her church family.

"I don't care if there are people who are using my tax dollars to game the system. Because I care more about the people who are being helped instead of hindered in their struggle for basic human necessities. And a decent life.

"So please, let's not ever pretend poverty doesn't exist, or that poverty is the fault of the ones who have no means and no voice. Because there are people who have to live in the poverty of 'not enough,' but they just may have richer souls than those who judge and condemn them through ignorance and arrogance.

"Go in peace. Amen."

There was absolute silence.

Irena forgot to play the postlude.

Harold and Ellen forgot to get the cookies up from the kitchen for coffee time.

Martha Babcock, known as the nosy police dispatcher and a recent visitor to Loving the Lord, turned bright red. She abruptly pushed out of her pew and left the church. Sadly, the two people she had been talking with weeks ago were standing in their pew like statues. Unknown to the rest of the congregation, Chester and Doris Walters had received a direct hit. They finally exited the church and walked slowly home, not saying a word.

The next morning, the Monday after All Saints' Day, Maggie took her mother's advice. She drove to The Grange carrying a satchel with a hymnal, a liturgy book, a pad of paper, and a pen. She sat with Cassandra for two hours. Cassandra took complete control, if not of her death, then at least of her burial.

"No. I don't want the children to see my body once I've died. I want them to remember me alive," Cassandra said calmly.

She continued, "No casket. Cole Porter knows I wish to be cremated with my ashes buried in the Cherish cemetery. The children do not need to know what cremation is until they are much older. When they go to church for the funeral, I want them to feel at home in a place they go to every week."

"What would you like the service to be like?" Maggie asked, pen poised over paper.

"I want lots of singing. Tell Irena to let it rip on that organ of hers. Please ask Marla about the songs the children know from Sunday school. Sing every single one." Cassandra's eyes began to glisten.

"I don't care if this is right or wrong, but tell Carrie . . . and . . . Carl," she stifled a sob, "that I am watching them every day. I am proud of them. I want them to laugh a lot and be happy, and I want them to cry when they feel sad. Tell them we will be together again. And that I love them." The sob snuck out, and Cassandra covered her face with her hands.

Once she regained control, she said, "I want everyone to wear bright colors. And if possible, lots of Mrs. Popkin's treats on the Sunday morning coffee table. That will be comforting for Carrie and Carl. No ham-on-buns or green Jell-O in the basement. And for heaven's sake, tell people not to cry in front of my children. That will really piss me off!"

Maggie looked up from her pad of paper. She gave Cassandra a wink and a nod. "You got it."

"And no sermon," Cassandra finished. "No offense, but no one wants to hear a sermon at a funeral. But I do like the first eighteen verses of Psalm 139. Read those. Please."

The two women continued to talk over different aspects of Cassandra's life and death and the future she wished for her children.

After the two hours had passed, Maggie was surprised to hear a light knock on the door. Mary stuck her head in and said, "Cassandra, Mr. Brinkmeyer is here for you."

"Thank you, Mary." Then to Maggie, "I'm taking care of a lot of business today. Thank you, Pastor Maggie. I feel better now."

Maggie packed up her things, gave Cassandra a kiss on the cheek, and left. She saw Harold in the hallway.

"Hi, Harold. How are you?"

Harold smiled his handsome smile. "Great. You too?"

"Yes, just visiting Cassandra," Maggie said.

"Yeah. Me too. There's a lot going on."

Harold squeezed Maggie's arm in support and walked down the hallway. Maggie headed back to church. She decided, thanks to Cassandra's input, the content of the funeral would be focused on Carrie and Carl.

But as she drove, she couldn't help wondering why Cassandra had called for Harold. Harold had been incredibly helpful when Cassandra was diagnosed, taking care of her estate and drawing up adoption papers for William and Mary. He gave his time for free and smoothed the way for Cassandra to focus on life and death, not finances. But that work was done. Why was he there today?

15

November 21 & 22, 2015
Cherish, Michigan

Three weeks had passed since Maggie's Poverty Benediction. Much to her secret relief, no one had dared challenge her. Her bravado had quickly given way to insecurity once that church service ended.

Now, Maggie was hopeful for the Sunday before Thanksgiving for two big reasons: first, the assembling and delivering of Thanksgiving baskets, and second, the beautiful rose window. It had been destroyed by Redford Johnson in October and now would be completely restored. There was much to be thankful for, indeed.

The stained-glass experts had been working tirelessly to complete the window before winter hit in earnest. They succeeded, but just barely.

Saturday saw the first blizzard of the year. Eight inches of snow fell and covered Southeast Michigan in a fluffy, white frosting. Maggie wondered and fretted throughout the day. Jack watched her pace and agonize and stare out the window every ten minutes.

"What are you doing, wife?" he asked.

"Oh, you know, bits and bobs, odds and ends, this and that," she said distractedly.

Finally, he said, "The basket items will be collected and delivered." He looked at his unconvinced wife. "Okay, okay, let's just say it snows and no one can open their front door. We still have three more days before Thanksgiving to get the baskets where they need to be. And there is no need to worry about the rose window. They are shining up the inside of it today."

Maggie grimaced. "Am I that obvious to you? It's like we've been married forty years already. How am I ever going to keep any secrets from you?"

"Why would you want to?" Jack asked.

"You know, birthday surprises, Christmas presents, pregnancy."

Jack's eyes grew wide. "What?"

"Ha! I guess I can fool you when necessary. Good to know." Maggie giggled.

Jack took a deep breath. "I think we should have a honeymoon before we have a baby. What do you think?"

"We probably will be married forty years before we have a honeymoon. Probably too late for a baby by then." Maggie pulled out the popcorn popper. "Would you like some popcorn and hot chocolate? We might as well settle in for this blizzard."

"Yes, please."

The morning after the seemingly unending blizzard, the church was full of parishioners talking loudly as they hung up their coats and hats.

"What a snow!"

"I don't remember a blizzard like that."

"Took me hours to scoop out my driveway."

Irena was hissing away, to no avail, so she played the organ as loudly as possible.

Snow plows had worked all night to clear roads. Last-minute Thanksgiving donations were brought in to church, covering the steps and platform of the altar. The twenty-two turkeys that had been donated were already in boxes, still frozen, waiting for delivery.

The worship service was full of familiar Thanksgiving hymns, a short sermon, and a long Thanksgiving prayer from Maggie, who had the congregation make a circle around the sanctuary so that all could see the newly restored rose window. As the sun shone through the sparkling stained glass, more than one pair of eyes glistened with thanksgiving as everyone was reminded of how brokenness and ugliness can be made whole and beautiful once again.

Maggie kept her eyes on Julia. Redford was her ex-husband. He had terrorized her, as well as the church and the original rose window. But Julia stood tall and held Hannah's small hand. Julia was becoming whole and beautiful too, Maggie thought.

Once the service was done, everyone got to work. Charlene had the high school students perfectly organized, separating the food donations and bringing them to the tables set up in the basement. The parishioners placed cans and the fresh items in the boxes and baskets that had been brightly decorated by the children in Sunday school. After talking with Grace in Action, other items that the families might need had been gathered as well.

Ellen had the forethought to order fifteen large pizzas from It's Not Your Mama's Pizza to feed the workers. The smell of pizza filled the church, and Ellen received a loud ovation from her parishioner friends.

"You can always count on a nurse!" Harold shouted. Then he kissed Ellen, which caused another ovation.

Soon cars and trucks were packed with food, and the deliveries began.

Martha Babcock had tried to sneak out of church before the closing hymn. However, Police Chief Charlotte Tuggle stopped her at the door and said, "Martha, it would be great if you could stay. Fred has a cold today, and I am driving his truck. Would you be on my team?"

Although it sounded like a question, Martha took it as a command. Charlotte was Martha's boss, after all. Martha had only pure respect for Police Chief Tuggle, but she did not want to be part of that charity nonsense.

"Well, I was going to head home and shovel my sidewalk, but I guess I could stay for a bit," Martha said, torn.

"Good. Let's go down to the basement and get started."

Charlotte led Martha downstairs as if she were a prisoner.

Doris and Chester were going for the coat rack when Hank and Pamela stopped them.

"Howdy doody, you two," Hank said in his folksy, slightly dorky way. "Let's say the four of us make a team. Those who work together, make Thanksgiving baskets together, right?" Hank grinned, but Pamela rolled her eyes.

"We're going to deliver five meals. Will you help us?" Pamela entreated.

Chester and Doris didn't know what to say. Then Doris saw Irena and that Ann Arbor detective making their way down to the basement, holding hands. *What in the world?* Doris was not going to miss out on that piece of gossip. Besides, if Irena was staying, Doris was staying. There was no way that little foreigner was going to do more church work than her.

Once all the baskets were done, the groups loaded their cars and headed out to make their cheerful deliveries.

The first house on Hank's list of deliveries was just north of town. Doris and Chester were silent in the backseat. Pamela talked about the new stained-glass window and the good work of the youth group. She prattled on happily.

"Yessireebob! It sure is nice to have the church all back together again," Hank said cheerfully. "The new rose window is something to be truly thankful for this of all weeks!"

No response from the backseat.

Hank pulled into a well-plowed driveway and stopped the car.

"Hey, Chester, you grab the turkey, and I'll grab the other food. Let's go."

Hank popped the trunk with a button next to the steering wheel and got out of the car. At first, Chester didn't move, then Doris elbowed him hard in the ribs. Chester opened the door and retrieved the turkey box from the trunk. He followed Hank up to the front door and watched him ring the bell.

The door was opened by a boy of about sixteen. His hair was shaggy, and he was wearing a Vulfpeck T-shirt. He looked like the rest of the boys at church. "Shaggy" seemed to be in again.

"Hi, there!" Hank boomed. "We're from Loving the Lord Community Church. We have a delivery here for you and your family."

"Mom!" the boy called.

A woman with short brown hair, brown eyes, wearing jeans and a University of Michigan sweatshirt came to the door holding a bottle of Pine-Sol and a sponge. She smiled at the two men.

"Hello." She looked at her son. "Bobby, did you say hello?"

"Hello," Bobby said, running his fingers through his hair.

Bobby reminded Chester of his own grandson, who was the same age, with the same long hair.

"We're just stopping by with a delivery from Loving the Lord Community Church," Hank said.

"That is fantastic. I'm sorry, my name is Cecelia. Chance. Cecelia Chance." She quickly set her cleaning supplies on a small table near the door. "Bobby is my son, and my daughter, Naomi, is around here somewhere. Thank you so much for this." She stepped aside so Hank and Chester could bring the food into the house. It was spotless. Chester couldn't help but look around and notice not a thing out of place. It smelled like Pine-Sol and Lemon Pledge.

"My husband, Jim, has been out of work for the last four months." Cecelia spoke nervously and rapidly. "He drives a forklift at The Mill. Four months ago, he and a coworker accidentally collided when a load dropped from above their lifts. Jim's back was broken."

Chester looked at Cecelia. She seemed embarrassed, and he felt a tinge of something. Empathy?

"He's got a ways to go before he'll be able to work again. Lots of physical therapy. There will be an insurance settlement of some kind from The Mill, but it's taking longer to go through the system than we expected." Cecelia motioned to the men where to set the boxes. She peeked inside Hank's.

"Oh, this all looks yummy." She smiled.

"Yessireebob. We are so sorry to hear about your husband, Cecelia. We hope this food helps and also brings you some joy."

Hank stuck out his hand and shook Cecelia's. Chester stood awkwardly. Cecelia held out her hand to Chester and shook his heartily.

"Thank you, again, for giving us a Thanksgiving dinner. I didn't know what I was going to do."

Just then, a girl with long brown hair slung up on top of her head walked into the kitchen. She was all elbows and knees. Her eyes looked like exact replicas of her mother's.

"This is Naomi, my daughter," Cecelia said.

"Hi," Naomi said shyly, her voice almost a whisper. She looked at the food. "What's this?"

"It's Thanksgiving dinner," her mother answered.

"We truly wish your whole family a wonderful Thanksgiving," Hank said, "a good recovery for your husband, and a Merry Christmas when it rolls around. And you're always welcome at Loving the Lord Community Church. It was actually our youth group who put all this food together. Great bunch of kids!" Hank let his inner salesman shine.

Cecelia, Bobby, and Naomi walked the two men to the door.

Once they were gone, Naomi said softly, "We have a turkey for Thanksgiving."

Cecelia hugged her kids and sighed deeply. A mix of gratefulness and embarrassment comingled in her soul. She had never taken a handout in her life.

The people from Grace in Action had called Cecelia after she had gone in to ask for help with food and money to pay bills. The people at GIA asked her if it would be possible to use her name and have a local church bring a Thanksgiving dinner to her and her family. GIA always used anonymity with the community members in need, but a special request had been made by Loving the Lord Community Church. They wanted to meet the people who were receiving the food. They wanted to know who their neighbors were.

Cecelia had no problem with people knowing who she and her family were. It would give her a chance to thank someone in person, and she was certainly thankful. The food was a blessing. She reminded herself she didn't need to be embarrassed about Jim's accident or asking for help. They were going through a rough time. Loving the Lord Church seemed like a kind and understanding group of people.

The next house on the Thanksgiving route was west on Old US 12. When Hank pulled into the driveway, they found themselves in several inches of snow. He drove through the snow slowly. Fortunately, there was gravel underneath to give occasional traction. The house was a small, single-story rental. It was in need of fresh paint, and the roof looked weary. Half of one shutter hanging on the front window was absent, making the house look like it was missing a tooth.

"Well, come on, Doris," Pamela said. "It's our turn now."

Pamela got out of the car as Hank popped the trunk. She grabbed two bags of groceries. Doris made her way to the back of the car and stared into the trunk. She didn't seem to know what to do.

"Could you grab the turkey, Doris? And that box of diapers." Pamela barely kept the small note of frustration out of her voice.

Doris picked up the turkey and diapers and mutely followed Pamela up the wooden front porch steps. Toys were scattered on the porch.

Pamela set one bag of groceries down and knocked on the door. It was opened by a little girl of about five. Her head was wreathed in fluffy black curls, her dark-brown eyes round and surrounded in thick black lashes. She was wearing a pair of shorts that were too big, leaving one side hanging down her small hip, and her long-sleeved ruffled blouse fit too tightly across her torso and down her arms. Her nose was running, but her small pink mouth formed into a smile when she looked up at Pamela and Doris.

Pamela smiled back and knelt down. "Hi. My name is Pamela, and this is Doris. What's your name?" she asked.

"Gabby," the little girl said, suddenly looking shy.

"We have brought some things for you and your family. Is your mommy or daddy here?" Pamela looked Gabby in her beautiful brown eyes.

"Mama!" Gabby shouted into Pamela's face.

A woman wearing a faded yellow apron with a dish towel thrown over her shoulder came to the door. She had soft brown skin, which glistened. She looked at the two women on her porch.

"Hello?" she said with a slight accent.

Pamela stood up, patting Gabby's curls as she did so.

"Hi. My name is Pamela Arthur, and this is Doris Walters. We're from Loving the Lord Church, and we have brought some food and other items for your family for this Thanksgiving holiday. Are you Maria Gutierrez?"

"Yes. And this is Gabby, my daughter." Maria smiled.

"We've met Gabby. She is delightful," Pamela said, picking up the bag of groceries she had set down. "May we bring these things in for you? We don't want to let the cold air in."

Maria stepped aside. "Thank you, yes. The kitchen is in the back."

Doris followed Pamela through a small living room, an eating area, and into the kitchen. The house was worn but not dirty. It smelled of onions, peppers, and garlic, which made Doris feel a little hungry. The kitchen was very small, and there was a little boy about six months old sitting in a highchair, eating Cheerios. He looked at the strangers with his own set of large, dark eyes. His lower lip began to protrude, then tremble slightly.

"Oh, no, no, no, Marcos! Don't cry."

Maria leaned down to the little boy and kissed a Cheerio off his cheek. She removed his highchair tray and gently picked him up. She began singing a song in Spanish, ending with a splash of kisses on his face. Marcos laughed and grabbed his mother's hair, pulling with glee. Maria looked at her guests.

"He's not used to strangers."

"I don't blame him," Pamela said, putting her two decorated grocery bags on the small counter. "We have a turkey here too. Where would you like it?"

Pamela pointed at the box Doris was holding under one arm. Doris looked like an awkward mannequin for an old ladies' department store.

"The refrigerator would be very good," Maria said, reaching over to open it.

Doris set down the box of diapers, then looked inside the refrigerator. She saw a half-gallon of milk, four oranges, a bin with peppers and garlic, and some margarine. There was plenty of room for the fifteen pound turkey. Doris slid it onto the top shelf and closed the door.

"This is so good of you," Maria said. "My husband, Juan, just got a job at the gas station, so things will get better for us."

Pamela felt bad that Maria needed to explain anything to them. She didn't want Maria to feel embarrassed or guilty for taking their gifts.

"I do cleaning, you know," Maria said too abruptly.

The women didn't know.

"I clean the Catholic Church at night. It's a good job."

Maria gave Marcos another kiss. By that time, Gabby was hanging on her mother's leg, vying for attention. Maria reached down and wiped her daughter's nose with a tissue from her apron pocket.

Doris processed that new bit of information from Maria.

"Gabby, I think there is something in this bag you might like," Pamela said, reaching into the paper bag. She pulled out a puzzle with farm animals and handed it to Gabby, whose large eyes became larger.

"Let me help you get it opened," Pamela said, sitting down on the kitchen floor and tearing off the plastic.

Gabby helped herself to Pamela's lap. Pamela knew Hank and Chester were waiting for them, but she didn't care.

Doris watched as Pamela and Gabby went through each animal, its name, the sound it made, and what it ate on the farm. They took the pieces out of the puzzle base, and Gabby slowly figured out how to fit the pieces back in the correct spots. She giggled every time an animal slipped into place.

"There are some other things for you and Marcos and your mommy and daddy in the bags," Pamela said, giving the little girl a squeeze, "but we need to go now." Then, looking at Maria, she said, "We hope you and your family have a wonderful Thanksgiving."

"Can you come back?" Gabby asked, looking from Pamela to Doris and back to Pamela.

"I think you might see us before Christmas," Pamela said, and then, thinking to herself, *Even if Grace in Action doesn't give us this family to care for at Christmas, Hank and I will be back on our own.*

Hank, Chester, Doris, and Pamela pulled out of the driveway watching Maria, who was still holding Marcos, and Gabby wave goodbye from the porch.

Doris swallowed hard. Maria cleaned at the Catholic Church at night. She had two little ones and an empty refrigerator. Her husband worked at the gas station. And Maria was smiling.

Doris thought of her own life. She cleaned Loving the Lord Church. She didn't have to. She wanted to. She and Chester both had good retirement benefits. Their house was paid off. They even took a yearly vacation to Florida or the Upper Peninsula.

So how did the Gutierrez family land in Cherish? And how would they ever survive here?

On another Thanksgiving delivery route, Police Chief Charlotte Tuggle had an unwilling victim in the form of Martha Babcock sitting next to her in Fred's pickup truck. They were on their way to Willow Tree Apartments in the middle of Cherish.

Charlotte was peripherally watching Martha, who hadn't said a word since leaving church. Martha was picking at her fingernails and nervously tapping her right foot.

"Martha!" Charlotte barked.

Martha jumped and slammed her head on the roof of the truck.

"Good God, Chief. What in the world?" Martha rubbed her head. Her wispy, shoulder-length gray hair stuck out in all directions.

"You seem nervous. I just wanted to settle you down," Charlotte said, turning onto Wilkinson Street.

"You gave me a concussion," Martha squawked. "Why are you making me do this, anyway? I don't believe in handouts, and that's that."

"Yeah. I know. I've been trying to figure out why you have been coming to church the last few Sundays, listening to Pastor Maggie's sermons, and hearing her say from the pulpit that we have people in need in our town. Then you honk like a goose about 'no poor people in Cherish.' You know better." Charlotte sniffed.

"There may be poor people," Martha capitulated, "but by their own actions. You see those folks on TV and all over. People who just live off the government, unwilling to work. In a word, *lazy*. I work hard and live on a budget. Why don't they?"

"Martha, with all due respect, you're an idiot," Charlotte said as she pulled into the Willow Tree parking lot. "I don't know what you watch on TV, but quit it. I know you listen to the police dispatch all day long at work. You hear for yourself about homes in crisis, single parents getting evicted because they can't pay their rent, abused children. How can you pretend Cherish is immune to the harshness of life?"

Charlotte knew she was the police chief of a very fine town, but she also knew long shadows were cast by the brightest lights. Charlotte was regularly in the shadows of Cherish society, the darker places.

Martha didn't know quite what to say after the chief's tirade.

"I just think too many people avoid the work of living responsibly," she mumbled.

Charlotte picked up one of the grocery bags sitting between the two women and pointed to the other, giving Martha a nod.

"Grab that one, will you?"

The two women made their way into the apartment building and up to the third floor.

"Do you know who we're bringing this to?" Martha asked.

"I do," Charlotte clipped.

"Well, who is it?" Martha wanted some warning so she could adjust her face to smug.

Charlotte kept walking down the long hallway until she got to the very last door. She knocked. They could hear someone coming toward the door.

"Just a minute, I'm here. Hold on."

A chain lock slid back, and then a deadbolt. The door opened.

The women saw a shock of white hair, all standing straight on end.

"Well, hello, ladies! What a treat. Two beauties visiting me today. Well, well, well."

Winston Chatsworth smiled a toothy grin, then stepped back so the women could enter his small apartment.

Martha had to tell her face to close its mouth, which was hanging open in unbecoming disbelief.

Chester and Doris sat at their kitchen table, eating chicken sandwiches with bowls of butternut squash bisque from the soup committee. Their freezer was crammed with soup. They had completed three more Thanksgiving deliveries with Hank and Pamela before getting back to church and then, finally, home. They ate in silence.

Then Doris spoke. "I didn't expect to see what we saw today."

"I didn't either," Chester said, staring at his bisque.

"Cherish has always been a good place to live, full of good, hard-working people. No poverty." Doris sounded almost defiant.

"Well, yes, but don't you remember old Mrs. Becker? Pastor Maggie said at her funeral last year that every weekend she would make a complete home-cooked meal, pack it all up along with Jennifer and Beth, and drive it over to that young widow with all the kids by the train depot. She did that every week." Chester was lost in thought.

Doris wiped her mouth and nodded. "We all knew the widow who lived by the train depot. We all knew she had a litter of kids. Mrs. Becker did what was practical and helpful. I never would have thought to bring a meal, even though we always had plenty."

"The boy at the first house we went to today reminded me so much of Charlie." Chester pictured his grandson. "The boy's name is Bobby Chance. He has the same stooped shoulders and shaggy hair, just like Charlie. Kind of a shy kid." Chester couldn't finish his thought. It was too much to think of Charlie going without food, or Chester's own daughter having to care for her family because her husband was injured on the job. "They're normal folks. They have a nice house. It wasn't the husband's fault he got hurt. Now he can't work for months, at the very least."

"I've never seen Mexicans here before," Doris blurted out ignorantly, "but that baby was about the cutest thing I've ever set my eyes on.

And Pamela just sat down on the kitchen floor and did a puzzle with that little Gabby. And Maria cleans at the Catholic Church. She does the same thing I do, Chester, but her refrigerator was empty. And here I am walking around with thirty extra pounds around my rump because I have all the food I want, and more." She sighed.

Their meal continued in silence as each of them processed the happenings of the day. The faces of parents and children flashed through their minds in a never-ending reel.

Chester looked at his wife and saw a tear on her cheek.

Martha sat across the table from the chief. Charlotte had suggested they grab a bite to eat after they finished their deliveries. She knew it was important to give Martha a chance to "debrief" on the day and not let her go home alone to brood.

"Thanks for coming along with me today," Charlotte said, taking a bite of her double cheeseburger.

"I didn't think I had a choice, did I?" Martha sounded petulant, but it didn't keep her from diving into a pile of crispy onion rings.

"You didn't have a choice today, but I hope you will help next month for Christmas."

"Don't count on it," Martha said.

"What did you think about today?" Charlotte asked a little more quietly.

"I saw a lot of people getting free food. People who should be able to take care of themselves. I don't believe in it." Martha picked up another onion ring with a little less gusto.

"What about Winston?" Charlotte asked.

"Well, that was a surprise. He's a nice guy, but why can't he support himself? Doesn't he get Social Security, a pension?"

"I have no idea. I just know that Grace in Action deemed him worthy of receiving some good food for Thanksgiving," Charlotte replied.

Martha decided to switch tactics. "Another thing is that Ghana trip. How do people know their money is going to those kids? How do we even know if there's an orphanage?"

Charlotte put her burger down and looked at Martha in awe.

"Martha, what happened to make you so suspicious?"

Martha looked at her boss, angry tears smarting her eyes. Her voice became low, menacing. "They're leeches. They're takers. I work. I pay taxes. They steal." Martha got up from the table. "It's time for me to get home."

Charlotte also got up. "I'll take you back to church to get your car. It's cold."

The two women split the bill, at Martha's insistence, and walked out to the truck. Once back at church, Martha got out of the car.

"I'll see you at the station tomorrow," Charlotte said.

But the door had already shut.

Martha walked into her apartment and dropped her purse on the floor. She turned on a lamp and saw the bright eyes of her housemate, G. Gordon Liddy Kitty.

"Meow," G. Gordon said.

"Hello, G," Martha said, her face softening, "Sorry I'm home so late. It's been a ridiculous day, Gordon."

G. Gordon Liddy Kitty wasn't concerned about Martha's day whatsoever. It was past his dinner time.

"I bet you want your dinner, don't you, Liddy." Martha made her way to the kitchen and pulled out a can of cat tuna. G. Gordon Liddy Kitty hopped off the couch in a hurry and began writhing around Martha's ankles while sending up waves of purrs.

As the kitty eagerly ate his pungent meal, Martha knelt down to stroke his back.

"The chief dragged me out for the afternoon delivering meals to people who supposedly can't buy their own. It makes no sense, Gordon.

People who want to work and live decent certainly can do so. It's their choice, right, Liddy? I saw some lazy folks today."

G. Gordon Liddy Kitty had his small nose down in his food dish, eating with gusto, grateful someone opened a can of food for him every day.

"I don't think I'll be going back to that church anymore. I don't care what the chief says. A lot of naïve people in that church, G. But I'm no fool."

G. Gordon Liddy Kitty finished his dinner and sat back with a full tummy, fixing his green eyes on his mistress. He sensed tension, so he did the only logical thing. He washed his face, jumped on the couch, and curled up for a nap.

16

January 8, 2016
Bawjiase, Ghana

After breakfast, Lacey took a few minutes alone on her bunk bed. She pulled her diary from the bottom of her bag and slipped the pen from the leather holder on the side of the diary.

> *January 8, 2016*
> *Today we will go to United Hearts. I can't wait to see the children! I hope I'm doing something worthwhile around here. It seems like there really isn't quite as much to do as we all thought there would be. But I'll do whatever it takes to make my penance. Coming this far to work with the poor must count for something. The thing is, these kids seem to have what they need. They sing all the time. They're happy. I can't ever remember feeling that way as a kid. Or as an adult. I wonder, if my parents knew I was here, would they talk to me when I got back? What the hell do you have to do to find forgiveness?*

Lacey hid her diary back down in the bottom of her bag. Then she took her phone and slid it into her pocket. She wanted to get some more pictures today. She also took her smaller bag and slung it over her shoulder. She had a plan, and she couldn't wait to surprise the kids.

When she walked out of the bedroom, she heard some commotion. Everyone was laughing. Bryan was trying to brush a huge, gnarled matt out of Obolo's fur, and the dog writhed on the floor, desperately trying to get away from Bryan's brush.

Lacey saw Maggie and Dana standing on the porch, watching goats. Lacey stuck her head out of the doorway.

"Hey, PM, when you have a chance later, can we have a chat?"

"Sure, Lacey." Maggie squeezed Dana's arm and smiled. "We'll figure this out, Dana, I promise."

Maggie walked toward Lacey. "Is everything all right?" Maggie tried to banish the cranky mood that was beginning to settle in her soul. And on her face.

"Yeah, I think so. I just have a couple of churchy questions for you. You're practically Mrs. God, so I expect answers. Ha!" Lacey laughed.

"I'm not sure, but I think calling me Mrs. God could be blasphemous. You may be going straight to hell." Maggie laughed back, obviously joking.

But Lacey was caught completely off guard. She tried to control her face, but couldn't. It crumpled.

"Lacey, oh good grief. Lacey, what's the matter?" Maggie gently moved Lacey to the far end of the porch. "Lacey, I was just kidding. I didn't mean that at all. It was a stupid thing to say."

Lacey quickly reestablished her nonchalant face. "No. I mean, yes, I know, PM. Sorry about that. Maybe it's the malaria medicine. I'm sorry about that," she repeated.

"Don't be sorry, Lacey. If you still want to talk later, I'll try to keep my dumb jokes to myself. Maybe we could find some time before dinner, once we get back here from United Hearts." Maggie was almost pleading.

"That would be great. Let's plan on it," Lacey said.

She walked back toward Bryan, the rest of the group, and the hapless Obolo.

Maggie walked toward the bedroom and wondered what had bothered Lacey so much. Something in her bad joke had affected Lacey dramatically. Maggie guessed it was the word "hell." Not that the word itself scared Lacey, but perhaps it was more about the person in her past who told her she was going there.

She was almost to the bedroom when she heard someone in the bathroom.

Someone was vomiting. Violently.

Maggie cringed. She was glad the others were in the big room, laughing over Obolo's antics. She stepped into the bedroom and waited to see who came out of the bathroom.

"Hey!"

Maggie jumped. She turned around and happily saw Jack's arms coming toward her. "Mmmm." She nuzzled her nose into his chest.

"How are you doing?" Jack asked. "Things don't seem quite right this morning."

"I know. I feel the frustration of our group. But I can't do anything about it. Bryan seems different here than when he was in Cherish. I don't know what's going on. What do you think about the week so far?" Maggie asked.

"I agree it hasn't been exactly what we all expected. But then, maybe our expectations were unrealistic. I know Dana's frustrated not being able to care for animals. Charlene, Ellen, and I had all hoped to do some work at the clinic. And Bill thought he'd be building a school. I do think something needs to change to keep up morale. The people going to United Hearts seem to be satisfied," Jack said.

Just then there was another retching sound from the bathroom. Jack dropped his embrace and turned to look.

"Shhh," Maggie whispered. "I don't know who it is. I was waiting."

Both Jack and Maggie heard a bucket of water being poured down the toilet. The lock slid open, and the door swung open. Sylvia walked out. She turned into the bedroom and stopped short when she saw Jack and Maggie staring at her.

"Oh, hi," Sylvia said. She looked pale.

"Sylvia, we didn't mean to startle you," Maggie said as she walked closer. "Are you all right? It sounds like you aren't feeling well."

Sylvia's face flushed red over the paleness. "I'm embarrassed. I'm having a bit of trouble with the food. I'm not really keeping much down. I've been lucky to have use of the bathroom, if that's what you can call it, when the rest of you are together in the other room. But this morning, it was particularly rough."

"Do you have any other symptoms?" Jack asked, reaching for Sylvia's wrist to check her pulse. "A fever? Chills? Headaches?"

"No. I don't think so. Well, last night I felt a little chilly, but I had kicked off my sheet. And I don't know how I would tell a fever from the heat on the farm all day." She gave a wan smile. "I'm just exhausted. Every day. Working at the farm is taking a toll. This is different kind of work than I do in Cherish, but it's only for another week. You can do anything for a week, right?"

Sylvia waited for Jack to let go of her wrist. Once he did, she went to her bunk bed, grabbed her sunscreen, and began to apply it to her arms and face.

Jack and Maggie looked at each other.

"Sylvia, do you think it might be a good idea to stay back today and get a little rest?" Jack asked. "Maybe a long nap will help you. I'm worried about you going to work in the sun with no food on board, and you're probably dehydrated."

"I can't stay back today," Sylvia said. "Bill and Dana are coming to the farm today. I want to show them what Nana and I have been doing. Plus, I miss my husband." She looked at the ground, then squeezed some more sunscreen into her hand. Finally, she just sat down on her bed. "Maybe I'll hang back tomorrow," she said, looking at Jack and Maggie hopefully.

Maggie sat down next to Sylvia on the bed.

"Sylvia, are you pregnant?" Maggie asked.

Addie skipped into the room, then stopped in her tracks.

"Well, what are you three doing?" she asked with her infectious smile. Addie seemed to be the only person completely happy on the trip.

"Just chatting," Maggie said.

Sylvia laughed. She looked at Maggie and Jack and said, "The answer to your question is 'no.'"

"This is going to be such a fun day!" Addie said as she pawed through her suitcase, searching for something apparently of great importance.

Maggie and Jack looked at Sylvia, who winked back at them.

"I've got to get to the farm." Sylvia walked out of the room.

"Yes, Addie," Maggie said. "Today is going to be a fun day. I'm glad you're here!"

Maggie impulsively gave Addie a hug. Then Maggie followed Jack out of the bedroom and went back to the porch, where Dana still stood like a statue. The two women stood, side by side, each one sifting through her own thoughts.

17

After delivering Thanksgiving baskets, the days that followed sped along until it was the Wednesday morning before Thanksgiving. Maggie had already had two blissful days with Bryan, ensconced in the parsonage. She and Jack had picked him up Monday evening from Detroit. Maggie's joy was complete. She was with her husband and her brother. Cate Carlson got home from the U on Tuesday night for Thanksgiving break, and the foursome had enjoyed a delicious and lively dinner at the Cherish Café. Bryan and Cate went off on their own after that, to do some much needed catching up.

Now it was Wednesday morning, and Maggie and Irena were going at it hammer and tongs over the *Manger Baby* concert. Irena had written six more pieces to add to her "masterpiece," which was going to extend the three-hour musical an extra hour.

"Four hours is too long, Irena. No one can sit here that long, no matter how amazing your concert is. Think about it." Maggie was exasperated.

"Dis ees vy ve hev de interrmission. You get de cookies and de punch. Ve hev a snick, den morre museek." Irena glared.

"Irena, listen to reason. People don't have time for this the month before Christmas. You've got to shorten it to two hours. Tops!"

Maggie was ready to wring Irena's skinny neck, and it didn't help that Irena had just used her kitchen sink to dye her hair a purplish gray. She was somewhat difficult to look at. When Maggie asked her about the new hair color, Irena said, "Dunt you look at de magazines? All de young ladies hev gray hairr now."

Maggie had seen it and thought it was revolting. Irena helped solidify her feelings on the matter.

"The museek cannot be cut!" Irena shouted.

Blessedly, Maggie's door opened. Irena was just about ready to continue her tirade when she saw Hank's face. Maggie saw his face as well.

"What is it, Hank?" Maggie asked, no anger in her voice, just fear.

"I think you should get over to The Grange, Pastor Maggie. Judy from hospice just called. Something is changing." Hank looked stricken.

Even Irena, who mainly lived in "Irenaland," knew what that meant. She knew what it was to lose a mother too soon.

"Pastor Maggie, you need to go," Hank said firmly.

Irena nodded her purple-gray head solemnly.

Maggie grabbed her jacket, walked out of the church to the parsonage driveway, got into her car, and drove towards Dancer Road and The Grange.

The fastest way was through the cemetery.

As Maggie drove down Dancer Road, she saw Jack's Jeep in The Grange's circular driveway. She parked behind him and quickly made her way to the front door. Pamela opened the door before Maggie could knock, wiping away tears with a tissue as she stepped back to let her through.

Two evenings before, on Monday, Pamela had helped Cassandra get ready for bed. At least she tried to help. Cassandra was agitated, confused, and frustrated.

"I have to go now. I have to get there. Carl . . . sick," Cassandra was mumbling over and over again, shaking her head, and trying to stand up.

Pamela sat on the edge of the bed.

"Cassandra, may I help you with your dress?"

"Got to get there. Carl has the flu. He's sick." Cassandra kept buttoning and unbuttoning as she mumbled.

"Cassandra, Carl is in bed. So is Carrie. It's nighttime. Carl is fine. It's time to sleep now. You'll see Carl and Carrie in the morning. Then, later this week, is Thanksgiving. You will be with the children all day long."

Pamela tried to sound normal as she searched for Cassandra's morphine. She found it in the top bathroom cupboard where Judy, the hospice worker, had put it, broke one of the tablets in half, and brought it with some water back to Cassandra.

"Cassandra, take this pill and a drink of water. You will feel better," Pamela said softly as she slowly put the half tablet in Cassandra's mouth and lifted the glass of water. Cassandra swallowed. Pamela realized she had been holding her breath and exhaled.

"Let's get you into your nightgown," Pamela continued in her forced light tone as she helped Cassandra to the bathroom, then into her nightgown, and finally into bed.

Once she could see Cassandra's even breathing, Pamela called Judy and asked her to come over. She also called Hank to say she would be home a little later than planned after she updated Judy on the change in Cassandra's behavior.

Hank hung up the phone, remembering again why he loved his wife so much.

Judy arrived with her medical bag after another somewhat frantic phone call from Pamela on Wednesday morning and went immediately to Cassandra. Pamela stayed in the spacious Grange kitchen and rewashed the breakfast dishes. She had nothing to do but wait. When Judy came to the kitchen, Pamela was filling the sink with soapy water for the third time.

Judy said, "I need to call Dr. Elliot. Cassandra's vital signs are falling too quickly." The nurse was already pulling up contact information on her cell phone.

"How about Pastor Maggie?" Pamela asked, swallowing the lump in her throat.

"Yes, I'll call the church next." The nurse had worked with Pastor Maggie before at the Friendly Elder Care Center.

When Maggie entered the small room at The Grange a short while after Judy's call, the blinds had been closed. The room was quiet, dark, and warm. Maggie could smell Cassandra's perfume as she passed by the closet and a very faint whiff of urine in the room. The woman was lying against several pillows, eyes closed, covered in a brightly colored quilt. When Maggie got closer, she saw the quilt was made with pieces of baby clothes. They must have been Carrie and Carl's. The clothes that once covered their tiny bodies now covered their mother. Jack was sitting on the side of the bed, stethoscope in his ears, listening to Cassandra's heart. Judy was standing on the other side of the bed, watching Jack. Pamela was standing in the doorway behind Maggie, sniffing quietly.

Cassandra's breathing was irregular. A few shallow breaths, then nothing. Then a deep breath from out of nowhere. Maggie heard the slight rattle from Cassandra's lungs. *The death rattle.* Jack turned around after listening to Cassandra's heart.

"Hi, Maggie," he said quietly. "I don't think it will be long now."

Maggie nodded and moved toward the bed. Jack moved aside so Maggie could sit next to Cassandra and hold her hand.

"Hi, Cassandra," Maggie said in her normal voice, "this is Pastor Maggie, and I'm right here next to you." She gave Cassandra's hand a gentle squeeze. "Pamela is here, as well as Judy and Dr. Jack." Maggie brushed her hand across Cassandra's cheek. "We are here with you and we love you."

Maggie turned to Pamela and mouthed, "Where are Carrie and Carl?"

Pamela mouthed back, "At school."

Maggie nodded. That was good.

Carrie and Carl each held one of Mary Ellington's hands. Carrie skipped down the hallway of the elementary school, singing a song about sunshine and rain clouds and snowflakes. She was pulling Mary and Carl along with her. Carrie enjoyed being in first grade. Carl did not enjoy being in pre-kindergarten. Both children were in school all day, which was a change from the carefree life they had lived before moving to The Grange. As a young mother, Cassandra felt she could teach her children everything they needed to know at home. Then Mary stepped in and registered the children for school, with Cassandra's agreement. She brought them to visit for a short time each day until they began full-time.

"Carl, what did you think of your class today?" Mary asked, looking down at the little blond head.

Carl looked up with his solemn blue eyes. "Miss Marwy, I think I would like to just play at youw house."

"What did your teacher do with your class today? Did she read a story?" Mary persisted.

"She said I had to sit in my chaiw," Carl said unhappily.

"Did you have fun with your new friends?" Mary asked carefully.

"Well, it was Wyleigh's birthday today. She gave us cupcakes from Mrs. Popkin," Carl said reluctantly. "I guess I like Wyleigh okay."

Mary realized that "Wyleigh" was really Ryleigh.

"But why isn't Cawie in my class?" he asked.

"Because I am older," Carrie said patiently. "I have to be in first grade. You are in the before kindergarten class. But school is fun, Carl. Did you play at recess?"

"I stayed by the mommy," Carl said, looking miserable.

"You mean the teacher," Carrie said and then burst into her sunshine song again.

Mary's heart cracked just a little watching Carl's face. There would be so many sudden changes in his young life. They stopped by the kindergarten classroom and picked up Hannah.

Hannah had been in school full-time a little longer than Carrie and Carl. She had tried to alleviate their fears and talked about her new friends. Hannah enjoyed the socialization of school after having been isolated with her mother for so long. She was thriving now, and Julia was thankful for the work Mary had done to get Hannah enrolled.

When Mary had prepared the children for school earlier that morning, Judy had been there examining Cassandra, who was unresponsive. Carrie and Carl had bounded in and jumped on their mother's bed to begin their morning hugs and kisses. Cassandra remained very still, eyes closed.

Judy smiled at the children as they called to their mother and shook her shoulders.

"Mama! We're going to go to school again today," Carrie reported. "Miss Mary is bringing us. I am wearing my new school clothes. Do I look pretty?" Carrie stood on the bed and twirled.

"Mama," Carl said, "I think I would like to not go to school today. I want to stay here at Miss Marwy's and see the cows." Carl waited for a response.

"Carrie, Carl," Judy said, helping them off the bed, "your mama is too tired and sick to visit right now. Do you understand?" She smiled gently at them, even as she saw their smiles disappear and glimmers of fear dot their eyes. Cassandra had been unresponsive for two days now. The morphine kept her asleep, and kept the horrific pain away.

"Is she going to heaven today?" Carrie asked directly.

Carrie knew her mama was heading for that elusive place called heaven, but no one could tell her exactly when that day was. It caused a great deal of discomfort and consternation in Carrie's small soul.

"I don't know, Carrie. She is very sick."

Judy was used to talking to all ages of people about death and the pain of losing a loved one. Not surprisingly, children asked the most direct and startling questions, and they deserved the most direct and unstartling answers she could possibly give them.

"Tell her what you especially want her to know today," Judy encouraged.

Carrie got on the bed a little more carefully. "Mama, I especially want you to know that I will be a very good girl at school today. I promise. I will do what the teacher says, and I will tell you about it later. Please don't go to heaven today, but if you do, please tell Jesus hello and that I am being a good girl."

Judy caught her breath. Then she looked resolutely at Carl.

"And you, darling Carl, what would you especially like to tell your mama today?"

Carl crawled on the bed and right onto his mother's shoulder. He tucked his head under her chin and wriggled into the crook of her arm.

"Mama," he whispered, "I especially want you to know that, if you don't like heaven, you can always come back herwe. I'll wait fo you."

Carl was sure he felt a squeeze around his back. He closed his eyes and wrapped his arms around his mother's neck.

Now, as they skipped and walked down the hallway of the school, Mary wondered to herself what kind of hell would be unleashed on these little ones and what she could possibly do to help. Taking them to the Treehouse for some playtime instead of going to The Grange was the first step. They would stay there until it was over. Dr. Jack had said it wouldn't be long now.

Maggie, Jack, Judy, and Pamela sat around Cassandra in the dim bedroom. They had been there together for the past five hours.

As the morphine began to wear off, Cassandra once again became agitated, her face showed pain as her eyebrows pulled together and her mouth opened in silent agony. More morphine was administered by Judy, and Cassandra lapsed back into unsteady breathing, with the death rattle sounding more and more often.

A little before four o'clock p.m., Cassandra's breathing slowed severely. As the time lengthened between each breath, Maggie took Cassandra's hand and nodded to the others. They all touched Cassandra as Maggie began to pray.

She began by saying, "Cassandra, you may go now. You have fought hard, but you don't have to fight anymore. We love you, and we love Carrie and Carl. We will guard them, love them, and protect them in every way. They will hear stories about you as they grow, and they will know how much you love them."

Maggie continued with a petition to God for Cassandra's peace, wholeness, and the joy of heaven.

Suddenly, Cassandra sat straight up, opened her eyes, and gasped.

"Oh, hello! I've missed you so!"

Maggie stifled a small scream. Pamela did not stifle hers. Judy quickly put her arm around Cassandra's back in anticipation, and Jack grabbed his stethoscope.

Cassandra's eyes closed, and Judy helped her limp body back onto the pillows.

Jack listened to Cassandra's heart, then he looked up at the women and removed the stethoscope from his ears.

Cassandra had stepped across the threshold of death into eternal healing and joy.

18

November 25 & 26, 2015
Cherish, Michigan

Jack and Maggie prepared to leave The Grange after Cole Porter had taken Cassandra's body to the funeral home. Judy cleaned up the room as she waited for hospice to come and take the larger supplies away.

Pamela had left once Cole was gone. The first stunning slap of grief struck Pamela as she rode her bicycle home to Hank. Her heart felt like it was hemorrhaging, and Hank would let her hemorrhage every emotion of that sad day until her tears were exhausted. But it would only be the first wave of grief on this journey of loss.

Jack, Maggie, and Judy heard the small voices of Carrie and Carl coming up the stairs toward their mother's empty room. The three adults were quietly waiting when William and Mary brought in the children. Judy had taken the sheets off the hospital bed in preparation for hospice to pick up and take the bed to a new patient. She had also opened the shades on the windows, which brightened the room, but showed the starkness of the empty bed.

When they had returned to The Grange, Mary told Carrie and Carl that mommy had died that day. She didn't elaborate. She gave them time to assimilate the most difficult words they had heard in their little lives.

"So, she's not in her room now?" Carrie asked, her blue eyes wide with earnestness and fear.

"No, Carrie, she is not in her room."

Mary put her arms around both children.

"Can we see?" Carl asked, needing more proof than words.

"Of course."

Mary had no idea if that was a good idea or not, but she believed it would be worse not to let the children see for themselves. William and Mary, each taking the hands of Carrie and Carl, walked upstairs to the bedroom.

The adults watched as the children entered the room, not knowing what to expect. Carrie and Carl hesitated in the doorway, then stepped through. They stared at the empty bed.

"Hello, Carrie and Carl," Maggie said softly.

She walked toward them and got down on her knees. They walked into her open arms, and she squeezed them tightly. She had no idea what to say next, so she said nothing.

Carrie and Carl looked around the room some more. They saw Dr. Jack, Nurse Judy, and William and Mary. But no mommy. So they decided it must be true.

Their mommy went to heaven today.

Carl yelped and abruptly pulled away from Maggie's embrace, then darted across the room. He ran into the closet and threw his small arms around a hard-sided green suitcase just inside the closet door.

"Mommy fogot her clothes. She didn't take her suitcase to heaven!"

Carl clung to the suitcase, and tears and jagged little sobs began to fill the room. Carrie instinctively moved toward him but looked up at Maggie.

"Why didn't mommy take her suitcase, Pastor Maggie?" Carrie whispered.

She stared expectantly at Maggie.

Maggie didn't know what to say. Once again. She wished her mother was in the room. She walked Carrie over to the sobbing Carl. Then she pulled both children close, somewhat prying Carl from the green suitcase.

"I don't know for sure, but I think everything is brand-new in heaven," she said slowly, then inhaled deeply, "and your mommy didn't need to bring any old things, or even a suitcase. She'll have all new things and everything she needs." Maggie stumbled on her words.

"But won't she miss her nighty and slippers?" Carrie said, seeing the items on top of the dresser where they had sat for days.

"What kind of nighty and slippers do you think she would like to wear in heaven?" Maggie asked, hoping it was the right direction to go.

"Well, I think pink. Maybe with feathers," Carrie said thoughtfully.

"I wonder if you might like to keep her nighty and slippers for when you are a little bigger. Then you could wear them, just like she did . . you know . . . since she has all new things now." Maggie felt like she was drowning.

Silence.

"I would like that." Carrie finally decided, reached up on her tiptoes, and pulled the nighty and slippers onto the floor. It seemed too much for her to pick them up.

"What about me?" Carl said with a small sob.

"What would you like to have?" Maggie asked.

"Did she leave her Mickey Mouse shirt?" Carrie butted in. "Remember, Carl? You like Mickey Mouse."

Carl nodded then buried his head under Maggie's arm.

Mary came closer now.

"I know she left her Mickey Mouse shirt, Carl, because I just put some of her clothes in the drawers. It's right here." Mary opened a drawer of the dresser and pulled out the T-shirt. "I wonder, would you like to sleep with Mickey Mouse tonight?" she asked as she gently picked him up and hugged him.

Maggie realized how important it was for Mary and William to be in charge now. She picked up the nighty and slippers from the floor and handed them to William.

Maggie, Jack, and Judy watched, quiet once again, as William and Mary took their children from the room and led them down to the kitchen.

The morning of Thanksgiving came early for Maggie. She, Jack, and Bryan had been up until midnight the night before, preparing for the dinner. And now Thanksgiving was here.

When Maggie and Jack had finally left The Grange the night before, the rolling grief that had propelled them through the long day at Cassandra's bedside retreated briefly. They returned to the parsonage and found Bryan and Cate waiting for them.

"Cassandra is gone. I'm sure you have already heard," Maggie said, her emotions depleted. "I just need to send a quick email to Hank."

Bryan stood in her way and wrapped his arms around her. Maggie could see Cate standing behind him with tears in her eyes.

"I'm sorry, Maggie," Bryan said quietly.

"We've made some supper, if you're feeling hungry at all," Cate said with a little sniff.

"Thank you," Maggie said, returning Bryan's hug. "That was thoughtful of you two."

Jack petted Cheerio, who had made her presence known on the kitchen table, then he absentmindedly picked her up and held her in the crook of his arm. She began to purr. Something about the tiny rumble caused Jack to take a deep breath. As a pragmatic man, and a skilled physician, Jack knew the many pieces that made up the puzzles of life and death. That day, something different had happened.

Maggie looked at her husband cuddling the cat. "Are you okay, Jack?"

He smiled at Maggie, then looked at Bryan.

"When Redford was arrested in the church basement for doing all the damage to the church a few weeks ago, I found your sister's shoes lying near the sanctuary door. After everything died down, I asked her why her shoes were there and not on her feet. She said it was because she had been on holy ground in the sanctuary that night. It was the same night she had been part of telling Carrie and Carl their mother was dying." Jack gave Cheerio another pet. "I didn't know what she really meant by that at the time, but that's how I felt today. We were on holy ground."

Jack put his nose on the top of Cheerio's head, mainly to lower his eyes. The emotional eruption was unnerving him.

"I've never held the hand of someone who stepped from life to death to new life before," Maggie blurted out. "She left us and met God while I was holding her hand."

Cate was openly crying now. Bryan watched his sister intently. It seemed no one knew what to do next. Maggie finally turned toward her study, walked in, and touched the "on" button of her computer. Within fifteen minutes, she had sent off an email to Hank, asking him to send it to all members of the church.

Dear Church Family,

As many of you know, Cassandra Moffet died today at The Grange. She died peacefully. Carrie and Carl are doing as well as can be expected. William and Mary are loving them and caring for them beautifully. We ask that you do not call The Grange or stop by with food or for a visit at this time.

Cassandra's funeral will be on Monday, November 30, at 11:00 a.m. in the sanctuary. This service to celebrate Cassandra's life is meant for all of us who loved her and love her children. Per her request, please wear brightly colored clothing. Please be prepared for a service of joy. I ask, if at all possible, we reserve our tears for another time and focus on Carrie and Carl during the service. There will not be a luncheon, but we will set up the Sunday coffee tables with treats the children love from The Sugarplum Bakery. But everyone is welcome to bring cookies for the children and everyone to enjoy.

Our work now is to support William and Mary as their family has shifted. Our love for Carrie and Carl is uppermost.

Thank you for truly being a church FAMILY.

God bless you,

Pastor Maggie

Maggie sent her announcement to Hank, knowing he would use his church database and have it out to the membership before anyone could say "Yessireebob." She slowly walked back to the kitchen.

Cate had taken a bubbling casserole of chicken and dumplings out of the oven. Bryan poured steaming green beans into a bowl and sliced a fresh loaf of Mrs. Popkin's peasant bread. Jack, along with Cheerio, set the table. They all sat down to the warm comfort food.

And they were comforted.

Following dinner, they shifted their psyches to the task immediately at hand: Thanksgiving Dinner. With twenty-two people expected around the large oak table in the parsonage dining room, along with the kitchen table to give everyone a little more space, there was some work to be done. Thankfully, most of the guests were contributing to the feast. Maggie had the job of cooking two turkeys, pies, and blueberry buckle. She was also going to make whipped butternut squash soufflé, due to the box of squash left at the back door of the parsonage with a kind note from Sylvia.

Cate began making pie crust, wanting to help and also excited to be one of the people sitting around the table tomorrow. Her mother had relented, knowing Bryan was in town, but Cate had promised to bring Bryan over in the evening so the Carlson family could enjoy him as well.

Maggie made the fillings for cherry rhubarb (having brilliantly frozen several bags of Sylvia's rhubarb in the summertime), pumpkin cream cheese, chocolate toffee crunch, and two large pans of blueberry buckle in honor of Detective Keith Crunch. Jack and Bryan peeled squash.

Maggie put Christmas carols on the iHome to lighten up the mood. The kitchen was pleasant, but not full of the conversation and teasing it might have been.

Bryan walked Cate home at ten o'clock, but he returned shortly.

"What can I do now?" Bryan asked Maggie, who had her hand up a turkey's bottom, a bowl of cranberry-herb dressing next to her.

"Well, once this turkey is stuffed, will you bring it over to the church kitchen and put it in the fridge?" She used the back of her wrist to wipe a stray hair from her forehead. "The second turkey can stay here."

"Sounds like a plan," Bryan said with a yawn.

Jack set the table in the dining room, sans Cheerio. He had already set the kitchen table.

"I didn't realize how many people twenty-two were until I set these plates out," he said from the next room. We're going to have quite a crowd. I'm glad we can spread them out in two rooms. Everyone will have enough space."

"I made a promise to myself last year that I would have Irena and Mrs. Abernathy over for Thanksgiving this year. They were each alone last year. But now Verna's married, and Irena has her Captain Crunch, and the rest of the guest list just grew somehow," Maggie said, stuffing one more handful of dressing into the turkey.

"Somehow." Jack laughed.

His family was gathering in Blissfield tomorrow, but he didn't think he'd miss it much. He was thankful to wake up with his wife and help host the crazy crowd of people.

Maggie, Jack, and Bryan finished their preparations and wearily crawled into bed as the clock struck midnight.

Howling meows from Marmalade began promptly at six a.m.

Maggie groaned. She pushed the orange face away from her ear, then was struck by the memories of the day before. She put her head under her pillow.

How will Carrie and Carl wake up this morning? How will reality hit them?

Then she remembered. It was Thanksgiving. She was hosting a dinner for twenty-two people that very afternoon.

I can't do it. I'm not leaving this bed. Until Christmas.

She felt a strong arm around her waist, pulling her close.

"Scram, Marmalade," Jack said, putting the cat on the floor. "Happy Thanksgiving, wife." He kissed her.

"Happy Thanksgiving, husband. I've just decided to stay right here until Christmas. Care to join me?" She snuzzled her nose into his chest.

"Well. Okay. But we do have some company coming today."

"Bryan will have to take care of it. We're unavailable." She smiled. It felt good to smile.

"This will be a very different Thanksgiving for all of us. But it's our first, so let's pretend we know what we're doing."

"I, my good sir, don't have to pretend. I am brilliant at Thanksgiving. My mother taught me how to stuff and cook a turkey when I was ten years old. I also know how to make everything to go with the said stuffed turkey." She kissed him. This self-pep talk got her moving. There was much to be done, and the day was passing her by.

"What time will your parents be here?" Jack asked, trying to keep her from moving by locking his legs over hers.

"Around eleven this morning. I am glad other people are bringing food for the feast, and we really got so much done last night with Bryan and Cate."

She tried to wriggle away but couldn't move. *Drat!* She was too small.

Cheerio jumped on the bed, and Maggie noticed her paw was bleeding.

"Oh dear! What did you do, Cheerio?" she said in her singsong voice. "Did Fruit Loop bite you?"

The blood was sticky and very, very red. Maggie noticed bloody paw prints on the bedspread. In one quick move, Maggie pushed Jack off, flew out of bed, out the bedroom door, and down the stairs.

Jack heard a scream from the kitchen and quickly went downstairs. He understood why his wife had screamed once he saw the kitchen floor. He could hardly believe his eyes.

∞

Priscilla Sloane was startled awake the night before Thanksgiving when her phone rang just after midnight.

"Hello?" she said groggily into the receiver.

"Pris, did I wake you?" the man asked.

"Who is this?" Priscilla tried to shake her brain awake.

"Mmm . . . has it been so long? You don't recognize—"

"Darcy!" Priscilla exclaimed. She sat straight up in bed and switched on the lamp. "Darcy? It's you, right? Where are you? Are you in New York? Wait! Are you okay?"

Darcy laughed. "Yes. It is I, your brother. I am not in New York. I just landed in Detroit. I am fine. I'm sorry to call so late, but I was wondering if you would join me for Thanksgiving dinner at my home tomorrow. Can you cancel your plans? Because I'm sure you have some." Darcy waited for a response.

Priscilla was fully awake. "Yes, of course. You're in Detroit. Do you need anything, like a ride?"

Priscilla knew he didn't. He would have arranged for a driver to be waiting.

"No. It's all arranged. I'll be in Cherish in about forty-five minutes. I called ahead to have the house ready and food prepared for tomorrow. I promise you a delicious Thanksgiving repast," Darcy said lightly.

"I can't wait! Something's happened since the last time we spoke. I can hear a change in your voice. I'll come over in the morning. You better not be asleep," Priscilla said with mock seriousness.

"Even if I am, I'll welcome you in my pajamas. I'll see you in the morning. Go back to sleep."

Darcy clicked off the phone.

19

Jack couldn't believe his eyes.

Dripping down from the kitchen counter, smeared and splattered everywhere, was cherry-rhubarb pie and blueberry buckle. The pans had been tipped over and then must have slowly slid to the floor. The mess was spectacular.

"Oh no!" Maggie's hands held her head as she took in the enormity of the fruity chaos.

Jack looked around the room and saw blue and red paw prints going in all directions. He walked into the living room to see blotches of cherry and blueberry splattered on the once-white-now-gray couch. The prints on the carpet led him into the family room. There must have been a game of kitty tag due to the amount of red and blue prints. Table cloths on both tables, along with plates, linen napkins, and even some coffee cups were decorated in the patriotic colors. The little paws went up and down the stairs, something both Jack and Maggie had missed on their separate but hurried journeys to the kitchen. Jack walked back into the kitchen.

There were more feet coming down the stairs. Bryan entered the kitchen, hair askew, his face showing a map where it had been smashed against his pillow.

"What's going on? Do you know what time it is?" Bryan sounded grumpy. Then he actually opened his eyes. "What? What is this?" Bryan was awake now.

"The cats," Maggie whispered. "The cats knocked over the pie and both pans of blueberry buckle. I left the desserts on the counter to cool."

"Where are the other pies?" Bryan asked.

"In the refrigerator. They had to be kept cold. Thank goodness." Maggie shook her head in dismay.

"Well," Jack knew Maggie needed a plan and a push. "Bryan and I will start cleaning up the messes."

"Messes?" Maggie asked, then looked around and saw the telltale paw prints. "Oh! Good grief!"

"Do you have enough ingredients to make more pie and buckle?" Jack kept going.

"Yes. Yes, I can remake the desserts," Maggie admitted, deflated.

"Fortunately, we're ahead of ourselves," Jack said with false optimism. "We got so much done last night, and Marmalade decided we should know about this mess sooner rather than later. He woke us up. We can get this done."

Jack got cleansers out from under the sink.

"Yeah, we can do this, Megs," Bryan said, following Jack's lead. He began to stack the dishes from the kitchen table and load the dishwasher. He looked at his sister. "Start baking."

The clean-up was not quite as easy as the valiant Jack had believed. Cherries and blueberries stubbornly resisted coming out of carpeting and furniture, along with Jack and Maggie's bedspread. Bryan's sheets also were covered in the colorful splotches. The two tablecloths were ruined.

Maggie began by cleaning actual kitty paws before any more prints could be sprinkled around the parsonage. The cats were utterly and completely offended. They took turns letting out howls of protest, then ran to hide after their grand humiliation.

The kitchen counter and floor were cleaned of globs of fruit and crust and buckle. But pale pink and blue stains remained. Maggie mopped the floor for the second time, using straight bleach. The floor looked a little better. Then she then pulled cherries, blueberries, and rhubarb out of the freezer. This baking felt like a chore. Her emotional hangover from the day before at Cassandra's bedside weighed her down. *Our help is in the name of the Lord, who made heaven and earth.* These words began every worship service and every funeral. Maggie tried to believe them. She mixed ingredients mechanically and was relieved to finally shut the oven door on her labors. An hour later, the kitchen smelled wonderful as the fresh desserts baked.

"I'm going to turn the ovens on at church," Maggie called as smells of bleach, carpet cleaner, and Pine-Sol mingled with bubbling fruit in her nostrils.

"Okay. Cate's on her way over," Bryan yelled from upstairs. "I called her and told her about the dessert disaster."

Maggie opened the back door to Cate's fresh and cheerful face.

"Hi! Happy Thanksgiving! I brought vinegar!" Cate exclaimed, holding up a large bottle. "I'm ready to clean up after those naughty, naughty kittens." Cate giggled.

Maggie smiled. "Cate, you are good for my disgruntled and unthankful soul. Happy Thanksgiving." She gave Cate a kiss on the cheek. "I'm popping over to church. Your boyfriend is upstairs cleaning with my husband."

"Righty O! I'm on my way."

The morning flew by. Tables were reset with borrowed church tablecloths, turkeys were put into ovens, many of the stains were removed from floors and furniture, and when the Westminster chimes rang, the four young people were as ready and relaxed as possible. Which wasn't much.

Dirk and Mimi Elzinga stood on the parsonage porch. Mimi, immaculately dressed, was holding a tidy basket with carefully placed ingredients for green bean casserole. Dirk grinned, seeing his daughter and son standing together. He was carrying a large Thanksgiving floral centerpiece.

"Happy Thanksgiving," Mimi and Dirk said in unison.

Their voices were cheerful, although their eyes belied them. They had been deeply saddened to hear of Cassandra's death the previous day. Maggie had called from the front yard of The Grange to give them the news.

"Happy Thanksgiving, Mom, Dad," Bryan said as he hugged his mother and messed up her perfect hair. She didn't care.

Maggie followed suit, feeling safe and that all things would be well once enveloped in her father's arms.

"I'm so glad you're here," she whispered.

Dirk and Mimi were ushered into the parsonage, surrounded by four people talking all at once. It was like being in a bird sanctuary.

"So we finished everything last night . . ."

"After Cassandra died . . ."

"Cherry-rhubarb pie and blueberry buckle . . ."

"Set both tables with extra chairs from church . . ."

"Stuffed turkeys . . . peeled squash . . ."

"So exhausted!"

"Cheerio . . . I thought it was blood . . ."

"Pie and blueberry buckle everywhere!!"

"Carpet . . . stains won't come out . . ."

"Tablecloths and dishes . . ."

"Bleach . . ."

"Vinegar is best . . ."

"Bedspread and sheets . . ."

"Naughty kittens!"

Maggie brewed Keurig cups for everyone as the chorus continued.

Mimi took her coat and Dirk's and hung them in the front hall closet, since it appeared no one else would do so. She ran her slim fingers through her hair to put it back in place, then reentered the kitchen, attempting to ignore the aromas of bleach and vinegar that competed with the cooking desserts.

"No use crying over pie and buckle," Mimi said over the din.

Everyone quieted down.

"It sounds like the devil has been working overtime to dishearten and deflate you," she continued, "but you have overcome. Well done.

Now, what needs to be done to be ready when the rest of the guests arrive?" She began unpacking her green bean casserole ingredients.

Maggie laughed. She felt like she could breathe again. Mimi would quietly put all things to rights. It was Thanksgiving, after all. It was time to act like it.

Dirk placed the centerpiece in the middle of the kitchen table.

"Where are the makers of the mischief?" He looked around for the cats.

"Hopefully, under a bed somewhere. Where they will stay for the next ten hours. I had to wash all their filthy, sticky paws, then they went running. Good riddance," Maggie said.

They all took a few minutes to sit with their coffee in the living room. Red and blue stains were faintly apparent on the once-white-now-gray couch. Even Cate's vinegar couldn't get the furniture clean.

Drat! I'll have to think about this later, Maggie thought to herself. The fact that everything in the parsonage belonged to the church, and not to her, was weighing heavily. Even the dishes on the two beautifully set tables were not her own. Marmalade had smashed several of the church's dishes the second month Maggie had been in Cherish. He'd saved Cheerio from the council members, who were meeting in the parsonage to do business. It was a disaster.

Maggie sipped her coffee and listened to the others recount every harrowing detail of the morning for her parents. She swallowed another gulp of coffee when the parsonage phone rang. She looked at Jack, then got up to answer.

"Pastor Maggie? This is Priscilla Sloane. I am showing terrible manners by calling this late, and I'm sorry. I won't be able to come for Thanksgiving dinner today. My brother just flew into town last night. Without notice." Priscilla said all this factually, without emotion.

"We'll miss you, Priscilla, but how nice for you to see your brother. When was the last time you were together?" Maggie asked, already moving to the dining room table to remove a place setting.

"Oh, he was here in September for a board meeting. We do speak regularly, but this is a bit of a surprise," Priscilla explained.

Maggie knew how hard it was not to see her own brother frequently anymore and figured everyone felt the same way.

"Enjoy your day, Priscilla, and Happy Thanksgiving to you both. I would love to meet your brother sometime."

"It will have to be somewhere other than church, I'm afraid. Darcy has sworn never to set foot in a church as long as he lives. Quite the heathen." Priscilla laughed. "I like to tease him. I can't wait to tell him how much I'm enjoying visiting Loving the Lord. Thank you for understanding all of this. I have prepared a roasted vegetable and orzo salad. Jennifer and Beth will bring it for me. Have a beautiful day," Priscilla said, then hung up.

Maggie brought the extra dishes into the kitchen and wondered what Priscilla's Thanksgiving Day would be like.

Darcy opened the large oak doorway, not in his pajamas, but dressed stylishly in gray flannel slacks, a gray button-down shirt, and a pale-blue wool pullover. Darcy was close to sixty but looked twenty years younger. His brown hair was graying at the temples, his blue eyes were set off by the sweater, he had acquired a few wrinkles around his mouth and eyes, but his smile was full of delight when he saw his sister standing in the doorway.

"Pris! Come in. It's cold out there." He grabbed her and gave her a hug, but his voice had a slight edge. "It's good to see you. Here, let me take your coat."

Darcy shut the door. Priscilla stared at her brother, reading him like a book. She handed him her coat and scarf, not taking her eyes off him.

"Darcy, why are you home?" Priscilla asked.

The Westminster chimes began ringing in earnest between noon and one p.m. Jack was the front door sentinel. Cate and Bryan took coats, hats, scarves, and brought them upstairs to one of the extra bedrooms. Maggie and Mimi finished putting together their own dishes in the kitchen, while Dirk checked on the turkey and some of the side dishes in the church kitchen.

"The church smells great," Dirk reported. "Maybe we should have set up tables over there since we're practically feeding the five thousand."

"We are feeding twenty-two, I mean twenty-one, now that Priscilla isn't coming. I want everyone to feel like they're 'home,' not at a church potluck," Maggie said, whipping up her butternut squash soufflé.

"That's admirable, Maggie, but it's still a church potluck. It's just over here," Mimi said, dumping cream of mushroom soup on top of her green beans.

Maggie looked up just as Ellen Bright walked into the kitchen.

"Happy Thanksgiving!" Ellen's large brown eyes twinkled as she placed a huge layered fruit salad on the counter. She threw her arms around Maggie and gave her a kiss on the cheek. "Hi, Dr. Elzinga!"

"Please, call me Mimi, Ellen. I consider you a niece." Mimi looked up and twinkled her own brown eyes back at Ellen.

"Yes, ma'am. Now, ladies, what are we doing here? I can't cook, so what else needs to be done?" Ellen always felt slightly useless at food events, although she loved to eat.

"You can shovel snow off the roof," Maggie said, deadpan.

"Great. Harold! Hey, Harold!" Ellen shouted.

Harold came into the kitchen with something in a casserole dish.

"Yes, dear?" Harold said mockingly.

"Pastor Maggie wants you to remove snow from the roof."

"Sure. Right after dinner. Where should I put my Brussels sprouts?" Harold asked.

Maggie wrinkled her nose.

"You're going to love them," Harold said.

"In the oven," Maggie said with a crooked smile.

Brussels sprouts made her gag. Maggie removed the turkey from her oven and added the Brussels sprouts.

The kitchen became overcrowded as Howard and Verna Baker, along with Winston Chatsworth, came through the door. Howard was holding a large tray of cheeses, French bread slices, grapes, and a small pot of honey.

"Appetizers," Howard said.

"Happy Thanksgiving, you three," Maggie said, putting her soufflé in the oven next to the Brussels sprouts. "How about appetizers in the family room?"

Dirk had already begun to pour coffees and ice teas as more guests were directed to the family room.

Jennifer and Beth Becker had arrived with Priscilla's orzo salad and two large pans of corn pudding.

"The salad can sit on the counter, but our puddings should be kept warm," Beth said.

Dirk took both pans and headed over to church, where there was extra room in the large ovens.

Jack took over beverage service.

A minute later, there was a knock on the back kitchen door. Maggie opened it to see one of her favorite faces.

"It's freezing out here, little one!" Marvin Green was in his wheelchair with a blanket over his knees and a bouquet of red carnations in his hands. "Let me in."

Marvin was a shut-in at the Friendly Elder Care Center. Having tried to start a war of wars with Maggie when she first came to visit him, Marvin had become one of her biggest fans. When she invited him to Thanksgiving dinner at the parsonage, he'd choked out a quiet, "Yes, please." As Marvin had aged, his frustration with being old grew into a begrudging acceptance. Maggie unwittingly had much to do with that change of heart. She decided to love Marvin, whether he liked it or not, and she did it with gusto.

"Marvin! I'm so happy to see you. And look at those carnations. They're my favorite. May I have them?" Maggie leaned down and gave Marvin a kiss on his leathered cheek.

She looked up and saw Bill and Sylvia Baxter standing behind Marvin's wheelchair. They had picked him up for Thanksgiving Day festivities at the parsonage. Maggie knew Sylvia must be missing her mother, who had also been on Marvin's floor in the FECC. Sylvia's grieving heart had moved down the hall to Marvin's room, and she was now his regular visitor.

"Bill, Sylvia, thank you for bringing my favorite parishioner to Thanksgiving dinner," Maggie said, stepping out of the way so Bill could push Marvin into the kitchen.

"I brought you these flowers to give that young husband of yours a run for his money," Marvin harrumphed.

"I'm sure he will be sufficiently jealous."

Maggie took their coats, while Mimi took the large pan of marshmallow-covered sweet potatoes from Sylvia and an even larger pan of cream cheese mashed potatoes from Bill.

Maggie realized she would need to divide food into separate bowls if she didn't want to be running from the kitchen to the dining room throughout dinner. She handed Cate the coats and began getting large bowls out of the pantry.

"Pastor Maggie, it smells wonderful in here," Sylvia exclaimed.

"I know. And there's another turkey coming from church yet." Maggie laughed.

She led the three guests into the family room where Lacey Campbell, Skylar Breese, and Arly Spink were helping themselves to mini egg quiches, homemade hummus and vegetables, and the cheese platter.

"The ladies who keep the economy of Cherish going," Maggie said as she saw the owners of the downtown businesses.

"That's us, PM," Lacey said with a mouthful of hummus. "We're the *lady-bosses* of this town."

"Mmmm . . . yes . . . I guess we are," Sky said in her silky and slightly otherworldly voice. The tall blonde had brought a beautiful fall arrangement of flowers, pinecones, and greens for the dining room table.

"Pastor Maggie, it's so nice to be here today," Arly Spink said, shaking Maggie's hand. "I've donated the quiches for the beginning of this feast."

"I'm so glad you are all here."

Maggie smiled. The house was full, happy, and celebrative, but everyone turned when a new voice screeched above the others.

"Vat you all doing herre?"

Irena Dalca wobbled in on her six-inch stilettos. She had her arm linked through the arm of Detective Keith Crunch.

They were met with silence.

Irena was wearing a skintight purple mini-dress. Her red lace bra was visible and barely holding her breasts in place. Maggie hoped she wouldn't bend over. Irena's makeup was actually color-coordinated with her dress and underclothes, but it didn't seem to help. The deep-purple eye shadow made Irena look like the victim of a collision with a telephone pole. Her red lips glistened with several layers of gloss.

Keith Crunch, on the other hand, was dressed to perfection in a gray suit and one of his signature blue shirts. His coiffed gray hair and startling blue eyes made some of the women in the room a little weak in the knees.

"Ve arre herre. Let's hev de fun!" Irena was actually happy.

Maggie closed her mouth and rearranged her face. She walked over and hugged Irena, then shook Keith's hand.

"Happy Thanksgiving! We're so glad you two are here," Maggie said a little too loudly.

"Happy Thanksgiving, Pastor Maggie and Dr. Jack," Keith said, handing Jack two bottles of wine for the dinner table.

Irena handed over two bottles of vodka. "Yes, I vould like de glass."

Jack laughed. "I'll get you a glass right away, Irena."

Everyone resumed chatting and eating the appetizers as Jack and Maggie went into the kitchen and retrieved wine glasses and a vodka glass for Irena.

Irena was cramming a mini quiche in her mouth when Jack held out the glass of vodka to her.

"Tanks." Irena accidentally spit some crust crumbs on Jack's sleeve when she spoke, but she took the glass and then a swig of her drink.

Jack grabbed Maggie, who was talking with Lacey, Sky, and Arly, and pulled her into the kitchen.

"This is the craziest Thanksgiving I've ever seen. Thank you for putting this crowd together." He finished his sentence with a very romantic kiss.

"Sorry to interrupt," Mimi chirped as she walked into the kitchen with the empty cheese platter. "Maybe we should start getting food on the tables. The appetizers are nearly gone." She smiled when she saw Maggie's startled face. "After your kiss, of course."

Mimi turned and went back into the family room to fill wine glasses, silently pleased to see that her daughter's new marriage was going so well.

The turkey and side dishes were brought from the church ovens, and Maggie divided up the other food into separate bowls while Jack and Bryan set them on each of the tables. It really did look as if they were feeding the five thousand. When the food was ready, Maggie went into the family room. The guests slowly ceased chatting, then turned and looked at her.

"Happy Thanksgiving," she said. "Jack and I are glad you are here. We know we have much to thank God for. We also know that at The Grange it is a very different kind of day. I'm sure you have heard that Cassandra died yesterday afternoon. So as we give God thanks for many blessings, let's also keep Carrie, Carl, and the Ellingtons in our hearts."

She took the hands of the two people closest to her, Marvin Green and Irena. The rest of the group made an oddly shaped circle around the furniture as they took one another's hands.

Maggie prayed. Then Jack and Maggie directed their guests to the two different tables. Maggie sat at the kitchen table, while Jack sat in the dining room. It wasn't until halfway through the dinner that Maggie realized she and Jack weren't sitting in the same room for their first married Thanksgiving, and it bothered her. In fact, as the dinner wore on, Maggie found herself more and more frustrated as she refilled bowls and walked from room to room, making sure everyone had what they needed. She heard snippets of conversations.

". . . and I just hate hunting season. Gunshots before I'm even out of bed in the morning." Sylvia helped herself to the butternut squash soufflé. "How do they call it a sport? They set out food. A hungry deer comes to eat. *Bam*, they shoot it. It doesn't sound like a sport to me." Sylvia was getting worked up, so Bill gently put his hand on her knee to settle her down.

"Oh . . . I agree . . . mmm," Sky chimed in with her fairy-bell voice. "It's all despicable and barbaric . . . mmm . . . yes. Horrendous."

Maggie stared at Sky. Although she despised hunting season herself, the conversation wasn't very Thanksgiving-ish.

"That seems a little harsh, Sky," Lacey said. "Some people hunt to feed themselves over the winter."

"Oh, do they? Good for them. Mmm . . . I find hunting for vegetables a much more humane way to go. You see," Sky actually looked Lacey directly in the eyes, "I've seen deer who have been shot, but not killed. They wander in pain and suffer a lingering death. The drunk or unskilled hunter who shot them can just walk away. Give guns to people who love guns. Just keep those people away from animals and those of us who hate guns. They can shoot each other instead." Sky's voice had lowered dramatically.

Maggie sensed that people were feeling uncomfortable now, as was she after Sky's last shocking statement, and no one seemed to know where to look. Jennifer and Beth Becker both stared intently at their forks.

"This is probably a conversation for another time," Jack said as he came in to refill water glasses and overheard part of the conversation. "Let's remember the meaning of the day." He smiled, which eased some of the tension.

"Yes, let's," Lacey said. "Sky, you're a huge bummer. Eat your Brussels sprouts and be quiet."

Sky put a Brussels sprout in her beautiful mouth and chewed. If anyone noticed, which they didn't, they would have seen her eyes narrow in anger.

Maggie made her way into the dining room with two more bottles of wine to refill glasses there. Jack was right behind her with a water pitcher.

"Good grief!" Maggie whispered to Jack in the doorway. "That was uncomfortable."

"The gun debate in our country is fierce," Jack said. "Now we know where Sky stands. I never thought she stood for anything."

They moved into the dining room and began refilling glasses with water and wine.

". . . I heard there were so many needy people in Cherish that over fifty baskets had to be delivered by area churches," Cate said, looking at Bryan.

"I'm sorry I missed out on the Thanksgiving baskets," Arly said, taking a sip of her wine. "But I will certainly help with the Christmas baskets. We're doing Christmas baskets, aren't we?" She looked up at Maggie, who was just over her shoulder.

"We absolutely are. I've already asked Grace in Action to give us some extra names."

Maggie glanced sideways at Winston. She didn't want to embarrass him. He picked up his knife and began to clink his water glass. Everyone quieted down. Winston stood up and made his way to the doorway connecting the kitchen with the dining room. He had the attention of everyone.

"You may think I clinked my glass to see Dr. Jack and Pastor Maggie kiss in front of us all, which is not a bad idea. However, I would just like to say that this church means more to me than anything. I am thankful for old friends, like ancient Howard Baker here and his young wife Verna. I am thankful for a seat in a pew to hear good sermons that keep me going all week long." Winston gave Maggie a smile. "I am thankful for music that makes my soul dance, even if the rest of my old, tired body can barely walk at times." He winked at Irena, who coquettishly dropped her gaze. "And I'm thankful that two people from this church came to my house on Sunday and gave me a Thanksgiving basket."

Everyone stopped eating. Forks and glasses were held in midair. No one knew what to do. Did Winston really receive a basket? Why?

"I worked for Chrysler all my life. I made a good living. I took care of my family. I was promised retirement benefits. It seemed to work out just right. And then some of my benefits were cut. My wife was diagnosed with a cancer that killed her by inches. You know, it's expensive to die by inches in this country. I was a hard worker, but now I am a poor man. The Thanksgiving basket was a real treat. It will add to my pantry generously. Being here today with my church family is even more of a treat. I guess I just wanted you all to know there are lots of ways to be rich, and there are lots of ways to be poor. I believe I'm the richest man in town. I'd like to make a toast to our hosts and to my real family, right here at these tables. May we always be rich in spirit. It's the only wealth you can count on." Winston raised his water glass.

Silently, all the glasses were raised.

"Hear, hear!" Howard said as he wiped away a tear. "Yes, hear, hear!"

Everyone clinked and smiled and sipped.

Arly got up and put her arms around Winston's thin, rickety body.

"My dad worked for Chrysler too," she whispered. "He lost some of his benefits, just like you did."

"I knew your dad," Winston said. "He was a good, honest man. I guess a lot of us took a hit. Yes, he was a very fine man."

Arly hugged Winston, then sat down and raised her glass again. The clinking continued. It seemed Thanksgiving Dinner had suddenly taken on a much deeper meaning.

20

January 8, 2016
Bawjiase, Ghana

As they stood on the porch of the volunteer house, Maggie and Dana heard a car coming toward them. It struggled on the rutted road and finally stopped in front of the volunteer house. A blonde ball of energy burst out of the backseat.

"Pastor Maggie!" Cate Carlson bounded onto the porch, squealing with delight.

The driver of the taxi let out a barrage of loud, seemingly angry, Twi in Cate's direction. Cate was oblivious as she hurled herself toward Maggie and wrapped her long arms around Maggie's neck.

"Pastor Maggie! It's so good to see you!" Cate sounded as if she hadn't seen Maggie in years. It had only been a week. Cate had traveled to Ghana with her school group one day prior to the church group's departure.

"I almost didn't get to come today. My professor wanted us to stay together as a group for the first weekend. I told him I would do some 'field work' at an orphanage in Bawjiase. He wasn't impressed, but he gave me permission to leave anyway."

Maggie suspected Cate got about anything she wanted just by smiling. Fortunately, Cate was unaware of her charms thus far.

The taxi horn began a nonstop blaring. The others came out of the volunteer house in the midst of the car horn and Cate's squeals. Joy headed over to the taxi and told the driver to stop the incessant honking.

"Cate!" Joy called loudly.

But Cate was in Bryan's arms now.

"Cate!" Joy called again. "You need to settle your taxi bill."

Cate ran back to the taxi as she pulled cedis out her pocket. Joy listened as the driver told Cate what she owed. It was double the appropriate amount. Joy put her face close to his and said something in Twi. Loudly.

Cate finally paid, after Joy told her how much for the actual cost of the fare. Joy also made a mental message to suggest to Bryan that Cate might need a crash course on traveling in Ghana. Cate would be in the country through April with her school program, and Joy knew Cate would learn much more than her coursework.

Cate's advent was exactly what everyone needed to lift the heavy spirit that had descended at breakfast. Even Dana smiled as they listened to Cate's stories of travel and the settling-in process with her classmates.

"Let's make the most of this weekend," Cate finally said. "What are we all doing?"

Silence.

It was Maggie who finally spoke, decisively. "Sylvia, Bill, and Dana are going with Nana to the farm to water vegetables. Joy, Ethan, and I are going to Market to get food, and the rest of you are going to United Hearts. There are two tasks at United Hearts. The younger children need to go to the health clinic for booster shots, and their National Health cards need to be updated. Also, Lacey has some super-duper secret thing she has planned for the kids."

"Oh, I want to go with Lacey," Cate said, looking at Lacey with a grin.

"First, we fetch water," Bryan chimed in, "unless you are going to the farm. Then you should probably be on your way."

"Has everyone taken their anti-malarial pills this morning?" Joy asked.

The anti-malarial pills needed to be taken daily on an exact schedule. There was a risk of getting malaria if pills were skipped or not taken at the same time each day. No one was interested in getting malaria. They had decided that after breakfast was the best time, since they were all together before scattering for the day.

Everyone went and got their pills, toothbrushes, and a baggie of pure water. Brushing teeth commenced on the porch. Actually, the brushing occurred on the porch, spitting occurred over the low cement wall of the porch. Pure water rinsed mouths and washed the anti-malarial pills down everyone's throats. Spit and toothpaste decorated the ground in front of the house.

Everyone usually needed to use the one and only toilet following breakfast. It taught patience to all. Sometimes the wait was longer than others. Maggie and Ellen discovered a large bush at the back of the volunteer house. It had served as a "bathroom with a view" once or twice.

Like any mission trip, personal habits became public.

Bill and Dana applied sunscreen, then grabbed hats and baggies of pure water. They chatted with Cate as they waited for Sylvia to collect her things for the day. She finally emerged from the house, hat in hand, a smudge of sunscreen on her nose.

"We're off," Sylvia said with forced enthusiasm. "We'll see the rest of you at lunch."

Sylvia was glad Bill was coming along to the farm. It seemed she hadn't really seen him or had time to discuss anything with him since they arrived. She fell, exhausted, into her bunk before anyone else at night. She was also happy to get away from Dr. Jack and Pastor Maggie right now. She didn't appreciate their hovering and was embarrassed they had heard her vomiting.

Nana was waiting for his three farmhands on the dirt road near United Hearts.

"Good morning, Nana," Sylvia said.

"Ah, more help! This is very good." Nana smiled, then set a fast pace to get to the farm. "I think we will get all the work done today," he said as they walked. "The heat dries the plants quickly. But with four of us, more work will get done."

"We can start with the plants we didn't get to last night," Sylvia said as she pictured the corner of the field that went without water the day before.

Bill and Sylvia followed Nana and Dana. Bill slipped his hand into Sylvia's.

"I miss you," he said softly.

"I miss you too. I'm glad you are working at the farm today. I hope you put on enough sunscreen," she said, looking at his red hair and fair skin.

"I have, and I brought extra. Your eyes look tired."

"They are. I'm pooped," Sylvia said. "But I can't imagine not helping Nana. Wait till you see what he has to do every day. He's only been farming with these plants for three months, and they have gone gangbusters."

Dana and Nana walked ahead in easy silence. Dana gave herself a little lecture. Her ego had taken over her psyche, but she had to put her ego away now. Her expectations had been single-minded. She thought she was going to take care of animals in Bawjiase. She had been told she would be able to do that and also work with a local veterinarian. But it hadn't happened. As hard as it was, Dana had to remember her will might not be God's will. Dana hated when that happened. She usually had an impressively awesome plan for each of her days. God just needed to give a stamp of approval. It seemed like coming on the mission trip was a mistake. There was just over a week left. She would do what she was told. Then she would get back to Cherish and what really mattered.

Back at the volunteer house, the rest of the group, minus Joy, who was getting a grocery list from Pastor via cell phones, grabbed their buckets and made their daily trek to the well. Their necks and shoulders were slowly getting used to the new burden. Bryan filled the buckets. By the time he filled the last one—Cate's—Maggie was back for her second bucket. Cate left, walking slowly back to the volunteer house, water sloshing onto her dress and shoes.

"Maggie?" Bryan said when Cate was out of earshot, "are you all right? This morning was a little rough."

Maggie's feelings were still stinging. She had been trying to sort out her part of the issue.

"No. I'm not all right." She set her bucket down on the edge of the well. "I'm trying to be a good follower of you and Joy. I'm also trying to be a good leader to my parishioners. But I really don't have any say in the situation here, so I can listen to others' frustrations, but I can't do anything about them." She took a breath. "You and Joy seem to enjoy telling us our expectations are too high, but you also set us up to expect something more than sitting around for two weeks. Do you understand that these good people took two weeks off work to come here? They paid money for plane tickets. Addie's missing two weeks of school." Hot tears stung her eyes, but she could see Ellen coming down the road for a second bucket. "I'm embarrassed," Maggie choked, then reached up to wipe her eyes. As she did so, her elbow brushed against the bucket and knocked it into the well.

"Damn it!" Maggie said without regret. It felt good to say it. She wanted to say it again.

"Oh dear," said Ellen, walking toward them and seeing the bucket fall. "Now that's a dilemma."

Bryan dropped the filler bucket down the well, being sure to hang on to the rope. It took several tries, but he finally hauled Maggie's bucket to the top.

Bryan filled the bucket with water, and Maggie silently lifted the bucket to her head. She began the walk back to the volunteer house. Her tears didn't stop, which was why she didn't see the tree root on the path. Her foot caught, and down she went, water splashing out first to make a muddy puddle for her to land in. A village woman and her three small children were sitting in front of their house, cooking something in a tin pot over an open fire. They just stared at Maggie and watched her fall. Maggie's humiliation was complete.

Jack was coming back for his second bucket of water, followed by Ethan and Charlene. Maybe the humiliation hadn't been quite complete after all. It definitely was now.

Jack set down his bucket and got to Maggie quickly, lifting her by the arms.

"Are you all right?" Jack asked.

"Yes. I was tripped up by a maniacal tree root." Maggie pointed to the offending root.

Ethan and Charlene took in the scene. Once they realized Maggie was okay, Charlene said, in an attempt to lighten the mood, "Well, at least now you'll have something to do today. Laundry."

Maggie's shorts and T-shirt were plastered with red mud. She was ready to make a sarcastic comment and join in with Charlene's frustration, but she stopped herself.

"It doesn't matter what country I'm in," Maggie said, forcing a smile, "I'm clumsy everywhere."

Ellen came from the well with her bucket perfectly balanced on her head.

"Hey! What happened to you, Pastor Maggie?"

"Keep walking, cousin," Jack said.

Ellen got the message and kept walking.

Maggie, Jack, Charlene, and Ethan walked back to the well. When they got there, Bryan looked at Maggie, but he didn't say anything. They hadn't had an argument in years, but now it felt like when they were children fighting over Saturday morning chores. He couldn't tell by her face whether she was on the verge of crying again or ready to haul off and slug him.

"We're ready for our refills, sir," Charlene said with a little bow.

"Yes, ma'am."

Bryan lowered his filler bucket into the well and refilled each bucket.

"What are you going to do today, Bryan?" Ethan asked. "Are you going to do booster shots or Lacey's secret activity or go to Market?"

Apparently, Ethan hadn't been listening when Maggie barked out the marching orders earlier.

"I'm definitely going with Lacey. She's doing something with the kids, but I think I'll bring a couple of new soccer balls I have been saving. They all love to play soccer." He lowered the filler bucket once again.

"That sounds like fun," Ethan said. "I'm eager to see how Market works in Bawjiase. I've spent time in Kenya, but not on this side of the continent. I enjoyed Market in Nairobi."

Bryan was caught off guard.

"You've been to Kenya?" Bryan asked Ethan.

"Well, yes. And South Africa as well. You know I teach African studies at the university, don't you?" Ethan laughed.

Bryan and Joy had never bothered to ask if anyone had been to an African country before.

The sound of laughter came first, followed by Cate, Lacey, and Addie as they walked up to the little crowd with the ever-present buckets.

"Bryan, did I hear you say you are coming with us?" Lacey asked, giving Bryan a high five. "I commend you! You're going to have a great day."

Bryan looked at Cate and grinned, knowing in his heart the real reason for his choice of activities. He would have done anything Cate was doing just to spend the day with her, and she was going with Lacey.

"What are you doing with the kids, by the way?" Bryan asked.

"None of your beeswax," Lacey said as she lifted her bucket to the top of her head. "Just hurry up. We should get to United Hearts."

On the farm, Nana and Sylvia also filled buckets. The moss-covered pond smelled like warm mold, mingled in with the aromas of mud around the water and the tree branches hanging low. It reminded Sylvia of her uncle's farm in Dexter, Michigan, when she was a child. Playing in the pond and breathing in the smells of summertime were happy memories for her. She wished she wasn't so tired and could enjoy it more. She wished her stomach would settle down.

Once they had buckets filled, Nana headed off to a plot of land where he would begin sowing young plants in the freshly turned dirt. Sylvia led Bill and Dana to the far corner of the farm to a plot of cabbages, which needed water first that morning. The walk itself was slow going as they carefully carried their buckets. They did not carry them on their heads. The water was too full of bacteria and contaminants for that. No one wanted an accidental mouthful of pond water. It was worse than the well water. Besides, that way, they could each carry two buckets instead of one.

The morning continued with walking back and forth from the pond to the thirsty plants.

"I can't believe you have been doing this all week," Bill said to Sylvia, wiping his forehead with a bandana. "No wonder you practically fall asleep at the dinner table."

"It's exhausting," Dana said as she bit off a corner of her pure water baggie and drank the contents. "But it feels good. Every row we water feels like an accomplishment."

Sylvia laughed. "I know. Every day I feel like I'm getting something done. I can't believe there are days when Nana has to come out here alone and try to keep this all watered and planted. It's good to be here during the dry season. We can really help." Sylvia sighed. "I know Nana appreciates it. The farm is one of the most sustainable projects for United Hearts. I've learned a lot from him."

Dana adjusted her sun hat. She had never felt heat like that before.

"I'm guessing that's because you ask him a lot of questions," Bill said.

"Sure. I know how I grow things in Michigan, how farmers grow things in Michigan. I know nothing about farming in Ghana. The way we farm at home wouldn't work here. The climate is different. The tools are different. What grows and thrives here is different. What people eat here is different. Nana knows what works. He has made this farm his personal project, and it's flourishing."

Bill stood for a moment and saw Nana two fields over, on his hands and knees as he dug a hole and then carefully placed a small plant in the ground. He used his bucket to water each new plant. Bill looked at the four fields surrounding them. The magnitude of Nana's work was staggering.

"Let's get more water." Bill headed for the pond.

At United Hearts, the younger children were thrilled when they saw the obronis coming toward them. They ran to meet them, jumped into arms, clung to legs, and laughed as they were hugged and kissed by Bryan and his crew. Cate, Addie, and Lacey had already decided they would keep the children outside playing games and share the granola bars they were carrying in their pockets. That way the "medical staff" could get organized with the National Health cards and then make a trip to the clinic.

Bryan, Jack, Charlene, and Ellen went inside United Hearts and were greeted by Pastor Elisha.

"Welcome!" Pastor said, grinning. "Thank you for the help with this task. It is good to keep our children healthy."

"What can we do first?" Bryan asked, although all he really wanted to do was go outside where Cate was and play.

Pastor Elisha retrieved a box from one of the shelves in the large room.

"These are the health cards. Some of the children need their registration renewed, some are fine for some time."

Ellen took the box and sat down. She had brought a small backpack and now pulled out a pad of paper and a handful of pens.

"Let's make a list of everyone and the date on their card," Ellen said practically. "Jack, Charlene, why don't you sit down and help me."

The two doctors took their orders from the organized and competent nurse, and they sat.

"Well, if you have this under control," Bryan said, slowly backing toward the door, "I'll check on the kids."

"And your girlfriend," Ellen said, taking the cards out of the box. She handed one third of them to Jack and another third to Charlene.

"Yep!" Bryan said. "See ya!" He was out the door.

∞

As she sat at the large table in the volunteer house and looked over her grocery list, Joy thought about the conversation from breakfast. She had made some presumptions that the group would be similar to other groups that had come through Bawjiase, but something was different. They weren't insinuating themselves into tasks where they weren't invited. The problem was, most of them weren't being invited into anything. She had to accept responsibility for that.

Maggie walked in from the porch.

"Maggie," Joy said, "do you have a second?"

"Sure."

"I want you to know, I heard you this morning. And I apologize. You were right to be frustrated."

"I guess it's just different expectations," Maggie said quietly.

"I have to confess that Bryan and I have our inside jokes about certain people or groups who have come here thinking they know best for the 'poor Africans.' They were people who had all the answers but were never willing to ask any questions. That's not the case for your group. You are more sensitive to the culture than most. You want to do something with the people, not tell the people what to do. Hopefully, today will be different." Joy realized her lack of affirmation for the group as a whole, and Maggie in particular.

"We'll do whatever you want, Joy. I told Bryan earlier that we just want to do *something*," Maggie said directly.

Joy had gotten used to telling groups and individuals what they shouldn't do in the Ghanaian culture and had often left off what they were doing right.

"Your group is different, Maggie," Joy said again. "You don't want to be in charge, like some other groups we've had. And you also don't want to lie around and do nothing, or go drink in the village every night, like some of the others. I don't want to waste the remainder of your time here in Bawjiase."

"Thanks, Joy," Maggie said as a small feeling of renewal washed over her. She just needed to punch her brother, and all would be well. "Let's make this next week a good one."

Maggie got up from the table and saw Joy bow her head.

Joy said a silent prayer. She prayed for her own understanding and beliefs, not only to be clarified, but opened. And she prayed for humbleness. Her own.

"Hey, Ethan!" Joy called, lifting her head. "Are you ready to go to Market?"

Ethan came in from the porch.

"First of all," Joy said, "thank you for helping me with this. Market days are crazy, but also a lot of fun. Ethan, I want you to know how much we appreciate the time you've taken to be here, the money Loving the Lord has donated for United Hearts and the new school, and your patience with a trip that hasn't met all of your expectations."

Ethan looked slightly confused.

"Thanks for that, Joy," he said haltingly. "I think we all have felt slightly underutilized. But we've also learned that to live by our watches and checklists won't do anyone any good."

"Now that we're talking about it," Maggie said, "I think that's important for everyone. We've got a week to do whatever you need."

Ethan nodded in agreement.

"Well, now get ready to shop," Joy said. "You're going to see some huge amounts of food. You've brought enough money to feed United Hearts for six months. We can't thank you enough."

And Joy meant it.

Maggie happily handed her the donation money from Loving the Lord, relieved not to have the responsibility of so much money anymore.

"Well, Happy Thanksgiving, Merry Christmas, Happy Easter, and Happy Birthday!" Ethan said with a loud laugh. "Let's go see what this Market is all about.

21

November 26, 2015, Thanksgiving Day
Cherish, Michigan

The fireplace crackled in Darcy Keller's living room. Although the central heating was on, the fire made the dark wood-paneled living room seem warm and cozy. Priscilla was settled in a soft leather chair, and Darcy was on a dark cherry-colored velvet sofa. Everything was spotless.

"Okay, you must have known you were coming back for some time now," Priscilla said with a little annoyance. "The house is spotless and smells of Murphy's Oil Soap everywhere. There is a Thanksgiving dinner cooking in the kitchen, and you have a maid. That doesn't happen in five minutes. What gives, Darcy?"

Darcy laughed. "You're right, Pris. I've planned to come home for a while. I didn't tell you because I had to talk myself into it first. I had to get out of New York. My ex-father-in-law and I had an offer on our business. I think he felt guilty because of what his daughter did to me. Anyway, we made a killing on the sale, and I got seventy-five percent of the profits. Being in New York just reminded me of my old life, so I decided I wanted to come back to my even older life. Back here to Cherish." Darcy stopped and stared at his sister.

"What . . . What are you . . . going to do? Here?" Priscilla asked as her head tried to catch up with her brother's words.

"I don't know. Do you want an answer right now? I'll remain Chair of the Board of The Mill. I guess I can be a little more helpful if I actually live here. And if I give a damn."

Priscilla looked at him carefully.

He continued. "I owe you an apology. Before the divorce, I acted like coming back here was a big waste of my time. My business in New York was more lucrative. My life more exciting. To be in Cherish felt like putting the brakes on, and I didn't like it. Maybe it's getting sucker-punched with divorce papers and seeing your best friend grab your wife's ass that brings a little clarity. Anyway, I'm sorry for being an idiot to you. I'm going to take some time and figure things out. So . . ."

Darcy got up and opened a bottle of champagne with a loud pop. He poured two slim glasses of the bubbly wine. Priscilla stood up and walked toward her brother as he handed her a flute.

"To new beginnings," Priscilla said, then clinked his glass.

"To new beginnings," Darcy agreed and took a large swallow. "And to hopefully figuring out who the hell I am."

Maggie pulled Jack into the study, where the three felines had hidden from the guests—and, thankfully, from the turkeys and desserts. The cats now began a tuneless chorus of meows.

"Happy Thanksgiving, husband." She kissed him.

He smiled. "Well, Happy Thanksgiving, wife. What's this all about?"

"I think I have felt sorry for myself all day. What a little idiot I am. Winston's toast was the kick in the rear I needed to remember just how happy and blessed we are. So I just want to say, I love you. You are a gift, and I'm not going to pout anymore." She looked up and smiled.

"I didn't notice you feeling sorry for yourself. We have a house full of people on a day that began with a dessert disaster. You helped a good woman die yesterday, and you're worried about her children. You own too many cats. You're newly married. Fortunately, you're married to me. Now, we're going to finish this dinner and enjoy a quiet evening with your family." Jack slapped her on the bottom. "Move it, wife."

Maggie laughed out loud, led him out of the study, closing the door on the hapless cats, and went back into the kitchen. The conversation had turned from hunting and guns to Christmas baskets. *Thank goodness.*

"Well, I think we will be given a list of the things people need. We usually find out special toys that the children would like to have." Jennifer Becker explained to Lacey how the baskets worked.

"Can we donate other items, special things for the adults too?" Lacey was thinking of her shop and all the pampering items that might go nicely in a basket.

"I'll double check with Grace in Action. In the past, we have usually stuck to a list they've given us," Jennifer said, looking at Beth for confirmation.

Beth was enjoying a mound of mashed potatoes but nodded in agreement.

Marvin Green had his wheelchair pushed up to the table and was eating everything he could get his hands on. *Finally, decent food. None of that nursing home slop.*

"There's no harm in putting in a little something extra," Marvin said gruffly. "More green beans. Please."

Maggie passed the green bean casserole and smiled at Marvin.

"Do you want to come to Ghana with us?" she asked. "We need people like you to stir things up a bit."

"I'm guessing the entire country of Ghana is not ready for me yet," Marvin said. "Otherwise, I'd be there and show you youngsters what's what." He looked back at Jennifer and Beth. "Your mother would have put a surprise in every basket, and you know it. She was a generous woman, and not only that, she had an imagination." He plopped a huge spoonful of casserole on his plate. "Make sure you use yours for those Christmas baskets." He resumed eating with a vengeance.

Jennifer and Beth smiled at each other. Marvin had known their mother for years, even before they both ended up at Friendly Elder Care Center. They'd spent their sunset years in friendship at the FECC as their bodies slowly trapped them into wheelchairs. Jennifer and Beth had visited their mother every day, but Marvin's two sons and one daughter had never darkened the doorway. Jennifer and Beth, with encouragement from their mother, brought Marvin home-baked treats when they visited, and it had been the highlight of his day. Now that their mother was gone, they didn't get up to Marvin's room as much as they used to. Both sisters were thinking the same thing as they watched Marvin enjoying his green beans. *Regular visits must be made. With treats.* Sylvia and Bill weren't the only ones who could smother Marvin with love, attention, and food.

In the dining room, Irena was holding court. The rest of the table listened as she shared her good news.

"*Manger Baby*. Dat's vat eet's called. I wrrote eet, ov courrse. Eet ees breeliant, and you vill luv eet."

She looked at Keith Crunch sitting next to her. He grinned.

"We can't wait, babe," he said, giving everyone at the table a moment of shock, quickly followed by nausea.

How did the handsome, perfectly manicured, brilliant, crime-solving man fall for someone as ridiculous and frightening as Irena?

"Your concert will bring us all into the Christmas spirit, Irena," said Ellen, who always had a word of encouragement to give. She smiled and lifted her glass. "To *Manger Baby!*"

Other glasses were raised and clinked. Irena basked in her own glory.

Verna was the only one unwilling to shine a light on Irena's magnificence, but Howard used his elbow to help her lift her glass.

He whispered, "It's Thanksgiving, Verna. If I remember right, you brought Irena a home-cooked meal last year because you knew she was alone."

Verna had forgotten that. She had brought Irena a meal, indeed. The two women had each been alone last year on Thanksgiving Day. What a difference that year had made. Verna worked a smile onto her face and raised her glass a little higher.

"To *Manger Baby*."

Maggie filled one of the church coffee pots that Bryan had procured for her earlier. She sliced pies and cut squares of blueberry buckle. Cate happily took orders from each table. Maggie dished up the desserts while Jack scooped vanilla ice cream on top. Both Cate and Bryan poured coffee into the church china cups.

Maggie couldn't help but sneak a look into the dining room to see how Keith Crunch was enjoying his blueberry buckle. His eyes were closed as he slipped another bite into his mouth. He was obviously in heaven. Mimi gave Maggie a smile and a slight nod of her head, which meant, of course, Thanksgiving was a success.

Maggie felt a tug on her elbow. She turned and found herself face to face with a Brussels sprout. Harold's face was smiling perfectly as he held the sprout on a fork.

"Try it," he said.

"Oh, Harold! I really don't like sprouts. Don't make me eat it," Maggie whined, trying to move away from the stinky vegetable.

Harold held on to her elbow. "Try it."

Maggie opened her mouth slowly, and Harold shoved in the sprout. Then he stood back and watched.

Maggie began her vomit face, but actually stopped when she tasted the cheese, cream, and onion encrusted morsel. She looked up at Harold, her eyes full of surprise. After swallowing she said, "Well, good grief, Harold! That was not a Brussels sprout. You fooled me."

Harold smiled so broadly, every one of his perfect teeth was on full display.

"Told you."

"May I have the recipe?"

"Nope. You just have to ask Ellen and me over for dinner more often. I'll bring the sprouts."

Harold patted Maggie on the shoulder and went to find his girlfriend.

Maggie laughed. A lukewarm Brussels sprout was a highlight of her day.

By the time coats were brought down from upstairs, filled leftover containers passed out, hugs given all around, Cate and Bryan on their way to Cate's family, and the cats released from the study, Maggie thought she just might fall asleep standing against the wall.

Dirk and Mimi had made it clear they would do the cleanup, graciously declining all offers of help from Jack and Maggie's guests, mainly to get them out of the house. Once the parsonage was empty, she ordered Jack and Maggie to sit.

"Dad and I will handle it from here. It was a wonderful day. Thank you."

She tied an apron around her small waist and helped her husband clear the dishes from the dining room table. They would be staying for the weekend. Mainly to see Bryan, but also to attend Cassandra's funeral. The little church in Cherish had become another part of their family. The celebrations and tragedies were also theirs.

Darcy and Priscilla enjoyed Cornish game hens, cornbread stuffing, roasted potatoes, and asparagus au gratin. Priscilla had to keep telling herself she wasn't living in a dream. Or nightmare. Her brother seemed to lose his genteel filters as the meal and champagne flowed. They were just finishing up pieces of pumpkin chiffon pie and cups of coffee when Darcy began another tirade about his ex-wife.

"Darcy, you're sounding more and more cynical. Have you, I don't know, talked to anyone about the whole divorce situation? A counselor or someone who could help?"

Priscilla knew the importance of getting a little help when going through a major life change. She had no qualms about seeing a counselor when she needed to sort out her life.

"It's a divorce. It's the end of a business agreement. Marriage is a business. It has a license. Sometimes the license runs out. The business is over. I think I get it." His voice was edgy and sarcastic.

Priscilla sighed. "Right, okay. You sound like such a fool right now. Listen to me, Darcy, you need some help. Your ego has been crushed, and you're a powerful man. Powerful men don't like their egos to be crushed. They try to ignore what's happening. Your wife left you for another powerful man, your best friend. That is a tragedy. You don't have to pretend that you're handling it all just fine because obviously you're not. You are out of a real business you seemed to enjoy. You have left an exciting city. You didn't come back here to take better care of the board of The Mill. You came back to hide and lick your wounds. Well, I'll let you do that for a little while, but not for long. I will be your worst nightmare if you don't get some help."

Priscilla wiped her mouth with the delicate linen napkin and stood up.

"Happy Thanksgiving" she said. "I'll be back tomorrow. And Saturday. And get ready for this, fool, you're coming to church with me on Sunday. Even if I have to bring you in a straitjacket."

She walked over to her brother, who was still sitting in his chair, dumbfounded. She leaned over and kissed his cheek. Then she whispered, "I love you, Darcy. We will do this together. I'm not leaving you. Ever. Thanks for dinner."

She retrieved her coat and left through the large front door. Then Priscilla sat in her very expensive car and prayed.

There were other homes in Cherish on Thanksgiving Day with food on tables, new toys for children, diapers for babies. Turkeys were roasted and served with mashed potatoes and gravy. There were fresh vegetables and boiling cranberries.

Maria Gutierrez made a traditional flan, the way her mother had taught her when she was a child. She proudly served it to her family as the dessert for their feast.

The Chance family gathered around their kitchen table. Cecelia had been cooking all day and was pleased to place their dinner of thanksgiving in front of her family. Bobby wheeled his father up to the table. Jim was hoping to be out of the cumbersome chair by the New Year. Cecelia noticed that Jim smiled as he stared at the heavily laden table. He hadn't smiled since his accident.

"I have an idea," Cecelia said, spooning sweet potato casserole onto Jim's plate. "How about we go to church this Sunday?"

Naomi and Bobby both groaned.

"Mom! No!"

"I'm not going!" they said, talking over each other.

"Loving the Lord Church brought us this dinner," Cecelia said firmly, "plus extra food to last us a while. It was their youth group who thought this whole thing up. I want to meet the kids who thought it would be nice to share Thanksgiving dinners with strangers."

Naomi and Bobby recognized the tone.

They were going to church.

"I'll stay home," Jim said. "This chair is too hard to move around, and that church probably isn't handicap accessible."

"You're going too. Now let's eat."

Cecelia never once forgot who was at the helm of her family's ship. And she ran a tight ship, indeed.

William and Mary Ellington sat at their large oak kitchen table with Julia Benson. They each had a glass of red wine to end the day.

"I think it went as well as could be expected," Julia said, looking at the tired couple in front of her. "The dinner was delicious, and the children had the freedom to stay in their rooms and play or go out to the barn with you, William. There was no pressure on anyone."

"I think we were all exhausted from yesterday. Carrie and Carl must still be shell-shocked, in a way. Poor little ones," Mary said.

She had tried not to hover, but she kept a close watch on the children and saw how many times they went into Cassandra's room out of habit.

Or hope.

They went looking for a mother who would never be in that room again.

"We knew this transition time was coming," William said, taking a sip of his wine. "We're in it now, but I don't know what that means. It's a strange relief that Cassandra isn't dying upstairs anymore, but she was the lifeline for Carrie and Carl. Now we're the lifelines. I don't think I'm ready for this. Does that sound harsh?"

"No." Mary looked at her husband. "You've got to cut yourself some slack. It's barely been twenty-four hours since Cassandra died. We're going to mess up. Probably a lot. But I know we'll get things right as well. Love and patience will overcome our ignorance." Mary looked at Julia. "I think your little Hannah is helping them more than anyone. She's the only one who talks to them normally. I heard her ask them today, 'So what is it like to have a mommy in heaven?'"

"What did they say?" Julia asked.

"They said she was with their daddy now, and she must be happy because Jesus was there too. And Jesus is super fun." Mary sighed.

"I think we all just need to get them through the funeral on Monday," Julia said. "Then we will be here to help them through these first days and weeks."

When the three adults went in to check on them before going to bed themselves, they saw three little arms linked together in sleep. Hannah had crawled into Carrie's bed along with Carl, Butterball, and Dusty. Dusty was at their feet. Butterball lay across the tops of their heads, like a furry guardian angel.

Martha looked over at G. Gordon Liddy Kitty, who was fast asleep in front of the heating vent.

She had spent her Thanksgiving Day at the police station, prepared to answer the phone, which didn't ring. After five hours of playing Candy Crush, she had jumped when the door to the police station opened abruptly.

"Martha, what are you doing here?" Charlotte was dressed in full uniform after a shift of patrolling Cherish, looking for any sign of

Thanksgiving hooliganism. There had been none. Now it was Officer Bernie Bumble's shift.

"I've been answering the phones and minding the dispatch," Martha said, sliding her phone into her purse so Charlotte wouldn't see what she had really been doing.

"Well, the phone calls will come directly to my phone now. I would like you to come to my house for Thanksgiving dinner. Liz, Mason, and Brock have been cooking all day. It's the only reason I have children, I'll tell you that for free. Of course, Fred has been overseeing the entire business, making sure there were no kitchen wars." Charlotte cracked herself up and couldn't help guffawing.

"No, thank you, ma'am, I have other plans for the day." Martha could barely force herself to look Charlotte in the eye.

"Is this over the basket delivery last weekend? You've got to get over it, Martha. We did a good thing for good and deserving people. Get that corncob out of your butt and come to my house for dinner." Charlotte was talking in her chief voice.

"I really can't." Martha sounded petulant.

"If you change your mind, just come on over. We can feed an army." Charlotte turned and left the station.

Martha waited several minutes to make sure Charlotte was gone. Then she locked the station doors, wrapped her scarf a little tighter around her neck, and headed home. She and G. Gordon Liddy would be sharing a frozen Marie Callender's turkey dinner.

But once dinner had been shared, and G. Gordon settled in for a nice eight-hour nap, Martha was left alone with her negative thoughts.

And her anger.

And not much for which to be thankful.

Sitting in a cell in the Wayne County Jail, Redford Johnson was seething. He had been rotting in the jail for almost two months. On the floor of his cell was a supposed Thanksgiving dinner. *What a joke!* Nothing in that place was edible. It was pure crap.

Redford was waiting for his final hearing. He was certain his lawyer would get a plea deal with the prosecutor. His lawyer was too. The jails were too overcrowded, and the judge would be lenient, his lawyer was certain. Then Redford would be out. He had been in that dump for too long, and for doing nothing bad enough to keep him there.

He had some revenge to take. He had some punishments to mete out. There were some people who needed to suffer for causing him to be locked up in that place. Redford spent his days making his plan. *They will suffer, oh yes, they will.*

He ran his fingers through his hair in agitation. Then he stood up and kicked the tray of food at the wall of his cell. The crash was loud. The food splattered everywhere.

The guttural yell that came from Redford brought the correction officer quickly to his cell. The officer observed Redford spinning into another unhinged rage.

Just more bad behavior to document.

22

Joy, Maggie, and Ethan walked into the village and found themselves in the midst of a large, loud gathering of people. Speakers were set up at one end of a huge circle, music blaring. Maggie observed at least one hundred people—some danced, some cried, some ate, and some drank. The music was so loud, she had to put her hands over her ears. Every person in the gathering was dressed in black or red clothing. The men wore suits and ties, and some were in traditional Ghanaian dress. One small group of people, all dressed in black, were surrounded by others who were wailing. It looked like a wedding reception. With crying and wailing.

"What is this?" Maggie shouted in Joy's ear.

"A funeral," Joy shouted back. "The community gathers for a day, or days, to mourn with the family. They are also very religious and celebrate God's goodness and thanksgiving for the one who has died."

Maggie watched the scene in front of her. Anguish and joy commingled. Maggie had never seen anything that dramatic before.

Joy watched as well, knowing it was an important piece of Ghanaian culture for Maggie and Ethan to experience. Joy herself was always awestruck by the tradition.

Ethan stopped when Joy did, but he knew exactly what was going on. He had been teaching the different historical and cultural aspects of all African countries for over a decade. He watched the funeral with interest.

The music was deafening, but Maggie had her focus on the people wailing for the dead. Their dramatic movements with arms and bodies fascinated the foreigners. Maggie thought about the stories in the New Testament, when townspeople would come to the home of someone recently deceased to begin to "professionally" mourn and wail with, and for, the family. An age-old tradition she had never seen in America.

What would it be like to wail for someone you didn't know, or someone you didn't know well? Was it a gift to give the bereft family, or an acting job? Shouldn't every death be mourned, even if the deceased wasn't known personally? As the scene played out in front of her, she felt emotions at their rawest.

Maggie searched the faces of the people who wore black, and she shivered. Grief poured out of those who had lost their loved one. At the same time, the joy over remembering the life of that same loved one was also overflowing. Food and drink and dance gave it a wedding reception feel. Where the funerals Maggie had been to, or officiated, were proper, sanitized, and grief was "appropriate," that funeral held nothing back. The people experienced the highest highs and lowest lows and everything else on the emotional spectrum. Their grief was sloppy and overdone. The family grieved openly. Some of the other guests were there simply to wail and mourn, whether they felt it or not. No one hid behind tidy clothes or worn platitudes.

Maggie felt as if the ground rose up—the spirit of the earth, the spirit of God unleashed. She closed her eyes. She had felt the same sensation the day she went walking alone. The day Hannah fell. It was frightening and powerful. It was uncontained and unattainable. It was indescribable and transcendent. She felt as if every sermon she had ever preached had been trite and neatly packaged for her listeners, but there was nothing trite or packaged about the spirit she felt swirling around her at this funeral. She closed her eyes and let herself experience the chaos in her own soul. Was that the reason she was here in

Ghana? Not to run a mission trip, but because God had made an appointment to meet her here, to wipe away her perfectly packaged faith and give her more questions than answers.

There were no whispers here. There was only a deafening roar.

"Are you okay?" Ethan gently shook Maggie's shoulder.

Maggie jumped, quickly opened her eyes, then lost her balance and leaned into Ethan's arm. He steadied her.

"Wow. Sorry, Ethan," Maggie said loudly over the music, getting herself back under control. "I think I got carried away in the service. I've never seen anything like it."

"It is fascinating," Ethan agreed loudly so Maggie could hear him. They walked a few steps away so they could hear each other. "What's interesting is that the family is responsible for the cost of the entire funeral. The more people who show up to the funeral, the better. It means the deceased person was a friendly and well-liked person in the community, but it also means more cost for the family. Sometimes, the poorer people go into great debt just to show the proper respect for their loved ones. It can be quite a burden. Billboards must be put up around the community. Special coffins are made to represent what the deceased person did in life. But it's mainly a huge party."

Joy turned and walked down a side street. Maggie and Ethan followed reluctantly. Once they were away from the loud music, Joy said, "It's fascinating to watch, but I'm afraid we stand out in the crowd."

That statement struck Maggie. She lived in a world surrounded by people who looked exactly like her. She now stood in a place where she was an extreme minority. Her skin color made her an outsider in that village, in that country, on that continent. She, Ethan, and Joy were different.

They were people of color. White.

A color with no hue.

As they walked to town, Maggie couldn't stop thinking of Cassandra, the last funeral she had officiated. The faces of Carrie and Carl. The congregation had surrounded them until there was standing room only in the Loving the Lord sanctuary.

Maggie's main goal had been to try and fulfill a request made by the children.

They did not want to tell their mother goodbye.

Maggie had never felt so inadequate.

23

November 28-30, 2015
Cherish, Michigan

Maggie and Irena called a truce on the *Manger Baby* war the Saturday after Thanksgiving in Maggie's office. Maggie was slightly shocked by Irena's willingness to cut the musical to two hours, instead of the original four. They settled on a date without argument. It would be the Saturday before Christmas at two o'clock in the afternoon.

Maggie had been most surprised by Irena's willingness to help plan Cassandra's funeral completely around the needs of the children. Irena had willingly agreed to the uplifting hymns Cassandra had requested, so unlike her own favored dirges. Irena agreed to each and every children's Sunday school song on the list Marla had given them and thought bright colors and coffee-time treats were the only way to go. Maggie looked at Irena and tried to keep her face normal.

"Thank you, Irena, for your willingness to do this for the children. They certainly must be comforted."

"Ov courrse."

Irena stood up, grabbed her ever-present stack of music, and abruptly left Maggie's office, teetering on her high heels. Maggie realized she shouldn't be surprised much anymore by Irena's erratic behavior. Irena was in love, and she had lived through a difficult childhood. Irena was a crazy person, in Maggie's estimation. But Maggie was thankful. She didn't have the energy to battle the tiny organist that weekend.

∞

Irena toddled from Maggie's office into the sanctuary, then climbed onto her organ bench, trying to set her stack of music down next to her. She missed the bench, and hundreds of sheets of music fell to the floor and scattered around the organ and nearby pews. She put her small hands over her face and let the tears drain from her eyes. There was no way to stop the years of sadness that had been stuffed down and held securely from flooding out. Irena tried to stifle her sobs, unsuccessfully. She cried for her mother. She cried for the years she had to hide who she was when she was a young girl in order to survive in Detroit. She cried for injustices suffered and pain freely aimed her way by strangers, landlords, and customers.

Something about being in the church was changing Irena's frozen, rock-solid heart. Irena, who had fought against God like a caged animal for so many years, played music that meant nothing to her personally and dared anyone to try and get close. The hard chunk of stone in her chest was turning to soft sand and gently blowing away. Maybe it was her Captain Crunch. Maybe somehow, some way, Pastor Maggie hadn't been lying Sunday after Sunday when she said they were all loved.

Irena wiped her eyes and blew her nose several times. Then she gathered up her music and turned the switch of the organ to "on." Irena began to practice for the funeral, for the children who no longer had a mother.

Jesus loves me! This I know,
For the Bible tells me so;
Little ones to him belong;
They are weak, but he is strong.

∞

The Sunday morning after Thanksgiving, Maggie wondered what to expect from the worship service. It was the first Sunday of Advent, everyone had just celebrated Thanksgiving, and they would all come back in twenty-four hours for Cassandra's funeral. Maggie imagined her congregation felt such a mix of feelings, they could not gain any emotional purchase. Their hearts and souls ran amuck. Grief, joy, pain, and thanksgiving roiled and rumbled in the members of Loving the Lord.

As she waited to begin the service, Maggie tried to figure out how to pastor her hurting flock. She was hurting, herself. She waited for a whisper.

Our help is in the name of the Lord, who made heaven and earth.

Maggie picked up her Bible, and her heart, and left her office.

She was surprised to see the sanctuary full as she came through the secret door. There were faces she did not recognize. She guessed these were neighbors and maybe some of Cassandra's medical caregivers over the past few weeks, but she was surprised to see two new families sitting toward the back. One family had a father in a wheelchair, sitting next to Marvin's. Marvin was having a spirited discussion with the visitor. Maggie secretly hoped Marvin wouldn't scare the new family away. The other family looked Hispanic. The mother held a baby, who enthusiastically chewed on some large, plastic baby keys.

Priscilla Sloane was sitting next to a very handsome man Maggie did not recognize. Perhaps her visiting brother? He looked unhappy to be sitting in a pew.

Jennifer and Beth Becker snuck into their pew next to Max Solomon after helping with the coffee time set-up. Jennifer was looking at her bulletin when she felt Beth's sharp elbow jab into her side. She looked with annoyance at her sister.

"What? That hurts," Jennifer whispered.

She looked at Beth and then followed her gaze.

Darcy Keller.

He sat next to Priscilla, six rows ahead.

"Did you know he was here?" Beth whispered to Jennifer.

"No. I had no idea. That must be why Pris had us take her salad to Pastor Maggie's. Why didn't she just tell us?" Jennifer asked quietly.

Beth sighed. "I have no idea. I thought she was feeling sick." She stared at Priscilla and Darcy.

The sisters' focus was brought back to the sanctuary as worship began. Jennifer gave a slight cough, then drew her attention to the Advent wreath.

Max Solomon gazed at the sisters. He looked forward to Sundays when these two friendly, and not unattractive, sisters sat in the last pew with him. They always had a nice visit after church as they nibbled cookies and drank church coffee. It was his favorite part of a lonely week.

Cole, Lynn, Molly, Penny, and Sammy Porter led the service by lighting the first Advent candle in the wreath. Last year, Sammy's arrival had kept the Porter family from carrying out their Advent duties. Maggie had promised they would all be summoned back the following year. She watched the family and was calmed. It was a gentle way to begin worship on that difficult weekend for Loving the Lord.

William and Mary had decided to keep Carrie and Carl home, knowing they would be in church the next day for their mother's funeral. Neither Carrie nor Carl would probably notice it was Sunday, due to the Thanksgiving break from school.

Irena played "O Come, O Come, Emmanuel." The voices of the congregation lifted the words toward heaven. Maggie closed her eyes and listened to Irena's unusually quiet organ. She knew the words of the hymn by heart, words begging for a Savior to come and take away all pain and suffering.

After worship, Maggie drove out to Dancer Road and joined Carrie and Carl in the big kitchen at The Grange. Mary worked at one of the counters, mixing up something that smelled of cinnamon and apples. The children sat at the large kitchen table, coloring in coloring books and making bird feeders out of pinecones, peanut butter, and bird seed. Maggie sat at the table, took one of the extra coloring books, and listened to Carrie and Carl talk about their mother. She carefully took notes in her coloring book without the children realizing. She wanted to hear their own words about their mother and what she had meant to them.

"I think Mommy is feeling better today," Carrie said, picking up a yellow crayon.

"Is she awake?" Carl asked, taking a break from his work of art.

"Of course. It's heaven. Mommy is talking to Daddy and Jesus and probably eating a punkin' spice donut," Carrie said decisively.

"What else is she doing?" Carl asked.

"I don't know. Maybe she's taking care of the stray animals," Carrie said more thoughtfully.

"Like the kitties? Like the mama kitty who died in the stweet?" Carl remembered taking care of the three little orphaned kittens. All three now had homes in Cherish.

"Yes. Mommy is petting her."

Carrie took a drink of milk. Mary had put milk and cookies on the table when Maggie arrived.

"Can you tell me something?" Maggie asked slowly. "What would you two like to have happen at church tomorrow for your mommy's special service?"

Carrie stopped coloring and looked up at Maggie.

"Why are we having a special service when Mommy isn't even here?"

Maggie paused. "It's a way to say goodbye. For now."

"What do you mean?" Carrie asked, confused.

Maggie took a breath. What did she mean? And how could she explain it to these two little souls? "It means . . . it means we will all go to heaven sometime. Then we will see the people we love and who got there before we did."

"When?" Carrie's blue eyes were staring straight into Maggie's.

"It's different for everyone," Maggie said, but she felt spiritually wobbly.

Carrie sighed. She decided to give up on the topic. Pastor Maggie didn't seem to really know all that much about heaven.

"I don't want to say goodbye," Carl said quietly. "I would be sad. Would you, Carwie?"

"Yes. I would too, Carl."

Carrie put her arm around Carl's shoulder, brushing her forearm through a blob of peanut butter, then accidentally wiping it through Carl's hair.

Maggie looked at the two of them and felt another piece of her heart crack off. She steadied her voice and smiled at the two little orphans.

"We won't say goodbye, then. We absolutely will not say goodbye. We'll just do our favorite things at church with our friends. How does that sound?"

"Will there be cookies?" Carrie asked. "From The Sugarplum?"

"Of course. We always have cookies from The Sugarplum," Maggie said, trying to wipe some of the peanut butter off Carrie's arm and Carl's head with a napkin.

"Would it be all right if we sing some songs?" Carrie asked as she picked up a purple crayon and continued coloring in her book, spreading peanut butter on Mary's table.

"Yes, we will sing some of the songs Mrs. Wiggins has taught you in Sunday school."

"Okay. We'll come," Carrie said, glancing at Carl, who nodded somberly.

"Great. I will be happy to see you in the morning, my darlings."

Maggie stood up and kissed each child on the head, receiving a gift of peanut butter on her lips from Carl's hair.

"I love you," Maggie said.

Carrie got up from the table and threw her small arms around Maggie's waist.

"We love you too, Pastor Maggie."

Carl joined in the group hug.

"Can we bring Black and Blue?" Carl whispered.

The two canines were blissfully snoring under the table.

"Absolutely. I'm sure Mary and William will be happy to bring them along tomorrow."

Maggie looked up at Mary, who nodded wordlessly. Maggie took her coloring book, and Mary walked her out to the porch.

"What time should we be at church?" Mary asked, wiping her hands on a towel then throwing the towel over her shoulder.

"How about ten fifteen? Everyone else will arrive a little before ten o'clock. I would like a chance to remind people of the tenor of this service. Cassandra wanted it to be uplifting for the children's sake. Do you mind bringing the dogs?" Maggie thought of Black and Blue back in church so soon since they were part of the animal blessing service.

"We would bring every animal on this farm if that's what Carrie and Carl wanted," Mary said.

"Please don't offer. God bless you, Mary. I'll see you in the morning."

Maggie drove home, sticky with peanut butter on her upper lip and around her waist. She didn't notice.

Cassandra's funeral went exactly as she herself had planned.

Maggie stood on the altar and saw the church, once again, full of people. There were people lined up along the back of the sanctuary. They even stood in the gathering area. It was standing room only.

Our help is in the name of the Lord, who made heaven and earth. Maggie silently breathed in the foundational words. Then Maggie spoke with a clear, strong voice.

"Good morning. Just a reminder as we prepare for this service, we are gathered here to remember Cassandra Moffet, but more importantly, we are gathered here to surround her children with support, kindness, and familial love. Cassandra requested that you wear bright colors."

Everyone had shown up in colorful clothing.

"Cassandra also asked that no tears be shed in front of her children. This may be harder to manage, but let's do our best."

Her voice became a little less strong when she said, "The children do not want to say goodbye to their mother. They want to sing songs and eat cookies. And they are bringing their dogs."

Everyone seemed to understand, even if they didn't necessarily agree. After all, funerals were meant to be sad. It was a time of good-byes. Shouldn't the funeral be devastating, with or without pets?

Just as Maggie finished her instructions, William, Mary, Carrie, Carl, Black, and Blue entered the sanctuary. Carl wore a little blue and white seersucker suit. Carrie was resplendent in a gold and silver tutu, golden rhinestone ballet slippers, and a royal-blue crown studded with what looked like sapphires.

The congregation was too quiet.

It was as if everyone had ceased to breathe.

The children looked around in confusion.

"Hello, Carrie and Carl," Marla said.

She had been sitting in the second pew with Addie and the other children. She walked up the aisle to the family.

Molly, Penny, and even little Sammy Porter ran, although Sammy toddled, to Carrie and Carl. Hannah Benson was also there in a flash. Kay and Shawn Kessler went over to the little group, prompted by their parents.

"I'm sorry about your mommy," Molly said to Carrie.

"But I'm glad you brought Black and Blue," Shawn said, petting the dogs, who were unaware they were in the midst of a tragic moment.

The dogs began to lick the children, and Blue's tail knocked Sammy over on his bottom. Penny picked him up, then almost dropped him. Kay caught him, set him back on his feet, and then gave Carrie and Carl hugs.

"I love your tutu, Carrie."

Carrie smiled.

"And Carl, your suit makes you look like a grown-up," Kay continued.

Marla and Addie each took a turn hugging Carrie and Carl, then herded the entire bunch to the front of the church. Maggie sat down on the top step of the altar.

"Would you all mind sitting here with me?"

The children ran to Maggie, along with the dogs.

From their pews, the congregation watched as the children hurled themselves up the steps and on top of Maggie. The dogs began barking and writhing with all the excitement. William and Mary sat in the front pew, while Marla and Addie pried the children off Maggie and tried to make the dogs sit still. It was crazy chaos, but even Verna Baker couldn't come up with a criticism. It was all she could do not to burst into wailing tears, which she had never done in her entire life.

Maggie opened her Bible and read the first eighteen verses of Psalm 139. The congregation barely held themselves together as Maggie finished.

"I come to the end—I am still with you."

The children whispered and giggled and didn't listen to a single word.

With a nod from Maggie, Irena, who was dressed in neon orange from head to toe, began playing the organ. The children stayed seated on the steps and sang every Sunday school song they had been taught by Mrs. Wiggins. They did the hand motions to "Deep and Wide" and broke into fits of giggles when their arms collided with one another on the word "wide." Each song got louder and louder. The congregation began to clap along with each new number, and the children rose to the excitement. When Marla finally directed them to sing "He's Got the Whole World in His Hands," the children stood up and began to dance as they named all who were held in God's great, good hands.

> He's got you and me brother . . .
> He's got you and me sister . . .
> He's got Loving the Lord Church . . .
> He's got the little bitty baby . . .
> He's got the whole world in His hands!

At the very end, when Marla finished directing the song and the children began to sit back down. Carrie stayed standing. Her small voice rang out.

> He's got my pretty,
> pretty mama, in His hands.
> He's got my pretty,
> pretty mama, in His hands.
> He's got my pretty,
> pretty mama, in His hands.
> He's got the whole world in His hands.

The silence was absolute.

Carrie looked around. Then she turned to Maggie, who pulled the little girl onto her lap in an embrace. Carrie wriggled away.

"Pastor Maggie, can we eat cookies now?"

24

January 8, 2016
Bawjiase, Ghana

Maggie followed Joy to Market, lost in thought over Cassandra's funeral. She realized that Cassandra's funeral was more like a Ghanaian funeral than not. Cassandra's funeral was sloppy and chaotic, full of emotions ranging from joy to despair to hope to thanksgiving. There was singing and even dancing from the children. There was celebratory food. There wasn't any wailing, and the parishioners stealthily hid their tears, as they had been directed to, but it barely resembled any funeral that had been attended by the good people of Cherish, before or after. Cassandra had the chance to plan her funeral to protect her children and to take the sting out of death.

If everyone had the opportunity to plan their own funeral, would they? What about the people who were so afraid of death they were unable to begin the discussion? Maggie thought, when she got back to Cherish, she would offer a class for anyone who wanted to talk about life, death, and eternal life. She would emphasize the good sense of planning their own funeral. It certainly would make it easier on the family—and selfishly, easier on Pastor Maggie herself. No one wanted to watch a family squabble about how to bury their mother.

Maggie's thoughts wandered back even further to the funeral of Katharine Smits—a woman who was also loved well, like Cassandra. And she also left a child behind.

But earlier in the fall, Maggie had been ask to officiate a funeral for a man named Abe Jones. She had never met the man, but had been contacted by Cole Porter and asked to officiate the funeral. Abe had one daughter, Melissa, who Maggie discovered despised the father who had abandoned her. As it turned out, there was no funeral at all. Irena had saved the day. She had read the situation and encouraged Melissa to share her hatred and then move toward the possibility of forgiveness. Cole had the body buried with no one in attendance.

Maggie wondered what it would be like to get to the end of life and not have one single person show up at the funeral. She almost walked right into Ethan as Joy stopped at one of the Market stalls. That jolted her back to the present.

Joy quickly spoke in Twi to the owner of the stall. The owner and her sons dragged bags of rice and beans from the back of a small brick attachment. Thirty pound bags of rice and beans were stacked up in front of the Americans.

"How will we get this back to United Hearts?" Ethan asked Joy.

"I've already ordered a taxi to meet us here. It's the only way to get the amount of food we will buy back to United Hearts." Joy was all business.

Maggie watched Joy, but then looked at her surroundings. Stall after stall was set up with canned goods, fresh and dried Ghana red pepper, cooking oil, clothing, homemade soaps, meat, which was sitting in the sun and covered in flies, school supplies, fresh pineapple and watermelon, yams, cassava, oats, colorful squares of fabric, and a plethora of other goods. Each stall was run by women. Some of the women had babies wrapped on their backs as they sold their wares. They were laughing and talking to each other in Twi. Some of them seemed to be arguing. Small children, too young or poor for school, were chasing each other around in and out of the stalls. Older children, who were out of school, helped their mothers. There were speakers set up, and Ghanaian music played loudly. It felt like a city festival. Maggie was reminded of being at the Bazaar in the Old City of Jerusalem when she lived there after college.

She breathed deeply and smelled the spiciness of the red pepper, the familiar smell of the red dirt, baskets of fresh tomatoes, sliced pineapple, and the occasional wafts of burning trash and excrement. These smells were becoming less offensive and more normal to Maggie's nose.

The women in the stalls took notice of Ethan right away. They did not hide their pleasure in seeing an obroni man. They looked at him, then at each other, and raised their eyebrows, smiling. Then began a torrent in Twi with what must have been their version of wolf whistles.

"They like you," Joy said to Ethan. "They think you are very handsome, and they wonder if you are married."

Ethan was quite happy about that bit of information. His five-foot-eight-inch frame, full beard, and paunchy tummy had never garnered him many compliments. He had always been the smart one, never the handsome one.

"Well, now," Ethan said, smiling, "I'll have to tell Charlene she's got some competition. Can we come back to Market on Tuesday?"

The women seemed to swoon as he spoke.

Ethan smiled and began to pick up items from several different tables around him.

"Do we need those things?" Maggie asked.

"I don't know. I'm just trying to help the local economy," Ethan said, smiling at the women.

Maggie playfully punched him in the arm. The women did not like that and began pointing at Maggie and speaking angrily.

"They aren't happy that you hit this fine specimen of a man," Joy said. She immediately said something to the women to settle them down.

"What did you say?" Ethan asked.

"I told them Maggie was your sister. She's allowed to hit you, and now she's not a threat to them. You're available," Joy said as she picked up several cans of tomato paste. "Would you please grab about ten baggies of that dried red pepper?"

"I can't wait to tell Charlene," Ethan said again, smiling at the woman with the red pepper on her table.

Joy also took Maggie and Ethan to the pharmacy. There were no doctor prescriptions necessary. All antibiotics, anti-malarial tablets, pain relievers, bandages, and other medical supplies were set up in one of the small shops near the stalls, and Joy purchased what they needed.

"I had no idea medicine was so readily available," Maggie said, "and so inexpensive."

"Ghana's National Health is one of the best on the continent. Getting medicine to remote villages like Bawjiase is a real blessing."

After they completed many purchases and loaded the items into large canvas tote bags Joy had brought with them, the trio walked back to the first stall. The pre-ordered taxi was parked next to the stall with the rice and beans, and the trunk was loaded with bag after bag of rice, beans, and large plastic containers of cooking oil. They sardined themselves into the car, surrounded by their many purchases. The taxi ride to United Hearts was bumpy and painful. As the taxi lurched over and through potholes and rocks, Maggie and Ethan bashed into one another. Joy sat in the front seat and hung onto the door handle for dear life, clutching her canvas bag with all her might. They drove past the funeral, which was still in full swing. Maggie watched out the window until they had passed by.

When the journey finally ended, Maggie felt relief as all the big boys came from the direction of the school-yet-to-be and unloaded the car. The bags and other containers of food were brought to the indoor kitchen of United Hearts. Marta laughed happily as she organized all the good food for the residents of United Hearts. Maggie's heart soared, knowing that the money the church had raised would feed those dear ones for months to come.

Jack, Charlene, and Ellen brought their small charges home from the clinic. It had been quite harrowing as soon as the children realized they were going to the clinic for a needle in each arm. Even with promises of ice cream, a rare treat, the children still threw themselves into hysterics once they got close to the clinic. Keeping all twelve of them moving was a challenge.

The clinic was packed with new moms holding their babies—the mothers, once again, dressed in their finest clothes.

"We'll be here all day," Ellen muttered to Charlene. "How will we ever keep the children calm for such a long wait?"

The children cried, some began to scream, and Ellen had to bring the loudest screamers back outside to calm down. Jack looked around and felt the desperation of having to sit there for several hours. A light tap on his shoulder brought him face to face with Dr. Obodai.

"Good morning, Dr. Elliot and Dr. Kessler. It is a pleasure to see you today." Dr. Obodai smiled and patted little Dougie on the head. Dougie clung to Jack's arm.

"Good morning, Dr. Obodai," said Jack. "We're here with the youngest members of United Hearts for their updated vaccinations. Is there any way to expedite this process? I realize you have many patients waiting."

"I have an idea," Dr. Obodai said.

Jack, Charlene, Ellen, and twelve crying children followed Dr. Obodai to the small room where the CBC machine had been set up.

"I will have one of the nurses bring in the vaccines. I expect you all know how to administer the needle," Dr. Obodai said.

"Yes, we do," Jack said, "but I suspect Ellen will be the best. Nurses get stuck, so to speak, with giving vaccinations in the U.S. We doctors get out of the room as fast as we can."

"That's very true, Dr. Obodai. They are quite useless when it comes to making children cry," Ellen added.

"Well, my nurse will have the proper dosages of the DTP and MMR vaccines, also polio drops. If you can help her administer these things to the children, you'll be out of here quickly."

Dr. Obodai left the room, and the children whimpered and huddled together, awaiting their torture.

When the nurse entered, she carried a large tray with syringes and the needed medicines. She looked at each child's National Health card and filled syringes. Then she called the name of a child and handed a syringe to Ellen. Both nurses gave the injections, double-teaming the children. Jack and Charlene held the children and distributed the polio drops into opened mouths. There were wild yelps and dramatic screeches from some of the little ones, but most were busy swallowing their drops after being poked. It worked perfectly until Dougie threw up his polio drops. He cried so hard, his nose and eyes created small streams of tears and goo down his sweet face.

"It's all right, Dougie."

Charlene turned the little boy away from the other children, who all watched with fascination. It was fun to watch someone else get jabbed. Vomiting was just an added bonus. Charlene cuddled the inconsolable Dougie and cleaned his face. He had received his shots from Ellen but still needed to redo his drops. He was having none of it.

"Dougie," Charlene whispered in the crying boy's ear. "Dougie, what kind of ice cream do you want from town? Chocolate? Banana? Pineapple?"

Dougie tried as hard as he could to keep up his hysterics, but the thought of ice cream deflated some of his determination. Charlene wiped his nose and eyes, then gave him another squeeze.

"Ice cream sounds so good! I think I will have pineapple," Charlene said as she licked her lips.

Dougie tried to get down from her lap. Yes, ice cream sounded very good. He was ready to go.

"Wait," Charlene said. "You need to have these little yummy drops first."

Dougie began to relodge his complaint with a loud yell. As soon as his mouth was open, Ellen swooped in and quickly deposited the drops as far down his throat as she could.

Dougie swallowed them without even knowing it. Another outrage.

"Good job, everyone! Let's get some ice cream!" Jack said loudly as he took back the cards from the nurse with a smile.

Dougie swallowed his pride along with the drops. He grasped Charlene's hand, stuck his tongue out at Ellen, and followed everyone out of the little room, out of the clinic, and back onto the street.

Jack stopped Dr. Obodai in front of the clinic.

"Thank you for helping us get through the vaccinations. We really appreciate it."

"You are welcome." Dr. Obodai smiled, then made his way to the room with the gurneys.

Jack went out of the clinic and picked up the two smallest children. It was another quarter of a mile to the main road of Bawjiase and the ice cream vendor. Then the long walk back to United Hearts.

As they walked toward the ice cream stand, Jack pondered the differences in medicine in that country and his own. A lot was taken for granted in the United States. Dr. Obodai treated diseases Jack had never seen before. He didn't seem to complain and worked long hours every day in his clinic. Dr. Obodai had few of the necessities to help him with his doctoring, but he made do. He was thankful for what he did have. He had a true doctor's heart.

Jack loved being a doctor. He loved seeing his patients and treating medical ailments. But he was surrounded by a staff who did whatever he told them to do. He had cutting-edge information about the latest treatments. He could order tests to be done. Immediately. He could send his more serious patients to specialists. Jack and Charlene both worked in an immaculate environment and could create a schedule that gave them a life outside of their offices. They could also turn away patients who didn't have insurance or who were on Medicare, though they never did.

But Jack knew some of his colleagues chose to see only patients with insurance. Some doctors had more of a heart for money than a heart for their patients. They misused their staff, took days off without warning, and suffered a "God Complex." What would those doctors do in a place like Bawjiase? Would they still want to be doctors?

Jack determined that skill, humbleness, and hope were the tools Dr. Obodai brought to work every day. He cared for his clinic full of patients until the last one walked out the door at night.

Somehow, that sounded very satisfying to Jack.

∞

Earlier, before leaving for the clinic, Ellen had given Cate, Bryan, Lacey, and Addie the task of updating the older children's health cards, while she, Charlene, and Jack took the younger children to the clinic.

With no children to play with, the four adults sat down to the task. Cate began adding to Ellen's chart with birthdates, immunization records, and dates to renew the cards. The other three read off the information, then placed the cards in one of two files: "Up To Date" or "Renew." It was a laborious task to do everything by hand.

"I can't read some of the writing of whoever did this last," Cate said. "If we can't read the date, how do we know if the immunizations need to be renewed or not?"

They all took turns trying to figure out the dates of the last immunizations. The room was getting hotter, with little breeze making its way through the small windows.

"So, Lacey, what is your secret plan for the kids today?" Bryan asked as he tried to decipher another card.

"None of your business."

Lacey had brought a zipped carry-on bag with her from the volunteer house and hidden it in a corner behind a small table in the front room of United Hearts.

"It's sort of my business," Bryan said, disgruntled.

He was second in command for the project and still stinging from the argument he and Maggie had earlier. He didn't like feeling that they weren't on the same page. But Maggie didn't understand that she couldn't control the happenings of these two weeks. She just didn't get it. He would try to help her understand what being in a different culture meant, but she wasn't making it easy.

"It's a surprise for when the children all get home. You just have to wait."

Lacey read the name and dates off a card for Cate to add to the medical chart.

"I'm sure it's going to be fun," Addie said, then read off her card information.

"Well, there are some things that might not go over so well, you know, culturally." Bryan was trying to regain a little control. "It would probably be good to run it by me first."

"I'll take my chances, boy-wonder. I heard Maggie call you that once."

Lacey read off more information for Cate.

Cate wrote it down, but she could sense Bryan wasn't happy. Lacey was being playful, but Bryan's ego wasn't playing. Bryan was just about to remind Lacey one more time that he was in charge when they heard a car pulling up near United Hearts. They also heard the big boys laugh and run toward the car. Bryan went out the door.

The taxi had arrived from Market with food, Joy, Ethan . . .

And Maggie.

As soon as the taxi left, everyone could hear Jack, Charlene, and Ellen returning with their charges—tummies full of ice cream.

Addie and Cate ran out of United Hearts to gather as many children as they could hold and hear about their horrifying morning with the needles.

Maggie was still in the kitchen with Marta and Joy, helping to put food away or at least stack it neatly against the wall. When she heard the children, she looked out the window and saw little faces with traces of ice cream and huge smiles. She piled one more bag of rice on top of the others, then went out to the group. When she saw Jack, she felt a pang in her heart and realized she missed him. They had been do-ing different things during that first week, and even when they were together with nothing to do, they were with the other members of the mission trip. She wanted to take his hand and walk down the red dirt road away from everyone.

Maggie went up to Jack and gave him a kiss. "I'm so glad to see you," she whispered in his ear.

Jack surprised her by picking her up and swinging her around. The children squealed, watching Maggie fly around in a circle.

Joy walked out to the crowd. As she did so, Sylvia, Bill, Dana, and Nana all came down the road from the farm. They looked hot and sweaty, and Dana looked annoyed.

"Well, the gang's all here," Ethan said.

Everyone began talking at once until Joy gave a loud whistle.

"We've all got stories to share. Why don't we adults head back to the volunteer house for lunch. Then we will come back here for the afternoon." Joy looked at Marta for approval.

Marta smiled and waved them away, then yelled to the retreating adults, "Thank you for this food. God bless you."

Joy and Bryan waved. Joy said something in Twi, which made Marta laugh.

"What did you say?" Maggie asked.

"I just told her I hoped it would be enough food for dinner tonight."

Joy led the adults down the road. Everyone walked rather slowly after the hot, busy morning. Fifi had made them groundnut soup with a large rice ball in the center of the bowl. There was a platter of sliced pineapple in the middle of the table. Everyone grabbed two baggies of pure water, tore a corner off with their teeth, and drank thirstily.

"Let's sit down and eat," Joy directed. "I'd like to hear about your mornings." She looked at Fifi. "This looks wonderful, Fifi. Thank you again for feeding us."

Everyone else chimed in with their thanks.

Looking at her bowl of groundnut soup, Cate tried to control her face, but Bryan caught her.

"I think you might like it," Bryan said. "It's a little spicy, but the rice tempers the pepper."

After Maggie prayed for the meal, everyone began slurping.

"Hey, Megs," Bryan said as Cate wiped soup from his chin, "can we go for a walk after lunch?"

All Maggie wanted to do was to talk to Jack about her spiritual awakening, her argument with Bryan, the sensations of being at Market, and her doubts about coming on the mission trip. She didn't know if she was ready to deal with Bryan yet.

"Sure," she said unenthusiastically.

25

December 1, 2015
Cherish, Michigan

The day after Cassandra's funeral, Harold Brinkmeyer's law office was full. His assistant readied the conference room with plenty of chairs for the large table and several bottles of water. Harold sat at the end of the table with a small stack of legal papers.

William and Mary Ellington sat together across the table from Harold. Marla Wiggins sat next to Mary. Pamela Arthur sat next to William. Maggie and Jack were next to Harold, and Julia Benson sat alone across from Maggie.

Maggie looked at each face with curiosity. It seemed like an odd little grouping.

"Good morning," Harold said. He smiled and at once put everyone at ease.

"Thank you for coming this morning. I realize we have all been through an emotional time with Cassandra's death and the funeral yesterday, but I have asked you here because it is what Cassandra ordered me to do." Harold chuckled lightly. "She had some very specific ideas about everything in her life. And her death. She wanted this taken care of the day after her funeral."

Maggie nodded. She remembered back to the day she and Cassandra had planned the funeral—or the day *Cassandra* planned her funeral and Maggie jotted down notes. That was the same day she had seen Harold at The Grange, also calling on Cassandra. Maggie had wondered what Harold was doing there at the time. Perhaps, now she would know.

"I want to make this easy," Harold continued. "No one likes to listen to legalese, except lawyers." He chuckled again and then formally said, "On this day, Tuesday, December first, twenty-fifteen, I, Harold Brink-meyer, the executor of these trusts, will share the wishes of Cassandra D. Moffet." He took a deep breath. "Cassandra had a great deal of money and assets to consider before she died. When Cal was killed, he had a large life insurance policy. Because he was a military veteran, she received money from the government for herself and her children. There was also a payment from a car insurance policy." Harold coughed.

It had been William and Mary's car insurance policy. Both William and Mary cringed when Harold mentioned Cal's name. They had also received life insurance money when their son Michael's car had crashed into Cal's, killing both men. It was the worst check they had ever accepted. Dark money.

Harold continued. "She developed a very specific plan of how to distribute her assets and money. I am implementing her plan through the development of trusts and distribution of monies today. Here are her decisions."

Harold opened an envelope, pulled out a letter, unfolded it, and read:

> Dear friends gathered around the table,
> I guess I am speaking to you from the dead, but at the time of this writing, I am very much alive and my brain is working just fine. Harold has all the legal documents in order. I wanted to tell you in my own words what I wish to have done with my money and property. I'd appreciate it if you didn't blab this stuff around town. Some of my wishes will cause others to take notice. One of my wishes, in particular, will need to be made public. But please be discreet.

Carrie and Carl have trust funds of $250,000 set up in each of their names. The money will be for their use when they reach the age of twenty-five. I expect Mary and William to teach them about responsible money management before they get their hands on their trusts. Ha! Thank you.

Also, to you, William and Mary, there is a trust of $500,000 meant for you to raise my children and also make your lives comfortable. We have already talked about what I would like you to teach my children and the experiences I would like them to have. Again, thank you. Harold is the executor of all three trusts.

Pamela, what can one say to a friend who held the trash can every time I puked? More than anyone, you never treated me like I was sick. You joked around with me. You brought me food I shouldn't have eaten every time I asked. You washed me, cried with me, stayed with me into the darkest nights. You were my angel. Angels probably don't need money, so do what you wish with $50,000. It would buy a lot of Kentucky Fried Chicken!

Pamela's eyes filled with tears, which seemed to be contagious to everyone else at the table, except Harold, who had no choice but to remain professional and continue reading.

Pastor Maggie, I know you did a beautiful job with my funeral yesterday.

Maggie shuddered. It was surreal to hear Cassandra's words. She reached up and fingered the gold cross around her neck.

You and Dr. Jack have done a great deal for me and my children. I am grateful they will be raised in Loving the Lord Church and have contact with you regularly.

232

Harold has a check for $150,000 made out to Loving the Lord. I don't want people fighting over what to do with it. That would just piss me off. So, my wish is that Loving the Lord will open up some kind of day care center. A FREE center for children under school age. I want part of the money to go into a trust for a director's salary (Harold's work to do). My hope is that Marla Wiggins will run the center. I realize this request can't remain a secret. But it is my wish, and my money will pay for it. Don't let any old biddies or cranks in the church keep it from happening.

Maggie had a fleeting thought. Opening a day care center at church would mean the building inspector, Fitch Dervish, would be called in again to assess the church's capacity to have such a center. Fitch had caused the church nothing but trouble when Maggie first arrived and the handicapped ramp had to be replaced. Fitch had returned to town after a few months away—blissful months. Now he'd be in the thick of things at Loving the Lord once again. Maggie sighed, then noticed Jack staring at her. She shook the thought of Fitch away. For now.

Marla was still recovering from the shock of the day care news when she heard her name again.

Marla, you did more for me and my children than I can ever thank you for. I'm sorry my secrecy about being ill put such a burden on you and your family. Harold will hand you a check from my trust for $50,000. Go get a massage or something.

Marla smiled, then tried to stifle a sob. She covered her face with her hands, her breaths ragged. Mary put her arm around Marla's shoulder.

Julia Benson. Hello.

233

Julia jumped. It was creeping her out. She began pressing the finger-nails of her left hand into her right until they made deep, red marks. Maggie instinctively got up, walked over to Julia's side of the table, sat down, and took hold of Julia's marked hand.

> Harold has been so helpful to me. He told me how to make these trusts. He helped me sign documents to make sure all things could happen on this day for the people I have grown to love. And so, I have signed the necessary documents to transfer my home on Freer Road to you, Julia, without encumbrance. Harold will explain all that. The house is yours today. You and Hannah can move in whenever you wish. You will also receive a check for $50,000 for new paint, furni-ture, carpet, anything. The only thing I ask is that you will have Carrie and Carl over for sleepovers once in a while. I think they would like that. You will make happy memories in that house, and I am grateful.

Julia sat, frozen, not really processing what Harold had just read.

> Harold will do the rest of the business. He's been great, and don't worry, he's been paid.

Harold cleared his throat and smiled.

> Thank you all for what you have done, and will do, for my family. I will leave this world relieved to know this letter will be read to you.
> Cassandra Darlene Moffet
> November 2, 2015

Harold folded the letter and placed it back in the envelope. Then he stared down at the rest of the papers in front of him. He couldn't look up quite yet. He finally took a deep breath and looked into the faces and emotions flowing around the table. He, William, and Mary were the only three people at the table not completely staggered by the letter. Cassandra had made her wishes known to the three of them, but to no one else.

"Cassandra had this all figured out," Harold said quietly. "She told me what she wanted, and that she wanted it to be immediate. So I have these checks prepared for you."

He stood up and walked around the table, passing out the checks like a teacher passing back homework assignments. He stopped next to Julia with a large envelope.

"Julia, this is the deed to your new home. Cassandra was most excited about this decision. I hope you and Hannah will feel settled and happy there."

Harold handed Julia the envelope, and she looked up at him.

"Who does this?" she asked, her voice raspy. She seemed to be in shock. "Who does this kind of thing? Who just gives a house away? Who writes checks for fifty thousand dollars or one hundred fifty thousand dollars?" She was beginning to talk faster, a little out of control. "Who does this??"

Maggie slipped her arm around Julia's shoulder, and Harold sat down on the other side of her.

"Julia," Harold said gently, "this has come as a shock to you. It's crazy. It doesn't make any sense. Your questions are legitimate. Not many people do this. But Cassandra was very clear about what she wanted done with her money and home."

"I thought William and Mary were insane to let me stay at The Grange when I couldn't even pay. I had never been given that kind of a break before." Julia looked up at William and Mary, who nodded back.

"I'm sorry that's the case," Harold said. "Now you've been given another break. I hope you can accept it, and enjoy it. That's what Cassandra hoped for too."

The small group remained for another half-hour as Harold patiently answered questions and reassured everyone that there were no mistakes. The mix of emotions kept flowing.

"How do we go about opening a child care center?" Maggie asked. She was taking Cassandra's wish seriously and, in true Maggie style, was ready to go buy toys for the grand opening, which should probably be tomorrow.

"It will be a process," Harold admitted. "The city will need to be involved. We'll need to see if our old church can be approved, but we don't need to figure this all out today. It should be on the next agenda for the council meeting."

Harold truly wondered if that one wish of Cassandra's would be possible. There were legal issues and licensing involved, not just determination to make it happen, but he knew he would help where he could.

"Thank you, Harold, for all you have done." Marla's quiet voice rose across the table. "I know this news has shocked me. To be honest, I don't want Cassandra's money. Is there another use for it? Something for Carrie and Carl?"

"Cassandra said you might be one who would refuse her wish," Harold said. "I don't recommend you do that. She said she would come back and haunt you." Harold smiled, then laughed. "She was a very different kind of woman. I'm personally glad I got to know her. She was thankful for the way you loved Carrie and Carl when she was trying to accept the fact that she was dying. Please keep the check."

Pamela was ready to join Marla in the refusal of the check. She opened her mouth to speak, but Harold cut her off.

"And you, Pamela. Cassandra thought you might be another."

Pamela closed her mouth.

"Julia, if you would like, I can take you over to your new home," Harold said.

"Mary, William," Julia's voice sounded small, like a child, "will you come along too?"

Mary and William both nodded.

"We are happy for you, Julia, and for Hannah," Mary said. "We have some extra furniture in our attic. If there is anything you would like, we'll get it moved for you."

For a few more moments, everyone around the table sat in silence to absorb the enormity of what Cassandra had done. She had changed their lives through her death. The people and the projects she was investing in would assure Cassandra lived on for her children, for Loving the Lord, and for Cherish.

After saying goodbye and leaving Harold's office, Maggie looked up at Jack.

"I'll see you at home later," she said.

"How about a date?" he asked. "Let's go to Ann Arbor tonight, find a quiet corner in our Italian restaurant, and just sit."

Maggie took a deep breath. "That sounds perfect. Just the two of us for a whole evening."

She was emotionally exhausted. She could feel her body refusing to move. Her brain was shutting down, and she felt foggy. The last week had taken its toll, and that morning in Harold's office had depleted the last drops of energy.

"I'll pick you up at six." He kissed her before heading back to his office.

Maggie walked slowly around the corner from Harold's office and down Main Street. She wanted to clear her head just a little bit. She turned down Middle Street and climbed the steps to the sanctuary doors. She heard Irena playing what could only be something from *Manger Baby*.

Before she opened the door, she could smell onions frying. The soup committee. It was Tuesday, but of course, they couldn't have made soup yesterday, on their regular day. They were all at Cassandra's funeral.

As Maggie entered the church, she saw several people bustling around the music-filled sanctuary. Hank, Doris, Chester, Verna, Howard, and Winston were opening boxes and taking out fake greens, the large Nativity set, and Christmas tree decorations.

In all the distraction of Cassandra's death, Thanksgiving, and preparation for the funeral, Loving the Lord Church members had forgotten to hang the greens on the Saturday after Thanksgiving in order to be decorated for the first Sunday of Advent. Doris only thought of the Advent wreath ten minutes before worship the past Sunday. So, the "Greening of the Church" had commenced a little later than years past.

Maggie looked in bewilderment as her brain was only working on one cylinder.

"Good morning, Pastor Maggie."

Maggie looked toward the basement stairs. Bill and Sylvia carried a fake Christmas tree into the gathering area.

"Here's the mitten tree," Sylvia continued.

The mitten tree was set up without decoration. As the season of Advent continued, donated hats, scarves, and mittens would slowly fill every branch. These needed items were then taken to Grace in Action.

"I completely forgot about the greening of the church," Maggie said softly.

"We all did." Verna Baker walked over to Maggie. "This hasn't been a typical start to the holidays, has it Pastor Maggie?"

Verna did something very un-Verna-like and placed a long, bony hand on Maggie's shoulder.

"No. I guess it hasn't."

The organ music paused.

"Pastoor Maggie," Irena screeched, "you leesten to dis! I em playing *Manger Baby.*"

Irena dove back into her music.

Maggie wondered if there would be any singers for the fiasco. The choir at Loving the Lord was at best hit and miss. With Irena as the director, more people left the choir than joined. Maggie had seen different configurations over the last year and a half. Sylvia, Marla, Ellen, Jennifer, Beth, Hank, Winston, William, and Howard had all given choir practice a try. Irena had successfully dispatched them all with her biting remarks and harsh criticisms. The past Sunday, Addie and Charlene made the choir into a duet.

Bill and Sylvia put the mitten tree in its stand, then walked over to Maggie and Verna.

"We're catching up on soup today too," Sylvia said cheerfully. "It's good to see you, Pastor Maggie. What a week you have had. I don't know how you're standing. Bill and I want you to know how much we enjoyed Thanksgiving dinner at the parsonage. You and Jack made us thankful for being part of such a loving church family."

"We really are, aren't we?" Maggie said. "We're good for each other's souls in this place."

"You betcha," Sylvia said. "How do you like the decorations so far?"

Maggie looked around the church and watched the transformation. Wreaths were hung, candles were placed carefully in the windows, the nativity set was joyfully celebrating the baby Jesus, and the large Christmas tree was covered with handmade Chrismons and white twinkle lights next to the pulpit. Hank, Doris, Chester, Winston, and Howard were unpacking a few more boxes with the outdoor decorations.

"I think," Maggie said slowly, "I think we are on holy ground."

"We certainly are," Verna snapped. "This is God's sanctuary. It can't be anything but holy. Now I think it's time to check the soup. Will you have some lunch with us, Pastor Maggie?"

"Yes, please," Maggie said and let Verna lead her to the basement.

After soup and conversation, Maggie felt revived from some of the heaviness of the past week. She knew she had a visit to make and decided to put it off no longer. She wrapped up in her coat, scarf, and mittens and walked toward Main Street, passing many familiar businesses decorated for Christmas. She took a deep breath of the crisp air, then opened the door of Pretty, Pretty Petals Flower Shop.

Skylar was on a small ladder, hanging twinkle lights around the windows of her shop. Her long legs and arms teetered slightly as she draped the string of small lights. Maggie thought she had never seen anyone so beautiful.

"Hi, Sky," Maggie said.

Sky looked down with a bend of her swan-like neck.

"Oh! Pastor Maggie . . . you'll never believe who was just . . . mmm . . . well, no." Sky stepped gracefully from her ladder.

Maggie was still getting used to Sky's inability to finish most of her sentences. She decided to soldier on.

"Sky, I was wondering if you were busy or if maybe you had a few minutes to chat?" Maggie asked awkwardly.

"Oh . . . I have time to chat. Yes, always to chat." Sky smiled.

She led Maggie to a room behind the counter stocked with large glass-fronted refrigerators full of beautiful flowers, a long table covered with colored tissue paper, ribbon, scissors, and underneath, rows of different sized vases. There were also two chairs tucked back in the corner with a small round table set between. It was covered with half-filled coffee cups and granola bar wrappers. The room smelled glorious.

"So this is where all the miracles happen," Maggie said with a chuckle. "It smells like heaven in here. I always say that about The Sugarplum too, but this might be more heavenly."

"Thank you. It's all Sylvia's doing . . . mmm . . . She grows every flower I sell." Sky smiled as she absently gathered the trash from the round table and threw it into a bin of flower stems and bits of ribbon. "Please, sit down."

Maggie sat. Sky stared at her guest. Maggie looked at Sky and couldn't speak. Why had she thought it would be so easy?

"How can I help you?" Sky asked, her gray eyes wide.

"Uhh . . . I was wondering . . . umm . . ." *Good grief! I sound like Sky!* Maggie took a breath. "Sky, I was wondering if I . . . if I could ask you something," Maggie stammered.

Sky nodded her head.

"It's just that I overheard part of a conversation at Thanksgiving dinner . . . and I was curious . . ." Maggie felt completely inept.

"Was it about hunting?" Sky had no problem with her words.

"Well, yes. You . . . sounded so . . . intense. I didn't know where that came from, and I realized I don't know much about you at all," Maggie finished.

Sky stared at Maggie, unblinking.

"I have a story. Like everyone else," Sky said, now sounding desolate.

Maggie wished she hadn't brought up the subject. Somehow, it felt too intimate. She wanted to run out the door and back to her cozy office at church.

Sky stood up, went to the long table, and began to fold the delicate pieces of tissue paper with her slender fingers.

"I . . . lost a loved one . . . to gun violence. That's . . . mmm . . . the story that belongs to me." Sky blankly stared at a piece of tissue paper.

Maggie sighed. "Sky, I'm so sorry."

Sky turned and looked at Maggie. "Yes. I am also sorry. I didn't want this story." Sky sat back down and looked at Maggie. "No one but my parents know this story. I've never told Sylvia or anyone. Do you . . . mmm . . . do you understand?"

"I'll never share your story, Sky. And you don't even have to tell me. I do not need to know." Suddenly, Maggie didn't want to know.

Sky sighed and sat back in her chair. "I was married once. Yes . . . to a wonderful man. We . . . mmm . . . we eloped when I lived in Traverse City. I had left Cherish when I was young to, uh, 'find myself,'" Sky looked wistful, "but he . . . he found me first. After we married, we settled in Traverse City. He ran hotels. I worked in a marketing department for the city."

Sky took a breath as she gathered more words, discovering that sharing the story out loud came surprisingly easy. Probably from all the times she had played it through from beginning to end in her mind.

"It was hunting season." Sky's voice cracked slightly. "We lived in the woods in a beautiful log cabin. Well, that sounds . . . mmm . . . misleading. It was quite an extraordinary home. I've . . . mmm . . . never been in anything that compares to its beauty."

Sky silently walked through the ghostly rooms of her past. Maggie remained quiet.

"My husband was up early one morning. Mmm . . . he often was. He went outside for some reason. I'll never know why." Sky's eyes began to fill. "The . . . uh . . . the gunshot woke me up."

Maggie took Sky's hand. It was almost too much to bear.

"It was a hunter?" Maggie asked.

Sky wiped her eyes and looked at Maggie. "Yes. She was fourteen. It was her third day hunting with her father. He was farther away in the woods when she accidentally shot and killed my husband. We had been married for . . . mmm . . . eight weeks."

Maggie held Sky's hand for another hour as she heard about the funeral. She heard about the fourteen-year-old girl who had to go on with her life after that horrific day. She heard about Sky's agonizing work to sell the home and receive assets she didn't know she had. Maggie heard how Sky decided to come back to Cherish—her true home.

Both women were startled when the front door of the shop opened and two customers came in, giggling.

Maggie hugged Sky before she left and whispered, "You are an amazing woman, Sky. I'll be praying for you, but more than that, I am here for you."

Sky wiped her eyes and mouthed the words "thank-you."

The happy mother and daughter in her shop needed Sky to help plan flowers.

For a wedding.

Maggie's heart broke for Sky again as she headed out the door to her own happy home and marriage.

Jack walked through the parsonage kitchen door at six o'clock with a large bouquet of red carnations. They were wrapped in a vase with a Pretty, Pretty Petals sticker on the front.

"For my wife," he said, kissing Maggie.

"This is the best part of a crazy day," Maggie said, burying her face in the flowers.

"My extraordinary kiss?"

"Nope." She laughed as she placed the vase on top of one of the kitchen cupboards, away from the cats and next to Marvin's bouquet from Thanksgiving. "I see we were both at Pretty, Pretty Petals today."

"I know I was," Jack said. "I went during my lunch hour. My office smells like carnations."

"Lucky you," Maggie smiled. "I was there after lunch for a little visit. It's quite a shop, isn't it? I saw the area in the back where Sky keeps her flowers and decorations."

"I've always wondered how she was able to buy that shop," Jack mused as he helped Maggie with her coat.

"Thank you," Maggie said, slipping into her coat and shaking off the memory of the day, then added, "I'm starving, let's go."

She would not share Sky's story. It wasn't hers to share, and Jack didn't need to know. There wasn't a medical issue to share. Just a broken heart. No doctor could fix that.

They drove to Gratzi in Ann Arbor. He had called earlier to request a quiet table in the back of the restaurant. Once they were seated, Maggie felt a flood of relief. They were alone. They both left their cell phones in Jack's car. No interruptions for one whole evening.

"How are you doing?" He watched Maggie closely.

"Sometimes you look at me as if I'm one of your patients," Maggie said.

"I can't help it. I'm brilliant, and I can see things in your face and body language. Then I just have to see if your words are telling the truth or not." Jack smiled at himself.

"I'm pooped," Maggie said.

"Yes, that's true." Jack nodded somberly.

"I don't know how we have made it through the last few days."

"We didn't have a choice."

"I'm so thankful you were at The Grange when Cassandra died. I've been meaning to tell you that," Maggie said earnestly.

"You have told me. Several times. I'm glad I was there too. I don't usually step into hospice situations like that, but this was different. I'm thankful Judy called and asked me to come."

A waiter arrived at their table to take their drink order, and Jack selected a bottle of Chardonnay.

243

"Christmas is next," Maggie said, working herself up. "Then Ghana. But before that, we have three Advent services and Irena's crazy concert. I need to plan a staff Christmas lunch. Marla is working on the children's Christmas program. I haven't even helped. We need to buy presents. I don't think I can handle the parsonage full of people again."

"Then we won't host Christmas dinner. You can handle these things. Advent services are full of traditions that are already in place. Your sermons will be uplifting, as always. The church needs the hope of Advent, especially now. Your staff lunch will take one phone call to the Cherish Café. Irena is in charge of her crazy concert. Let that one go. Marla also is completely capable of handling the children. We'll make a list of people and presents." Jack took a breath. He was tired too. "And, what do you think of this?" Jack wanted Maggie to love the next idea. "What if we spend our first married Christmas alone? No parsonage full of people."

"Just the two of us, alone on Christmas Day?" Maggie asked.

"Well, and the cats," Jack said with a smile.

"That's better. I'm in." Maggie got up, walked around to Jack, and kissed him. "You just gave me brand-new energy."

"Good. I plan to put that to use." He smiled broadly.

Maggie raised her eyebrows as she sat back down.

"Making a Christmas present list!" Jack said in faux shock.

"What will we tell our families?"

"To leave us alone."

A nice basket of warm Italian bread was placed before them, along with a bottle of Chardonnay. The server waited for Jack to taste, then poured the glasses of wine and took their dinner orders. Maggie tore off a piece of bread and dipped it in the small dish of olive oil and spices.

"Jack, what did you think of this morning? Did Harold blow your mind like he did mine?"

"I'd love to say I saw it coming, but I had no idea of Cassandra's wealth. She lived a frugal life," Jack said as he sipped his wine.

"I think we should organize a housewarming for Julia," Maggie said. "She doesn't have any household goods. We could have a party at church, no, a party at her new house, and bring gifts to her and Hannah." Maggie completely envisioned the parade of presents.

"Yes, that's a great idea. But we won't plan that tonight," Jack said, trying to bring Maggie back to their dinner table.

"And what about this day care center she wants us to open? I don't have any idea how to go about that," Maggie said, her energy once again deflating.

"Like Harold said, it is something for the council to figure out. We'll do our best, but you and I won't figure this out tonight." Jack sighed, then continued, "Back to Christmas. Let's tell our families this week that we would like to be exempt from Christmas this year. Christmas Eve will be busy at church, and Christmas Day will be ours. We will have our own celebration. Along with the cats." Jack was quite pleased with his plan. "I think they will understand our wish to be a couple, but also, we will be leaving for Ghana just over a week later."

"Yes. Let's do that. Maybe next year we can do something different." Maggie already felt relieved. Then she changed gears. "So we leave for Ghana in just about a month. Unbelievable."

"I think part of it is we don't really know what to expect. Bryan and Joy have been helpful, but it's different for them. They've actually lived there."

Bryan had gone to Zeeland with Dirk and Mimi after Casandra's funeral. Tomorrow morning, they would be driving him to Grand Rapids. He would fly to Ghana, where Joy was already waiting.

"I think this could very well be what my grandma called 'a trip of a lifetime,'" Maggie said. "Which reminds me," she put her piece of bread down on her plate, "my mother said you and I should probably sit down with Harold and make a will, or a trust, or change names of life insurance beneficiaries." She picked her bread up again.

"How did Ghana remind you of our finances?" Jack asked, once again marveling at the way Maggie's mind could free-associate.

"I thought about Bryan in Ghana, then grandma—you know, 'trip of a lifetime,'—then my inheritance, then Harold's office this morning and Cassandra's trusts," Maggie said simply.

245

"What do you mean your inheritance?" Jack asked. It dawned on him that, due to their brief courtship and hurried marriage, they had never talked much about finances.

"Both sets of my grandparents left trust funds for Bryan and me when they died. I haven't looked at this month's statements yet," Maggie said. "To be honest, I don't read the statements with any regularity. I usually forget I even have the trust. My parents explained it all to Bryan and to me, about the money, but until the age of thirty they would have to sign-off on us taking any money out of the accounts. Or unless we got married. Which I did. So the money is ours now. My parents made it very clear it should only be used for something important, something big. Not to be frittered away on the ordinary things of life." She took a drink of water. "The thing is, I don't have any needs. My education was paid for. I live in a parsonage—I mean, *we* live in a parsonage. My salary from church has taken care of everything I've needed. And now I have you. I don't need an inheritance. I'm the happiest girl alive. I'm sitting across the table from my husband!"

She stopped as the waiter brought their entrées to the table. Hers was a spinach and feta lasagna, while Jack received a plate of steaming chicken Alfredo.

"Well, what's the ballpark figure of these trusts?" Jack asked, taking a bite of chicken, peas, and creamy Alfredo sauce.

"It's right around three hundred and thirty thousand dollars," Maggie said as her fork sliced through layers of spinach, cheese, and noodles.

Jack choked on his food, and Maggie looked up, startled. He reached for his water, but ended up knocking it all over the bread basket. He finally stopped coughing, then stared at her with his mouth gaping. The waiter returned to check on his guests.

"Is everything okay?" Then he noticed the spilled water.

"May we have some more water and another bread basket, please?" Maggie asked with a playful smile.

26

January 8, 2016
Bawjiase, Ghana

After the groundnut soup and rice balls, Bryan gave Maggie a look, which she tried to ignore.

"Hey, Megs," Bryan said finally.

"Mmm?" Maggie said, looking at her brother.

"Let's go for a quick walk. We can head to United Hearts."

Bryan stacked bowls from the table, and Maggie brought bowls from her end of the table into the kitchen. The plastic tub of water and a bar of soap were ready. Maggie put her stack of bowls in the tub, then soaped up her hands and began washing the bowls and setting them on a plastic drain rack. Bryan walked in with more bowls. He watched silently as Maggie washed the bowls and placed them on the rack to air-dry.

"Megs, I want to figure this out," Bryan said as Maggie wiped her hands on her shorts.

"I want to punch you," Maggie said, looking Bryan in the face. "Joy and I had a talk about all this earlier this morning. I think we both understand each other."

"But *we* need to understand each other," Bryan said.

Maggie turned and faced her brother. "I don't recognize you here in this place. I don't recognize you from the guy who spoke to our church and got us all fired up about this trip. I know you have been here more times and longer than we will ever be, but we came to help. Not to control, just help. You're being rude and condescending. I don't like it."

Bryan took a step back. "Hey, wait a minute. I *have* spent more time here, and I understand the culture. Joy and I are here to help you and your group."

"No, our group is here to help you. I've heard from Joy that other groups have come and tried to force their ideas on United Hearts without asking Pastor or Marta any questions about what they need. She also said you have had lazy groups that just went out and got drunk at night. Ignorant and arrogant and elitist groups have come through here, but we're not one of those. No, we don't know everything. Yes, we did have expectations of doing things here that are not happening. *You* gave us the expectations. I told Joy that we would do whatever is needed for the rest of our time here. I'm going to meet with the group to chat about this later. No, you're not invited." Maggie glared. Bryan was ready to launch another attack, but Maggie put up her hand. "Our relationship is different here. I don't understand you. And I can't figure this out any more now. Maybe later." Maggie turned and walked into the large dining room.

"Jack?" Maggie struggled to keep her voice under control.

Jack looked up from the table. Maggie came closer and said quietly, "Can we head back to United Hearts right now, just to have a little time to talk before everyone else heads over?"

"Sure," Jack said as he stood.

Maggie looked at the rest of the group. "When you all are ready, head back to United Hearts. Jack and I are going now. Lacey, we can't wait to see what you have planned." Maggie forced a smile. "We'll see you there."

Maggie and Jack left while the rest of the group hung back. It was very apparent they didn't want company on their journey.

Outside the volunteer house, Maggie felt the sun and smelled the baking dirt below her feet. The choir of chickens, a rooster, goats, sheep, and a stray dog barking at Obolo, who stayed on the porch, growling, filled Maggie's ears. She loved each sensation and breathed deeply.

"Let's walk," Jack said, taking Maggie's hand. Once they were headed toward United Hearts, Jack spoke again. "I feel like I haven't seen you for four days. I miss you."

"I miss you too," Maggie said.

"You are in another world. What's going on?"

"You know what's going on. We're all frustrated, except Cate and Addie, but they're young and idealistic." *Of course, so am I, or at least I used to be.* "To be honest, I am so mad at Bryan right now. I feel like an idiot. He was so positive at home, but I feel like we're all in his way around here. And he's let me know it."

"Okay, you're right, we've been a little disillusioned this week. But don't you think Bryan is just trying hard to show you this is his world? This is his place of expertise?"

"I know it's his world. I've never claimed it's my world. I just feel responsible for all of you, the sacrifices you have made to be here. It feels like we're just taking up space." Maggie's frustration was rising.

"This trip is out of your control. It isn't what we thought it was going to be, at least not so far. But we have a week left," Jack said.

"Joy and I had a good conversation before going to Market. I think she will help us figure out some tasks. It's Bryan who's bugging me right now. I thought we would have so much fun these two weeks together. It is not fun."

"If nothing else, we've learned a lot about this culture. The time we spend with the people of Bawjiase is time we see what life is truly like for them. I think I'd like to volunteer at the farm on Monday. I would love to go to Market on Tuesday, just to look around. Playing with the kids at United Hearts will give us a chance to really know them." Jack gave Maggie what she needed, a plan, though he actually needed one too.

They passed by Adua's house and saw Kofi and Kwashi playing outside.

"Let's go in and check on Hannah," Maggie said.

Kofi and Kwashi saw the two obronis and came running. Jack and Maggie scooped them up and hugged them.

"Orphanage?" Kofi asked.

"Mama?" Maggie asked back, looking around for Adua.

They went to the doorway of the home. Kofi and Kwashi wriggled down and ran inside, talking loudly and quickly in Twi. Adua came outside to see Jack and Maggie. Through few words and many hand signals, Adua made it clear the boys could go along to United Hearts with Jack and Maggie.

"Hannah?" Maggie asked.

"Mmm . . ." Adua nodded her head and waved Maggie and Jack into the house.

Hannah was sitting in a chair, twisting twine around very thin and reedy branches. She was making a broom. She smiled when she saw Maggie.

"Hannah, how is your head?" Maggie spoke too slowly and too loudly (as people do when trying to force someone who doesn't speak their language to understand).

Hannah smiled again. "Yes. Good." She gently touched her forehead.

After more clunky communication, it was decided Hannah could come along to United Hearts with her brothers.

As the five of them left the small house, they saw the rest of the group coming from the volunteer house. They were each carrying an empty water bucket.

"Hi!" Maggie shouted. "What are you doing?"

"We're going to United Hearts, silly," Lacey said.

"What's with the buckets?" Jack asked.

"Part of the fun surprise," Addie said as she set down her bucket and picked up both Kofi and Kwashi. The little boys threw their arms around her neck and kissed her.

The group commenced down the red dirt road. Maggie noticed Cate at the back of the pack, but there was no sign of Bryan or Joy.

When they arrived at United Hearts, they still had to wait over an hour for the older children to get home from school, but Lacey was ready to begin. She went and found Marta.

"Hello, Marta," Lacey said slowly. "May we have water? For our buckets, please?"

Lacey had expected to be taken to the well next to United Hearts. She knew there wasn't warm water available. But Marta surprised her. Marta led Lacey to the back of United Hearts where large holding tanks stood. During the rainy season, they were full to overflowing, now they were less than half full. But the water was warm, sitting in the sun all day. Marta opened a spigot and began to fill Lacey's bucket. Lacey raced around United Hearts.

"Come on, everyone, and bring your buckets!"

The adults mixed in with the younger children and went to the back of United Hearts. Warm water filled each bucket.

Lacey led the group back to the large front room in United Hearts. It took only a few minutes to set up all the chairs in cozy circles. Lacey retrieved her small case hidden under the table. The other adults watched with interest.

Lacey opened her case and pulled out a mini salon. She unpacked liquid soap, bottles of lotion, several bottles of colorful nail polish, nail clippers and files, body spray, and pairs of soft foam rubber flip-flops.

"Lacey! You have brought a spa to Bawjiase!" Cate exclaimed.

"Yep. I have." Lacey grinned. "I had this small bag wrapped in my clothes in my big bag. I was relieved to find nothing had burst or broken during the flights," Lacey said, almost giddy.

"What a fun idea," Maggie said. She felt a lift in spirit at the creative and even luxurious gift for the children.

"I was thinking we could give every child a manicure and a pedicure. Whoever wants paint on their nails can have it. Unless . . . is that breaking cultural laws or anything?" Lacey looked a little unsure.

"Are Joy and Bryan coming?" Maggie asked in a neutral voice. "They would know."

"They said they would be here by the time the older kids get back from school," Charlene said.

"We still have some time. What shall we do with the kids?" Cate asked.

Maggie thought for a second. "Maybe we could have the children walk us to the farm. It would be good to see the work Sylvia, Bill, and Dana are doing. Then we could get back here by the time the older children arrive."

Hannah was the oldest of the children. Even though she didn't live at United Hearts, she led the way to the farm. Everyone in the country-side knew the farm. As they walked, the children began to sing.

Trust and obey,
For there's no other way
To be happy in Jesus
Than to trust and obey!

Maggie caught her breath as she listened to their young voices sing a traditional old hymn. She looked at the red dirt of their incredible country. The children sang with a faster pace for the familiar tune. They sang with joy, unlike the funeral dirge it had sounded like in Maggie's childhood church in Zeeland. She had known the words of the hymn since Sunday school, but somehow the meaning had quietly faded away. *Trust and obey.* Maggie could feel tears well up and was angry. She was angry at Bryan. She was angry about the failed mission trip. She was angry about feeling useless. She was mostly angry with herself. She desperately wanted a whisper from God.

Then the warm air blew.

∞

Bryan looked up from his cup of tea. "I don't get it. Maggie is acting irrational. She might be the pastor of her church at home, but she is not in charge here." He sounded defiant. "She just doesn't get it."

Joy listened to Bryan but said nothing. He needed to hear himself first. She took a swallow of her sugary tea.

"They all need to learn about 'Ghana time.' They're just living in their American fast-paced world, but that doesn't work over here. We were hoping they could work on the new school, but we can't build without supplies. We're on Ghana time." Bryan tried hard to convince himself of his sentiments. He looked back at the silent Joy.

"Bryan," Joy said, "do you remember the first time you visited each new country connected with Africa Hope?"

"Of course." Bryan looked quizzical.

"Do you remember your first few days at each site? How it felt? How each place was different from the others and couldn't all be lumped together as just one 'picture of Africa'?" Joy took another sip of tea but kept her eyes on Bryan.

Bryan thought back. He remembered each place they visited. Schools in rural villages. A brand-new clinic in the countryside of Uganda. The project in Kenya to rescue children from the slums and give them a safe place to live. He remembered his first days in Bawjiase. Pastor Elisha, Marta, Fifi, Nana, and the children.

Joy watched as Bryan's memory book of experiences turned page by page in his mind. She remembered his fears in the slums. She had held him when he was overcome by grief at what he saw in the eyes of the sickest children and the most hopeless. She remembered, as he remembered, the time in the middle of the night when he took little Zinabu to the clinic in Bawjiase, wondering if she was going to live or die. She lived.

Joy spoke softly. "I often forget that, when volunteers come to us, they come without experiences of this particular culture. They often bring their own ways of doing things from their sterile worlds to us, and it annoys us. But for the people who come without all the answers, it's important to allow them to experience life here and come to the reality of it on their own. Your sister's group are those kind of people. They are absorbing the experience. You don't need to force them to do it. And I don't either. But we do need to include them and encourage them and give them experiences. I apologized to Maggie this morning, and I would like a chance to apologize to the entire group."

Bryan sat still as all the images of his first trips—and now the visit from this group, these people he knew by name—swirled in his head. Then he looked up at Joy and nodded.

"I've been thinking," Joy continued, sounding a little more upbeat, "what if we plan a beach day for tomorrow? I can get permission from Pastor, and you can order a tro-tro. We can all play in the Atlantic for a day and then begin fresh on Sunday."

"That's a good idea, Joy," Bryan said quietly, "and thank you for that lesson you just taught me over your teacup. I got it."

"None of us ever stop learning," Joy said, finishing her tea. "I discover that each and every day when the person I was raised to be clashes with people who were not raised like I was. I always try to remember how much I don't know and how much others can teach me. There. That's my sermon, along with my culture lesson. You should be good for a while." Joy smiled.

"I like the idea of the beach day," Bryan said. "I'll call for the tro-tro. Then I want to get to United Hearts. There's a sister I need to find. And I also really want to know what Lacey is up to."

Maggie, the other adults, and the chorus of singing angels arrived at the farm. The first thing Maggie noticed was how large the farm was. She looked at Jack.

"For some reason, I thought this would be like a large backyard garden," she said quietly.

"This is impressive," Jack said, looking at the large fields. "Now I see what Sylvia has been telling us every day."

At the far side of one of the fields they could see Nana on his hands and knees—digging, planting, and watering. They looked in the opposite direction and saw Sylvia, Bill, and Dana with buckets and watering cans, carefully watering a row of small cabbages.

The children scattered, running toward Nana and the three obronis. Cate and Addie followed them.

Nana stood up when he heard the children. He yelled something loudly in Twi. The children stopped and looked down. It was obvious he was telling them to stop before they completely crushed all of his hard work.

The children turned and carefully walked back to Maggie and the others.

"Maybe this wasn't such a good idea," Charlene said.

Ellen nodded her head. Addie and Cate picked up two children each and got them back to the road. Sylvia, Bill, and Dana had all turned when they heard Nana shout. They set down their buckets and walked over to the group.

"What are you guys doing here?" Dana asked, looking at the faces of the children.

"We thought we would come on a little field trip. Literally," Maggie said.

"Well, we could certainly use the help," Sylvia said softly.

Jack and Charlene both noticed Sylvia was white as a ghost.

"Sylvia," Jack said, "are you all right?"

Charlene stepped forward, repeating Jack's movements from earlier in the day. She took Sylvia's wrist, and Jack watched as Sylvia's eyes fluttered just slightly.

"Sylvia, what is that?" Ellen sounded frightened. She was standing behind Sylvia, staring down at her lower leg.

"What?" Sylvia said, trying to follow Ellen's eyes.

"Just above your sock?" Ellen said, kneeling down.

She gently pulled down Sylvia's sock, and Sylvia winced. Jack and Charlene helped Sylvia sit down and extend her right leg.

"Are you feeling cool?" Jack asked.

"Just a little chilled," Sylvia said.

Sylvia's lower leg was bright red with inflammation. Jack discovered there was an infected cut, and the pus that oozed from it was alarming.

"Maggie," Jack said quietly, "why don't you get the kids and the others back to United Hearts. We need to get Sylvia to the clinic."

Maggie's stomach lurched into her throat at the look in his eyes. She had never seen Jack scared before.

"Of course."

"We'll help take care of the kids," Lacey jumped in. She looked at Addie, Cate, and Ethan.

Nana made his way over to the group once he saw Sylvia on the ground.

"What is going on?"

Jack quickly explained.

Nana looked at the children, particularly Hannah, as the oldest, and told them to go back to United Hearts. He then pulled out his cell phone and made a call.

"The taxi will be here. He will take you to the clinic."

"I can stay and help you, Nana," Dana said, knowing she wouldn't be needed at the clinic and Lacey had the afternoon at United Hearts under control.

Maggie, Lacey, Addie, Cate, and Ethan marched the children back to United Hearts, talking lightheartedly to keep them calm. Hannah sang "Kum ba yah," which instead of sounding like youth group sappiness sounded more like a poignant and sincere prayer. The other little ones joined their voices with Hannah's.

Lacey looked at Addie and said, "What are they singing?"

"Come by here, my Lord," Addie said.

Lacey's heart had all it could take. Her guilt, her fear, the feeling of rejection, and the voices of these children asking God to please stop by was too much. Lacey walked ahead of the group, trying to wipe away her tears so that no one would see.

A taxi rumbled by United Hearts just as the small parade was coming down the road. It headed toward the farm.

When Maggie and the rest of the group entered United Hearts, Bryan and Joy were sitting with Marta in three of the chairs set in a circle. They all stood up when the group came in.

"Hi, there," Joy said. "How was your walk?"

"We went to the farm," Maggie said quietly.

Lacey moved some of the buckets around so she didn't have to look up.

"Yeah," Cate walked over to Bryan, "we saw the huge amount of work that has to be done there. It's awesome. How does Nana do it when volunteers aren't here?"

They all heard the rumble of the taxi coming back down the road.

"Where's everyone else?" Bryan asked.

"With Sylvia. Sylvia's sick. That taxi is taking her and the others to the clinic," Cate replied.

"What?" Joy asked, surprised.

The taxi drove past.

"Sylvia has some kind of a laceration on her right lower leg. It has become infected," Maggie said, looking at Joy. "Jack, Charlene, and Ellen are with Sylvia and Bill. Dana stayed to help Nana water as much as possible."

Bryan and Joy looked at each other. Marta also looked concerned. She knew enough English to understand that Sylvia needed to go to the clinic.

Then the older children came into the large front room of United Hearts, home from school. Once they saw the obronis and the buckets of water, they smiled and ran to their rooms to put their books away.

Joy said, "I think I should get to the clinic. Bryan, what would you like to do?"

Bryan wanted to go to the clinic too, but decided he wouldn't be necessary.

"I'll stay here and help Lacey," Bryan said, subdued, "but will you call when you know something?"

"Of course."

Joy left quickly, her long legs moving fast.

The older children rushed back into the large room, excited. Something different was happening after school today.

Lacey had pulled herself together.

"Okay, quiet, everyone," she said loudly. "We, the obronis, would like each of you to sit down and please take off your shoes or sandals."

Lacey made a small bow from the waist and smiled broadly. She had quite a flair for the dramatic. "And now, watch the miracle of bubbles!"

Lacey went by each bucket and put a squirt of liquid soap into each one. Maggie, Addie, Cate, Bryan, and Ethan followed Lacey's lead and swirled their hands in the water to make the soap foam into frothy bubbles. The children laughed, mouths open at this soapy extravaganza.

"Children!" Lacey said dramatically. "Welcome to the Bawjiase Spa!"

27

The taxi finally arrived at the clinic. Sylvia held tightly to Bill's hand as they walked into the building. Jack, Charlene, and Ellen went ahead, looking for Dr. Obodai.

The clinic was packed, as usual, with mothers and babies lined up on the benches. Jack walked to the front of the clinic, where one of the nurses was sitting with a young mother and her baby. She looked up.

"Yes, hello."

"Is Dr. Obodai here?" Jack asked.

"Yes. In the room." The nurse pointed to the room with the gurneys.

"Thank you," Jack said as he turned and walked into the room.

Dr. Obodai was wrapping the wrist of a young boy. The boy's mother was standing on the other side of the gurney. Jack waited until Dr. Obodai finished with the procedure.

"Hello, Dr. Elliot," Dr. Obodai said.

"Hello. We have a problem with one of our group members. I believe a laceration on her leg has become infected through some standing water."

Charlene, Ellen, Bill, and Sylvia entered the room.

Dr. Obodai pointed to a clean gurney, and Bill helped Sylvia sit then lie down. Sylvia turned onto her stomach so they could see the back of her leg better. Dr. Obodai pulled down her sock and examined her leg. The flesh around the cut was an angry red, and pus was continuing to ooze out of the wound. All three doctors, along with Ellen, could see that the infection had spread down her leg to her foot and was also moving up toward her knee.

"She needs antibiotics immediately," Dr. Obodai said.

Bill watched silently, but the shake in his hands caught Ellen's attention.

"Bill," Ellen said quietly, "Sylvia will be all right. They've got to get her started on IV antibiotics. We'll find out for sure, but I would guess this will take a few days."

Bill's eyes opened wide. "What do you mean, 'a few days'? We're only here for a few more days."

"We'll check her progress each day and see how the infection heals. It's good we found it now."

Ellen moved out of the way as Dr. Obodai and one of the clinic nurses brought in IV equipment and an extra sheet to cover Sylvia, who now shook with chills.

"Bill, you come with me. They will clean Sylvia's wound and get the IV set up. Then you can come back in and sit with her. I think." Ellen didn't know exactly what the protocol was.

"I can't leave her here for the night or anything like that," Bill said, the most animated Ellen had ever seen him. "She's not going to stay in that room with strangers."

"Let's see what the doctors say when they come out. Jack and Charlene will have information for us," Ellen tried to reassure him.

Bill was not reassured.

Dr. Obodai numbed the area around the infection on Sylvia's leg. He then probed the laceration to make sure it was open and could drain. Fortunately for Sylvia, they had also given her a mild sedative. She was falling in and out of consciousness. The IV was placed in her arm and the healing antibiotics began to flow.

Joy got to the clinic and saw Ellen and Bill as they stood outside the gurney room.

"What's happened?" Joy asked quickly.

Bill just shook his head.

"Sylvia needs IV antibiotics to get rid of an infection in her leg," Ellen said.

"How are you doing, Bill?" Joy asked.

"I just want her to be okay. I don't know how this could have happened." Bill's hands began shaking again. "They might keep her for days."

Joy looked at Ellen, who gave a slight nod.

"She really is in good hands, Bill. Dr. Obodai and Jack and Charlene know how to take care of these types of infections."

Joy leaned up against the wall next to Bill. They waited in silence.

When Ellen, Bill, and Joy were brought back in, Sylvia was covered in a blanket and resting on her back, her eyes closed.

"Bill," Jack said, trying to ease Bill's concerned face, "Sylvia is going to be okay. It is good that this clinic is here, and they have an experienced doctor and excellent supplies."

Bill couldn't take his eyes off his wife.

"Sylvia will need to stay here for a few days to receive the antibiotics through the IV. She is in very good hands." Jack saw Bill's shoulder twitch.

"Why can't she come back to the volunteer house?" Bill asked, looking as if he might just pick up Sylvia and run.

"Bill," Charlene said, "she has to be monitored here. Her bandage will need to be changed, and they have to make sure the infection doesn't spread. There will be nurses here all night."

Bill glanced around the large, bare room. Just gurneys. No chairs.

"I would like to stay here with her tonight. Please."

Jack had expected that. It was exactly what he would do if it were Maggie lying on the gurney.

"I'll ask if it's okay and try to find a chair," Jack said without argument.

Jack, Charlene, Ellen, and Joy all hugged Bill and kissed Sylvia, who was slightly aware they were there. Then they left Bill with a metal folding chair and his sleeping wife.

"I'll bring you dinner later," Ellen said.

Bill didn't respond.

At the Bawjiase Spa, children and adults were having a sudsy time with the buckets of soapy water. Lacey got on her knees in front of the children and washed their feet and calves. She used a large file to smooth the rough skin on their heels and the balls of their feet. The children squealed because the fingers and file also tickled. Maggie, Addie, Cate, Bryan, and Ethan all followed Lacey's lead. They washed and filed. Then they used Lacey's soft towels to dry the clean feet and toes. Lacey clipped toenails carefully. The other adults again followed suit.

"What is this?" Cynthia asked, pointing at the nail polish.

"It's called polish," Lacey said. "In America, girls like to have polish on their toes and also on their fingers. But you don't have to."

"Yes, I would like it," Cynthia said.

"Me too!" agreed Grace.

"I would like it," Amanda chimed in.

Soon all the girls agreed that polish would be good for them.

"What about the boys?" Promise asked.

Lacey was about to say "Whatever you want" but Bryan cut her off and said, "I have some soccer balls ready to be kicked around. Would any boys like to play soccer?" Bryan wasn't sure painted nails on boys would go over so well at school.

That took care of that. The boys took their brand-new clean feet and went running out into the red dirt as Bryan fetched soccer balls and followed them out to organize a game.

"Well, their feet were clean for a minute," Lacey said wryly.

Actually, Lacey had been surprised when she found out the children took two bucket baths each day, morning and night. Cleanliness was important to their culture.

Ethan decided to go outside and observe the soccer game. While he knew very little about the game, he enjoyed the grins on the boys' faces. Lacey, Cate, and Addie took the buckets to the back of United Hearts and got some more warm water from the holding tanks while Maggie stayed with the girls.

"Your feet look beautiful," Maggie said. "Do they feel different?"

"Oh, yes, yes, yes!" the cacophony of voices shouted.

"What color polish do you think you would like? You can have one color on your toes and a different color on your fingers."

Maggie watched as the girls chose different bottles and shared easily with one another when a color was chosen by two or more. The manicures began when the fresh buckets of water arrived. More suds. More clipping and filing. And finally, the polish.

Maggie carefully painted purple onto the nails of Zinabu. The little girl squealed as she saw her toes and fingers become little pieces of jewelry.

"Now just a minute," Maggie said as Zinabu squirmed to get down. "Let me blow on them so they will dry." She blew on small fingers and toes.

"May I have pink and orange on *my* fingers and toes?" Amanda asked Addie.

"Do you mean on one finger and then the other color on another, every other finger and toe?" Addie tried to clarify.

"Yes, yes, yes!" Amanda giggled.

"Absolutely." Addie opened two small bottles.

Cate sat with Grace. "What color would you like Gracie-girl?"

"Blue," Grace said definitively.

Cate opened a bottle of blue polish.

The manicures and pedicures continued down to the tiniest little fingers and toes of baby Leah, who wiggled when the polish brushed against her toes. Maggie watched the girls show one another their beautiful nails. She stared into the eyes of Leah. Then Maggie heard the whisper.

These children are mine, Maggie. You are mine. I hold each one of you. Learn about me from them.

Maggie shuddered. The joy, openness, and trust of the children brought Maggie's faith to another level. She felt another shift in her soul as God kept growing out of the boxes Maggie had been raised with and had learned in seminary. There were no parameters or boundaries on God's goodness and grace, she realized. The old words and phrases weren't going to work anymore. God was truly loose in the world— God gone wild—all fiery and shockingly powerful and unexplainable. She came back to that. God was unexplainable. God could only be experienced. It was just that she had usually decided how spiritual experiences would go. Or her pastor had. Or her youth group leader had. It was all very tidy, God tucked away in some memorized Bible verses. But even the Bible couldn't hold God.

Maggie came back to the moment when Lacey clapped her hands loudly.

"We're not finished!"

Lacey made another dramatic display as she pulled lotion out of her magic bag—like a funky Mary Poppins—and began to rub the lotion on hands and feet once the polish was dry.

"There you go," Lacey said to Cynthia. "You look beautiful."

Cynthia smiled. "Thank you. This is pretty. I must go now to help with the washing."

Lacey shook her head, then looked at Maggie, who understood immediately.

"Sit here for just a minute," Lacey said to Cynthia.

Lacey went out to find Marta. She was with some other women, who were cooking dinner. Lacey smiled, and Marta returned the smile.

"Marta, may I ask you something? Is there, please, any way Pastor Maggie, Addie, Cate, and I could do the washing for the girls today? Just today, so they can keep their nails nice for a little while? *Please?* I know we're guests, but we really want to give the girls this fun, pretty gift."

Marta looked at Lacey and considered.

"Yes," Marta said, "just this once. You may do the washing in place of the girls."

"Thank you," Lacey said, beaming.

Then she brought her good news back into the large room.

"Girls, you may all go out and play, or go to your rooms and do homework, or just sit and look at your pretty nails. We are going to wash for you today."

The girls stared at Lacey in disbelief. They didn't have days off from their chores. Everyone had to work hard to keep clothes clean, dishes washed, and to care for the younger children.

"Shoo!" Lacey said. "Go do something fun."

The big girls jumped up and began clapping their hands. The smaller girls watched the bigger girls and copied them. All the noise scared baby Leah, who began to cry. Maggie was holding the tiniest member of United Hearts and kissed and cuddled the frightened baby. The girls ran from the large room to do . . . something, squealing all the way.

It was time to do the laundry.

Maggie and Cate found a piece of fabric and wrapped baby Leah on Maggie's back, mimicking the way the mothers in Bawjiase carried their babies.

Lacey used her liquid soap as she, Addie, Cate, and Maggie refilled the buckets for the third time.

"I'm not going to try and use a bar of soap to clean the piles of dirty clothes sitting out in the dirt," Lacey said, making more froth with her hands. As she stirred the water, she quickly raised her wrist to wipe her eyes before others saw the tears.

As the women made their way to the front of United Hearts, Maggie watched Lacey closely. Something was wrong. Lacey was almost frenetic, especially once she began to wash her pile of clothes. Lacey scrubbed and wrung out clothes as if she were trying to wash away more than the children's stains. It wasn't the first time on the trip that Lacey had behaved oddly, but Maggie wasn't sure how to approach her friend about it. Right then, in front of everyone, was certainly not the time.

When the last little shirt was drying in the sun, the women emptied out their buckets and walked over to Marta.

"We have finished the wash and will head back to the volunteer house now," Maggie said as Marta carefully helped unwrap baby Leah from Maggie's back.

"Thank you for doing this work," Marta said.

Then she handed Maggie, Lacey, Cate, and Addie each a small buttoned coin holder made of beautiful Ghanaian kente cloth. Earlier in the week, Bryan had told Maggie that Marta made many things with the fabric to sell. Maggie knew it was an extravagant gift to receive.

"These are beautiful. Thank you, Marta. We will use these and always think of you."

Maggie hugged Marta.

"Thank you for this day you gave the children. It was good." Marta smiled.

Dinner was waiting when everyone returned from United Hearts. Spaghetti with tomato sauce and fried chicken were eagerly devoured as everyone shared their stories of the day.

"Sylvia will stay at the clinic for several days," Jack said as he twirled spaghetti on his fork. "Her infection is deep in the tissue."

"When will be Bill be back?" Maggie asked.

"I'm going to bring him some dinner when we're done eating," Ellen said. "I hope to talk him into coming back with me tonight, but I have a feeling he won't leave Sylvia's side. He is pretty distraught. I'll bring a pillow and sheet, just in case."

Ellen ate quickly. Fifi had prepared a plate for Bill with extra food in case Sylvia was hungry for a snack.

"I'll help," Charlene said. "Maybe two of us can be more persuasive. How was United Hearts today?"

"Amazing," Maggie said. "Lacey made a 'Bawjiase Spa' for the children." She went on to describe the manicures and pedicures, then the process of washing all the children's clothes.

Bryan sat quietly over his dinner and listened to the descriptions of the day. It had been fun to watch the kids so excited over their spa experience. The boys had played soccer for the rest of the afternoon, elated by the special attention they received. There had been a lightness in spirit and joy in the freedom to play for such an extended amount of time. Bryan looked at Maggie as she happily shared more details of the afternoon. At one point, she caught Bryan's eyes looking into hers and smiled.

"Well, at the farm this afternoon, we watered like crazy," Dana said as she reached for a slice of pineapple. "Nana stopped planting so we could get everything as drenched as possible. But we did it," Dana said, contentedly. "I'll go back tomorrow and help again."

"Tomorrow may be different for everyone," Joy said. "I hope it's okay, but we've planned a beach day."

She grinned at the anticipated reaction.

The next morning, everyone awoke with the roosters. Fifi had already been up for two hours making a huge pot full of jollof rice. He knew Marta and some of the women staying at United Hearts were doing the same thing.

"Good morning, Fifi," Maggie yawned into the kitchen. "It smells wonderful in here."

"Thank you," Fifi said, giving the rice a stir. He was also making fried egg sandwiches for breakfast.

"May I take some of these out to the table for you?" Maggie asked.

"Yes, please."

Fifi handed her a plate, then began cracking more eggs. Everyone, except Bill and Sylvia, sat at the table and made cups of instant coffee with the boiling water Fifi set out. Bill had chosen to stay the night at the clinic with his wife. In fact, he said he would stay until she was ready to leave.

Charlene took a sip of coffee, then said, "I'll go to the clinic now, before the tro-tro gets here. Bill will need enough food for breakfast and lunch."

Fifi came back into the large room with two covered plates. One held three egg sandwiches, the other a mound of jollof rice. He handed the plates to Charlene.

"These are for Bill and Sylvia."

Ethan stood up. "I'll help. I would like to see how Bill and Sylvia are doing."

Ethan grabbed several bags of pure water and an egg sandwich, which he shoved into his mouth.

By the time Ethan and Charlene returned, everyone was getting into the tro-tro. The couple grabbed their towels, sunblock, and hats. The adults were loaded up when a second tro-tro passed the volunteer house. It was full of the children from United Hearts and all the adults, singing and laughing as the tro-tro whizzed by. They were jammed in like too many books on a shelf, sticking out at odd angles, but no one seemed to mind.

"Sylvia looked slightly better this morning," Charlene told the others as the tro-tro bounced down the rutted road. "The antibiotics are working. She had much better color, and she had slept through most of the night. She does have pain in her leg, but that's to be expected."

"Bill looked like hell," Ethan said, shaking his head. "He sat in that folding chair all night. It would be good if we could get him to come home tonight for some sleep."

"They both ate the egg sandwiches," Charlene continued. "Bill was going to save the rice for their lunch. The clinic is also providing them with some food, but yours is the best, Fifi."

Fifi nodded his head under the praise. He was a good cook, and he knew it.

"Maybe Bill will feel better about coming back if Sylvia has a good day today," Maggie said. "We'll make a trip to the clinic when we get back from the beach."

The tro-tro picked up speed on the paved road. Maggie watched the large palm trees swaying in the wind as they sped past. They went through small villages and also larger towns. It was becoming familiar to see the bright colors of Ghanaian fabric wrapped around women and wrapped around the babies on their backs. Maggie observed the people in the streets as they sold fried rice, fufu, breads, and so many other items. She closed her eyes and breathed in deeply until someone shook her shoulder.

Maggie opened her blue eyes and turned to stare into Bryan's.

"Can you come back here a second?" Bryan asked.

Maggie was going to say no because she was stuck in her seat, but she wiggled around, crawled over Jack and Ellen, and squeezed herself next to Bryan.

"Listen," Bryan said softly, "I owe you an apology."

"Yep."

"Megs, I am sorry. I was busy being an ass because I was trying to be the boss. I was rude and patronizing to you. I want you to know that I get it now. You came, not just with hopes, but promises of work to be done. I just want to say—"

"Bryan," Maggie interrupted, "thanks for the apology. I believe this trip has been a surprise for everyone. We have one more week. We'll do what we can, as you and Joy direct us."

"Thanks. I'm sorry for being such an idiot to you."

"I'm sorry for being such an idiot to you. Although, you were a bigger idiot."

Maggie punched him in the arm, which shoved him into Joy.

"You two calm down," Joy said. "How did your mother ever manage you?"

"Are you kidding?" Bryan asked. "She just had to look at us. Mimi can be very frightening when she needs to be."

"She is an excellent mom," Maggie said. "She never budged when she set a boundary, no matter how hard Bryan tried to push it. He was always a problem child."

The teasing and apologies broke the frostiness between the siblings. Maggie never wanted to be in that frost with her brother again. The Ghana trip threatened to leave a small shadow over all the other good memories, but Maggie hoped the next week would chase the shadow away.

After an hour and a half, the tro-tros pulled onto a grassy area under several palm trees. The warm air blew through the open windows of the tro-tro. Quickly, everyone piled out. When Maggie extricated herself from the back of the tro-tro, she caught her breath. The Atlantic Ocean crashed and rolled up onto the beach, wave after wave after wave. Along with the wind through the dancing palm trees, it was a song to Maggie's ears. She breathed in the salty air. Joy was right. It was exactly what everyone needed.

Cynthia, Mary, Grace, and Promise were the first ones out of their tro-tro, and they ran as fast as they could toward the water. The rest of the children followed, screaming with excitement. One after another, Maggie watched them splash into the ocean. The big boys followed, making sure to help the smaller children.

Maggie grabbed Dougie and followed the others. Addie, Cate, Ellen, Charlene, Ethan, and Jack each had a little child in their arms as they made their way to the ocean. The waves crashed and rolled and chased the squealing children up the beach.

"This is amazing!" Maggie shouted to Jack, who was carrying Zinabu. "I can't believe there are people who think Lake Michigan is the same thing as an ocean. This is completely different."

"It's awesome!" Addie yelled as she ran in-between Maggie and Jack, carrying baby Leah.

The children laughed, splashed, and swam. The big boys made a kind of barrier so no one could go out too far or get pulled by a rip current.

"Let's let these little ones feel the water," Maggie said.

She got to where the waves were rolling in, then sat down in the sand with Dougie. She let his feet feel the wet sand first, then the water as it rolled over his toes. Dougie giggled. The other volunteers held their little ones so the water could wash over their feet as well.

Jack sat down with Zinabu, who immediately began splashing her hands in the water and squeezing the wet sand until it oozed out through her small fingers. She squeaked.

Fresh air, salty water, and sunshine filled everyone with overflowing fun.

"Look at Marta," Maggie said to Jack.

Jack turned and looked back toward the tro-tros. Marta was sitting on a bench under one of the palm trees. Her eyes were closed, legs stretched out.

"I wonder how often she gets a day like this," Jack mused.

"And the children," Ellen joined in the conversation. "They work so hard at school and United Hearts. This is a great day for them."

"We try to do this whenever we can," Joy said. "We have to pay for the tro-tro, or tro-tros, and usually some extra food. It's amazing how hungry we all become after we play in the sun and water all day."

Dana had been quiet, not only on the ride to the beach, but ever since they arrived. She watched Nana throw the smaller boys into the waves, then pull them out again.

"What about the farm?" Dana asked Joy. "It seems impossible to skip one day of watering."

"They haven't skipped a day," Joy said when she saw where Dana was looking. "Nana was up at three a.m. He took his torch, uh, flashlight and got a good portion of the watering done. He'll finish tonight when we return."

"Unbelievable," Dana said, more to herself than to anyone else.

At noon, everyone enjoyed bowls of jollof rice and boiled eggs. Maggie listened to the children laugh and tease one another as they shoved handfuls of rice into their mouths. Then she noticed Cynthia as she began to gather the empty bowls. Maggie stood up and walked over to the girl.

"No way, missy! You go back and play. We'll wash up today." Maggie took the bowls from Cynthia. Then she stopped and looked over at

Marta and Joy. "May we please wash the bowls?" Maggie asked, perturbed that she had to ask.

Joy looked at Marta, who slowly nodded.

Maggie and Cate collected bowls and took them down to the beach to wash them in the salty water. Addie and Lacey followed with the two large pots that had held rice and the larger bowl that held the boiled eggs. The cleanup party began.

The afternoon was a mix of water play and naps on the soft green grass near the tro-tros. It was a luxurious day of relaxation for Marta, the older girls, and the other adults from United Hearts. By the time everyone was soggily packed back into the vehicles, Maggie thought she would pass out from non-luxurious exhaustion. But she and the other members of Loving the Lord were thankful to give the gift of a day of relaxation to their new friends.

It wasn't until they were settling in at the volunteer house that Maggie noticed Dana wasn't with them.

"Where's Dana?" she asked.

"She wanted to ride back with the United Hearts tro-tro," Bryan said.

"Why?"

"I don't know. Are you going to the clinic?" Bryan questioned, seeing Jack, Charlene, and Ethan getting ready to leave.

Maggie nodded. They had all changed their clothes, but the salt was itchy on their skin and clung to their hair.

Fifi, who hadn't changed his clothes but had quickly gone to the blue store, came into the volunteer house.

"I am so sorry!" Fifi exclaimed. "Bawjiase is completely out of chicken! No chicken in Bawjiase!" He looked frantic.

Maggie couldn't help herself. She began to laugh. Bryan and Cate laughed, and Addie and Lacey couldn't control themselves. Everyone fell apart with amusement.

"What?" Fifi was confused. "I can't make your dinner."

"Fifi," Maggie said, "there are chickens *everywhere* in Bawjiase. You can't walk two steps without treading on one, you nut."

Fifi looked confused, then he smiled. "True, Pastor Maggie. But no chickens in the store tonight."

"How about this?" Jack said, trying to bring a tiny bit of order to the slapstick of the moment. "We will go to the clinic, check on Sylvia, and try to bring Bill back with us. Then we will stop in town and buy fried rice. You don't have to cook for us tonight, Fifi. You must be as tired as we are."

Fifi smiled. "Yes. And thank you. Thank you very much."

"It will take a while. Eat a biscuit if you're starving," Joy chimed in.

When Jack, Maggie, Charlene, and Ethan returned two hours later, they had several containers of food, bottles of beer, and Bill.

"Oh, Bill." Cate gave Bill a hug.

He looked like he was going to cry, and he immediately did.

Everyone gathered around him. Bill received a group hug in the truest sense of the word. In the midst of so many loving arms, Bill sobbed out his fears, his tiredness, and his frustration at being in that country, on that trip, doing nothing of consequence, and watching his wife lie on a gurney hooked up to an IV.

"I . . . don't know . . . why we came . . . here. There is no . . . point. I want to get . . . Sylvia home. This was . . . a mistake. We shouldn't have come."

They waited for Bill to run out of tears. Then Jack helped him sit down at the large table.

"Eat a little bit, Bill," Jack said. "Then you'll sleep."

Bill obeyed. He was delirious, having had no sleep for over thirty-six hours. He was distraught over his wife. He was confused about what the mission trip was all about. He ate some fried rice and then walked to his bunk. When Jack checked on him a few minutes later, he was sound asleep.

At the clinic, Sylvia awoke to a loud scream. She opened her eyes in fear and looked at the doorway. The nurses helped a very pregnant woman into the room. She could hardly walk and cried and pleaded in Twi. The nurses tried to soothe to her as they helped her onto a gurney. They had her almost lying down, but she heaved herself back up again with another scream.

Sylvia cringed.

One of the nurses came over to Sylvia and quickly said, "The maternity ward is filled. I am sorry. We must bring this woman here. It is her first baby." The nurse quickly went back across the room and pulled a curtain-on-wheels to give the woman some privacy. The curtain was sheer enough for Sylvia to see her silhouette. She screamed again.

A little girl, whom Sylvia guessed to be about five years old, had been brought in earlier, suffering with malaria. The little one had also been asleep when the pregnant woman was brought into the room. The mother of the girl had to leave the child at the clinic to go home and care for the rest of her family. Hearing the screams, the little girl began to cry. Sylvia could see the child was confused and frightened.

"What a mess this is," Sylvia said to no one.

Sylvia slowly sat up and made sure she wasn't feeling dizzy. Once she was sure of her steadiness, she stepped down off her gurney and, taking her IV pole with her, she walked over to the little girl. She felt a stab of pain in her leg but slowly pulled the little girl's gurney next to her own.

There was another lengthy scream from the laboring woman.

Sylvia struggled to climb back on her gurney, then pulled the little girl close to her and began to softly sing "Jesus loves me! This I know." She rubbed the little girl's back as she sang. It struck Sylvia that there was no way to communicate effectively with the child, or really anyone. The nurses knew little English. Sylvia knew no Twi that could help her situation. It was a little frightening.

Another scream, and the little girl jumped and began to cry again.

Sylvia kept singing as she wiped the sweat from the brow of the fevered girl.

It was going to be a long night.

Dinner at the volunteer house was subdued after Bill's arrival. Dana returned from the farm.

"Nana and I finished watering the rest of the plants. What a day."

"Thank you for all your help, Dana," Joy said. "It is a hard job, and to grow enough food depends on the daily water. You've been a real, practical help to him."

Dana smiled a tired smile, but she looked happy for the first time all week as she sat down for a quick dinner.

Joy continued. "Tomorrow is church. After church, we usually eat at United Hearts, then come back here for the afternoon. How does that sound?"

"That will be fine," Maggie said. "I wonder if, after dinner tonight, we could all gather in a circle on the floor. I think it's time to have our own church."

No one at the table thought that was a good plan. Maggie received half-hearted nods from her parishioners. Then she had an idea.

28

December 5, 2015
Cherish, Michigan

On Saturday afternoon, Jack and Maggie sat in two leather chairs in Harold Brinkmeyer's law office. Harold sat behind a beautiful mahogany desk, opening file folders and humming to himself.

"Well, so you want to combine your assets and make a trust. This should be easy to do. You're both young and uncomplicated." He looked up and grinned. "It looks like you married up, Jack. Maggie's trust must have come as a surprise. For richer, for poorer, eh?"

The bit of unprofessionalism was ignored by both Jack and Maggie.

"The only property you own is the condo, Jack, is that correct?" Harold asked.

"Yes. We aren't sure what we are going to do with it yet. We've talked about living in it. We'd have a little more privacy, but it is quite a bit smaller. Or we could rent it, if we wanted to. For now, we'll keep it."

Jack looked at Maggie. They had tried to figure out what to do with the property. After a consultation with Jack's dad, they decided to keep the condo as an investment.

"And you have quite a sizable retirement account and some investments. Not so bad." Harold shuffled through Jack's investment portfolio. "It's a good thing neither of you ever invested with Redford. How did you get away with that? That guy was relentless when it came to harassing possible investors."

"He tried," Jack said, "but I knew it would be wise to leave my accounts with my financial advisor in Blissfield. The company has worked for my family for generations. I don't know about Maggie."

Jack and Harold looked at Maggie.

Maggie was daydreaming.

She knew the meeting would bore her. It bored her silly when her parents explained her trust funds in the first place, but she loved the stories of her grandparents. Her two sets of grandparents, both living in Zeeland, had been wise with their money. Her maternal grandfather had delivered oil and gas for Standard Oil. He drove out to the farms of West Michigan, chatted with the farmers, and filled their tanks with whatever they needed. He was given stock as part of his compensation throughout his years of work. When those stocks split, he reinvested. Over and over again, he watched his money grow. Not being a big spender, he undramatically became a very wealthy man. No one knew that but his wife, and they left large inheritances for their family members.

Maggie's other grandpa owned a furniture factory in town. He was also wise with his money. When a large Chicago factory came in to buy the small Zeeland business, her paternal grandfather was able to retire at the age of fifty with a very full bank account. Again, it was not news anyone was privy to, including Maggie's father. Dirk had been shocked when his mother died, ten years after his father, and he was told by an executor there was a large trust for him, his sister, and each of their children. Maggie and Bryan, along with their cousins, were the next generation to benefit from the familial generosity.

"Maggie?"

Maggie started and looked at Harold.

"Yes?"

"We were just talking about Redford Johnson," Harold said. "And how smart it was that you didn't invest with him. It's been a hassle for his investors, even though it should all get worked out eventually."

"He never tried to get me to invest with him, not seriously," Maggie said quietly. "He thought I was just a poor little pastor. He knew my salary, of course, and I guess he didn't think I had anything else to offer."

She wondered about Redford, locked away in his jail cell. At some point, they would find out his final sentence. She knew Keith Crunch would let her know.

"Well, that was smart on your part," Harold said with a nod. "Now, do you want both of your trust accounts to be put in a single trust with Jack's assets?" Harold asked.

"Yes. One trust. The Jack and Maggie Elliot Trust. Although, I suppose you'll have to use my legal name of Margaret." She smiled.

"I just want to make sure that you don't want to keep anything separated."

Harold watched her closely to sense if she had doubts. Maggie had already consulted her parents regarding that question. They had encouraged a single trust.

"Nothing separated. I'm sure." Maggie looked at the clock on Harold's desk, wondering how much longer the meeting would take.

"Fine. The next thing is to choose an executor. I can do that, or you can choose someone else."

Jack and Maggie looked at one another. They had already discussed that as well.

"You," they said in tandem.

"Fine," Harold said again, writing his own name on the checklist.

"What about beneficiaries? If you two perish in a plane crash on your way to Ghana, who gets your stuff?" Harold laughed at his own crassness. "I know that isn't going to happen, and whenever you two procreate, we'll change everything for your children to benefit. But for now?"

"We've decided to split our assets between Loving the Lord Church and Africa Hope. We have more specific instructions for the uses of the money. We want to make sure Loving the Lord is using the money for the church, but also for the community. Here is exactly what we would like."

Maggie pulled out a thumb drive and handed it to him.

"Okay. I will have the documents drawn up, and you can come in sometime next week to sign them. This is easy." Harold grinned. "It's been nice doing business with you two lovebirds."

The three shook hands, then Jack and Maggie left Harold's office.

"Well, that's done and dusted," Maggie said. "Good for us."

"It's good to do these things correctly from the beginning. Of course, now that we've made it legal, I can confess I only married you for your money."

Jack put his arm around her waist and kissed the top of her head.

"You didn't know I had any money before you married me. That's what a hurled-together wedding can do to a couple. You forget to talk about some things. Plus, I thought you married me for my cats."

"Ah, and the truth is now revealed," Jack said with a sad shake of his head. "All I wanted were those crazy, lazy beasts."

"Lucky you. Now you have them." Maggie smiled. "I'll see you later."

"What do you have going this afternoon?" Jack asked as they stopped in front of his car.

"Oh, bits and bobs, odds and ends, this and that," Maggie said. "Love you."

She walked down the sidewalk, headed toward church.

"Love you more," Jack called after her.

Darcy Keller brooded in his bathrobe. He sat alone in his dark, wood-paneled study, ticking off his complaints with life, one by one. If he had a rosary, he would have used the beads, not to pray, but to curse the world. Holding each tiny bead, he would remember all the wrongs done against him. He had come back to Cherish and thought he was leaving his pain behind in New York, but all the pain and embarrassment he had suffered were packed up like his suitcases, ready for the long trip home. And now they were lying bare in front of him. He had come home determined to be fine—determined to be happy—but he couldn't actually remember what that felt like. Happiness. So he playacted for a while, but it only lasted a few short days. Then he couldn't play or act anymore.

Darcy's self-pity was a delicious cup of poison he just couldn't stop sipping.

Since the previous Sunday, when Priscilla had dragged him to church, he had slowly turned his anger toward God. If what the short, blonde pastor said on Sunday was true, God only wanted to love and protect his creatures. He rescued a whole nation of Israelites from Babylon. He promised them a Savior. Where was Babylon, anyway? He would have to Google that later. The fact was, God was nowhere. God didn't give a shit about Darcy, about his cheating wife, or about his business ventures. God was probably laughing. *Bastard.*

Darcy was called back to reality when his doorbell rang. He knew the maid would answer, but when he heard the small, quick steps of his sister coming down the hallway, he groaned inwardly.

"Darcy?"

The door opened, and Priscilla marched herself right into Darcy's study.

"Good grief, turn on some lights," she said sharply. She began switching on lamps around the room. "What are you doing sitting in the dark? Feeling sorry for yourself? Well, knock it off."

Priscilla, having illuminated the situation, sat herself down in a luxurious leather chair.

"What do you want, Pris?" Darcy said as coldly as he could muster.

"How long are you going to lick your wounds? You look awful. Have you even showered since Sunday?" Priscilla sounded like their mother.

"I didn't come home to be harassed by you," Darcy said, petulant.

"Too bad. It's my number one job until you pull your head out. Now," Priscilla reached into her large handbag, "I have brought you some back copies of *Time* magazine, *Cherish Life and Times,* and *The New Yorker.* If I'm right, the only thing you read while you lived in New York was the stock market. And for that, you just looked at your fancy phone. Why don't you get a peek around the world? There have been some big things going on. Way bigger than your injured ego."

Priscilla stopped to take a breath but dove in again before Darcy could gather any words.

"We'll be going back to church tomorrow. It's Sunday. And I also signed us up to bring Christmas baskets to some poor people in town." Priscilla didn't care how condescending she sounded. "That's in a couple of weeks. I've never done it before, but you need some purpose in your life, and I'm here to give it to you."

"I'm not going back to church," Darcy said. "I'm surprised a thunderbolt didn't hit me the first time I walked in there."

"You will go. Now, clean up and get dressed. You're taking me out for dinner. I'll tell you about the Christmas baskets." Priscilla lifted her hand up before Darcy could speak. "Don't say a word."

Maggie pulled up in front of Cassandra's house. Then she remembered Cassandra didn't live there anymore. Julia and Hannah did. She pulled into the driveway, walked up the familiar sidewalk, and felt her heart clench as she rang the doorbell.

Within seconds, the door was opened.

"It's Pastor Maggie!" Carrie squealed.

"Pasto Maggie!" Carl pushed past Carrie and clung onto Maggie's legs.

"Pastor Maggie!" Hannah chimed in.

Maggie knelt down and hugged all three children.

"What are you doing here, Carrie and Carl?" Maggie asked.

"Wea having a lumba pahty!" Carl said excitedly.

"It's a 'slumber' party, not a 'lumber' party, silly," Carrie said to her brother.

The door opened wider, and Julia stood behind her daughter.

"Hello, Pastor Maggie. Would you like to untangle yourself and come in?" Julia smiled, and Maggie was shocked to see how pretty she looked.

Maggie stood up and took Carl's hand as she entered the familiar home. She immediately smelled fresh paint. The living room was empty of furniture, but Maggie could see paint cans, rollers, and brushes in the middle of the floor.

"It smells so good in here. I love the smell of fresh paint," Maggie said. "Are you painting the entire house?"

"Maybe eventually. I really wanted to get the living room and kitchen done first," Julia said. "But we decided we would have a slumber party here tonight anyway. Didn't we, guys?"

Squeals and shouts of "Yes!" came from the small bodies.

"We brought our sleeping bags and pillows. And stuffed animals," Carrie explained. "We're getting pizza for dinner too!"

Maggie looked at Julia. "This is amazing. What a perfect house for you and Hannah."

"And us," Carrie added. "We get to come here when we want to."

"Of course. Is it fun to be in your old house?" Maggie asked.

"Yes," Carl said soberly. "We lived hea with Mommy."

"Yes, you did. What do you think of your mommy giving this good house to Miss Julia and Hannah?" Maggie questioned.

"It was very nice. It reminds me of Jesus. He would do something like that," Carrie said thoughtfully. "Mommy is like Jesus."

"Yes, she is." Maggie looked at Julia, who looked at Carrie lovingly. "Well, I just wanted to stop by and see if anything was going on over here. I was so glad to see the living room light on. Do you need anything I can help you with?"

"I think we're okay for now. We'll take our time moving in. Mary and William have been unbelievable, as always. We can take as much time as we need." Julia's voice sounded as light as air, and her smile completely changed her face.

Maggie remembered seeing her in the basement of the church only two months before, looking scared, angry, and hopeless. Now Julia was a woman who was completely safe. She was happy, and she had all the hope in the world.

When Maggie got back in her car, after many hugs and kisses from the children, she closed her eyes and thanked God for the transformations life brought. She had no idea one was headed her way in a month's time.

Darcy Keller was back in his study after an irritating dinner with his sister. Coming home had been a bad idea. He should have gone on a cruise or moved to Paris. Priscilla was relentless about his church attendance and the delivery of some sort of gift baskets around town. *Ridiculous*. She sounded like an imbecile.

Feeling the chill in his huge home, he decided to start a fire in the large fireplace. Priscilla had left the stack of magazines and newspapers on his desk. He grabbed the top copy of something, balled it up in his hands, and put it in the grate. He repeated this with several newspapers. Once wood was added and a match struck, Darcy poured himself a large whiskey and sat in the firelight. He saw a *Time* magazine on top of the remaining stack on his desk. He looked at the date: October 19, 2015. The title was: *Exodus*. It was almost two months old already. He threw the magazine into the fire. Just as it caught the flame, he saw something and leaned over to pull it out of the fire, spilling his whiskey on the Persian rug in the process.

"Damn it!"

He hit the magazine on the stone hearth until the flame was extinguished.

There it was. The cover picture he had spotted. A little girl on her father's shoulder, holding a ball. The father was holding the little girl's legs so she wouldn't fall. They were surrounded by mothers and fathers who carried children or held their hands. They were from Syria, on an exodus to another land. The little girl was looking to her left. She didn't look sad as she looked at something out of frame of the picture. She was safe on her father's shoulders, and she had a ball in her hand.

Darcy stared at her face. It didn't show fear. Perhaps she didn't have any idea the danger she was in.

Darcy had known about the Syrian war. He knew people were fleeing. People were fleeing from Africa too. He'd seen images of the boats filled to overflowing. Dead bodies on faraway shores. But that was somewhere else. Not his concern.

But what about that little girl? Completely unafraid, she held a ball and knew her daddy would not let her tumble down. He wasn't sure why the photo affected him so dramatically, but it did.

He found the article about the exodus. Some of the pages were singed, but he got most of the story. He saw more pictures. For the first time in Darcy's life, he tried to imagine what it would be like to know you could never go home. For so many years, he avoided coming home as often as possible. But he always knew he had a home to come to.

What would it mean to him if that home was gone forever?

29

December 5 & 19, 2015
Cherish, Michigan

Maggie stopped at church after her visit with Julia and the children. Hank had gone home for the night, his perfectly typed bulletins sitting out, ready for the morning. Maggie grabbed a copy and turned out the lights in the offices. As she left, the sanctuary doors opened. In walked Irena, dressed like a leopard. She wasn't alone. Detective Keith Crunch was with her. Irena looked as if she had been crying. Mascara was mixed in with green eye shadow and bright-pink blush. It looked ghastly. Irena was as startled as Maggie was to find someone in the church.

"Vat you doing herre?"

"I work here, Irena. What are you doing here?" Maggie tried to glare, but she really wanted to laugh. "Hello, Detective Crunch."

"Hello, Pastor Maggie. It's nice to see you."

Keith Crunch flashed his swoon-worthy, bright-blue eyes.

"I just stopped to get a bulletin before heading home," Maggie said. "Are you here to practice, Irena?"

Irena didn't answer. She just looked down at her tiny feet in their stilettos. Then she sniffed.

"Irena?" Maggie looked at Keith. "Irena, are you okay?"

"No. I em nut okey," Irena said with a slight catch in her voice. Then she elbowed Keith in the side.

"Irena was just telling me about her mother, Catrina. I believe you already know this story." Keith was straightforward.

"Yes. Irena was kind enough to share it with me." Then Maggie turned to Irena and tried to take her small hand, but Irena pulled away forcefully, almost toppling off her shoes. "Irena, I'm sorry you feel sad about your mother. Is it because of the holidays?"

Irena elbowed Keith again. Apparently, he was her spokesperson.

"Kind of," Keith said. "I also think she hasn't talked about it before, and telling the story to you kind of unleashed . . . stuff," Keith said less straightforwardly.

"Can I help?" Maggie asked.

Irena shook her head.

"We were just going to sit here and talk for a bit," Keith said. "Irena feels safe here."

Maggie stepped forward, and before Irena could look up, Maggie wrapped her arms around the small leopard-print shoulders. Irena tried to wriggle away but was off balance due to her shoes.

"I love you, Irena. And I'm so sorry about your mother. You two stay here as long as you want."

Maggie pulled away quickly, before Irena could bite her or pull her hair.

"Thank you, Pastor Maggie. We'll be sure to lock up when we leave," Keith said.

Maggie headed across the lawn to the parsonage. It looked like a package had been left on the front porch. She walked up the steps and picked up the box. Then she unlocked the front door and carried the package into the kitchen.

"Jack?" Maggie called.

His car was in the driveway, so she knew he was home.

No answer.

She walked to the stairs and called, "Jack, are you up there?"

Silence.

She walked into her study and saw three furry bodies sitting side by side, staring out of the floor-to-ceiling window. She stared too.

Jack was on a ladder next to the middle pine tree, carefully stringing lights round and round the gorgeous tree. He had already done one. It was beautiful. Maggie knelt down next to the felines and continued to watch. They sat in silence as Jack began and finished the third pine tree. The backyard looked magical.

When Jack came in through the kitchen door, his wife hurled herself into his arms. He smelled like pine sap.

"They are breathtaking! You decorated the trees!"

After kissing him several times, like a small bird pecking at his cheek, she took his hand and led him into the study so he could see his handiwork.

"Hey, they look pretty good."

"This might be all the decoration we need this year," Maggie said.

They walked into the kitchen, and Jack saw the box.

"What's this?"

"I don't know."

Maggie grabbed a knife and slit the box open. Inside was a beautiful evergreen wreath, wrapped in a red and silver bow. A small gift card fell from the wreath.

> *Dear Jack and Maggie,*
> *We hope you enjoy this wreath of Christmas cheer.*
> *Merry First Married Christmas!*
> *Mom (Mimi) and Dad (Dirk)*

"I guess she had to clarify who it was from," Maggie laughed. "Well, this will be our other decoration. We'll put it on the front door. Does that sound good?"

"It sounds perfect."

Jack washed the sap off his hands, and Maggie leaned on the counter next to him.

"You know, I think I know two people who should see what you have done," Maggie said thoughtfully.

"Who?" asked Jack, who had hoped for a quiet evening alone with his wife.

"They're in the church right now."

"Who?" Jack asked again.

"Irena and Keith."

"I'll order a pizza," Jack said.

It was not what he had planned for the evening. Living in the parsonage could make the church a little too close for comfort, he realized once again.

"Thanks," Maggie said. "They won't be here all evening. I think we will have some cuddle time, and I don't mean the cats."

Maggie went upstairs and grabbed a blanket out of the linen closet. She also pulled some clothes out of her dresser drawer and laid them on the bed. Downstairs, she set the blanket on the kitchen table, grabbed some items from different cupboards, and walked out the kitchen door toward church.

On the phone with the pizza parlor, Jack watched his wife with curiosity. He'd learned quickly about her impetuousness and how she skipped from one idea to another. His brain was much more linear.

"One large supreme pizza and an order of breadsticks," Jack said into the phone. "Delivery."

He wasn't about to leave the house for a pick-up. He wanted to see what was going to happen next.

Maggie opened the sanctuary doors and could hear Irena crying softly. She almost turned back. Perhaps it was a bad idea.

"Who's there?" Keith's voice rang out.

Maggie moved into the sanctuary. "It's just me." She could see Keith and Irena on the steps of the altar. He had his arm around Irena's small body. "Jack and I wondered if you two would join us for pizza, but if this is a bad time, we'll pick another night."

Keith looked at the tear-stained Irena and waited. And waited.

"Vell, yes, okey." Irena sniffed, then wiped her runny nose on the sleeve of her leopard dress. "Ve vill come to pizza in a few minutes."

"Great. We're glad you can come."

Maggie waved and went back home.

Keith saw a box of tissues in the front pew and gently handed it to Irena.

"They're on their way." Maggie sounded victorious as she walked into the kitchen.

She grabbed the blanket and kitchen items.

"What are you doing?" Jack asked. He held a stack of plates.

"You'll see," Maggie said. "You can put those away if you want."

Keith and Irena arrived within fifteen minutes. Maggie had one more plan. This one, however, could possibly ruin the entire evening, but she had to try.

"Irena, come with me a minute."

She led Irena up the stairs and hoped the organist wouldn't trip on her shoes, fall down the stairs, and break her neck.

Maggie brought a confused-looking Irena into the bedroom.

"I'm going to take a risk here, Irena." Maggie looked straight into her eyes. "I've set out some clean clothes of mine, some sweat pants and a long-sleeved T-shirt. Now, I know I'm a little taller than you," Maggie realized she had never said those words to another adult before, "but I think they'll work okay. I just want you to be comfortable, and if I'm honest, that dress looks like a python trying to suffocate you. So if you would like, put these sweats on and just relax. Here are some slippers for your feet. The bathroom is in there, if you want to wash your face or anything."

Irena stared at Maggie and tried to compute these new messages.

"And Irena, I'm so sorry about your mother, and I'm really sorry for all the pain you are feeling right now. I want you to know how much I appreciate you, and I love you too."

Maggie quickly left the room, not waiting for Irena's response. She closed the door behind her and went downstairs.

In the kitchen, Jack and Keith each drank a beer and waited for the pizza. Maggie came in just as the Westminster chimes rang out.

"I'll get it."

She paid for the pizza and brought it into the kitchen.

"Where's Irena?" Keith asked.

"I hope she's getting comfortable. I suppose I mean that both figuratively and literally."

Jack handed Maggie a glass of red wine, and the three waited. And waited. And waited.

Maggie stuck the pizza and breadsticks in the oven to keep them warm.

Finally, after twenty minutes, Irena Dalca came downstairs without any click-clack of her heels. She shuffled into the kitchen in Maggie's soft sweatpants and fluffy slippers. Her face had been washed clean.

Both Jack and Keith couldn't help staring. Maggie felt like her heart was singing.

Irena was beautiful. She was beautiful in a vulnerable way. It made the other three adults want to take care of her. Maggie realized the excessive makeup and revealing clothing certainly were the perfect mask for a woman who carried painful emotional wounds from her childhood.

"Irena," Keith said, moving close to the tiny woman, "you look so . . . young. And so . . ." Keith couldn't get a grasp on his vocabulary. "I love your face," he said somewhat lamely.

Irena tried to toss her head, but it looked more like she had a crick in her neck.

Maggie did not want to make Irena feel uncomfortable, so she retrieved the pizza and breadsticks from the oven. Then she herded her husband and guests into her study.

On the floor in front of the large window was the blanket. On the blanket were paper plates, glasses, napkins, a bottle of wine, and a pitcher of water.

As they entered the study, Irena, Keith, and Jack stopped and stared. The three evergreens in the backyard were twinkling with Christmas lights, which cast the loveliest colors into the dark room. Maggie had lit two apple-cinnamon scented candles on her desk, and very softly in the background, Christmas carols were playing. The room pulled them in like a longed-for hug.

"Well, let's sit down and eat," Maggie said. "Didn't Jack do an incredible job with the lights? Go ahead, have a seat and grab a plate. Would you like a little wine, Irena? May I get you another beer, Keith? Oh, don't mind the kitties. They'll just want to hang out with us."

Maggie kept up her chatter until everyone had a plate and a full glass.

The Christmas picnic commenced.

"Keith, where did you grow up?" Jack asked the detective.

"Wait," Maggie said, putting her piece of pizza down. "Are we allowed to ask you personal questions? Are you supposed to remain private and unknowable due to your secretive job?"

"Maggie's watched too many *Midsomer Murders*," Jack explained as he took a huge bite of pizza.

"I can tell you," Keith said seriously, "but then I'll have to kill you."

Irena looked at Keith and said, "Den you must hev grrown up in Romania."

Jack and Maggie looked at Irena to see if she was serious.

"Vat you look at me like dat? I can tell da joke! You dum-dums." Irena smiled at Keith.

"I was raised in Los Angeles," Keith said with a smile. "I'm the son of the man who ran the Los Angeles Homicide Department of the LAPD and a mother who worked in the county hospital as an emergency room nurse. I have two older sisters. It was an interesting life. Dinners were never boring."

"Oh my gosh. Your life must have been like two of the greatest television shows ever thrown onto one kitchen table every night," Maggie said, eyes wide. She imagined the homicide stories mixed in with the emergency room details. Death and destruction everywhere. How exciting.

"It was pretty wild. You don't have to guess how I chose my profession," Keith said.

"But how did you end up in Ann Arbor?" Jack asked. "As great a city as it is, it can't possibly compare to Los Angeles."

"When I was thirty-two, my dad died of colon cancer," Keith explained. "It was bad. My dad was afraid of the doctor, so his cancer had spread by the time it was diagnosed."

Jack nodded.

As if on cue, Marmalade crawled into Keith's lap and snuggled in. Keith absentmindedly started petting the orange cat.

"My mother's family were all from Lansing," he continued. "We were in Michigan for a couple of weeks every summer, and sometimes for Christmas, while I was growing up. Such a difference compared to living in California. Michigan seemed like a safer place. But it's like everywhere else, perhaps on a different scale. My mom wanted to move back to her family after my dad died. She lives in Lansing and works for Sparrow Hospital now. I hope she'll think about retirement in the next couple of years. I wanted to work in Lansing, but the Ann Arbor position opened up first. So I took it. One of my sisters lives in Lansing with her family. My other sister stayed in LA."

Keith dipped a breadstick in a tub of marinara sauce.

"Wow," Maggie said inarticulately. "What a fascinating life. I'm sorry to hear about your dad. Is your mom doing well?"

"She loves her job. She loves her church too, the First Presbyterian Church of Lansing. I have to tell you, she's very happy to know I have been coming to your church." Keith grinned.

"Eef Redforrd did nut be de villain arround herre, dere vould nut be my Captain Crunch." Irena said. "So, eet's okey. Now de villain go to jail. Goot."

Maggie silently wondered if Keith's mother had met Irena yet.

"I don't want to ruin the mood," Maggie said, "but do you have any updates on Redford?"

"His hearing is in early January. He'll certainly be heading to prison. We'll have to wait and see just how long he'll be there. He did some pretty bad stuff," Keith reported unremarkably. "May I have a little more water?"

Jack topped off everyone's glasses. The subject of conversation changed to Irena and her musical, *Manger Baby*.

Maggie listened as Irena animatedly shared the details of each scene. She loved seeing Irena stretching easily in the soft pants and T-shirt. She looked like a maniacal ballet dancer as she waved her arms and described the animals singing to baby Jesus at the manger.

Midnight snuck up on the foursome. They were surprised to see the time, especially Maggie and Irena, who both had to be prepared and ready for church in the morning.

"Let us help clean up," Keith said, gathering plates and glasses.

Irena watched. She wasn't going to help.

"No, we'll take care of this. It's nothing," Maggie said. "And Irena, why don't you just wear my sweats home? No need to change back into your dress."

Irena couldn't express how the soft clothes made her feel. At first, she was embarrassed. Her figure was completely covered up. That was no good! But as she sat on the floor, leaning against Keith's strong arm, and ate and talked and laughed under the twinkling lights, she breathed again. She thought maybe she hadn't taken a real breath since the day her mother died. Her tired feet luxuriated in the fleecy slippers. No one could see as she wiggled her toes in the softness. For that one evening, life had lost some of its harshness. A gentle blanket of safety surrounded her.

"Yes," said Keith. "I'll carry you to the car so the slippers don't get dirty." He was feeling unusually giddy. "It's a good thing I'm not on duty tonight. The moonlight, tree lights, and this beautiful woman have rattled me a little."

Maggie smiled to cover up her utter shock at the blatant, gooey honesty from the ever-professional Detective Keith Crunch.

"Yes, dees ees okey. Tek me home, my Captain Crunch."

Irena only had water to drink through the evening. Maggie had offered her wine, but Irena declined. As out of character as it was, she didn't want to feel fuzzy from alcohol in any way. It was a dream she didn't want to forget.

Maggie grabbed Irena's things from upstairs and put them in a bag.

"We'll see you in the morning. We'll all need some extra coffee, I think."

Keith picked up Irena with her bag of clothes and carried her out the door. Jack and Maggie followed.

"Careful! Dun't hit my head!" Irena barked.

And the quiet night was interrupted, but only until Keith tucked Irena in the car and shut the door.

"Thanks for this evening. I haven't experienced anything like it in a long time. And I know she hasn't either, if ever."

Keith waved as Irena shouted something from inside the car, but without any makeup on, she wasn't nearly so scary. She looked like a weary child in need of a good night's rest.

Two weeks later, on Saturday afternoon, the sanctuary was full once again. Maggie had asked, nudged, cajoled, and threatened her flock to show up for *Manger Baby*. Two large candelabras were lit, along with the Christ candle and the Advent wreath. Irena crawled up onto her organ bench. Although it had been two weeks since the Christmas picnic in Maggie's study, Irena had not returned Maggie's clothes or slippers. Maggie secretly hoped Irena would keep the clothes and enjoy them often.

Instead of sweatpants, Irena was bound tightly in an emerald-green satin dress. Her breasts were almost completely on display, barely covered by her lacy black bra. A large red ribbon was tied in a bow around Irena's slim waist. She looked like an odd-shaped Christmas present. Purple suede stilettos, in honor of Advent, covered in rhinestones, raised Irena six inches taller than her true height. Maggie noticed her makeup was less startling than usual, but the jingle bell headband drew all eyes to the top of Irena's small head. Every time she moved, two bells jingled. The headband appeared so heavy, it was a mystery how her neck held it up.

The parishioners held bulletins meticulously typed on Hank's church computer. Hank had to decipher Irena's handwritten lyrics for *Manger Baby*. It had taken four days.

Once Irena was securely perched on her bench, Maggie stood up in front of the congregation.

"Greetings!" Maggie said with robust enthusiasm. "Welcome to this special Christmas concert written and performed by our own Irena Dalca." Maggie smiled and looked around the sanctuary. "You can follow the story and read the words in your bulletin. Please remain after the concert for hot chocolate and gingerbread, and to thank Irena for her beautiful gift of music." Maggie hoped that would be true. "And now, *Manger Baby!*"

Maggie quietly sat down next to Jack, who was sitting next to Keith. Doris, who stood in the back of the sanctuary, slowly dimmed the lights, as Irena had fiercely ordered her to do.

The concert began in candlelight.

Irena began playing softly, creating the image of a quiet space, with farm animals tucked in for the night. The music changed and lifted when a young couple were led into the barn by an innkeeper. Irena was able to create the feeling of anxiety in the animals as their slumber was interrupted.

Maggie sat, dumbfounded. Without a single person or animal in sight, Maggie was transported to the manger. Staring at the candelabras in front of her on the altar, Maggie could hear the sounds of the animals, the tenseness of a baby being born, the relief of a tiny cry, and surprisingly, the joy of the animals—the first witnesses to the Christ child. There was not one single spoken or sung word for the entire two hours. And yet, Irena brought every emotion of the birth of Christ into the Loving the Lord sanctuary.

Irena played as if in a trance. Her eyes were closed as her fingers and feet hit every memorized note perfectly. Her body moved dramatically to the music as she unfolded the timeless story of Christmas. At the end, instead of a jubilant and triumphal musical piece, Irena reprised her opening. The quiet barn, the sleeping animals, the exhausted parents, and the tiny baby swaddled and resting in the manger. Irena held the final note, then let it fade gently away, like a dream.

The sanctuary was absolutely silent.

Irena had brought the entire congregation to Bethlehem with her fingertips.

Maggie wiped her eyes, then she noticed as Keith removed a handkerchief from his suit coat. He held it to his own eyes, then loudly blew his nose. Other sniffles and blows were heard as the congregation attempted to control their emotions.

Then there was the sound of clapping.

Maggie turned to see Darcy Keller on his feet—facing Irena and clapping loudly.

Others began to stand and applaud. They all took Darcy's lead and faced Irena on her organ bench. The applause continued, building in enthusiasm.

Finally, Irena climbed down and took a small bow. Her jingle bells, which had jingled during parts of the concert (somehow appropriately), now jingled as she shook her head.

"Tank you, tank you!" Irena said. "I em glad you liked eet, my concerrt. Tank you!" Instead of her usual haughtiness, Irena seemed truly surprised at the response.

Maggie saw something else. Irena looked embarrassed. Maggie walked to the altar and spoke loudly to get all eyes off Irena.

"Irena, we have always known how gifted you are. Every Sunday you show us. But today was a masterpiece. We are thankful for you. Now, everyone, let's make our way to the basement for refreshments and a chance to share some Christmas joy."

Maggie pointed toward the stairs, hoping people would begin moving out of the sanctuary. She made a beeline toward Priscilla and Darcy.

"Hello, Priscilla and Darcy. It's so nice to see you here today."

"Good afternoon, Pastor Maggie," Darcy said. "This was certainly a delight. My annoying sister forced me to come, completely against my will. I'm so glad she did."

Maggie was struck by how handsome Darcy was with his model good-looks and smooth voice. She thought she might like to have him read a scripture passage on Christmas Eve.

"Yes," Priscilla added. "He is a pain in my side. I have to threaten him with torture to get him to leave his house. Just kidding. He's been pretty good coming to church these last few weeks. But this concert was a slice of heaven, wasn't it? Whoever would have thought scary little Irena could pull something like that out of her own brain?"

"It was amazing," Maggie agreed. "Listen, you two, we're putting together Christmas baskets tomorrow after church. Is there any way I could beg you to help? Or guilt you? Does guilt work on either of you?"

Priscilla laughed. "Never. But tell us about the baskets." Priscilla wanted her brother to hear from Maggie herself.

"We will fill boxes and baskets with food and personal hygiene items, then deliver them to folks in town who are in need. We did it at Thanksgiving and received many more names of families for Christmas." Maggie left it at that. "Just think about it. We'd love to have your help."

Maggie turned to go downstairs, but as she did so, she bumped right into Keith Crunch.

"Sorry, Maggie," Keith said. "But I need to talk with you about something important. Do you have a minute while Irena is busy in the basement with all her fans? It really is important."

"Of course. Let's go to my office." Maggie's curiosity was piqued.

30

Maggie let the others burn the trash from the fried rice dinner as she grabbed a bucket of water, a bar of soap, and a T-shirt. She waited for everyone to come back to the large room.

"I know you're tired from the beach. It was a great day. But let's sit on the floor in a circle for a few minutes," Maggie said.

Everyone sat down obediently. No one was interested in devotion time. They just wanted a bucket bath and their lumpy bunk beds. Maggie was just about to begin when the lights went off. It was the first time the group experienced what the Ghanaians called "light out." When electricity went out in the village, it went out everywhere in the countryside, at least those places in the countryside that had electricity. The fans that had been blowing, stopped. Maggie had never experienced such darkness. She felt blind.

"Okay, everyone sit still," Joy's voice said from wherever she was sitting. She pulled her phone out of her pocket and clicked it on. "Let there be technological light!" She got up from the circle and made her way slowly to the bookcase. "We've been lucky not to have 'light out' for an entire week, but now it has struck. If the electricity doesn't come back on, you may get a little warm in the night without the fans. But stay under your mosquito nets. Here, here we go." Joy was carrying something back to the circle. She set down two candles, then lit them with wooden matches. "We have more candles, but your flashlights or phones should do the trick in the night without risk of fire."

Maggie looked around the circle at the tired, candlelit faces.

"Let's pray," she said, bowing her head. "God, You are light, the ultimate light. You shine in every darkness and bring truth to the blackest parts of our lives. You abolish our secrets. You forgive. You warm us with your spirit. You hint of your eternal history by being present with us in this beautiful land that is unlike our land. You are powerful and scary and comforting. How do you do that? Please continue to reveal yourself to us in the days to come. Give us patience and willingness to follow you. Startle us into action, and move us out of our mediocrity." Maggie paused. She felt so full of emotion, the emotions of a week where God was unleashed in her world, and she didn't know what to do about it. "And . . ." she swallowed, "be with Sylvia tonight at the clinic, and with Bill here in his bed. Thank you for healing our ills and restoring our souls. Amen."

Quietly, Maggie picked up her bucket of water, bar of soap, and T-shirt. She moved everything in front of Cate, who was to her left. Without speaking, Maggie dipped the soap in the bucket, then made a lather in her hands. She carefully took Cate's right foot and washed it gently. Maggie washed each toe. She dipped her hands back in the water and wiped the soap off Cate's foot. Then Maggie took her T-shirt and dried Cate's clean foot. Maggie repeated the process with the other foot.

Everyone watched in silence.

Maggie made her way around the circle. She kept a slow, quiet pace so that every foot received the gentlest of care. Addie giggled quietly when Maggie got to her since her feet were particularly ticklish. Joy smiled as Maggie washed her feet. Maggie could feel the blisters and calluses on each foot. She felt the dryness of the salt from the ocean.

Everyone gently fell into the peace of the moment.

Jack closed his eyes as his wife washed his feet. After she wiped them with her shirt, he took her hand and kissed it.

Then Maggie found herself in front of her brother. She lathered her hands and took his foot. She had known that foot since the day he was born. Bryan's foot was as familiar as her own. They had the same shape toenails. Maggie looked into Bryan's eyes. Her love for her brother overwhelmed her. As she washed his feet, her tears mingled with the water. She slowly dried his feet then whispered, "I love you."

"I love you too."

Lacey was the last in the circle. She had been silently crying since Maggie's prayer. What did it mean to have a God who could shine a light in all the darkest parts of her life and then forgive?

Maggie began her ritual with Lacey's feet. Lacey's quiet tears turned into sobs.

"I don't deserve this," she gasped.

Maggie stopped and looked up at Lacey's tears. "Why not?"

"I just don't." Lacey put her head in her hands.

"Lacey, let me finish. Please?" Maggie whispered, feeling Lacey's embarrassment.

Lacey kept her head down but allowed Maggie to finish the foot washing. Maggie sort of dried Lacey's feet with the now very wet T-shirt. Then she turned to the rest of the circle and slid next to Lacey, feeling a need to protect her. Then Maggie spoke to the group.

"We have had an interesting week, haven't we? Another week awaits. Let's expect God to have some more surprises for us. It's the only expectation we can have. Thank you for being here."

They sat in the candlelit circle for a while longer. No one seemed in much of a hurry to have a bucket bath and go to bed. Lacey was sniffling, but Maggie sat next to her and tucked her arm through Lacey's. The past week had surprised everyone with emotions they hadn't known before, but she sensed something more was going on for Lacey.

Jack was the first one to move. He stretched out his long legs, then kneeled.

"I think this was exactly what we all needed tonight. Thank you, Pastor Maggie." Jack winked at his wife. He stood and said, "I'll check on Bill, and then I'm hitting the hay. Good night, everyone."

The others slowly stood, all sharing their good-nights with each other. Finally, only Maggie and Lacey were left in front of the two glowing candles.

"Are you okay, Lacey?" Maggie asked.

"No. Nothing is okay," Lacey said with a little hiccup.

"Is it the trip?"

"No." Lacey shook her head.

"Do you want to talk about it?" Maggie was now beginning to fight her own tiredness. The heat in the room had been rising without the fans.

"I don't think you would get it." Lacey sighed.

"Maybe not. But you could give me a chance. Why did you think you didn't deserve to have your feet washed tonight?"

"God doesn't want me around," Lacey whispered. "I'm not a real Christian."

"Who told you that?" Maggie asked staring into Lacey's huge, sad eyes.

Lacey just shook her head.

"Please, Lacey. I care about you, and I think you believe some lies right now. God loves you." Maggie heard herself and how trite it sounded. "God doesn't just love you," she stumbled, "God *knows* you. God created you. You look just like him. Just like everyone else here."

"You don't know anything about me. And neither does God." Lacey had an edge to her voice now.

"Lacey, tell me what's going on." Maggie lost her patience.

"I am the worst of sinners. I never believed in that word before, but now I know how true it is. You know how I found out? By coming to church. I realized what a sinner I was when I came to Loving the Lord. I told my parents I was going to church and then heard what a blasphemer I was to set foot in a church. I had to look that word up. *Blasphemer.* I thought coming on this trip might pay for my sins. I thought God might accept me. I wanted to believe in all that forgiveness you preach about week after week after week. But there are some things that can't be forgiven. You shouldn't preach about it so freely, Pastor Maggie." Lacey took a deep breath and held Maggie's gaze.

"You know the mind of God so well?" Maggie fired back. "You know what God forgives and doesn't forgive? I'm impressed. But you're wrong, and I'm sorry your parents said such a hateful thing to you about coming to church. They used harsh words. I choose to believe differently. What would be the point of Jesus coming here, dying and rising again, if it wasn't to redeem the world and make all things right with God? Whatever you have done, it's not as bad as the amount of good in God's love. Do you get that?" Maggie wanted Lacey to believe that so badly, she felt hot tears sting her eyes. "What have you done?"

"It's not what I've done. It's who I am. I am a lesbian. And I'm going straight to hell." Lacey let her head drop into her hands.

"Wait," Maggie said, forcing Lacey to lift her head and look at her, "so all of this is because you're gay?"

Lacey gave a slow nod.

Maggie was furious.

"Lacey, you have been lied to. You are not a sinner. You are not going to hell. Good grief, I thought you were going to tell me you did something terrible. You're a lesbian. What a relief." Maggie threw her arms around Lacey.

"My parents say the Bible says I'm going to hell," Lacey said emphatically, pulling away. "That was seven years ago, and it was the last time I saw them."

"Well, they are wrong. To tell you not to be a lesbian would be like someone telling me I couldn't be a heterosexual and in love with Jack. Can you imagine?" Maggie shook her head at the ridiculousness of that thought. "That's just an impossibility. Lacey, you are a beautiful, generous, kind, loving, hilarious human being. And you are created in the image of God, who is absolutely crazy about you."

Lacey stared long and hard at Maggie's face and saw she wasn't lying. Maggie gave Lacey another hug.

Suddenly, both women jumped as the house came alive again. Electricity.

The fans blew.
And the light came on.

Sylvia tried to sleep while holding her hand gently over the ear of the little girl next to her. The laboring woman behind the curtain was now in nonstop pain. Sylvia hoped it would be over soon, for everyone's sake. The problem was, she herself felt sick again. She had thrown up her dinner and now had dry heaves. She desperately wanted some water, but there was no one who could help her with that now. Her stomach retched. She tried not to make any noise, but couldn't help a low groan. Her leg throbbed again, and she worried the infection was getting worse.

For over an hour, there had been no lights or fans in the clinic. Sylvia was glad she had pulled the little girl's gurney next to hers before the lights went out, but it was over an hour of heat and the unnerving shadows of a flashlight on the ceiling next to the woman trying to give birth. Finally, light and fans returned, but they didn't banish the chaos of the night.

The laboring woman screamed and sobbed. Sylvia watched the shadows through the curtain. One nurse held the woman's hand. The other nurse checked the baby's heartbeat. She said something in Twi to the first nurse. The two nurses helped the mother sit up a little higher and then told her what to do next. The exhausted woman shook her head "no" and sobbed so pathetically it brought tears to Sylvia's eyes.

As another contraction racked the woman's body, she let out a piercing scream. The little girl who was snuggled next to Sylvia jumped awake. Not remembering where she was, she began to cry. She took the little girl in her arms and made soothing noises. Then she rubbed the girl's back until she settled down. Sylvia was certain the clinic occupied one of the lower levels of hell as she retched again.

Back on the other side of the room, the nurses shouted at the agonized woman, who was unwilling or unable to obey. Fortunately, her body kicked in, and she pushed because it told her to. Sylvia listened in agony for another forty-five minutes as the woman pushed and sobbed and begged and screamed.

Until she didn't.

There was a quiet moment then, filled only with the sound of her ragged breathing.

Then a new little voice began to cry.

The nurses scurried around, caring for mother and child. The mess was horrendous—blood puddled on the floor, stains on the thin curtain. Sylvia could smell the mustiness of amniotic fluid and the sharp odor of the fresh blood. It made her sick all over again.

After they washed the woman and the baby, the nurses carefully moved the mother from behind the curtain to a clean gurney near Sylvia. Then one of the nurses placed the swaddled baby in her arms. Sylvia watched as the mother's face changed. It glowed. She looked at her baby, and her exhaustion slowly washed away. She touched her baby's nose, then kissed it. She held her baby's tiny hand, then marveled when the baby gripped her finger. She looked up at the nurses, whose faces wore tiredness and some well-deserved pride for their skilled good work. They said something kind to her in Twi, and the new mother smiled.

On her own gurney, holding the little girl, who was now sleeping, Sylvia watched the woman across the room and the intimate moments between mother and baby. Sylvia's senses brought the sights, sounds, and smells of childbirth to light in a true and unexpectedly realistic way. It always looked so sterile and scripted on television, with actresses screaming and sweating, a doctor choreographing minute-by-minute instructions, and then a fake bloody baby being handed to the relieved mother. But what Sylvia had just witnessed was exactly how millions of real women brought life, and sometimes the tragedy of death, into the world. Every day, in every country. Many in less comfortable places than even that uncomfortable clinic.

Sylvia remembered back two weeks to the Christmas Eve service at Loving the Lord Community Church. It was all very tidy and sweet and perfect. Mary walked down the aisle, pregnant, then the music changed and she was holding baby Jesus, wrapped in a soft, white, fringed blanket, while shepherds bounded up to the altar to take a peek.

Sylvia thought about the real Mary. She thought about having a baby in a strange place—a dirty place, a comfortless place—and Sylvia realized she had just witnessed Christmas for the very first time.

Jesus showed his face in the arms of a loving mother, in a tiny clinic, in a rural village in Ghana.

"Congratulations," Sylvia said quietly.

The new mother looked up at Sylvia, smiled, and shrugged her shoulders, not comprehending the foreign language.

Sylvia pointed at the little bundle of a baby. "Baby." Then Sylvia impulsively blew a kiss to the mother.

The mother smiled and said softly, "Me da wo ase." (Thank you)

Sunday morning at the volunteer house was a proverbial beehive of activity. Since most everyone bypassed their bucket bath following Maggie's foot washing, there was a scramble to get clean, get clothed, eat Fifi's breakfast of Ghana pancakes with strawberry jam, and walk hurriedly to United Hearts for church.

Bill had slept like a boulder all night long and awoke eager to see his wife. He took a heaping plate of pancakes to the clinic for Sylvia. He also brought some instant coffee packets, having seen a pan of hot water available by the nurses' desk.

Behind United Hearts, just past the water holding tanks, speakers blared as Pastor Elisha prayed in Twi. Then the congregation of children and adults from United Hearts and the countryside began to sing.

Joy led the volunteers to a bench in the makeshift church, where they filed in and sat down quickly. The church service moved from songs to prayers to testimonials from Pastor and other adults from the Ghanaian congregation. Everything was in Twi, except the hymns. They were mainly British colonial hangovers, along with a few others brought to Bawjiase by other foreigners.

Maggie felt the heat of the sun in the airless tent. She could smell stew cooking over the outdoor fire near the kitchen. Peppers, tomatoes, and onions were boiling down into a thick stewy sauce to go over rice or beans. She listened to the prayers and testimonials. She enjoyed the lilt of the Twi dialect. Then she smiled as everyone sang:

> What a friend we have in Jesus,
> All our sins and griefs to bear!
> What a privilege to carry
> Everything to God in prayer!

Maggie glanced over at Lacey. Lacey stared down at the hard earth, miserable. She wondered if Lacey had gotten any sleep at all the night before. Lacey's burden had been cemented onto her soul for so many years. How would she ever be able to break free of the lies and be able to love herself? Would she ever believe God loved her?

> Oh what peace we often forfeit,
> Oh what needless pain we bear,
> All because we do not carry
> Everything to God in prayer!

So Maggie prayed. During the rest of the service, with her eyes wide open, Maggie prayed for Lacey, Lacey's parents, Lacey's classmates, Lacey's enemies. Maggie prayed for God to release the guilt in Lacey's heart, to fill her with love and acceptance of herself, and to give her joy.

After two and a half hours, church ended. The congregation hugged and kissed one another with smiles and laughter. As they began to leave the tent, Maggie felt the arms of the children around her legs and waist. They all clung together on the short walk to the steaming lunch, then sat on the ground.

Pastor Elisha looked at the children.

"Now," he said in English, "repeat after me: God is good!" The children shouted the words. "God loves you!"

As the children shouted, Maggie leaned over to Lacey and said in her ear, "God loves *you*, Lacey."

Lacey looked down without responding.

Pastor continued, "God gives us food to eat and water to drink!" The children, all worked up by now, shouted these words with all their might.

Maggie resolved that those children would continually be able to say those words. They would have the food they needed and the tools to grow and buy it. From now on, Loving the Lord had a sister church in Bawjiase.

Lunch commenced. Everyone enjoyed heaping bowls of stew mixed with cabbage and black-eyed peas, plantains, and thick slices of watermelon.

"This is like Thanksgiving, only better," Cate said to Maggie as she enjoyed her stew. "I wish I didn't have to go back to school today."

"We'll miss you this week, but will you be back on Friday?" Maggie asked.

"Yes. I'll be here Friday, spend the night, and then go to the airport with you to say goodbye. Then back to school."

Cate smiled as Bryan came up behind her and gave her a squeeze.

"Hey, Megs," Bryan said, smiling. "I've got some good news. We just found out from Pastor that the cement mixer is being delivered early tomorrow morning. For real. We can get to work on the foundation for the school." It felt good to have something positive to tell his sister.

"Perfect! Let's make a work plan this afternoon."

Maggie's sense of relief was immense. She had pictured watering the farm and playing with the kids for the next five days. Which wasn't bad, but they had plenty of workers to get the school building started, and that seemed much more important.

At the clinic, Bill was somewhat shocked to see a little girl wrapped in Sylvia's arms and another woman holding what looked like a very tiny baby. Very tiny. All four patients were sleeping soundly. Bill set the food down and went back to the nurses' desk.

"Good morning," Bill said shyly. "May I have a cup and some hot water?"

"Of course. Your wife is good. Her leg is better."

The nurse poured hot water into a ceramic mug with a daisy on it. Bill wondered where it had come from.

"That's good news. Who is the little girl?" Bill asked.

"She has malaria. Your wife takes good care of her." The nurse smiled.

Bill went back in to Sylvia, shook her shoulder gently, and saw her eyes flutter open. She immediately turned away from the child, with dry heaves racking her body.

"Sylvia, are you okay?" Bill set the hot water down.

"Shh," Sylvia whispered. "Don't wake up the little girl."

But it was too late. The girl had been startled by Sylvia's retching. She opened her eyes and looked at the unfamiliar surroundings. Sweat had formed a sheen on her forehead, and Sylvia could feel her shake with chills.

"It's okay, shh, shh," Sylvia whispered. "Did you bring food?"

"Yes. Are you hungry?" Bill was hopeful.

"No, but she might be. Poor little one."

Sylvia wrapped the blanket around the girl. They helped her sit up a little, then Bill gave her the plate of pancakes. She looked at him with watery, fevered eyes. Then she took a bite. Then another. She slowly continued to eat the pancakes.

The wail of the newborn baby broke the silence of the room and startled his mother awake. She immediately began to nurse him, not noticing Bill was in the room.

"We've had quite a night," Sylvia said, trying not to retch again at the smell of the pancakes. "I'd really like to see Jack or Charlene. I think my leg is worse, and I can't stop these dry heaves."

"I'll get them. Just stay down."

Bill sprinted out the door. Nursing mothers, fevered child, and his wife probably dying from a cut on her leg—it was just too much. He ran as fast as he could straight to United Hearts and quietly pulled Jack and Charlene out of church.

When the trio reached the clinic, the doctors both checked Sylvia's leg and could see the infection hadn't spread. Sylvia wasn't dying.

"It's looking better," Jack said.

"But I feel so sick," Sylvia said, confused.

"Your body is fighting hard. Are you still getting fever and chills?" Charlene asked.

Sylvia thought a moment. "No, I'm not. Those seem to have gone away. But I can't stop throwing up."

"Let's see how you do today," Jack said calmly. "It doesn't sound like you got much rest last night." He glanced at the little girl cuddled up against Sylvia and the new mother and her baby.

"No, last night was unreal. But I don't want to talk about it now. I'm tired," Sylvia said. She didn't want to stay in the clinic any longer. How could she possibly rest there?

"Get some sleep," Charlene said, trying to sound hopeful. "We'll be back later and see if you can eat anything. At least the IV is giving you fluids and antibiotics. You really will feel better."

Sylvia just turned toward the little girl and closed her eyes.

The next day, Monday morning, began a busy week. After he visited his wife in the clinic and found that she was continuing to improve, Bill hurried back to United Hearts, where the older boys, Fifi, Isaac, and Joe were mixing cement. Bryan, Ethan, Jack, and Charlene waited for directions.

"Put the forms in first," Isaac instructed as he helped fit the forms along the large rectangle of the school's foundation. Bill knew exactly what he was doing. He followed Isaac and pushed the forms into the ground. The work was precisely what he needed to stop worrying about his wife.

Several feet away from the cement mixing, Maggie, Lacey, and Addie set up games for the smaller children while the older children were in school. Addie made a hopscotch with thin sticks in the dirt and showed the girls how to throw a rock into each square and hop around it. Lacey helped with puzzles from the volunteer house, and Maggie shared simple Bible picture stories with a small group of five children.

At the farm, Joy, Dana, and Ellen watered with Nana.

At lunchtime, gathered around the large table in the volunteer house, everyone talked at once.

"I can't believe the foundation is poured." Bill dove into his yams and fried chicken.

"We'll have everything watered by two o'clock, I'm sure of it," Dana said. "Then we can help Nana with some weeding. There's never time to get to the weeds."

"Who would have known that hopscotch could turn into such a competition?" Addie laughed. "The girls were determined to keep score. Once Hannah showed up with Kofi and Kwashi, she took the lead in no time flat. Her head is completely healed now."

"Lacey, did you have fun with the puzzles?" Maggie asked, sipping her tea.

"Yes. They liked the animal puzzles best. They kept saying, 'hipp-ohhh-pot-uhhh-moose.' They are so cute and silly." Lacey laughed.

Maggie smiled because Lacey was laughing.

After lunch, Jack took Maggie's hand and led her out to the porch.

"Let's go for a walk," he said, his brown eyes looking into her blue ones. "I miss my wife."

"I miss you too! Let me tell Bryan," Maggie said, heading inside.

Maggie stopped Bryan on his way to the kitchen.

"Jack and I are going for a walk. We need to reintroduce ourselves. We'll walk over to the clinic and check in on Sylvia before dinner."

"Sounds good. Hey, today is going great, right?" Bryan grinned.

"It's fantastic," Maggie said.

Jack and Maggie left the volunteer house, hand in hand.

"How do you think everything's going?" Maggie breathed in the wind and sun.

"Today has given everyone new energy. We'll be able to lay bricks at the school tomorrow, the kids are getting fun attention, and Nana doesn't have the work of the farm on his lonely shoulders. I wish Sylvia wasn't sick. This week will be different, that's for sure. I don't like being separated from you, however. We haven't been married long enough for that to be okay."

"We'll never be married long enough for that to be okay," Maggie said. "I won't mind crawling into our bed in Cherish on Saturday night."

"Mmmm, yes, please." Jack smiled.

"After we have scrubbed off all the dirt that seems to cling so desperately to every square inch of our bodies," Maggie said. There seemed to be a constant layer of dirt she couldn't quite get off her face.

"Thank you for washing our feet last night," Jack said. "I've never had anyone wash my feet before. It's a vulnerable and intimate act. I think it comforted everyone."

"Good. I didn't have any idea how it was going to go."

She decided not to mention her visit with Lacey. Lacey's story was her own. She could share it, or not.

Jack and Maggie went to the ice cream stand in the village and each got a prepackaged chocolate ice cream cone. The shouts of "obroni!!" had become so familiar, they hardly noticed anymore.

"Should we get some fried rice for Sylvia?" Maggie asked.

"Yes. She hasn't been eating, but maybe that would tempt her."

When they arrived at the clinic, Dr. Obodai waved them into the gurney room.

"It's good to see you," Dr. Obodai said. "Sylvia's leg seems to be responding to the antibiotics. The infection hasn't taken hold."

Jack and Maggie looked over at Sylvia. Bill had neglected to tell them that she was "nannying" a little girl. Sylvia smiled at them. The girl, whose name Sylvia discovered was Elizabeth, was curled up in Sylvia's arms.

"Hi, Sylvia." Maggie swooped over and kissed Sylvia on the cheek. "Who is this little one?"

"Elizabeth. She has malaria. They just hooked her up to an IV because she was getting worse. She cried herself to sleep, poor one." Sylvia used a small towel on her lap to wipe Elizabeth's sweating brow. "And over there is Helen and her new baby, Robert."

Jack and Maggie looked at the woman feeding her baby on the gurney across the room. She smiled at them but didn't speak.

"We had quite a night in the clinic the other night." Sylvia smiled, then kissed Elizabeth on the head. "Elizabeth's mother was just here. She has four other children to take care of so she had to leave Elizabeth. I asked the nurse to ask her if I could take care of Elizabeth since we were both in here together. She said yes."

Maggie took in the whole picture. A brand-new mother with her brand-new baby. Sylvia, not a mother at all, but loving a sick child as tenderly as if she were her own. Elizabeth's mother having to go home to four other children in need of her. Mothering had so many layers and patterns.

"I guess it really does take a village," Maggie said. "How do you feel?"

"Better, finally. My stomach was sick through the night, but I also didn't get much sleep. You know that tired feeling when you're over-exhausted and almost delirious? That's what it felt like. My stomach couldn't quite handle the smells and the lack of sleep. But after a nap this morning, I'm much better. My leg isn't throbbing as much either." Sylvia looked at the bag Jack was holding. "What's that? Flowers? A box of candy? A stuffed animal?"

"It's some fried rice. Are you hungry?" Jack asked.

"I just had some soup and bread, but why don't you see if Helen wants to have some. She must be starving after all she went through with her delivery. The soup couldn't possibly have been enough for her."

When Helen heard her name, she looked up. Dr. Obodai asked her in Twi if she would like some fried rice. Helen nodded her head, and Jack gave her the bag of rice.

"Thank you for that," Dr. Obodai said. "She will enjoy the extra food. She goes home tonight, maybe early tomorrow morning. She is doing well." He left the room.

Jack and Maggie quietly visited with Sylvia. They promised that Bill would be back at dinnertime.

"We'll make sure he has extra food for Helen and Elizabeth too." Maggie smiled at Helen.

Jack and Maggie walked back to the volunteer house, but not until they stopped at the blue store and bought several packets of biscuits, a bag of oranges, bread, and two dozen eggs.

"That should help support Sylvia and her new best friends," Maggie said. "I hope Fifi doesn't mind cooking a little extra."

"Maybe we can help since he's working at the school this afternoon. Let's see if he has anything going at the volunteer house," Jack said.

Stew was simmering on the stove when they got back. Fifi must have started dinner right after lunch. Maggie filled a large pot with water from the rubber trash can and put it on to boil. Then she added all two dozen eggs. *That should be plenty.* It was.

Tuesday, Wednesday, and Thursday were repeated variations of Monday. The only difference was on Tuesday morning when the entire group of adults took the younger children to Market and bought them ice cream and new cups and bowls.

Tuesday morning also found Sylvia with a new roommate at the clinic—a teenage girl named Lydia with a badly twisted ankle. Helen and her baby were gone. They had left after a breakfast of kenkey, a fermented corn dumpling, and fish.

Sylvia waited for Bill to bring her breakfast from the volunteer house. Just the smell of the kenkey and fish, as Elizabeth and Helen devoured theirs, made her stomach twist into a painful knot.

On Wednesday, Elizabeth was so much better, she was able to go home with her mother. Sylvia hugged the little girl as she prepared to leave. Addie had brought one of her secret stuffed animals to the hospital after Maggie told the group about Elizabeth. The girl went home with a small pink giraffe. Lydia left a few hours later with her foot tightly bandaged and part of a branch to be used as a walking stick.

After Elizabeth and Lydia were gone, Sylvia was impatient to leave the clinic.

"Dr. Obodai, please can I leave soon? I'm feeling so much better, my leg is healing, and I promise to be careful. I'm missing out on a whole week of our trip," Sylvia pleaded.

But even as she made her request, she knew she hadn't missed out on anything. She had just had a different mission trip than the others. She realized her experience was just as enriching, especially now that her leg infection wasn't going to kill her.

"I think tomorrow we will put you on oral antibiotics and you can leave. You must be a patient patient." Dr. Obodai chuckled. "Will that do?"

"Yes, and thank you for all of your good care. Your clinic is beautiful. I am grateful to you and the nurses. I never expected to be here, but I'm so glad you were here for me to come to. Does that make sense?" Sylvia asked.

"Yes, it makes sense," Dr. Obodai said. "I wish you good health and every blessing."

By Thursday evening, Sylvia was back at the volunteer house. She was on heavy-duty oral antibiotics. She knew, when they got home, Dr. Jack would have blood tests done to make sure she hadn't abandoned the IV too soon.

"We've missed you so much," Dana said, giving Sylvia a huge hug, "but you should know that we have not only kept up with watering at the farm, we have also weeded all the fields. My back will never be the same, but they look wonderful!" Dana hadn't cared for one village animal, but Joy had finally taken her to the local vet, where Dana left her suitcase full of veterinarian supplies. The local vet was grateful for the medicine and surgical tools.

"We have three layers of bricks laid on the foundation for the school," Ethan said, proud as a peacock that he had learned how to make cement and had become a bricklayer in three days.

Lacey and Addie shared their stories of games, art projects, and a second "Bawjiase Spa" day.

"The biggest surprise was when Cynthia, Mary, Amanda, and Grace sat us down and painted our nails," Lacey said. "They gave us manicures and pedicures, and all the little girls just squealed with laughter. It was so much fun."

Maggie listened and laughed. She'd had her nails painted too, and she loved having a different color on each finger and toe.

They had also spent the afternoon giving the children their new clothes from the congregation. Squeals of delight erupted as each child opened their large Ziploc bag and tried on their new outfits. Maggie snapped pictures on her phone as fast as she could. Besides the clothes, Polly Popkin had donated a Beanie Baby for each child. The soft toys were tucked into each bag, and the kids were thrilled.

It was a joy to see their faces as they tried on their new clothes, but Maggie had the realization that the children had exactly what they needed and wanted before she unpacked the Ziploc bags. The clothes would be well used. They would be worn and passed down to the younger ones. But these children were content with life. They certainly had dreams and goals, but their contentment with life was worth everything. Maggie thought she had never felt that kind of soul-settled-peace in her own life. It was a poverty of the soul. Maggie slipped into contemplation of true poverty and true wealth, until Zinabu crashed into her with a three-year-old hug and very wet kiss.

315

And before they knew it, it was Friday.

Cate showed up in a taxi, ready for the Friday evening celebration.

Joy had informed the group when they first arrived that the older boys at United Hearts would have a special goodbye evening planned for them. They did this for every group that visited.

Maggie had waited her turn to have a bucket bath on Friday afternoon. Then she put on a new dress made by a seamstress in town. Everyone had bought Ghanaian fabric on Tuesday, Market day. The women went to the seamstress, who promised to have dresses done by Friday. And they were. The men had gone to a tailor with their fabric for new shirts to be sewn. Now everyone dressed in their new clothes.

"What do you think the celebration will be tonight?" Addie asked Maggie.

"I don't know, but I can't wait. I can't believe it's Friday night already."

As they walked, Maggie smelled the fire before any of them could see United Hearts. She looked at Bryan.

"It's a bonfire," Bryan said. "You won't believe how fun this is going to be."

"I can't believe this is our last night, Bry. The first week seemed to drag by, but this week has disappeared. I don't think I want to leave tomorrow." Maggie slipped her arm through her brother's. "I wonder how long it will take for this trip to actually sink in and unpack itself in our lives. We've learned things we don't even know about yet."

"Look at that bonfire!" Cate yelled as it came into view. She stole Bryan from his sister and dragged him to the fire.

Maggie and Jack stood side by side and watched the flames reach toward the sky. The sun was almost gone on the horizon, the sky painted in pinks, oranges, and purples.

All of the children, including Hannah, Kofi, and Kwashi, danced around the fire as Ghanaian music played from speakers on the ground. Maggie watched Lacey, Addie, Cate, and Bryan as they danced in a circle around the fire with the children. Lacey and Addie had brought bags of biscuits from the blue store and handed them out as the children circled around them. Dana stood with Nana, Charlene, and Ethan. They all clapped their hands to the music.

Maggie looked toward United Hearts, where some plastic chairs were set out. Sylvia, Bill, and Ellen were sitting there. Ellen kept a close watch on Sylvia, but not as close as Bill did.

That week had terrified him. He had to admit to himself that he and Sylvia did not have the most exciting of marriages. They had a comfortable marriage. They hadn't been married a year yet, but they could easily be mistaken for an old married couple. Their week changed all that. Bill realized that every emotion he had never felt in his long, boring life had exploded through his senses when he saw Sylvia in the clinic—an IV in her arm and a little girl snuggled up against her. Bill had fallen madly in love with his wife for the first time.

He leaned over and kissed her on the cheek.

"What are you doing?" Sylvia looked at him, surprised, then she looked at Ellen and felt embarrassed.

"I'm kissing you. Because I can," Bill said.

"Good for you, Bill." Ellen laughed. "I'm thinking of a man I would like to kiss right about now. Oh well, tomorrow."

Bill stared at Sylvia.

"I just want you to know that I love you. And I'm glad you're not in the clinic. And I can't wait to get on the plane tomorrow. And I think you're the most beautiful woman in the world." Bill took a deep breath. He wasn't used to saying so many words at once. Sylvia wasn't used to it either.

"I love you too, Bill," she said a little awkwardly.

But there was a tiny jolt of excitement she had never felt before. Bill suddenly looked so handsome. Then Sylvia sat back and watched the dancing and the fire. Her eyes landed on Baby Leah. Cate had her cradled gently in her arms. Sylvia saw a version of Christmas once again.

"Pastor Maggie!" Pastor Elisha headed toward Jack and Maggie, grinning. "Welcome to this celebration. We are glad you are here. Come! There is food for all of you."

"Thank you!" Maggie said loudly over the music. "You are too generous," she said as she shook Pastor Elisha's hand.

Pastor Elisha shook his head and brushed off the compliment. He looked up at the sky, then down to the brilliant fire. He looked at the children. He considered each one his own. He turned to Maggie and leaned closer to her ear.

"God told me you two met here. God is happy you have heard the whispers and roars. You found God in this land. God met you in another land once. The land where Jesus walked, on the hillsides where the angels sang."

Maggie tried to hide her surprise, but failed. "How did you know?" she asked.

"God told me. There is hard work coming for you. You will go home to struggles. It is why God whispers to you. You will work hard. There will be pain. God will be with you."

Maggie searched Pastor Elisha's eyes. The frisson that shook her body frightened her. What was coming?

Marta came up to them and handed bowls of fufu, stew, and chicken to Maggie and Jack.

"We are so happy to know you. Thank you for your help, for food, and for love," Marta said. "Please, come to the fire."

31

After the Christmas Eve service at Loving the Lord, Jack and Maggie ate their "Happy Birthday, Jesus" cupcakes, hugged parishioners, and finally turned out the lights, locked the sanctuary doors, and walked across the yard to the parsonage.

The house was empty except for three naughty kittens, who were batting Christmas ornaments off the tree then rolling them around the living room. Jack and Maggie came in through the kitchen in time to see Fruit Loop leap on Cheerio and slam her into the once-white-now-gray couch. The glass Christmas ornament she had been playing with smashed into the end table.

"Hey, hey, hey!"

The cats scattered. Maggie ran into the living room and began to pick up the pieces of the ornament. She threw them in the trash.

"I think we need to move the ornaments up a branch or two," Jack said as he took Maggie's coat and hung it in the front hall closet.

"Agreed. Let's get in our pajamas and open Christmas presents. I have an idea."

Maggie headed upstairs. When she came back down, she once again unfolded a blanket in her study. She had two pillows, a Christmas bag, and a bottle of wine. She went back in the kitchen, opened the oven, and slid in a prepared tray from the fridge.

"Can you grab two glasses?" she asked Jack.

Jack brought the glasses and a wrapped gift into the study.

"I just put the pigs in blankets in the oven. Yum! They should be ready soon."

"I love your Dutch traditions." Jack grabbed her around the waist and kissed her. "I take it we're opening presents in here?"

"Yes. Our picnic with Keith and Irena was so beautiful. I want to enjoy your handiwork as much as possible before the evergreens aren't wearing their lights anymore." Maggie looked at the three beautiful trees. "I've been thinking about Keith and last week," Maggie continued. She remembered her conversation with him in her office after the *Manger Baby* concert. He had asked to speak with her in private and had presented her with quite a startling thought. "I wonder how Irena will react to his idea."

"He certainly cares about her to do all the work he told you about." Jack opened the wine. "Whoever would have thought those two would get together?"

"I know, but something clicks with them. Enough so that he will do anything to give her peace and comfort."

"Do you think you'll ever get your sweats back?"

"I hope not. Irena doesn't have many comfortable clothes, at least none I've ever seen. I did get her some soft pajamas and a robe for Christmas. I hope she likes them."

Maggie had given Irena the gifts privately, after the staff Christmas lunch at the Cherish Café, where she had given Irena an unadorned bottle of vodka.

"Vet ees dees?" Irena had asked, trying to sound grumpy, but the hot buttered rum she'd had at lunch mellowed her out a bit. She was confused by the pretty Christmas bag in Maggie's office.

"They are pajamas and a robe. They are super soft, comfortable, and warm. I hope you like them. Merry Christmas, Irena."

Maggie hugged Irena, who'd pushed her away.

"Vell, I dunt know. Maybe I vear dees tings. Merry Chreestmas. I hev to prractice now. I go."

Irena had walked toward the sanctuary, holding tightly to her Christmas bag. And her vodka.

But if Keith did for Irena what he had told Maggie he was going to do, it would be the greatest gift of all.

"I suppose we'll find out sometime." Maggie got up to check on the pigs in blankets. "About fifteen or twenty minutes for the pigs."

"Good."

Jack handed Maggie her present. She carefully unwrapped the shiny paper, feeling a wooden frame and the pane of glass. She turned it over, saw the beautiful calligraphy, and read:

The Mission

To connect the rich with the poor,
the healthy to the sick,
the educated and skilled to the uninstructed,
the influential to those of no consequence,
the powerful to the weak,
to do the will of God on earth.

Catherine McAuley, 1831

"I love this," Maggie said softly, rereading it. "Where did you find such a beautiful quote?"

"I was at a meeting at St. Joseph Hospital in Ypsilanti a couple of months ago. I saw this hanging in the lobby, and I thought of you. I found out Catherine McAuley was a nun who started the Sisters of Mercy, an order that began in Dublin, Ireland. A group of nuns from that order came to America in the 1800s to care for those sick with the plague and also the poor. This wasn't just their statement of faith, it was their statement of life."

Maggie reread *The Mission* out loud.

"So," Jack continued, "I scribbled it down and went to Arly Spink. She did the calligraphy and the framing." Jack was pleased at Maggie's reaction.

"Arly is so talented. Jack, this means everything to me. Where shall we hang it?"

"Wherever you would like. I didn't know if you might like it here at home or in your church office."

"Yes, we'll think about it," Maggie said quietly.

"Ahem," Jack gave a small cough.

Maggie looked up.

"I believe it's my turn. You know, my Christmas present?"

Maggie laughed, then kissed him.

"Very nice. Is there anything else?" Jack tickled her.

"Wait, wait, wait!" Maggie squealed. "Here's your present!" She handed him his Christmas bag.

"This is very light," Jack said. "Are you sure you remembered to put my present in here?"

"You'll have to look and see."

Jack began removing piece after piece of crumpled tissue paper. Finally, he reached the bottom of the bag. There was a small, white envelope. On the outside it said, "Get-a-moon."

Jack laughed. "What is this?"

"Well, I didn't want to plan a honeymoon without you, but I thought we should have something to look forward to before our twentieth anniversary. So, I remembered a place my mom and dad took us one summer when we were kids. I went online to see if it would work for newlyweds. I think it might be a perfect 'get-a-moon' location. You know, a getaway-sort-of-honeymoon?"

"I get it! Where are we going?" Jack opened the envelope. A card read, *Biltmore Estate in Asheville, North Carolina.*

"We'll be gone for two weeks in January, then we'll be back and get ready for Lent and Easter. So, we could go on our 'get-a-moon' the week after Easter: March twenty-eighth to April first. What do you think?"

"I can't wait. We have so much to look forward to. Thank you for planning a 'get-a-moon.' I've heard of the Biltmore, but I've never seen it."

"I have a feeling it will be a lot more romantic than when I was eight." Maggie smiled.

"You are quite Maggie-nificent!"

"I have one more thing, but it's for the two of us. I guess the Biltmore is too, now that I think about it, but anyway, here it is."

Maggie pulled a large album out from under her desk. It was the album of their wedding cards. On the front of the album was Jo's beautiful stitched lace with Shakespeare's *Sonnet 116*. Jack looked at each page, reading the cards from their surprise wedding. So many people had sent the couple good wishes and an abundance of love.

"Maggie, you will always be my fixed mark," Jack said. "And also, I'm starving."

The Christmas Eve picnic commenced with pigs in blankets and wine.

"I'm so glad we chose to spend tonight just the two of us," Maggie said.

She curled up in Jack's arms and looked at the twinkling lights outside the window. Their heads were on the pillows, looking upward. Three cats made their way in and licked up crumbs from the picnic. Soon the three cats and their two humans were fast asleep under the lights on the evergreens.

Priscilla Sloane pulled into the driveway of Jennifer and Beth Becker's home. She had offered to pick them up on her way to Christmas Eve dinner at Darcy's home. They had all been in church earlier for the service. Then Jennifer and Beth returned home, exchanged small gifts with one another, and waited. Jennifer brushed her hair again and put on a little perfume.

Beth didn't say anything about the preparations. She just smiled.

The past Sunday, both Jennifer and Beth had been surprised to see Priscilla and Darcy in the basement after church, helping to assemble Christmas food baskets and boxes.

"Darcy thought we better help with this business," Priscilla had said to Jennifer and Beth with a wink. Priscilla looked around as church members worked their way around tables piled with cooking supplies, canned fruits and vegetables, bags of potatoes, and so on. "I pushed him to come to church to get him out of his funk, but I think he may have gone a little off the deep end. He's acting strange."

"Oh, Pris. This is such a fun day," Beth said. "Just like last month when we did the Thanksgiving baskets."

"We look forward to this every year," Jennifer chimed in. "This year, Pastor Maggie asked for more names of families who needed help to make their holiday special. Last month, we met wonderful folks when we delivered Thanksgiving baskets. We'd never met the people we donated to." Jennifer grabbed a can of pumpkin and a box of pie crust mix for her basket. "Pastor Maggie got permission from Grace in Action, and the families in need, to meet them face-to-face. It's humbling for us."

"But are there any *really poor* people here in Cherish?" Priscilla followed suit and grabbed pumpkin and pie crust.

"Yes. There are," Beth said.

She had overheard Martha Babcock at Thanksgiving when she called the poor "lazy." Beth had been infuriated. She had also noticed that Martha hadn't been in church the past four Sundays.

"Well, where are they?" Priscilla demanded.

"Each basket represents someone in need," Beth said.

As they worked, Jennifer had looked across the tables to where Darcy was tearing the plastic off twenty-four boxes of Easy Corn Muffin Mix. He then went back into the kitchen and brought out another plastic-wrapped load. He continued to do that as everyone made baskets with added boxes of corn muffin mix.

When the baskets and boxes had been loaded for delivery, Darcy surprised the Becker sisters and asked if they would like to join him and Priscilla for Christmas Eve supper. Priscilla was more surprised than the sisters. Darcy had been in church every Sunday since the first time Priscilla dragged him there. He had even gone to Irena's *Manger Baby* concert. It had only been a month, but something was changing in her brother. This was an example of his strange, new behaviors.

"I would enjoy having you over for a festive meal," Darcy said, "and I also have an idea I would like to run past you."

Priscilla had looked at her brother in shock. What in the world was he up to now?

Beth had waited for Jennifer to answer, but Jennifer smiled and said, "That would be very nice. Thank you."

So, Beth and Jennifer put on their coats and scarves when they heard Priscilla pull into their driveway on Christmas Eve. Jennifer tried to ignore the friendly, fluttering butterflies in her stomach.

Christmas Eve dinner at Darcy Keller's mansion. Whoever would have guessed such a thing?

Martha sat on the couch with G. Gordon Liddy Kitty. She was not quite halfway through the movie *A Christmas Carol* with George C. Scott, and Liddy Kitty was sleeping.

Just before the ghost of Christmas Present was about to blow Scrooge's mind with the terrible truths of Scrooge's selfishness, there was a loud knock on the door.

G. Gordon Liddy Kitty jumped, as did Martha. She certainly hoped it wasn't Jacob Marley. She went to the door and saw Charlotte Tuggle standing in the doorway.

"Good evening, Martha. Merry Christmas. Please join me and my family for Christmas Eve dinner." Charlotte stared directly into Martha's startled eyes.

"No, thank you," Martha squawked.

"Enough of your nonsense. I'm not leaving this doorway until you leave with me."

Martha tried to make a stand but finally sighed, turned off the television, went to the closet to get her coat, and locked the door behind her.

G. Gordon curled up in the warm spot Martha's ample rear end had made on the couch and happily went back to sleep.

32

The group finally left the bonfire after food, dance, and lots of play with the children. Bill took Sylvia back earlier so she could lie down and get some rest. Everyone had the chance to thank Pastor, Marta, and all the other adults who had been in and out of United Hearts the past two weeks.

After many hugs and kisses from the children, Maggie led her tired group back to the volunteer house. They dropped Hannah, Kofi, and Kwashi back at their home with Adua and they said their goodbyes. Not with words, but with hugs and kisses.

The darkness of the night was only broken by everyone's beaming phones or flashlights.

"That bonfire was amazing," Addie enthused.

"They enjoy bonfires, especially when shared with groups of volunteers," Joy said. "I hope this week has been good."

The cacophony of happy voices gave her the answer.

"The whole trip has taught us so many lessons," Maggie said. "Sunday we will have to make sense of all we have experienced in order to share it with the rest of the congregation."

"I wish we could be there." Joy looked at Bryan.

"Me too," Cate chimed in. Cate didn't feel too bad. Bryan would stay in Bawjiase until the end of March. She would fly back to Detroit one week later.

Once they returned to the volunteer house, bucket baths commenced again. They would all need to be ready for the tro-tro at three a.m. No one had a lot of hope for sleep.

Maggie stood on the porch, breathing in as much of Bawjiase as she could. Part of her didn't want to leave. She didn't know how she could go back to sleepy little Cherish after God had shaken her to her core. She felt she had to deconstruct her perfectly constructed faith and belief system. *But how?*

Maggie felt a touch on her shoulder.

"Hey, PM," Lacey said. "Do you have a second?"

"Of course."

They sat in two of the plastic chairs. Lacey carefully looked around.

"No one's out here, Lacey. It's okay," Maggie said.

"Thanks. Thanks for everything. This trip has altered my life, to say the least. Thank you for washing my feet, even though I told you I didn't deserve it. I think it was the kindest thing anyone has ever done to me and for me. Thank you for . . ." Lacey's nose crinkled just slightly. "For accepting me for who I am. Thank you for telling me I'm not going to hell." Lacey stopped and sighed.

"Thank you for sharing yourself with me," Maggie jumped in. "I want more than anything for you to live in truth, your truth. You've had to hide for too long. It will never work for you to lie about who you are. It would just hurt you and the people around you. You are inspiring." Maggie leaned over and gave Lacey a hug.

"How do I fix things with my parents? How do I tell my friends?" Lacey sounded completely lost.

"I guess you will know when and how. You'll stay strong, no matter what others' responses may be. I also think that, if you can accept how loved you are by God, even if hurtful things are said to you, you will have a more powerful voice in your head that will remind you of that greater truth." Maggie believed that completely. She couldn't imagine what it would be like for Lacey to face her parents, who had turned their backs so cruelly on her.

"What about church?" Lacey asked hesitantly. "Will I be allowed to still come to church?"

That caught Maggie off guard, but just for a moment. Pictures of certain parishioners flashed through her mind.

"We are a Christian church. We believe in the value of every human in our midst. We don't judge. Lacey, you are a member of our family. And I'm so glad. We'll walk through this together."

Maggie wondered how the church would accept Lacey's homosexuality. It was a necessary conversation, whether or not Lacey had ever walked through the doors of Loving the Lord.

"Thanks, PM. To be honest, as scared as I am, life seems a little lighter now." Lacey wiped away a stray tear. "I think I'll pack. Well, the little I have." Lacey smiled.

Lacey left the porch, and Maggie closed her eyes.

God,

Be with Lacey. You created her and you love her. You know how scared she is. You must clear the way for her to be free from hiding.
Also, Pastor Elisha scared me tonight at the bonfire.
What do you have in store?
You have shaken me up on this trip in this amazing country.
Don't leave me.
Amen.

The group decided to leave most of their clothes and their luggage—which could be used for "dressers" or storage by the folks at United Hearts or the village—along with all of their toiletries.

Jack and Charlene had taken the box that had carried the CBC machine back to the clinic.

"We thought you might be able to use this to keep supplies safe or for extra storage," Charlene said to Dr. Obodai. "It has been a pleasure to meet you."

"Your clinic is impressive," Jack said. "We want to stay connected with you and hear about your work. Will you be in America again?"

"I may. And if so, I will come to Cherish and see what you do in your village." Dr. Obodai laughed. "Thank you for all you have done for us. This machine has already made a difference with proper diagnoses and the ability for speedier treatments. The young children at United Hearts are up to date with their vaccinations. You have shared good work with us. Please come back."

Dr. Obodai, Jack, and Charlene shook hands.

Jack and Charlene walked back to the volunteer house.

"I never thought I would say this, but I want to come back here," Charlene said as they walked.

"I would come back too," Jack agreed. "Now that we know this little bit about one small village, I would like to come back and do more. We have earned some credibility in Bawjiase."

The group of Americans was literally going home with the clothes on their backs, a new Ghanaian outfit each, and their purses and wallets. They buddied up with backpacks and small carry-on bags and planned to leave everything else behind.

On the porch a few hours before leaving, Maggie felt a soft lick on her hand. Obolo. The dog gave her a kiss, as he regularly did to everyone on the trip. Of course, he did so to get treats, which worked well for him. Dana had the opportunity to give him a second dose of dewormer medicine. She also explained to Fifi how to put the anti-flea medicine on Obolo every month. There would be at least one healthy dog in Bawjiase. Maggie and Dana both knew the importance of caring for all human lives, but the horrific state of the animals in the village, particularly the dogs and cats, had broken both their hearts.

Maggie gave Obolo a hug. "I'll miss you, buddy. I wonder what my spoiled cats will think when they smell you on my clothes?"

Obolo answered with more kisses.

Finally, Maggie took her turn with her last bucket bath. She washed her hair, tried to shave her legs, and scrubbed as much dirt off her skin as possible. When she crawled under her mosquito net, she attempted to fall asleep, but her mind was jumbled and whirring. Images of the past two weeks crowded her brain, vying for attention. But nothing had affected her more than the bottom falling out of her perfectly ordered faith.

How would it change her personal beliefs, and how would it change her as a pastor? She thought of how nothing had gone as planned on the trip, but somehow, it was exactly what everyone needed. Even Sylvia in the clinic. Even Lacey, who had been carrying around a suffocating secret.

Maggie was particularly going to miss the children at United Hearts. That thought brought tears to her eyes. She would miss Fifi, and Pastor, and Marta. New relationships had cemented themselves in her heart. She could hardly wait to print off the pictures of the children in their new clothes to share with the congregation. She wanted her parishioners to feel the excitement of the children and the power that land held. She craved the freedom of worship she had experienced there. She wanted to keep the feelings of God rumbling around in her soul.

How could she go back to Loving the Lord and the same old way of doing things? Round and round, thoughts and memories churned. Maggie looked at her phone. Two thirty a.m. There was no point in trying to sleep now.

But she did sleep, long enough for a dream.

Maggie walked down the red road, barefoot. It was dark, and she kept stubbing her toes. She knew United Hearts was just around the bend. She had to get there. She had an appointment to keep, so she ran. She ran and hit her toes again. She tripped and almost fell. She curved around the bend and saw what she had come for. The bonfire. It was blazing into the sky.

Maggie fell in the dirt, breathing hard. She saw her bloodied feet. She heard the crackle of the fire. She heard the wind whipping the flames. She saw the flames high in the sky, and they extinguished the stars.

She heard a voice.

"Maggie, wash your feet."

Maggie couldn't tell if the voice was male or female. It was neither. It was wind and the crackle of fire. She looked around and saw a bucket.

"Wash your feet," the voice said again.

Maggie crawled to the bucket and saw it was filled with water. She cupped her hands, poured water over each foot, and watched the blood wash away. The blood and the red dirt ran down her feet and made little puddles on the ground.

The fire dried her feet quickly, and her sores were gone. Disappeared. Healed.

"What do you want from me?" she whispered.

"Nothing," the voice whispered. "I want to give you something."

"What?"

"A mission. Don't lose sight of the mission."

"Why would I? What is going to happen?" Maggie gasped.

"I have sent you."

"I know. I wanted to be sent here." Maggie's voice blew away in the wind.

"Not here. I met you in Jerusalem and on the hills of Bethlehem. You listened to me. I called you, and then I sent you. To Cherish. Because there is work to be done. My voice must be heard. My people must know. I have met you in Bawjiase, Maggie, but this is not where I sent you. Don't lose hope. Don't waver in courage. Walk the path. Wash the feet. Speak the truth. My truth is good news. I give you hope in all things." The crackling voice faded in the wind.

"Wait! I can't do this. I'm not the one. I can't do more than I already do. I thought you sent me *here*. I have felt your spirit and your power *here*. I learned lessons I never expected *here*! This won't work in Cherish."

Maggie began to cry. She couldn't catch her breath, so she gasped for air. Her tears fell in the dirt and mixed with her blood.

And the fire was silent.

Maggie awoke and sat up so fast, she hit her head on the ceiling of the volunteer house bedroom. Her arm was tangled in the mosquito net, and she was covered in sweat. She had fallen asleep and then into a nightmare.

She untangled herself and got down from her bunk. Her very few possessions were in a small canvas bag. She walked into the shower room with a half bucket of water, took off her shorts and T-shirt, then she washed her face. She scrubbed her hair and the back of her neck. She washed her feet. Then Maggie sat on the cement floor and cried.

She was afraid. She felt the terror of the middle of the night when filled with a nightmare. Was it a nightmare? Was it God?

The cement was cold, and the cinderblock was rough on her back. She started to shiver. She put her clothes back on and walked onto the porch of the volunteer house. She looked up and saw the stars sparkling down on sleepy Bawjiase.

Then she heard something. It was so soft at first, she couldn't make out the sound. Maggie closed her eyes and focused. It was music. It was a congregation singing. It wasn't in the direction of United Hearts, it was somewhere in the village. *All-night church.* Maggie listened closely and recognized the hymn. It was sung in Twi, but Maggie knew the words by heart.

> Rock of Ages, cleft for me,
> Let me hide myself in Thee;
> Let the water and the blood,
> From thy wounded side which flowed,
> Be of sin the double cure,
> Cleanse me from its guilt and power.
>
> Not the labors of my hands
> Can fulfill Thy law's demands;
> Could my zeal no respite know,
> Could my tears forever flow,
> All for sin could not atone,
> Thou must save and Thou alone.

For richer, for poorer

Nothing in my hand I bring
Simply to Thy cross I cling;
Naked, come to Thee for dress,
Helpless, look to Thee for grace:
Foul, I to the fountain fly,
Wash me, Savior, or I die.

While I draw this fleeting breath,
When mine eyes shall close in death,
When I soar to worlds unknown,
See Thee on Thy judgment throne,
Rock of Ages, cleft for me,
Let me hide myself in Thee!

33

January 16 & 17, 2016
Cherish, Michigan

The weary travelers flew from Accra to New York and then finally to Detroit.

Maggie looked at the group. They had gone through customs in New York so were now walking toward the exit in Detroit, sincerely hoping someone would be waiting to take them home to Cherish.

"It seems surreal that this morning we were in Accra," Charlene said.

"It's almost one in the morning there right now," Ethan calculated the five hour time difference.

"No wonder we're pooped." Ellen yawned.

"I'm not pooped. I've never had so much fun watching so many movies in a row." Addie's young voice made everyone else feel even older. She had taken full advantage of her personal movie screen on the long flight from Accra to New York.

Maggie, on the other hand, had caught up on world news. The political climate in so many countries was at a boiling point. America was one of them, ten months away from a presidential election. Maggie realized how nice it had been to have two weeks with no news.

Bill and Sylvia were the last of the group. Sylvia was walking slowly, favoring her leg just a little. Sitting for so long had made it swell.

"I want our bed," she said quietly to Bill.

"We'll be there soon," Bill said. "I want a pizza."

As they stepped through the sliding doors, the whole group looked up in surprise.

Hank and Pamela Arthur, Doris and Chester Walter, Irena Dalca and Keith Crunch, Jennifer and Beth Becker, Max Solomon, Marla, Tom, and Jason Wiggins, Charlotte, Fred, Brock, Mason, and Liz Tuggle, Sky Breese, Cole Porter, Winston Chatsworth, Howard and Verna Baker, Dirk and Mimi Elzinga, and Ken and Bonnie Elliot were all waiting with handmade signs and balloons, welcoming members of their family home.

From behind the crowd, Harold Brinkmeyer stepped forward, carrying a bouquet of flowers, but he had eyes for only one person. He picked up Ellen and swung her around, kissed her, and handed her the flowers.

"You are a sight for lonely eyes," Harold said, grinning.

"I think I'm just a sight." Ellen laughed. "These are beautiful. Thank you, Harold."

Ellen's face was aglow. Maybe she wasn't as tired as she thought she was.

Everyone hugged everyone.

"How was the trip?"

"Are you just exhausted?"

"Pastor Nora did a good job preaching, but it's good to have you back."

"What was the food like?"

"Boy, it's been cold here. Snow too."

"You're all so brown. Didn't you wear sunscreen?"

"We missed you!"

"We missed you!"

"We missed you!"

Maggie headed for her mother.

"How was the trip?" Mimi looked Maggie over from head to toe.

"It was amazing. I can't even tell you. I think it will take time to put into words. Bryan is great, by the way. You don't need to worry about your baby." Maggie laughed.

Her mother probably didn't need to know about the difficulties her children had had with each other. At least not yet.

"Are you staying overnight?" Maggie asked.

"Yes. We thought Jack might let us stay in his condo. You two need some quiet and privacy. We can't wait to hear the stories at church in the morning," Mimi said practically.

"Excuse my interruption," Bonnie said, giving Maggie a squeeze. "We are so glad you're home. We'll be in church tomorrow too. We want to hear about Jack and Charlene's medical clinic and everything else."

Maggie loved her mother-in-law, but the stories would probably surprise everyone. Like the one where Jack and Charlene didn't have a clinic. In any way whatsoever.

"Pastor Maggie, I just heard Sylvia was in the hospital." Marla hugged Maggie, even as she clung to Addie's hand.

"But she's going to be fine, Mom," Addie said. "She just got a gash in her leg and it got infected."

Marla dragged Addie over to Sylvia so she could hug her dear friend. Maggie watched and thought Marla wasn't going to let go of Addie for about a year.

"Excuse me, excuse me, everyone!" Hank's voice boomed out, and everyone became quiet.

"I would just like to say we are so thankful to God to see you all home safely. Church wasn't the same without you, nosireebob, it wasn't. We have several different cars here, obviously, so ride with whom you wish. We can't wait for church tomorrow. We have a special lunch planned."

Hank's words helped the crowd disperse.

"Pastorr Maggie," a tiny claw gripped Maggie's arm, "eet's goot yurr beck." It was Irena. Her hair was a new shade of auburn. It almost looked like a real shade of hair color. "No morre you go avay."

She released Maggie's arm and turned to Keith, who was holding Irena's other small hand.

"You'll hear that a lot tomorrow," Keith said. "We've all been waiting for you to get back. Glad you're safe and sound. I wanted to let you know one thing," Keith said quietly. "Redford Johnson was sentenced while you were away. He received ten years in the Federal Correctional Institution in Milan, Michigan. He'll be up for parole before then. It was in the *Cherish Life and Times*, so everyone knows. I just didn't want you to be surprised." Keith put his hand on Maggie's shoulder. "It's done for now."

"Thanks, Keith. Wow, ten years." Maggie let the news sink in.

Then she hugged Irena, who tried to squirm away.

"I missed you, Irena. I have a hymn request for tomorrow. Is that okay? I'll have copies ready."

"Eet's okey dees time only." Irena tossed her small head.

Maggie and Jack rode with Dirk and Mimi back to Cherish. Ken and Bonnie would be driving up from Blissfield the next morning. Maggie watched to see that everyone had a ride home. Remembering losing Addie in Accra, she wanted to ensure that no one was left behind.

When they arrived, Maggie pulled herself out of the car, but she had things that needed doing before she took a break.

"Jack, can you take Mom and Dad to your condo?" she asked. "I'll grab some coffee out of the parsonage for you. I'm going to quickly run to the drugstore."

Maggie drove to the drugstore and went straight to the photo center. While pictures printed, she found poster board and grabbed two large pieces. She paid for her items and left the drug store just as Bill and Sylvia were walking in.

"Hey, you two," Maggie said, somewhat surprised. "Shouldn't you be in bed, Sylvia?" Maggie looked instinctively at Sylvia's leg.

"We realized we don't have any ibuprofen or aspirin in the house," Bill answered.

"It still aches a little," Sylvia said, looking down.

"Can I help?" Maggie asked, not knowing exactly what she could do.

"We'll grab the pills and head home. But don't worry, we'll be on time for church. We can't wait for the service. It's going to be great."

Bill used so many words. It confounded Maggie.

"If you don't feel well, please stay home and rest. We'll fill everyone in on the situation," Maggie said.

"Thanks, but we'll be there," Sylvia said.

Maggie drove back to the parsonage and found Jack going through the stack of mail on the kitchen table. Marmalade, Cheerio, and Fruit Loop all helped by playing with the rubber bands as Jack removed them from bundles of envelopes and magazines.

"How was the condo?" Maggie asked, taking out her photographs.

"Freezing. But I hiked up the heat and put the fireplace on. Of course, your mother has it completely under control. She was making the bed before I could even look for clean sheets. Your dad kicked me out. I guess they can take care of themselves." Jack laughed. "Hey, here's a letter for you. It's from Darcy Keller."

Maggie stopped what she was doing, took the envelope, and slit the top open with her finger.

> Dear Pastor Maggie,
> Welcome home from your trip to Ghana. I hope this letter finds you, and the entire group, well.
>
> I'm writing to ask you to consider a world situation with me. I have been reading and researching the issue of Syrian immigrants. These people are fleeing their country due to the civil war there. But you know all about this situation. It seems I lived under a rock in New York, quite unwilling to look beyond my own selfish ambitions. I am ashamed of my actions and my greed. I lived a shallow life.
>
> Dealing with a divorce, losing friends, and selling my business was, at first, a perfect excuse to be bitter and hateful. I was getting good at those two things. But I've recently been told by a pesky relative of mine that

the six weeks after a life-changing event are the most crucial to a person who wants to make changes in his or her life. I've come through my six weeks, and I want something different. I've had many options to consider. I've narrowed them down.

Would you consider the possibility of our church resettling a family from Syria in Cherish? I'm sure there is a church board or council that has to approve such things, but it would first have to be an idea you felt passionate about, or at least highly recommended.

I'm a rich man. I can do this project on my own. And I will do so if the church isn't interested. But it seems to me it would be a project that would do all of us some good, not just the immigrant family. Not just me.

If this is something you're willing to discuss further in person, let me know at your first convenience.

Thank you for your consideration, and again, welcome home.

Darcy Keller

Maggie handed the letter to Jack. She watched his eyebrows rise as he read Darcy's words.

"Well, this is interesting."

"What do you think?"

"I think it's too late tonight to think about it," Jack said, but he knew the idea would keep his wife awake all night. "Let's talk about it tomorrow. There's no rush. Let me help you with the pictures." Jack tried to move Maggie along to the task at hand.

But Maggie was always in a rush, jumping ten steps ahead. Within minutes, she could picture the family from Syria arriving in Cherish. She could imagine everything the church would do to give them a home, make them feel welcome, help them acclimate to a new life in a new land. Love them.

Jack watched her face.

"Maggie, stop," Jack said, a hint of frustration in his voice. "Ghana first, then Syria."

Maggie mentally came back to the kitchen table. She showed Jack the pictures of the children they had been with at the bonfire just the night before. She also had the pictures of each child in his or her new clothes from the congregation. Maggie and Jack glued pictures of the children on the poster boards. They wrote the names and ages of each child beneath their picture. Maggie had a second set of pictures to hand out to the church members who bought new clothes for the youngest members of United Hearts.

Finally, at midnight, Jack, Maggie, and three cats crawled into bed.

The next morning, church was full and lively. Irena didn't even try to shush anyone as she played her peppiest selection from *Manger Baby* as a prelude. Only Verna Baker was aware that it was almost a month since Christmas.

Looking out over the congregation, Maggie saw her parents sitting with Jack's. She noticed that the Chance family and the Gutierrez family were also there. They had each received Christmas baskets and invitations to come and be part of Loving the Lord.

Maggie looked around and saw Beth Becker in the last pew with Max Solomon, as usual, but no Jennifer. As she kept searching the sanctuary, smiling and waving at all the happy faces, she saw Priscilla, Darcy, and Jennifer Becker walking down the aisle together, looking for seats. Jennifer caught Maggie's surprised gaze and gave her a little wave.

Carrie and Carl were sitting with William and Mary, like a family.

Maggie was home. It was where she belonged. She couldn't wait to find out why Jennifer and Darcy came into church together and what Darcy's plans were for helping refugees. She couldn't wait to hug Carrie and Carl and find out how they were doing at The Grange. She wanted to visit the Chance family and the Gutierrez family. She'd do that this week.

She looked up and saw Julia Benson and Hannah. She thought of another Hannah in Bawjiase. *Grace.* Julia must have received the news of freedom that past week with Redford's prison sentence. Maggie wanted to plan a "love shower" for Julia and Hannah. The church would fill their new home with gifts and lots of love. She would plan it for Valentine's Day.

God would still whisper and even shout.

Then she felt a small chill as she remembered Pastor Elisha's words at the bonfire. *God told me. There is hard work coming for you. It is why God whispers to you. You will work hard. There will be pain. God will be with you.* She remembered her nightmare. Without realizing it, she reached up and touched the gold cross around her neck.

Finally, after the prelude, the group from the mission trip all got up together and stood in front of the congregation. Some had washed their new Ghanaian outfits, some had just put them on, slightly dirty and wrinkled. They were colorful, nonetheless. Each person shared a story from the trip. The common denominator was that nothing was as they had expected it to be. Dana was the most honest about her disappointment in not being able to care for animals.

"This trip was not what I expected. I found myself resentful and angry," Dana said, "and it took a few days for me to realize the trip wasn't about me. It was about the good people at United Hearts." Dana talked about the work on the farm, Nana, and her thankfulness to God, who adjusted her attitude so completely.

Ethan and Bill stood together at the pulpit and began their story in much the same way Dana had.

"I went to Ghana to build," Bill said quietly. "It wasn't the trip I expected in any way." Bill swallowed hard. His shyness had crept back in.

"And I went to pretend to build," Ethan said, which made everyone laugh. "Our first week left us all a little grumpy. I'll let Bill tell you about the second week."

But Bill couldn't. He moved away from the pulpit and stood next to Sylvia. He looked at Ethan and shook his head.

"I'm going to tell you about the second week, no matter what Bill says," Ethan said. He could see Bill's emotion rising.

"A cement mixer finally arrived at United Hearts, and I made cement for the very first time. We poured the foundation, layered bricks, and the older boys taught me so much about working with what you have, adapting when necessary, and how to let go of control. Bill is a shining example of these things right here in Cherish." Ethan gave Bill a nod. "This trip was better than I could have ever expected. I've been to other countries in Africa. This trip was by far the most meaningful."

"The trip was better than I expected!" Addie oozed enthusiasm. She giggled and cried and described the children in detail. "The best part was when Lacey surprised us all," Addie said, looking at Lacey to finish the story.

Lacey went to the pulpit. She looked at all the people in the congregation and wondered who they saw when they looked at her.

"This trip changed my life. It was not what I expected," Lacey began. "We enjoyed having a 'spa day' with the children, actually two spa days. We gave them all manicures and pedicures and had fun with bubbles. But that was just fun. It was play. For me, this trip taught me one true thing." Lacey looked over at Maggie. "For the first time in my life, I believe God loves me. Completely. Pastor Maggie taught me that, when we actually believe we are loved by God, we are able to love ourselves. No matter what. I have a feeling some of you might know what I mean. Some of us hold unbelievably large grudges against ourselves. This may sound selfish. I did work hard, and I learned so much from the joy of the children. But I mainly learned that I am loved. I hope you know you are too." Lacey stepped away from the pulpit.

Jack, Charlene, and Ellen all stood together and shared the fact that they did not work in, or set up, a medical clinic. The trip was not what they expected either. Ellen talked about donating the CBC machine. Jack described the clinic in Bawjiase, Dr. Obodai, and the good work being done for the people of the village.

Charlene looked over at Sylvia and reached out her hand. Sylvia came and stood by Charlene, Jack, and Ellen.

"Sylvia did not have the trip she expected," Charlene said with a soft smile. "Did you, Sylvia?"

"No. I thought I would work on the farm, which I did the first few days." Sylvia looked over at Bill. His face was almost as red as his hair. "But working at the farm caused a small accident. I received a gash on my leg." The congregation gasped in unison. "The gash became infected, and I spent the next few days in the clinic these three never got to work in." She smiled. "I helped take care of a little girl named Elizabeth who had malaria. And I saw a baby being born. And there was another patient who had a twisted ankle. The nurses were amazing. Dr. Obodai cured my infection. For several days of the mission trip, I was hooked up to an IV and lying on a gurney. I spoke a foreign language so we couldn't easily speak directly to each other. But you know," Sylvia coughed slightly, "I felt like we were a small family in that clinic ward. We could speak very few words to one another, but we could communicate. We communicated compassion and kindness, which means we can all do that whenever we are with people who aren't exactly like us. It was the best trip ever."

Someone began clapping, and the rest of the congregation joined in. Waves of emotion rolled over the people of Loving the Lord. Laughter, tears, and awe were evident on each face.

When they stopped, Sylvia leaned in to the microphone and smiled and took a very deep breath. "And lastly, Bill and I are going to have a baby."

After a moment of shocked silence, the entire mission trip group erupted on the altar. They hugged and kissed Sylvia, and then attacked Bill with affection. Sylvia whispered into Maggie's ear, "That's why we were in the drugstore last night. I thought something was wrong when I couldn't eat."

"I'm so happy for you."

Once again everyone had to calm themselves down. Maggie stood behind the pulpit.

"As you can see, it wasn't the trip any of us expected. I know that I went with ideas of 'doing good' and 'helping the poor.' I knew I was not supposed to pity the people in Bawjiase. But to be honest, I did. I felt that I had more to give them. Because I have money. Because I have an education. Because I live in a developed country. Because I'm white." Maggie paused and looked around the sanctuary.

"So the last few days I have thought about differences between a 'developed country' and a 'developing country.' It's not just about infrastructure, the economy, stable politics, education, or equitable healthcare. To be a developed country has something to do with an attitude toward the rest of the world. An attitude of openness, acceptance, human rights, and respect. I know our country is in a political election year right now. People who want to be president are speaking in ways that represent all of us to the rest of the world, whether we agree with them or not. I have read and heard words of exclusion and separation, instead of inclusion. To be very clear, the negative words, actions, and feelings are anti-Jesus Christ. These words are coming from a place of ignorance and cruelty. So what I have come to believe this week—as I watched children who are richer than I will ever be because of their joy, unbounded love, and universal acceptance of all—is this. We are living in a developing country. We aren't quite there yet. We haven't arrived. We have work to do to tear down walls of prejudice and judgment on every level. I met Jesus Christ in Ghana. Being a foreigner for the last two weeks made me realize the importance of being part of a good country, one worth representing. One that shows and spreads the love of God. I have left a piece of my heart in Ghana. I hope to go back sometime, not to retrieve it, but to leave a little more.

"Two nights ago, I was awake. We were leaving in the wee hours of the morning. I stood on the porch of our home, and one of the congregations in Bawjiase was having all-night church. Which is exactly what it sounds like—church all night long. I listened as music drifted over the countryside. They were singing in Twi, but I knew the hymn. I have put copies of the hymn in your pews. It is so old, it's not in our hymnals. Please stand and sing 'Rock of Ages,' and remember our sisters and brothers around the world, lifting their voices in praise to the God of us all."

Epilogue

The Mission
March 28, 2016—The day after Easter

Darcy Keller gave directions to his driver. He had an appointment in Ann Arbor. He was almost embarrassed at how quickly his request was answered. Being rich meant being powerful. It was time to do something good with his wealth and perceived power. His driver slowed, then stopped in front of a brick building.

"Mr. Keller, welcome." A young woman greeted Darcy inside the building. "This way please." The young woman led Darcy to the door of the director of the office. "Right in here, sir."

Darcy entered the office and shook hands with the director.

Darcy had been present at the last two council meetings at Loving the Lord. He hadn't expected them to be so contentious. He heard things in those meetings that made him wonder if he was really sitting in a church. It felt like a hate-hall. But Darcy persisted. And so did Pastor Maggie. She took some hits but wouldn't give up. Finally, the congregation had to vote on whether or not to support the resettlement a Syrian refugee family in Cherish. They needed two-thirds majority and just barely got the count. Darcy wondered what the fall-out would be for the church.

But he was here now, and there was work to do.

"Thank you for seeing me today," Darcy said.

∞

Bill helped Sylvia into the car. He was treating her as if she would crack into pieces if a gentle breeze blew.

"I really can get into a car all by myself," Sylvia teased.

"No, you can't. Remember how you almost died in Ghana?" Bill teased back.

"Oh, right. I forgot about that near-death experience."

Sylvia buckled her seatbelt. Bill drove the two miles it took to get to Dr. Jack's office.

It was time for their first ultrasound.

"Do you think it's a girl or a boy?" Sylvia asked.

"I think it's a baby."

They arrived at the office, and Bill helped her out of the car and up the sidewalk to the office door.

∞

Irena rode in the passenger seat of Keith's car.

"Verre arre ve going?" Irena asked, trying to sound grumpy but sounding adorable to him instead.

"You'll see," Keith said, heading east on Interstate 94.

"I should be prracticing de organ."

"No, you shouldn't. Yesterday was Easter and you played your fingers off. It was a fantastic service. You and Pastor Maggie are quite a team."

"Yes. Ve are goot, as long as she does vat I say."

"I love Easter. It's the most hopeful day of the year. Death never wins," Keith said.

They drove in silence for a long while. The fields were still brown, waiting for spring to show up and really mean it. They were getting closer.

"I spoke with Pastor Maggie about some of the things you and I have talked about. You know, about your mother and your childhood in Detroit," Keith said quietly.

A cloud crossed Irena's face. "Eet's not for us to talk about anymore. Dat's my old life. Gone." Irena noticed the road signs now. She didn't know exactly what Keith was doing, but she began to feel sick and afraid. "Pleese, don't tek me to Detroit."

Keith looked over at her. "I would never do anything to hurt you, Irena. You must know that. I wanted to give you an Easter gift." He had been confident, but looking at her face he started to think it was the worst idea ever.

Irena stayed quiet and stared at her hands. When Keith slowed the car, she looked up. They were at the entrance of a cemetery.

Keith pulled in through the stone gates, heading toward a Gothic chapel. He'd made the trip the week before so he would know exactly where to go. Now he wound the car past gravestones on the single-lane paved road. Finally, he slowed to a stop and turned off the engine.

"Vat ees dees?" Irena whispered.

"Please come with me," Keith said.

He got out of the car, grabbed something out of the backseat, then helped Irena out. Or pulled her out. He walked her a short distance to a plain headstone.

CATRINA DALCA
AUGUST 12, 1989

Irena stared at her mother's gravestone.

"I neverr knew vere she vent."

Keith opened the bag he was carrying and pulled out a bouquet of flowers. He handed them to Irena.

"I thought it might be nice to put these here. I think we should bring her flowers often. What do you think, Irena?"

Irena knelt down in her tight dress and fishnet stockings. Her knees sank into the wet grass, but she didn't seem to notice. She placed the flowers at the base of the plain stone and felt they made it look like someone was remembered.

Irena placed her small hand on the top of the stone. Then she leaned over and kissed her mother's name.

"I tink, yes," Irena whispered.

Lacey Campbell got into her car and started the engine. She headed south. Today was the day. She'd waited and procrastinated and talked herself out of this trip for over two months. But Pastor Maggie's sermon the day before, Easter Sunday, reminded Lacey that new life belonged to her too.

So she headed to Bloomington, Indiana. She hadn't called her parents to let them know. She didn't have the courage for that conversation. Not over the phone.

She would have five hours to retrieve her courage and put it on like a shield.

Then she would sit in the living room of her parents' home. The room where she had celebrated every Christmas and every Easter as a child and young adult. Not that there was ever too much celebrating. Lacey and her sister were reminded often about the sins of frivolity and self-indulgence. It was always better to make sure you had counted your sins and begged for forgiveness, or be damned to hell.

It was a scary and cruel message for two little girls.

Lacey hadn't spoken with her sister, Ruth, in months before last night. It was easier for Ruth to face her parents if she could say she hadn't had any contact with her sister. But Lacey called anyway.

"Hi, Ruth, it's me. How are you?" Lacey asked.

"Hi," Ruth replied.

"Listen, I'll make this easy on you. I'm driving down to Bloomington tomorrow. I'll be there around two p.m. I'm going to try talking with Mom and Dad again. If you want to be there, I'd love it. But I understand if you can't handle it." Lacey didn't have time for any "holier than thou" shit.

"I'll think about it," Ruth said.

"Great. Love you, Ruth. Bye." Lacey hung up.

After the long drive, Lacey stopped at a McDonald's for a coffee with three creams. She sat in the parking lot, sipped her coffee, and thought of Ghana.

Ghana was the place she first knew she was loved. Ghana and her coffee warmed her.

She pulled into the driveway of her old home. She got out of her car, walked up the sidewalk, and rang the doorbell.

She waited. Maybe Ruth had tipped off her parents.

But the door opened, and Lacey saw her father's face. He couldn't hide his emotion. It was a mix of fear and anger.

"Hi, Dad," Lacey said through the screen door.

"Hannah," he replied.

"My name is Lacey now. May I come in?"

Maggie drove her car south. She'd slept like a rock the night before from pure exhaustion. She had done everything she could the day before to make Easter happy and joyful, but she felt as if she was locked in a tomb. Hopefully, the Holy Spirit had gotten the message of her sermon out to the congregation.

She and Jack would leave for their "get-a-moon" to Asheville, North Carolina, and the Biltmore Estate that afternoon, but she had one important and difficult thing to do before she could leave with a clear conscience.

Maggie was emotionally drained. It had been a rough couple of months at Loving the Lord. More than once she had thought of Pastor Elisha's prophecy at the bonfire. Pain had certainly visited her. Darcy Keller's idea of helping an immigrant family was met with elation by some and a revolt by others. She had never anticipated the battles to come.

Council meetings were jammed with parishioners in January and February. The congregational vote was contentious and ugly. Maggie wished she hadn't seen certain faces or heard their voices. It left scars on her soul.

There was more fighting to come, she felt certain of it.

She remembered the fire and the wind of her . . . not her nightmare, it surely was a dream. A dream of a mission. God promised her the gift of a mission to accomplish. She wouldn't let God forget that promise.

But that day she had another task. She couldn't preach the good news of Easter without living it out.

Maggie drove for thirty minutes, then pulled into her destination. She got out of the car and walked inside. After showing ID, she was led into a small room with a metal table and two metal chairs. It smelled heavily of sweat and faintly of urine. She fingered the cross around her neck and breathed a prayer.

Then she waited.

The door on the other side of the room opened. A guard led a hand-cuffed man into the room.

"What the hell are you doing here?" Redford Johnson spat.

Maggie's hand slid down from her neck.

"I came to visit. I came to tell you Happy Easter, even though those words mean nothing to you because you are in here. I came to see if you would like to talk." Maggie braced herself for an onslaught of foul language. Then she decided not to wait for hate. "Redford, I'm not going to fight with you. I'm also not going to take your insults. I've never hurt you. I'm here because I care."

Maggie looked Redford straight in the eye.

And she waited.
The fire burned and roared.
The wind stirred and blew.
Whispers filled Maggie's ears.
And there was hope.

The End

BUT WAIT . . . THERE'S MORE!

DON'T MISS THE REST OF PASTOR MAGGIE'S STORY!

TO LOVE AND TO CHERISH
BOOK ONE

What's a young, idealistic, novice pastor got to learn from the congregation at Loving the Lord Community Church? A lot!

Twenty-six and single, Maggie Elzinga has just graduated from seminary and received a call to pastor a church in the town of Cherish, Michigan. Idealistic, impetuous, enthusiastic, and short on life experience, Maggie jumps in with both feet.

With her on the journey are a cast of colorful characters who support, amuse, and challenge her daily.

For Maggie it's a year of firsts: first funeral, first baptism; and the hope of a first wedding. But much more awaits her at Loving the Lord Community Church and in the little town of Cherish. Parking tickets, abandoned cats, and little white lies pop up to make her question what she believes is right and good and a sprinkling of romance provides a happy distraction.

Maggie faces her happiest moments and her deepest sorrow while serving the good people of her little church. She learns that being part of a community can be simultaneously suffocating and life-giving. Her bright attitude and hopefulness carry her through the difficult times, as she becomes a full-fledged pastor.

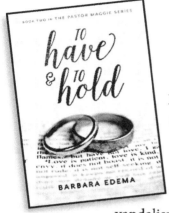

To Have and To Hold
Book Two

Welcome back, Pastor Maggie!

Pastor Maggie of Loving the Lord Community Church has settled into her new position and finally gained the trust and respect of her congregation, but they will all be tested when the church comes under attack through a series of malicious break-ins and vandalism. Maggie tries to hold everyone together and determine if the threat is from an outsider or someone actually sitting in the pews of her church each Sunday. Can she keep her beautiful church safe? Will she still be able to accomplish the planned mission trip to Ghana if the money from a fundraiser is stolen?

While Maggie desperately waits for a whisper from God, she also fears that a major event will be ruined by the well-meaning, very loving members of the church. How will she maintain her own blossoming romance with tall, dark, and scrumptious Dr. Jack Elliot and support the daily needs of her congregation through life-and-death matters when it all feels one step away from collapsing?

Will they catch the villain before he ruins everything?

FOR BETTER, FOR WORSE
BOOK FOUR

Is America at war?

It is the summer of 2016 and Pastor Maggie finds herself challenged in unimaginable ways. A national election is dividing the country, the city of Cherish, and Loving the Lord Community Church into splintered factions. To complicate matters, she is working with a local business owner to resettle a refugee family from Syria, but not everyone is happy to see the new arrivals. Maggie tries to guide her discordant flock but careens from one crisis to another. She knows that much good happens in a community where love and kindness reign, but how can she possibly overcome the judgment, divisiveness, and hate that permeates her parishioners and the nation? Can she hold her flock together through the storm?

In this fourth book of the series, the determined young pastor must marshal all the patience and fortitude she can to hold the vision of a harmonious and loving society.

GET YOUR EBOOK OR PRINT COPY TODAY AT
WWW.PEN-L.COM/FORBETTERFORWORSE.HTML

For Richer, For Poorer
Discussion Questions

1. Issues of wealth and poverty are juxtaposed in the book. If money is removed from these issues, where did you see emotional wealth and poverty in the story?

2. Cassandra Moffet surprised many of the characters in Cherish. Were you surprised by her final gifts? If so, why?

3. Which characters seemed to learn and change the most in their experiences of perceived wealth and poverty?

4. Lacey shared a painful secret with Maggie. What was your reaction?

5. What parts of the mission trip to Bawjiase, Ghana, surprised you? Which characters and stories in Bawjiase drew you into the culture? What Ghanaian food would you like to try?

6. Of the different character back stories that were revealed in the book (i.e. Irena, Keith, Skylar, Darcy, Priscilla, Lacey, among others), who most interested you?

7. What is your understanding of the phrase "poor in spirit"? Which characters would you describe this way?

8. Do you believe there are some people who aren't redeemable due to their own desires to hate, hurt, condemn, or harm others? Do the issues of racism, bigotry, misogyny, and violence affect your daily life? Where does God fit within these issues of redemption and human darkness?

9. Has anything changed in your personal beliefs about giving time, money, forgiveness, or acceptance? How?

10. Maggie has a faith renewal while in Ghana. Have there been times in your life when you felt God speaking and directing you in a specific way? How did you react?

Recipes

Maggie's Autumn Crock-Pot Dinner

Spray a large Crock-Pot with cooking spray then add:
1 lb. small potatoes, quartered
1 lb. baby carrots
2 small onions, diced
3 cloves of garlic, peeled and chopped
1 rutabaga, peeled and chopped
1 turnip, peeled and chopped
1 parsnip, peeled and chopped
Salt and pepper to taste
1 tablespoon dried Herbes de Provence
½ tablespoon dried rosemary

Toss vegetables with spices and herbs.

Place on top of vegetables:
6 uncooked, boneless chicken breasts, cut in bite-size pieces
28 oz. can diced tomatoes
6 oz. tomato paste
15 oz. can of tomato sauce

Cook for 10-12 hours.
When ready to eat, cook 1 lb. old-fashioned noodles according to package. Serve chicken and vegetables over cooked noodles. Will serve 6-8 people.

Maggie's Curried Orange Salad

Mix in large salad bowl:

9 oz. bag of baby spinach
9 oz. bag of romaine lettuce
11 oz. can of mandarin oranges, drained
½ cup red seedless grapes, sliced in half
½ cup green seedless grapes, sliced in half
½ cup toasted slivered almonds

Then toss and combine with dressing.

Dressing:
¼ cup extra virgin olive oil
¼ cup rice vinegar
1 small clove minced garlic
1 tablespoon brown sugar
2 tablespoons fresh chopped chives
1 teaspoon curry powder
½ teaspoon soy sauce

Maggie's Blueberry Buckle

Grease or spray 8x8 inch pan. Heat oven to 350°.

Mix together and press with wooden spoon into bottom of baking pan:
2 cups of Jiffy Baking Mix
½ cup of sugar
1 teaspoon cinnamon
¼ cup melted butter
⅓ cup milk

Spread 2 cups Michigan blueberries over Jiffy mixture.

In a saucepan, boil 2 cups water and 1 cup sugar together for 1 minute. Pour over blueberries.

Bake for 45 minutes. The top will look bumpy and slightly undercooked. Cool for 20 minutes. There will be a delicious syrup underneath the buckle. Serve warm with vanilla ice cream, if desired. Don't let cats on the counter!

Jollof Rice

3 medium white onions
2 orange habanero peppers
4 tablespoons vegetable oil
5 oz. tomato paste
1 teaspoon nutmeg
1 teaspoon salt
1 teaspoon tomato bouillon powder (or 1 cube)
1 ½ cups jasmine, basmati, or long grain rice
4 cups water or vegetable broth

Peel and thinly slice the onions and mince habanero peppers.

Heat oil in large pot. Add onions and pepper. Cook until completely softened, about three minutes.

Add tomato paste, salt, and nutmeg. Cook over medium heat, stirring frequently for 3 minutes.

Mix in bouillon cube or powder.

Add rice and stir until completely covered with sauce.

Add water or broth. Stir until mixed.

Let jollof simmer over low heat for 45-60 minutes (taste to know when rice is cooked). Stir every 15 minutes. Keep tight lid on pot to keep in the steam.

Acknowledgements

God whispers and roars. There is a constant challenge to do more good in this world.

My uncle, Craig Hubbell, was a cheerleader of my book writing endeavors from the very beginning. He was always honest with praise and criticism. He died on March 3, 2017. Uncle Craig had read the first chapters of the roughest draft of this book. I will miss his phone calls, critique, banter, and his unwavering love.

Thank you, Duke and Kimberly Pennell. Your authors are truly blessed. I know I am.

I am thankful for Susan Matheson and Meg Welch Dendler for their amazing editing skills. They are two truly talented women.

Thank you, Lauren, for introducing us to the amazing people at United Hearts and the beautiful country of Ghana.

G.M. Malliet, Maggie's (and my) favorite author.

Ethan Ellenberg, you gave me hope.

Five readers read the final draft of this manuscript before anyone else. They are all expert readers and writers. They also have different expertise, which helped direct this book. Thank you, Leanne Harker, Judy Elzinga, Joan Isenberg, Dr. Mimi Keller, and Dr. Doug Edema.

Susan Holmes Schrotenboer, thank you for sharing the history of your family, the history of the Jiffy Mix corporation (Quick Mix in the book), and permission to fictionalize the story of this incredible and generous company. Jiffy is a Chelsea, Michigan, landmark. For all of you who have ever eaten a Jiffy Mix, it was made and distributed from Chelsea.

Vicki Hubbell, thank you for your wealth of knowledge on all things real estate.

Peter Flintoft, Attorney at Law, your help was invaluable as storylines progressed in this book. I owe you several Manhattans!

Dr. Erin Harker, you shared your veterinary expertise, as well as your work with animals in developing countries. Thank you.

Thank you, Joy Nelson, Bonnie Walter, Lacey Campbell, Arly Spink, Priscilla Flintoft, Judy Teater, and Dr. Charlene Kushler. You've allowed me to use your names and fictionalize your lives. You are brave friends!

Bernard Boateng (Nana Bee), you are a treasure. Thank you for interpreting Twi into English. We miss you.

Doug, always and forever.

About Barbara Edema

The Rev. Dr. Barbara Edema has been a pastor for twenty-three years. That sounds astonishingly boring. However, she is a great deal of fun with a colorful vocabulary used regularly out of the pulpit. Barb has spent decades with people during holy and unholy times. She has been at her best and her worst in the lives of the people she has cared for. Now she's writing about a fictional church based on her days serving delightful and frustrating parishioners. Pastor Maggie is a young, impetuous, emotional, clumsy, and not to mention a crazy cat lady, who steps into ministry full of Greek and Hebrew but not much life experience. She learns quickly.

Barb lives in DeWitt, Michigan, with her husband, Dr. Douglas Edema. She is the mother of Elise, Lauren, Alana, and Wesley. Like Maggie, Barb is an avid feline female. Hence, she has collected an assortment of rescue kitties. Barb enjoys date nights with her husband, watching her children do great things in the world, a glass of good red wine, and making up stories about the fun and fulfilling life in the church.

Enjoy visiting Cherish, Michigan, and Loving the Lord Community Church. Pastor Maggie will delight you!

Visit Barb at:

www.Barbara-Edema.com
Blog: www.BarbaraEdema.Blogspot.com/
Facebook: The Pastor Maggie Series
Twitter: @BarbaraEdema1

Dear Readers,
If you enjoyed this
book enough to review
it for Goodreads, B&N,
or Amazon.com, I'd
appreciate it!
Thanks, Barb

Find more great reads at
Pen-L.com

Made in the USA
Monee, IL
05 March 2021

62016523R00207